MW00467149

Buried in Black

The fictional works of J.T. Patten do not constitute an official release of the Central Intelligence Agency (CIA), National Security Agency (NSA), or Department of Defense (DOD) information. All statements of fact, opinion, or analysis expressed are those of the author and do not reflect the official positions or views of the CIA or any other U.S. Government agency. Nothing in the contents should be construed as asserting or implying US Government authentication of information or CIA, NSA, or DOD endorsement of the author's views. This material has been reviewed for classification.

Buried in Black

A Task Force Orange Novel

J.T. Patten

LYRICAL UNDERGROUND
Kensington Publishing Corp.
www.kensingtonbooks.com

To the extent that the image or images on the cover of this book depict a person or persons, such person or persons are merely models, and are not intended to portray any character or characters featured in the book.

LYRICAL UNDERGROUND BOOKS are published by

Kensington Publishing Corp.
119 West 40th Street
New York, NY 10018

Copyright © 2018 by J.T. Patten

All rights reserved. No part of this book may be reproduced in any form or by any means without the prior written consent of the Publisher, excepting brief quotes used in reviews.

All Kensington titles, imprints, and distributed lines are available at special quantity discounts for bulk purchases for sales promotion, premiums, fundraising, educational, or institutional use.

Special book excerpts or customized printings can also be created to fit specific needs. For details, write or phone the office of the Kensington Sales Manager: Kensington Publishing Corp., 119 West 40th Street, New York, NY 10018. Attn. Sales Department. Phone: 1-800-221-2647.

Lyrical Press and Lyrical Press logo Reg. U.S. Pat. & TM Off.

First Electronic Edition: November 2018
eISBN-13: 978-1-5161-0862-6
eISBN-10: 1-5161-0862-0

First Print Edition: November 2018
ISBN-13: 978-1-5161-0876-3
ISBN-10: 1-5161-0876-0

Printed in the United States of America

To

Mom

You encouraged me to read, write, and dream

Acknowledgements

As always, I need to thank my wife, Shilpa, for being supportive of my writing, and my children who are equally as patient with my periodic time and focus creating stories. I know the laptop should not be an appendage wherever I go. A special thanks to Brad Taylor who made the introduction to my literary agent John Talbot. And to John who has always been forthcoming about where I need to be in this business, how to get there, and then putting this opportunity into motion.

Thank you to the boss, Steven Zacharius who opened the Kensington Publishing doors to me as an "indie" and encouraged Gary Goldstein to have that first chat. Gary, I've learned more about publishing and writing in a year than I ever expected. Thanks for your patience, mentoring, and friendship.

On the content front, it's always good to be able to share ideas with others and to gain some technical insights. Thank you to Joe Goldberg who is always willing to work through a storyline over BBQ. Thanks to my speed dial buddy, Josh Hood, who is there 24/7 to spit ball concepts and to talk about book doctoring. To Mark Greaney who continues to push and encourage, and to my "authenticity" reach-back team of Michael Scadden, Dave Powers, Sean Page, Erik Wittreich, Jack Murphy, and Scotty Neil. I also greatly appreciate the honest feedback from my beta readers Bodo Pfündl and Kathleen Herrin, and The Real Book Spy, Ryan Steck for acknowledging my works (and progress).

It takes a lot of help to kick one of these stories out, so thanks to anyone I've missed, and to the Thriller genre authors who have created such a powerful community to support and promote one another.

Author's Note

My apologies.

Unlike other novels, the story you are about to read is one of the few fictional works ever written that has been required to go through an extensive pre-publication review by multiple members of the Intelligence Community and select Department of Defense units.

As a result, the Central Intelligence Agency (CIA), the National Security Agency (NSA), and the Department of Defense (DOD) and its subcomponents weighed in on content and made suggested redactions even before the publisher could read a first draft. This allows me to uphold my public trust obligations that have protective controls to ensure that certain "equities"—or secrets—are not acknowledged, affirmed, or made known to anyone not authorized for such information. Even if such content may already be in the public domain.

So, some *even fictionalized* details have been cut out and other terms have been replaced with creative code names. But here's the fun part. Not many thriller writers have been involved with deep black Waived Unacknowledged Special Access Programs. While names, places, and things have been changed, the spirit of the forbidden world remains. You can't sanitize the adrenaline, fear, patriotism, brotherhood, wins and loss that happen day by day in the shadows. And I believe that still comes through loud and clear.

So, thank you for giving the Task Force Orange's story a try. And welcome to a thriller that is, indeed, blacker than black.

-JTP

Guide to acronyms, abbreviations, initials, and terms.

AFO – Advance Force Operations, A term used for low-visibility missions conducted by JSOC operators to prepare for possible future combat operations.

AO – Area of Operation

AOR – Area of Responsibility

AQ – Al-Qaeda

BBC – Baseball Card

BDL – Bed Down Location

CAG – Combat Applications Group, another term for Delta

CELLEX - Cellular Exploitation

CCO – Commercial Coverage Operative

CIA – Central Intelligence Agency

CONUS – Continental United States

COMINT – Communications Intelligence

CoS – Chief of Station (CIA)

CoS – Chief of Staff (White House)

CT – Counterterrorism

Daesh – Arabic language acronym for the Sulafi jihadist terrorist organization, Islamic State (IS)

Delta – 1st Special Forces Operational Detachment Delta (1st SFOD-D), an elite special mission unit of the United States Army under operational control of JSOC

DEVGRU – Abbreviation of Naval Special Warfare Development Group, a cover name for SEAL Team 6

DHS – Department of Homeland Security

DIA – Defense Intelligence Agency

DOD – Department of Defense

DOJ – Department of Justice

DOMEX – Document and Media Exploitation

E.O. – Executive Order

F3EA – Find, Fix, Finish, Exploit/Analyze

FBI – Federal Bureau of Investigation

FMV – Full Motion Video

Fort Bragg – Large Army post in Fayetteville, North Carolina, which is home to Delta Force and JSOC

HUMINT – Human Intelligence

IC – Intelligence Community

IED – Improvised Explosive Device

IMINT – Imagery Intelligence

IRGC – Iran's Islamic Revolutionary Guard Corps

ISA – Intelligence Support Activity

ISR – Intelligence, Surveillance, and Reconnaissance

Jackpot – JSOC term for a successful direct action mission

JIEDDO – Joint Improvised-Threat Defeat Organization

JSOC – Joint Special Operations Command, Command of Delta Force, SEAL Team 6, "Nightstalkers" 160th Special Operations Aviation Regiment

Mohawks – A name given to Iraqis that JSOC elements recruited and trained in espionage tradecraft

NAI – Named Area of Interest

NCTC – National Counterterrorism Center

NOC – Non-official Cover operative

NSA – National Security Agency

OCONUS – Outside Continental United States

ODA – Operational Detachment Alpha (standard 12-man Special Forces team)

OEF – Operation Enduring Freedom

OIF – Operation Iraqi Freedom

OPTEMPO – Operational Tempo

OPSEC – Operations Security

Orange – Color coded name for JSOC's Task Force Orange (TFO), the "Belvoir Boys" intelligence unit known as the Intelligence Support Activity (ISA)

OSD – Office of Secretary of Defense

PDB – President's Daily Brief

POTUS – President of the United States

Quds Force – The covert operations part of Iran's Islamic Revolutionary Guard Corps

ROE – Rules of Engagement

RPA – Remotely Piloted Aircraft (drone)

RUMINT – Rumor Intelligence

SAP – Special Access Program, often considered Black Projects that are especially sensitive operations and can be excluded from standard contract investigations

SAS – Special Air Service (British special forces)

SCIF – Sensitive Compartmented Information Facility

SECDEF – Secretary of Defense
SIGINT – Signals Intelligence
SMU – Special Mission Unit (within JSOC)
SNA – Social Network Analysis
SOCOM – Special Operations Command
SOF – Special Operations Forces
SOT-A – Special Operations Team-Alpha, a signals intelligence-electronic warfare element of the US Army Special Forces
TF – Task Force
UAS – Unmanned Aerial System
UAV – Unmanned Aerial Vehicle
USAP – Unacknowledged Special Access Program, a program made known to only authorized persons, including members of the US Congress special committees (often unconfirmed and verbal only)
VEO – Violent Extremist Organization
WMD – Weapon of Mass Destruction
WILCO – Will Comply
Waived SAP – Deep Black Programs, a subset of USAP whereas congressional members may be removed from the knowledge of such program existence

Prelude

Tunis, Tunisia, 20 years ago

"Allahu Akbar, Allahu Akbar, Ash-hadu alla ilaha illa-llah…"
CIA Chief of Station Alex Woolf heaved the metal spike down on target just as a blaring Muslim call to prayer echoed from Tunis's Al-Zaytuna minaret loudspeakers. The monotone muezzin's summoning startled pigeons to flight in the haze of the Mediterranean coastline, caromed through the ancient city's tumbled stone thoroughfares, and pushed its way into the rustic kitchen as the ice pick did its bidding.

Alex's thirteen-year-old son, Warren Drake Woolf, stood abreast sweating profusely under Africa's stifling heat as his father rhythmically stabbed the pick with force and requisite lesson. There was always a lesson. And that was just fine for Drake.

Today, however, would set a new standard for lessons learned, propelling Drake into a dark future as judge and jury of men.

Both males wiped their brows from the sweltering heat that the small room trapped like a prisoner barred from parole.

"Drake, when *you* do this, don't use one hand like me. Use both hands around the handle without interlocking fingers. Wrap them around…like a pistol grip." He demonstrated to his nodding son. "Thumb on top so the force of impact doesn't loosen your hold. Angle it slightly outward so it can't slip and go into your stomach. Come down hard. If it sticks, rock it a bit to go deeper or to get leverage to break off a chunk. Got it?"

"Yes, Sir," his son parroted back with scant emotion, still transfixed by the seven-inch carbon steel pick. The boy processed what he was instructed and tucked it away for future recall. From the corner of his eye, Drake watched his Tunisian friends outside. They were standing behind the short white-washed back garden concrete wall. Waiting. Drake had left them over an hour ago after a pickup soccer match in the adjacent lot so he could continue his Berber language lessons. The Woolf family was headed to Northern Mali next month, and Mother was adamant that Drake get a head start on yet another Sahara-Sahel Arab dialect. It would be easier to make new friends with language, she insisted. What Princeton PhD in linguistics working for the State Department wouldn't be so biased?

The kitchen must have been over ninety degrees. Alex wiped his deep Sahara-tanned forehead again. Perspiration beads collected under his mustached upper lip until they swelled and dropped from the weight.

"And why would it be bad for the pick to go into your stomach, Drake?" the spymaster tested.

"Can't sew it up."

"Correct. Deep punctures don't heal as well as shallow ones. Especially if they hit vitals. And why else?"

Why else? Drake's face distressed as he searched the catalogs of his mind for the right answer. *Was there something else?* His dark brown eyes drew up and to the left as he racked his brain. *What about the stomach? Something about stomach wounds.* Drake's tongue involuntarily clicked, a tic that validated aspects of a doctor's diagnosis back in the States. *God it's hot in here. It's always so hot.*

"Drake?" his dad pressed. "Why else?"

Dad was rarely cross. At least not with this son. Drake anguished at the thought of missing something important from a lesson. "Because… *because it would*…the stomach…"

"The stomach?" Dad crossed his arms. Head tilted.

The body language jacked with Drake's thinking even more. "I don't remember," he surrendered in a frustrated defeat. His head and shoulders slumped, but his fists balled, still in the fight. "Because it would…suck."

Alex Woolf's tight lips broke into a coy smile. "Exactly. It would suck. Especially with a deep puncture into the gastrointestinal tract. A field medic would have to plug it. Maybe use a tampon or something if he didn't have the right supplies. Not that a lot of guys have tampons in the field," he joked.

Drake visibly grimaced at the thought of blood. And of female hygiene products.

"Sorry." Alex grinned. "But anyway, use something to plug and absorb blood to buy time. Now that could also cause contamination, so you're not out of hot water yet. Either way, a doctor will have to open the patient up, find the source of the bleed, and also treat for infection." His eyebrows raised for impact. "It's pretty major." Alex popped an ice piece into his mouth. He lifted his son's chin to make eye contact and crunched the frozen chip. "But it would definitely suck, bud. And the question sure isn't important enough to stress over. Got it?"

Drake nodded in understanding. But being trapped in his own compulsions was something that he, himself, couldn't understand. He didn't think that was really the right answer. And that bugged him to the point of neurotic distraction.

The boy's IQ was as off the charts, as was his height for a young teen. Tunisian couscous stews and merguez sausage, Drake's food staple, were filling out his broad swimmer frame a plate at a time. Aside from his dark hair, he didn't take after his mother's lean Cypriot side of the family. But his OCD didn't come from his father. Nor did Drake's lack of confidence.

"Is that *really* the answer? I meant 'suck' like not good, not sucking wound. I can't remember the right word." Drake still wore a mask of heavy concern. His tongue clicked again as he contemplated.

"What?" Alex's blank look showed no clue as to what had been said. And then it changed to revelation. Drake was still wrestling with closure. "Sheesh, let it go, Buddy. You're maybe thinking pneumothorax? Like though a chest wall?"

Pneumothorax! Yes. Drake perked up. "That's the word. You taught me that last week." *Remember it. Pneumothorax. Pneumothorax. Pneumothorax.* He recited to himself.

Alex leaned against the tiled counter and lowered his voice. "Drake, no one in the field will say pneumothorax. They'll say 'suck.' And we don't need to talk about it, but the tongue clicking is getting louder again. There's no need to be so concerned about an absolutely correct answer. Life's not that clear."

Drake was well aware of the fact that the clicking drove his dad apeshit, but at least they had overcome the blinking tic.

"You are your mom's son." He put his hand on the boy's shoulders with another reassuring pat. "Drake, there could be lots of answers to a lot of questions. But in there somewhere"—he tapped his own head—"is also your dad. You've gotta let me out, too." He winked. "And most importantly, find yourself."

Tension continued to lift from the boy.

"So, a recap. And then I'm done lecturing. Rely first on what you've learned and how you've trained. Second, rely on your gut. Whatever your answer, whatever your choice, you won't be wrong. Because it's your choice. And there's rarely only one option. And you can't use your energy stressing on a decision. Make your decision and free your mind to respond if you need to make another quick decision." He rapped Drake on the noggin. "Mind memory is still muscle memory. It becomes second nature; instinct is developed with self-confidence. Believe in yourself, kid. That I can't teach. That's on you. That's your inner voice. Let your inner voice, not your tight head voices, get you out of problems," his father shared with the utmost of compassion to the family's fragile flower.

Drake affirmed again with a slow nod.

"And the problem of the day, my boy, is beating this heat."

"It's Africa, Dad. It's always hot."

"Well, if we were someplace cooler, you wouldn't learn how to chip ice. Right?" Alex Woolf lifted the pick and chipped a large corner of the ice block, sending tiny shards of ice into their faces. Both dad and lad had a good chuckle. Alex grabbed a small glass goblet and filled it halfway with the ice pieces scattered across the unevenly tiled countertop. He offered a small handful of the ice chips to his son.

"Yeah, we wouldn't want to be anywhere cool, would we?" The boy smirked as he dropped a few frozen bits onto his tongue.

"Ha...ha." Alex playfully stepped on his son's shoe. "Quiet, boy. Hand me that scotch, please. Because I decided a couple hours ago that I'm done working for the day." He smiled.

Taking the bottle, he searched Drake's dark eyes for a glimmer of courage. "You wanna taste it? Just make sure your mother isn't coming down the hall." Dad gave a wink and a nod of approval then tossed a glance to the kitchen door, encouraging his teen to take a peek before imbibing.

Their eyes re-locked. A knowing smile broke across each of their faces. "Check, check, checkmate." They recited the Woolf father-and-son catchphrase with a sneaky chuckle.

Drake pushed the thick swinging door out a crack and peered down the long hallway. He saw shadows shifting under the turquoise front door's threshold gap. Drake held his breath for a moment, wishing his brother had come back home. *No way is that happening.* Dad said not to worry. Mom still cried at night. The shadow was probably just Mehdi, the driver, coming back from the market.

Drake's mother descended the side stairs toward the kitchen. He stepped back and slowly guided the door to a partial close keeping an eye on Mother's whereabouts.

A faint knock on the entryway door beckoned Dr. Woolf to change course, which she obliged. Her long legs whipped the ruffled crepe panels of the draping yellow zest minidress along the way. It was a favorite off-the-shoulder outfit reserved for the house until Tunisia's women's rights could catch up to the less conservative Italian fashions she treated herself to when visiting the other side of the sea. Feeling elegant, she waved her arms widely as if they were gliding over clouds while giving the fabric an extra sweep of flutter. She hummed the Smiley Lewis song "I Hear You Knocking." Her head bobbed in rhythm with a touch of facial sass. "*Hayya 'ala salah...*" The dua, a second Islamic call to the late afternoon's Asr prayer, reverberated again, ping-ponging through the neighborhood. It summoned believers to line up. An unusually hastened call after the first.

Drake sensed from the singing that his mom was in a good mood today, but she was way too close to the kitchen. He wasn't going to chance it. The teen waved off the alcoholic spirits and detected movement from the back window. His buddies were still loitering in the garden. They were nodding. He extended his neck to view what they were looking at and saw a man. Drake squinted and stepped closer to the glass to see if he could recognize the stranger.

A loud noise from behind the entryway door jolted Drake. The bottle of scotch slipped from Alex Woolf's hand and shattered on impact, and the auburn booze splashed across the floor, onto their legs, and up to the cabinets, but neither looked down.

Their attention was laser-focused beyond the solid kitchen door.

A shrill scream pierced Drake's ears.

Shouting.

Alex grabbed his son and flung him toward the back door.

Automatic muzzle report.

Drake recognized the sound immediately. Kalashnikov. Same as he used in desert target practice with Dad and Tom Mendle, the embassy's regional security officer.

As noises flooded the house, his father, intently watching Drake without a word spoken, closed his eyes knowingly and then snapped to action in a controlled harmony of movement and directives.

"Drake. Out the back," the spook ordered in a muted voice. "I have to help Mom." He pushed his tearing son closer to the rear door and turned toward the melee in the other room.

Drake was rigid from fear. His hands wouldn't lift to the door handle; mentally they were one with his sides.

"Go, Drake," Dad commanded, his eyes frantic. "Get out *NOW!*" he mouthed. "Get the Marines at the embassy gate and find Tom." Alex Woolf pushed past the swinging door, looking back one last time. "I have my gun," he lied, patting his bloused overshirt. "I love you and I'll be with you." He winked. "Always." And charged toward death to buy time for his son's escape.

Drake Woolf touched the back-door handle. As the kitchen door swung closed, automatic gunfire erupted again.

Curses and wails from Dad filled his ears amidst the loud staccato snapping of rounds.

Drake was losing his own war battling the burden of decision and the anguish of losing Dad. Fear pitted Drake's core, clawing and gnashing at entrails demanding action of the pathetic weakling shell that locked rage in.

Mom? Dad? His lip quivered. "Dad?" He sobbed without sound as the emotions rushed over him.

Drake, get going. The inner voice commanded Drake. It roared, demanding to be released. He stared at the kitchen door. Dad wanted him to get Tom. Ordered him to get Tom.

Get out, Drake.

He turned to the back window and saw his local friends. They were smiling. Amir seemed to be particularly enjoying himself watching the large two-story embassy housing unit. The boys could no doubt hear the terrors from within with windows cast open and sounds of Hell resounding. Sounds that most certainly traveled to the minaret tower down the street.

Goddamn you, you stupid kid. More head voices were screaming.

Drake could hear Tunisian Arabic, *Derja* chatter starting up again. It was rushed and seemed to be growing louder, moving toward the kitchen.

Move, you shit!

The rage inside gripped him with terror. The voices were angry. Unlike anything he had heard before. His eyes locked on the steel ice pick resting on the counter.

Listen to Dad.

He looked at the back door. They would come for him next if he didn't run.

Trust your gut.

His tongue clicked. Hypomania boiled over.

Kill them all!

Drake seized the steel kitchen pick and rushed to his parents, barging through the heavy door.

As he moved toward the attackers, his surroundings slowed.

Three men. Tunisians. Who exactly, he had no clue.

Kalashnikov rifles. Lowered rest position. Facing parents on the floor. Deep pools of red blood.

Drake screamed a banshee war cry. It sounded distant. He sprang toward the closest man. Ice pick raising high, he whipped his arm down to the man's back. The long metal spike sank deep and true. Drake rotated his wrist to rip the piercing wound wide then yanked the pick from the bellowing intruder and hurtled himself at the next. Blood trailed the spike like a red ribbon whip.

The second man twisted in Drake's direction, but untrained muscle memory failed to raise the intruder's AK weapon.

Die!

In flight, Drake raised the pick for the attack and came down clenching it with both hands, thumb over top. He drove the steel in the chest of the surprised North African before him.

The ice pick hit bone, and Drake's wrists folded upon resistance. Drake's trailing legs found promise and sprang him up as he wrenched the pick to the side and heaved the steel again but deeper to an unprotected beating heart.

The invader's mouth fell agape. The man shuddered violently before his eyes rolled back.

As man and boy fell, Drake heard a crack. What felt like the hardest-ass punch he could imagine jettisoned him and the assaulter with massive force. Drake landed on the man, and another ghost punch hit Drake's side, flipping him over to the right. He felt like he was falling for an eternity in darkness before yet another shocking impact to his left shoulder sent him further into the empty and soundless abyss.

The ice pick rolled from his open hand into the growing pool of blood. A picture on the wall, two smiling brothers and doting parents, looked beyond the flaccid bodies bleeding out on the floor.

"*Qad qamat as-salah...*" sang into the house from a distance, and the late afternoon prayers began.

* * * *

Military Hospital, Place de Tunis, an hour later

He hadn't cried in decades, but Tom Mendle wiped watering eyes as he watched young Drake rushed to surgery down the mint green corridor with its peeling paint. Blood stained the white sheet covering the boy lying atop a gurney that looked like an abandoned asylum's rusted relic. Two Marines and the embassy deputy security officer stood by Tom's side.

"Tom, the kid took three 7.62s at close range," offered the deputy to his boss as a dose of reality. "He's probably not gunna make it. At least he grabbed your hand." The deputy shrugged. "He knows he's not alone." All eyes were on Tom, hoping he would accept the condolence to relieve his aching heart.

Mendle shook his head, rejecting the words. "We had warnings."

"Woolf had the same warning. It's not on you."

Tom Mendle bristled at the deputy's remark. "I mean warnings weren't on Woolf provided he stayed north and away from talking to the Tuaregs," he waffled. "Maybe it's random."

Tom filled his lungs. Stress constricted his chest. He tried to breathe it out. Fail. His insides grew tighter. Tom wished he had a baby aspirin just in case this was causing another grabber. "I've seen the two dead guys. This isn't random. Tunisia doesn't support this type of attack on Americans. But we're seeing more shitheads roaming around lately. There's something growing. I don't know... No one here wants Algeria's shit to spill over. Maybe the locals do. Alex had a better handle on it than I do. His wife heard chatter from the women she tutored in private. Bad shit's coming."

"Tom, our embassy people are pretty safe. They're hands-off."

Mendle was lost in his thoughts. "Woolfs were good people. Smart. Damn they were smart folks. And that kid. Sonofabitch, that twitchy quiet kid is aces. I mean the balls on Drake to go after those dudes with a friggin' what...ice pick? Holy shit. Never would have expected it from that bag of mis-wired nerves." Tom shook his head in disbelief.

The deputy security officer knew exactly what Tom meant. "I know. Pretty crazy. Alex would've done the same. Maybe he'll pull through, though. Clearly, he's a fighter. Who should we call? Langley first?"

"CIA is protocol. They'll handle it. I know the kid's uncle, though. Alex's NSA sister's husband. Robert. He and Alex were like brothers if you saw 'em together. Did same tours overseas." Tom blankly stared off into the hospital's empty corridors, looking at absolutely nothing.

"The uncle military or spook?"

"Huh?"

"The uncle. Was he prior military or Agency too?"

"Both," Tom replied. "Robert was Special Forces then CIA tactical advisor with the Phoenix program. Vietnam. He was one of the Blue Light plank holders and then did about five years with Delta after that. He's at Bragg now. Intel chief. Tougher than nails," he muttered. "Black program-type shit. He loves to be involved in the dirty stuff. They don't have kids."

The deputy's forehead lifted and eyebrows shot up in astonishment. "Wait. Bob? As in Robert O'Toole, the JSOC J-2 is the kid's uncle? *THE* O.T.?"

Tom exhaled a small pocket of air from his nose. He smirked at the deputy's revelation. "Yeah. *THE* one. So," he drew out, "we're letting Agency boys handle *that* call. O.T.'s going to make it worse here when he finds out." Tom stiff-fingered his deputy's chest. "We need to get hunting these goons and their links to any others before O'Toole has someone order us to. If it comes from Langley in the next week, believe me, it's coming from Bob. And we'll need bodies. Not names."

The deputy drew a quizzical expression, not exactly following the plan. Tom clarified. "O.T. may be intelligence, but he gives absolutely two shits about names unless they're on a list to get whacked."

"Holy shit, Tom. That's more of an Agency job. That's not on us. We're the watch, not a tactical team."

"Yeah," he said flatly, "But we're the closest thing to being able to. Alex didn't give an ounce of respect to the Agency's social party types who never walked the alleys and snubbed his way of getting intel. Plus, I think we need to start by finding Drake's brother and that band of holier than thou bearded assholes he hides out with. Talk about shame of the family." Tom tightened his lips for a moment then reflected in a low mutter, "Kid's been a struggle. Didn't stick out college. Army wasn't going to work. A real shady fucker. Streetwise and had the gift of languages like his mom. But never did anything with it. What a waste."

* * * *

When the Maghreb sunset prayers ended, a Range Rover appeared small and black on the road traveling into the vast Tunisian desert area south of Tataouine. Red sunlight faded from the purple African sky and men hugged in the shadows of old medina's winding streets. Dexter Woolf, scourge of his family, bounced along in the SUV. Even as the blindfold slipped, he saw nothing but darkness.

Part I
"Send Me"

Chapter 1

Sidon District, Lebanon, Present Day

From under a dust-covered rough and ready tarp tent, Drake "Birddog" Woolf eyed the persistent stare camera feeds on his laptop monitor. No movement in the structure. The high-value target appeared to be literally sleeping in his "bed-down location." Others in the two-story refugee flat were also in deep slumber according to the four image panes on his computer's dust-caked display.

Drake blinked dry, bloodshot eyes to focus and wiped the screen with the back of an equally filthy hand. Americans like Drake, in this secret unit, were no strangers to the Levant, their periodic and established presence dating back to the 1980s when they started conducting human and signals intelligence against militant cell phones and other electronic communications. To Woolf, this ancient battleground was home to many of his non-official cover missions against Hezbollah and other targets of opportunity using classic espionage tradecraft and new high-tech bells and whistles.

Let's go, Drake. The dark voice prodded from within.

It's not time. Drake had more targeting preparation to do before rushing in and needed to keep focused on tasks beyond the kill.

His IBM ThinkPad was recycled from India and procured from the Middle East to fit a closer pattern of life to his indigenous cover legend and backstops. This meant he had to look the part to play the part if he was caught. The computer's screen cast a dim, hazy glow on Drake's tanned and chemically bronzed face. His foul breath passed through a four-year-old beard that hung like dark cloth from his emaciated cheekbones and flowed over cracked and blistered lips.

Woolf's tongue was swollen from dehydration. It made a slight clicking sound as he contemplated his move after days of surveillance. The quiet clicks had persisted since he was a young teen. Ever since that day, and even before he decided to speak again to the aunt and uncle who brought him back from a zombie-like state of mental purgatory.

Woolf knew he needed to take his meds, but he couldn't afford slowing down his mind. They could wait. He had business to attend to. But the voices would persist.

Drake switched screen views to his network and signal monitoring utility feeds for COMINT, or communications intelligence. He had to continue validating the target and ensure there was a strong connection if he was going to get what he needed for the job. And to get what he wanted for himself.

An internet protocol, or IP, address mapped to the house's location in addition to the other triangulated bearings that targeted the exact position of the known violent extremist. This showed the team supporting Drake from afar who was in the house and where the signals were coming from. It confirmed the baseball card, or BBC, as it was often called when the detailed descriptions of an adversary matched.

In addition, the National Security Agency's Global Access Operations brainiacs had pushed the highly classified Y-LOCKCHECK communications surveillance data to Drake's system fields, validating a bunch of other techie mumbo-jumbo that basically said in bits and bytes and data blips that, yes, the asshole is indeed in the house and plenty of his nasty pals are nearby.

There was little to no risk of a technical blink occurring that would allow the target to vanish. Billions of dollars' worth of American technology pointed at a two-bit shithead in a shithole location to ensure he was the right guy and staying under watchful eyes. This wide-reaching system surveillance captured personal details, pattern of life, communication linked associates, and stored media. A comprehensive electronic snare locked the target to Drake, call sign Birddog, the digital assassin who'd stalked his prey for nearly a month in the region.

Drake's direction-finding and ranging Amberjack antennae also ensured the proximate lockdown. Once all the electronics and intelligence gave undisputable validation, then it would be old-school, roll up the sleeves, hardware meets flesh time. Of course, the latter was outside of his current mandate but well inside of Drake Woolf's comfort zone and the professional expectations of his uncle Robert.

As Murphy's Law would have it, the signal on Drake's feed stuttered for a moment. "No, no, no, no, no, no." Drake refreshed his setting with the last few hours' worth of technical signal bearings, pummeling frequencies to recapture the trace. The cell phone data indicated the target was spoofing a device MAC address to hide traceability. "You tricky little shit," he whispered with a self-assured smirk as the IMSI phone ping responded to his Harris Hailstorm stingray cell-site simulator and surveillance intercept tool. He reconnected.

Check, check, checkmate...motherfucker. Not sneaky enough. Drake gave the screen a middle finger. Nearing prep work completion, he keyed and pasted the code script for a payload hack to the phone that would remotely extract calls, contacts, and anything else from the target's phone to a cloud database.

Almost go-time.

His secondary tasking was to digitally capture bank transfer routing numbers that would also be swept up by the program written to search the target's device remotely. But personally, Drake needed a certain photo recognition from the crow, as he and his crew called terrorists. He'd handle that personally, and against orders. Drake knew the likelihood of a positive identification of the photo would be a million to one shot. Although, considering Drake's unofficial body count of those he'd shown the picture to, it was more like a million to upward of sixty when totaling all the up-close and personal terminations in the past decade. None of those men recognized the photo he presented at their time of final interrogation. And so he continued on his quest.

"Birddog to Halo Actual," Drake whispered. "Do you copy? Over."

"Halo Actual to Birddog. Good copy. Ready to come home? Over."

"Target handhold is locked. Just sent verification package to the mother ship. I'm clear to go say hello for final confirmation," Drake whispered. The tan skin-colored ear device and its four-millimeter boom microphone captured the fidelity and catapulted the communication up to the secure satellite relay.

"That's a negative, Birddog. You are red. Confirm. You are not green to shake hands. Stick to your script as fragged. You just help us develop the picture and confirm the BBC. Time to bug out. Do you copy? Over," the Operational Detachment Delta G Squadron commander, Blake Touhey, directed from the Beirut safe house over forty kilometers away.

Blake muted the mike and leaned to his right. "Man from Orange is on target. Chief, call our flyer. Temp hold payload on objective until he's outta there."

"Roger that. Not cleared hot on our end. I'll let 'em know," the chief validated.

"If they ask, tell 'em pre-strike HVI assurances are potentially compromised. We just need a minute to get him off the roof and headed for pickup," said the commander with a grin.

He had referred to *Orange* as Drake Woolf's unit—the Intelligence Support Activity, known as Orange, Centra Spike, Grey Fox, and a host of other terms to mask the true identity of one of the most secretive military elements in existence.

"Move the boys in for extraction. This crazy Activity bastard got closer to this crow in a week than we did in a year of deployments. Let's get 'em out before he does something stupid."

The channel to Birddog opened again. "Negative, Halo," Drake responded after the long pause, catching the commander off guard. Woolf continued, "I need to confirm. Getting a conflicting signal. Don't have *near certainty* anymore. Going dark and heading into the house for positive ID. Out."

From a snack-sized plastic Ziploc bag, Drake retrieved a small square of paper and placed it on his tongue. The microdose of lysergic acid diethylamide, a lesser fix of the recreational LSD hallucinogen, would heighten his senses and make him more productive for the hour. It was cool though, because the military gave it to him just as they used to give him performance-enhancing amphetamine "go pills" like Dexedrine. Oddly, he would have been discharged if they knew of his legit medical needs.

Birddog pinched the acoustic device out from his ear cavity and dropped it into a streamlined, discreet, zippered pocket within the seams of his customized button-down shirt.

Can't stop me if you're not here.

Now it's time to get some.

"Shit! He's going in. I knew he'd go in. Dammit." Blake was half frustrated and half tickled. "Birddog, do you copy? That is negative. You are not to engage."

Blake leaned back with a suppressed grin, "Fuck. Mister Sandman's going into that house. If it goes south, we're screwed."

"We were going to kill the crow anyway, your guy just didn't know it," quipped the large Native American Delta warrant officer nicknamed Taco.

"Pssht," he scoffed. "The video game boys were going to get the kill. I could give two shits about what Birddog does. At this point, we're observers—and a ride." Blake didn't hide his frustration. "Fucking drone strike in a refugee camp. We're so outta the game. Only the Pentagon could think this stupid shit up as an op worthy of green-lighting. Blame locals or some bullshit cover-up scheme." His face contorted in distaste of the plan as if Taco had farted. "Wait until someone puts the missile fragments up on social media." The commander kicked the chair next to him. "Birddog knew what was going to happen even if no one told him. All these joint task force ops are finishing with a push-button video kill. But not today."

* * * *

Drake pulled the black-and-white cotton keffiyeh scarf down to his dusty brow and draped fabric around his face to cover his nose and mouth. With a few taps on the Arabic character laptop keypads the hum of electrical generators immediately fell silent. Remaining lights in the surrounding hundred meters extinguished their glow in and out of the Ain al-Hilweh Palestinian refugee camp. Anyone awake would consider it a usual power failure. The reality, of course, was a remote power disruption device in the bag of tricks tradecraft from Drake's playbook.

Woolf inserted the USB port "brain killer" and waited for the loaded code scripts to destroy the digital content of the laptop's hard drive. Upon closing the tattered computer screen, he secured a small, sticky explosive charge on its underbelly and set the timed charge for thirty minutes. Drake slowly emerged from the hidden tarp and filled his lungs with the fresh albeit scorching hot Lebanese night air. First, he would give his fatigued eyes ample time to adjust. Then he would climb down from the rooftop. And then it was snuff the bad guy time. His favorite part. He whipped the antennae as far as he could onto another rooftop.

With eyes growing more attuned to the darkness and his senses getting a chemical tweak for high performance, Drake dashed across the narrow street. He hoped the lubricant he had put on the door hinges of the home earlier in the week had sufficiently quieted the wicked squeak. He took painstaking efforts to ensure an op would go down as planned. Even if it took days.

A dog barked in the distance. The LSD gave him an edge that could nearly hear the guttural canine growl from blocks away.

The sentry stationed at the door would be gone for another forty-minutes and the rest of his surroundings were silent. Three a.m. wasn't a busy time in the encampment. If a roach would have farted, he could have heard it.

Birddog inserted a shallow hook and lifter pick into the imported European door lock of the home. He manipulated the pins while using the centering fulcrum. Just like flossing teeth.

Success.

"What are you doing?" the voice from behind Drake asked in Lebanese.

Drake felt something hard pressed on his back. *Not good.* Woolf didn't turn. "You left your post," he scolded in the same tongue. "There was a noise coming from the house." Drake bent the lock picks into his palm, the steel long enough to jut from his clenched fingers.

"What noise? Who are you?"

"My mom called me Warren," he replied switching to Palestinian Arabic then spun catching a rifle barrel with his left and sending the lock pick fist into the man's throat. Like a tight rubber band, Drake's arm snapped back and then straight into the throat again while guiding the rifle out and away. The man's throat wheezed but not loud enough to cause a disturbance. Woolf dropped the picks and gripped the rifle butt then came back with a hammering blow to the man's head. The cracking feel confirmed sentry down. For good.

Drake scanned the streets. All was still clear.

He dragged the sentry into the home and left the body in a sitting room corner before moving to the modest kitchen. Drake found a half-full pitcher of water on a table, which after adjusting his scarf at a frantic pace, he brought up to his broken lips and gulped the cascading warm liquid of life. It was salty and foul-smelling but welcome, nonetheless. Drake guzzled it to the point of breathlessness. He wiped his dripping lips with his dusty shoulder sleeve only to smear water into mud.

His adhesive covered hands were sticky with blood but he gave them no thought. He was not going to make a clean exit regardless of what happened next.

A cleaver lay just as he had seen it on the camera feeds hours ago. To its right, a thick six-inch cutting knife. The latter was his quest.

In addition to Woolf and his unit entering a country under commercial cover, he was most always unarmed. At least conventionally.

Knife in hand, Drake continued up the narrow staircase.

Ho, ho, ho.

As the flooring beneath his feet creaked, his belly gurgled in seeming protest of the long-lost aquatic friend that had just invaded the withered cavity. It had been almost two days since he had had to piss. Add pissed-off kidneys to the list of furious bodily organs constantly pushed to limits.

Drake pressed at his gut, hoping it would recognize the need for silence. *Santa's not liking that eggnog.* Woolf was pleased with neither the sounds of his digestive tract nor the floor alarming anyone within lucid earshot.

The first room was the children's. That was off-limits. Personal code. Next.

The second chamber was the host's and his wife's. Later. Maybe. This was a flexible code determined by operational constructs. Namely, if shit went south it was cool to smoke them. He'd feel bad, but he'd be alive.

The third room, as the story goes, *was just right* and held the shady little Goldilocks—Syrian jihadi rebel leader and Iranian-sponsored moneyman Ali al-Hamad, a dude on the lam who the Israelis did not want to gain a foothold of influence within the camp. Somehow the Americans got the task. Tier one target for tier one troops. An opportunity gained was an opportunity seized.

Woolf crept up to the sleeping man's bedroll. He knelt down and gently put his latex liquid skinned hand over al-Hamad's snoring mouth. Ali stirred a bit but succumbed to deep slumber and breathed through his nose until the blade passed through shirt to skin.

Ali al-Hamad's eyes shot open, and forced air expired from his lungs, captured in the palm of Woolf's filthy rubberized hand.

Drake held out his mobile device, showing a glowing image of a man in his mid-to-late forties. The picture itself was dark and somewhat distorted. The bright glow made the target squint and blink until he could focus on the bearded man in the image before him, maybe Caucasian or a Turk.

Al-Hamad showed no apparent emotion at the sight of the picture save for the fear in his eyes of being awoken under duress.

Drake flipped to a sketched image saved on the device.

"Do you know this man? Both could be the same man. Have you ever seen him?" Drake asked in Arabic. "Think!"

Al-Hamad struggled and closed his eyes for a moment. He moved under Drake's hand, turning his head back and forth, signaling a denial of any knowledge of the photographic image before him.

"Asking again. For your life," Woolf whispered in a more than passable local accent.

Again, his subject denied knowing and moved his shoulders in an apparent shrug. Nothing. Another dead end.

Do it.

Drake Woolf pushed the knife between the man's ribs, the pericardial cavity, to the heart. Woolf's nostrils flared in frustration of the continual dead end with the photo. He took a deep breath and bent forward. "Sorry, pal," he whispered. "You're no help to *me*." Woolf's face was stone as he pushed the knife deeper before pulling it out with al-Hamad's passing life. He wiped the knife three times across the man's nightshirt. His thumb was not on the top of the handle. Drake had developed his own style over the years.

Woolf leaned in and with the room's faint light watched the man's eyes roll and the body succumb to the fate of a lingering Department of Defense Al-Qaeda network Executive *death* Order. Such orders permitted

US special operations to work in denied spaces without hindrance of legal or bureaucratic process to target and kill members of the AQN. Al-Hamad wasn't a card-carrying member of the terror group, but he was close enough to that charter and authorization that no one would raise a war crime eyebrow. But then again, Woolf didn't plan on signing his name or getting caught. Neither did his taskers or the president, himself. So, the point was moot. And Al-Hamad was no longer on the list.

Drake left his target lying lifeless save for the blood escaping to the floor. He rose devoid of emotion to his next task, retrieved the small camera from its nestled place in the bookcase stacked with magazines and newspapers, and proceeded to the host's bedchamber while stuffing the camera into a small cloth pouch.

Once in the bedroom of two sleeping adults, he placed the knife on the man's bedcovers in silence. It had just enough blood on the blade and handle to serve its purpose. Woolf looked with scorn at the man and woman who knowingly gave safe haven to a man capable of creating more problems for their own region. From a large hip pocket, Drake retrieved a bundle of Lebanese pounds. The US equivalent of roughly ten thousand dollars.

Judas. Drake, they have to die.

Drake placed the stack of currency on a small table.

You've been a little naughty too, Drake accused the man and woman to himself *But I'm going to let your neighbors and the local militia deal with that.*

After Drake left the soon-to-be-framed man and wife, he stood at the bedroom doorway where the children lay within, innocent under a blanket of assumed safety and security of their parents' watch.

"Shit," Drake muttered to himself. *We'll kill these kids ten years from now because of what I'm doing now. Kids like me.* He stood in the darkness. Silent. Deliberating.

Son of a bitch.

He looked at his watch. Five minutes tops before the militia would check in. They'd done it for days.

"Shit." Drake stared at the door to the children. *What do I do, Dad?* He softly clicked his tongue.

The vivid sound of Alex Woolf memory spoke to the soul of his son and over the voices in Drake's head. *"You know what to do. And it's not this."*

Drake rushed back into the host's room, picked up the knife, covered the startled man's mouth and stabbed him superficially just under the clavicle and waited for it. When the man fully awoke and realized what had happened, he flailed his arms defensively and yelled as the burning sensation set in. Woolf gave little effort to prevent the knife from flying from his own grasp.

And then there was the scream. He had anticipated it. Planned on it. And still, it cut deep into his own heart. After over twenty years, his mother's scream still left him breathless. This shriek of utter terror was universal. The images Drake had tucked away for years in the deepest and darkest corners of his mind resurfaced. His mother's sashay to the door. His father chipping ice for scotch. The men with guns. His friends laughing outside. The searing pain.

Drake swallowed hard and moved quickly away from the bed, snatched the money, and tossed it at the wife. "Hide this. Say nothing of it. An intruder has come to your house tonight and killed your guest," he said in Lebanese before fleeing the bedroom. He made haste before the children could see the killer in their home.

The cameras. Damn! He was supposed to get the other fish-eye. He'd have to leave the second camera upstairs.

Ruckus ensued above his head on the second floor. The children were awake now, calling and crying for their parents. Drake heard new noises coming from the front entryway. The militia men. Had he relocked the door? He had to have relocked it and checked again to be sure. And then checked it again. He was certain of it…he thought.

He was late. Woolf whirled to the kitchen, where he grabbed the third camera tucked between a shelf and the thin wall. The fourth was a fish-eye within the sitting room just off the front door. He couldn't get the second camera out of his mind and wrestled with the compulsion to retrieve it.

Drake heard the men opening the entry.

A pop resounded about twenty meters from the home. The laptop's set charge was just loud enough for the men at the door to turn around and stare at flames emerging from a rooftop across the way.

Right on time. Woolf rushed forward and seized the camera, then bolted for the back of the house. The door was barred and padlocked.

From Woolf's first discreet foray into the home weeks ago he had noticed this potential inconvenience for either future entry or escape and had returned to replace the bolts with smaller stripped screws with enough bite to hold the security framing in place. A dab of bronzer on the metal had given enough appearance of aging to camouflage the change.

Missions took days if not weeks or months depending on the complexity. It paid off with groundwork.

Drake gave a few tugs and the bar gave way as the militia men entered the home. Apart from these small preparations and backup plans, his ass was now flying in the wind. He had to leave, but he remained steadfast. *Damned camera.*

In the darkness of the room, he was still unseen, but the militia heard his movement in the back amidst the panicked cries upstairs.

From behind the door, guttural coughs of generators caused a pit in Drake Woolf's stomach. The man from Orange was a neurological blockade away from re-entering the heat of the Lebanese night. The lights were flickering back to life.

I need to get that camera.

Drake turned around and calculated his odds and the time—and the fact that he no longer had a weapon.

"Trust your gut. Screw your tight head," the sensory perception of Alex Woolf's imaginary voice said to his now warrior son. *"Leave the camera, Drake. It's untraceable. Move, boy!"*

Chapter 2

Drake turned from the militia men and kicked the door out to the alleyway, the remaining surveillance device be damned. He lied to himself that it was no big deal leaving it behind and mentally fought the compulsion to turn around every step of his escape. He couldn't disappoint Dad. Not again, anyway.

Woolf willed himself out of his head and accelerated to a full sprint to avoid any trailing pursuers. It was a process he had to consciously overcome on a daily basis to survive and succeed.

He took a quick right down a narrow passageway between the hyper-congested multistory cement block shelters in the overcrowded camp. His fear was not for any Lebanese army threats but rather for the numerous joint committees of Palestinian factions living within the impoverished and overcrowded coastal city. His extraction team would be just outside the walls, but other unexpected militia security forces would be a high risk to his escape and evasion plan.

As he emerged from the tight passage, he spotted a small group of Palestinian militants who he knew would not hesitate to gun down a stranger in this tension-filled shantytown at this time of night or any other, for that matter.

Fatah al-Aqsa Martyrs.

Shit.

Woolf checked his locally purchased knockoff Timex watch even though he knew exactly how little time he had.

The extraction team would come through Darb el Sim between two main checkpoints but not within the camp itself. Drake still had to make it through Fadlo Wakim and Hay el Sohoun, the camp's adjacent areas.

To Woolf, it didn't look good for an on-time ETA for pickup; to seasoned military planners, he was screwed.

Beirut safe house, Lebanon

"Wait a bit longer. He'll be there," Blake assuaged his pickup crew. "Asset had to do a double check. I don't think he engaged and no hostile contact reported. Should be clean coming in. Are you compromised?" The Delta Advance Force Operations commanding officer swiveled his bottom on the rickety kitchen chair and muted the headpiece again. He pointed to the BBMAT advanced tactical terminal screen and swatted at Taco for attention. "What does the Pred see on Birddog's position? Anyone approaching? I wanna give the knob-turner all the time we can." He waited for a response while Taco squinted. "I know some guys who worked with him in Iraq and Afghanistan. I'm sure he'll get there. He's good. Real good. I wish he would've stayed put. Shoulda known."

Taco gave a no-shit look sideward. "I know. He's pulled this shit before. We used to call him SOT-A Drake. He was one of the Task Force Sword SIGINT guys doing AQ and Taliban commo intercepts. They flew him in special for Operation Mountain Thrust when I was in Afghanistan."

"I thought he was a shooter. Eighteen-Echo, no?" Blake referred to an abbreviated Special Forces military occupation specialty of communications expert. "Wouldn't have had unit, rank, or name tape with the teams he was running with."

"Nope, Ranger-tabbed SOT-A," Taco corrected. "One of the few. Trust me, he's a shooter." The description he referenced pertained to another abbreviated role where SOT-A was the shortened name of Special Operations Team-Alpha, a downrange signals intelligence/electronic warfare element of the Army's Special Forces. A lesser-known capability to many outside of special operations, SOT-As are crypto linguists who detect, monitor, and exploit threat communications via intercepted communications and direction locating for the SFODA Forward Operating Base. But they also kill. A geek squad with guns.

Taco leaned back in his chair, nursing battlefield memories. "Team literally called him 'SOT-A Drake.' Badass linguist, too. Arab and a bunch of dialects. Big-ass geek. A-team kicked him out of Fallujah. Dude canoed a tango." Taco made a pistol with his finger. "Bam, thpbt," he said, with a tongue raspberry as both hands created a visual of a head splitting in half.

"RUMINT. That's why I thought he was Group. They kicked him off because he'd disappear at night and go into Iraqi homes interrogating dudes they didn't have a target package on or a green light to engage. Wasn't his call sign, but some guys on that team called him Werewolf."

"Cuz he was tearin' shit up at night? Like on a full moon." Taco laughed while leaning forward and checking the UAV feed again.

"No, Werewolf for Where's Woolf? They thought he was AWOL but he was out hunting in the darkness. From what I heard, the team he was supporting was forward but just sitting around all night with hurry up and waits, and he'd just disappear. They didn't have much oversight, so they just let him do his thing for a bit. He'd say he was scrounging for signals at night. But then they needed to cover their ass when he became like folklore legend and shit and he started freaking out locals who said there was some djinn demon coming into their homes, sometimes killing people, sometimes asking them questions. They asked the FOB team to help hunt this ghost down, and the whole time, the ODA knew it was Drake."

"That's weird."

"Did you pull the view up, yet?" The major leaned over for a look.

"Just about. I was waiting for it to pop back up while we shoot the shit. The target space still isn't back into view." Taco shifted to another laptop.

"Let me have them re-route a hair and take a look-see. Coordinates?"

"Let me confirm. Hold one," replied Blake.

Taco restarted the conversation. "Yeah. SOT-A Drake." Taco nodded. "Quiet guy. Killed what he stalked on the airwaves. I also heard that during OEF and OIF, he was on a JIEDDO team doing Attack the Network Counter-IED shit, too. Took out a cell linked to the Haqqani network like the first week. Found all their money and froze or rerouted it for SOCOM. That's how he got the Birddog call sign—sniffing out and pointing to the prize. NSA's Central Security Service military guys used to go into SOT-A Drake's hooch to get trained on the down low when they were the guys who were supposed to be giving the training. SOT-A Drake punched a guy on the teams when they called him 'Support.'"

"Seriously? That's gotta be more bullshit. I knew he had more TIC than most on the teams," he said, referring to Drake's time in combat.

"That's just what I heard...." Taco turned to the commander with a knowing look. "I do know he teamed with Delta before us when he went to Orange. Dude had invitations from *two* SMUs," he emphasized, given the few operators who received invitations to go through Special Mission Unit assessment.

Taco continued, "He was one of the dudes who trained the Mohawks in Iraq. Sniff out the bad guys' phones on the front end doing combat intel—then poof. Goes from Tactical Technical Tradecraft to Direct Action. Taught the Mohawks the same. Grim reaper carrying a laptop and an M4. Hey, we got any more of that jerky?"

* * * *

Drake Woolf was trapped between the streets but yet undiscovered in a narrow alleyway. He pressed his back against the wall and extended his legs out to the opposite building. Keeping his feet pressed to the parallel surface, he pushed with his hands and wiggled with his back and shoulders to ascend. After each move, Drake stepped up and pressed back with force to secure his position while shimmying up the wall as quickly as possible. Within minutes he reached the top.

Now what? Woolf remained elevated but had nothing to grab at the top. The roof to his shoulder line had hammered tin sheets sloping down and bent over the building facade. There were no hand- or footholds to support his weight. If it were raining, Drake couldn't have been any more wet than he was between the perspiration from heat, physical effort, and sheer dread of his precarious situation.

The opposite building had a flattened rooftop, but it was impossible to maneuver without falling roughly thirty feet down in the shadows.

Below, he heard whispers approaching his position then watched as silhouettes of a militia crew turned into the alleyway.

Woolf stretched his arms to be as flat against the façade and his body as straight across as possible. From the ground, at first glance, he ideally resembled a homemade bridge between buildings as was common in the area. And this was his intent during this ten-minute ultimate abs survival workout.

His left foot, however, was starting to slip.

With his right foot, Drake pushed as hard as he could. He pressed his clammy toes in third-hand Adidas runners against the surface. Gripping with isometric pressure, the traction gone decades ago, his ass began to drop.

Woolf could hear the grating of his left shoe sliding down. But with no leverage to his body, he had nothing left to raise his leg short of spasming abdominal muscles.

Sweat poured from his face; his right leg started to send signals of a coming muscle seizure. He prayed the cameras wouldn't clank in the bag and that his phone wouldn't shift from his nearly inverted pocket. He was as functional as a screen door on a sub and about as dry.

Drake fought against his body, waiting for the militia men to come closer to his position and hoping to the gods they wouldn't look up. He contemplated his only option. The voices drew closer. They were under his position. Drake's left foot completely slipped. *This is going to hurt.*

* * * *

The four-man Delta team kept vigilant as they waited for their package. "Halo Actual, this is Halo Two. Any update to ETA?"

"Negative, Two. Sit tight. I'm sure he's just strolling your way. He may be in warrior mode but he's still a support dork. You are still clear of hobos jumping your train."

The operators laughed. "That's a bit of a stretch, Halo. But thanks for the visual. Standing by."

"Roger that, Two. And who ate the last of the jerky? Can't find it. Over."

"We brought it along," the operator paused for response.

One of his crew whispered as he chewed the dehydrated meat, "Someone's approaching, better go."

Halo Two's lead, Charles Upton, a man they called Upchuck or Barf, laughed. "Uh, we gotta go, someone's coming, Halo Two out." The operator snickered. "That was pretty funny. I thought for a second you were serious about hostile approach."

"I am serious. Look!"

* * * *

Back in the safe house, a Predator feed showed the visual of white bogies approaching by foot and a vehicle turning in their direction. "Can we order the Nevada joystick monkeys to launch the Pred's Hellfire?" he asked, referring to the Creech Air Force Base fliers safe back in CONUS.

"We can't do anything unless engaged. They're not going to let us use a Hellfire for close air support. Shit. That's almost a White House sanction request."

"So, we wait?"

The XO, or commanding officer, sat flipping a pen end over end. He tapped it on the table as he thought through options. "Our dudes aren't here.

None of us are except the bird. But that's sanctioned. We got the target, so that was sanctioned to validate the crow's position. I'm wondering if we could schwack the bogies, right?" He searched his colleague's wide face for any sign of reassurance.

Nothing.

"See if we can get a connection to that Beechcraft King Air. It's gotta be flying arcs above the camp. Just like back in the sandbox. OGA's probably been airborne triangulating with SIGINT listening posts to support Birddog with signal feeds. ISR coverage would be too sparse. Maybe they even have microwave to spot their guy, right? Or maybe they have someone with like native language ears picking up and translating any shit going hot. How is it that we're the guys cut off from the bigger mission plan? I feel like Airborne," he jested under the futility of options.

Taco nodded and interjected an affirming grunt, "God forbid anyone direct connect them to us in case we needed them for *our* work."

"Dude, what even *is* our work here?"

"Support." Taco laughed as he feigned a duck from a punch.

* * * *

Drake craned his neck over a quivering shoulder. He looked down to the adversaries below.

They remained unaware of his presence and precarious situation.

High above their heads, the man from Orange had the three core tenets of close-quarters battle in his favor: stealthy surprise to gain an upper hand, speed against his enemy's immediate recovery, and an ability to inflict violence of action to further destabilize the men below. That was if he didn't screw up.

Newton's law of universal gravitation would make for a powerful weapon. At roughly twenty-five feet off the ground it would take only a second coming in at nearly twenty miles per hour to twist into a reasonable attack position with minimum damage to himself and maximum to the goon below. *Fuck it.* He thought. If an Olympic high diver or gymnast could do it in half the distance, he could at least get off a half-gainer with a twist and stick a landing on top of an unsuspecting goon.

And so he let go.

But even as he contorted his body while plummeting to the ground, he wished he had a better option. Woolf positioned his buttocks and hips, raising his knees just shy of a cannonball to ensure his legs were available to stabilize after the fall.

As he hoped, he landed just off-center of the middle man's head and hammered down on his foe's neck as it bent forward, breaking the bone and rupturing the spinal cord. Drake twisted to the left as the man crumpled under his legs, cushioning the impact and buttressing downward momentum. Crouched to a tripod, Drake snapped his leg outward, catching the next man's knee and driving it at a ninety-degree angle inward. As Woolf extended the kick, he could feel the break of bone and joint and hear the distinct snap as the lower leg flopped upward in a limp swing.

The militia man let out a cry and collapsed with hands covering his face then grasped down to hold the broken leg.

Two down—for the moment.

Drake flipped to the right, back over the dead Palestinian. His feet met the ground, and rolling momentum helped elevate him to a combat stance. His opponent, too, was preparing for battle starting with a trigger pull as he raised the weapon in Drake's general direction.

The muzzle flash was blinding for both men in the alley's darkness.

Drake leapt to the nearby wall and immediately pushed off with his right leg to carom into the assailant.

In the darkness, Drake miscalculated slightly, but both men still collided and hurled into the adjacent wall.

The militant's grip on the discharging weapon softened upon impact.

Drake regained balance and threw multiple devastating body hook punches into his foe's side until he heard the dull clank of the weapon hitting the ground.

The man grasped Drake's shoulder, to which he hammered his arm down and whipped out a balled fist, striking the militia man's face. Drake brought his arms back parallel, seized the man with fists full of clothing, and flung him against the opposite wall. He then yanked him back again into the other wall. When the dull thud of the man's head smacking the concrete sounded, Drake took a step back and watched the body drop like a stone.

All men were down. But the wounded man wouldn't quiet.

Killing a surrendered wounded man was a war crime, but an act of mercy was more acceptable. In this case, the injured man was a liability and technically still a combatant and Drake didn't have a humanity supply of morphine. Time was fleeting and if Drake didn't move out, he'd be a dead man, too His only recourse was to disengage the brain from the body. He did so with multiple swift kicks. The act would change most men forever, but Drake just added it to his tab.

Now he needed his own act of mercy to get to the exfil point. He was already on borrowed time and had to make contact. The plan came to him, and he began to search the bodies for mobile phones. Each had one.

Drake picked up a weapon and began firing down both ends of the alleyway, raising the fire upward and shouting in what little Hebrew he knew, "He's on the roofs!"

Woolf rewrapped his headscarf and headed out in the direction of the corridor the militia men had entered.

Chapter 3

John "Skidmark" Turdington chuckled from his position within the Beechcraft King Air. Not an Agency man, but rather, a member of JSOC's High Value Targeting task force, he was monitoring the airplane's SUMERIAN code-named geolocation system with another virtual base-tower transceiver to vacuum up the camp's data emitting from routers, computers, phones, and other devices within range.

The men's recurring mission over the past week was to re-map from the aircraft the ever-changing digital footprint of Ain al-Hilweh, while still keeping an eye—or ear—to their boy on the ground. "Hey, Waldo, someone on the ground just called Papa John's Pizza in DC. I didn't even know they delivered out here." He half-laughed, assuming someone in Lebanon must have a family member franchising back in the States. Pizza businesses were great for laundering money, so the call was highly plausible given the characters they monitored at just over twenty thousand feet.

The pilot, Herb "Waldo" Waldren, had a quizzical look on his face. He wasn't sure he understood and called back through his headset, "Papa John's Pizza? What the Hell are you talking about?"

Skidmark responded through his headset microphone, "Looks like about a kilometer south from Birddog's spot. Device originating call has stayed in the same place. Hey! I got another one. Holy shit!"

"It's him, right?"

He nodded to himself, now aware of the distress signals. "I'm bettin' yes." Another call to Papa John's from a second phone. Another half kilometer down. "He's evading and dropping us bread crumbs with the phones he's probably tossing behind."

"Think he'll talk unsecured?"

"Nope, just paving the way to give us heads-up. He's running hot. And getting pursued or he's on his way and doesn't want the bus to leave." The pilot replied, "Get to his extraction team. He's banking on us picking it up. Fucking Drake. Yeah! Run, Birddog, run."

"Whatta we do about the chatter we're getting near their extraction team?"

"Trust me, Deltas have better SA on their position than we do," he said, referring to the situational awareness of the extraction team on the ground. "We need to start heading back. Between the heat and the wind up here, I need to either climb or bug out. Not sure if their Pred is really watching our airspace. He'll make it. Always does."

"Roger that. I'll ring up the FOB commander," Skidmark replied, hoping the Forward Operating Base leader could pass the word that their man was on the way.

"Call the in-position boat, too. We may need them. Drake knows they're his secondary ride. Way to make your own luck, Birddog. Godspeed, brother."

* * * *

Drake dialed the pizza delivery number on the third phone. Given the devices had no password blocks, he assumed they were just burners, but he hoped his unit would pick up on the anomalous calls from Lebanon to the States. Though winded and nearly tapped out of energy, he also hoped someone would find a little humor in his resourceful plan. What good were high-speed ops if you couldn't have a bit of levity to cut the absolute panic that could take over your ability to execute? The winding-down chemical edge had certainly helped, too.

Woolf kept up a quick pace shrouding himself by shadows, fortunate that despite the commotion, most residents would be slow to wake and respond. His footfalls landed constantly on street trash and debris from the slum. Piss, shit, decay, and the hot salty sea air assaulted his sense of smell. He laughed, thinking it could very well be his own stench he was taking in. The brief moment of lightness pushed him on to quicken his gait.

Thanks for the nudge, Dad.

He tossed the third phone to his side while it rang thousands of miles away to his local go-to pizza place.

The diminishing sound of "Papa John's, will this be pickup or delivery?" broadened his smile as he gritted through uninvited massive fatigue and pain.

* * * *

Nearly two hundred meters away, armed militia men crammed into a jeep and smoked cigarettes and sipped coffee while patrolling their micro-territory. They remained parked with engine running in the shadows of Ain al-Hilweh. Waiting for anything unusual. Drake was already upon them when he recognized the new shitshow he had fallen into.

Four men popped to ready stance. "Stop!" they demanded, and further requested in Lebanese for Drake to show identification.

Woolf accelerated his breathing, which didn't take much effort, and bowed down into the shadows. His complete exhaustion was used to bolster cover credibility.

"There." He pointed backward without raising his head, "The Israelis. They're snatching our people. Like evil spirits." He spoke in Lebanese. Drake then rose and spread his right hand before his own face, miming a superstition of casting evil wards away. "We heard their animal whistles and they came. Dozens of them from the rooftops, from the shadows, they are everywhere," he panted while speaking their native tongue and casually sat down on the street waving them on, his job seemingly fulfilled and delegated to men tasked with camp security.

In no time, the jeep revved and the men started making frantic calls while hanging on with free hands as the vehicle lurched to life and headed toward the attacking Jews. Cigarettes were thrown to the sides, the butt sparks rolling behind the truck.

Drake reared his head back for a good laugh of relief before starting up. Tempted to stay down, he took another deep breath and looked in the low light toward the suckers heading toward his bluff before forcing himself to get up.

The single working red taillight alerted him, however, that the jeep was stopping. And it hadn't gone the distance. He squinted, thinking maybe they were pointing back at him, when he heard the crack of gunfire and saw the flash of the muzzle in his direction.

He let out a gallows humor sigh and smile. *Good Lord. From bad to worse.* As Drake bolted from his spot, the report of shooting followed behind him.

Rounds ricocheted off walls, the metal shards sparking from the high-velocity friction.

Shit. A fragment of something hit him. He wiped at his stinging cheek and knew he was still about a five-minute run away from the pickup location. "Pick it up, buddy," he pushed himself.

* * * *

"Commander, this is an air element covering one of our men in support of your activity. Can you hear me?" asked Waldo on the other end.

"*My* activity? Who is this? How did you get this sat phone?"

"So, you *can* hear me. Good. We need—"

"I asked who this is." Blake Touhey knew the answer, that it was one of the spooky outfits, but pressed anyway. *Screw these spooks and their secret squirrel shit.*

"Sir, we can either address the issue at hand or I can school you on things a Ranger won't understand anyway. May I continue?"

Are you kidding me? "When you check the Ranger jabs, you can have my attention, asshole."

"We picked up signal that our man is headed to exfil. From what we can tell of communications coming from him and from your team to you, he should be five minutes out but is on his way."

"Roger that," Blake acknowledged. "Are you able to provide any close air support? Our team may have been compromised. I may have to move them out in the next minute."

"That's a negative on our end. We're heading back to refuel. We've already left the area. Figure out a way to wait for the first sergeant. He's doing his best to get to you. Uncle Sam would appreciate if you could wait few more."

"Roger that. Thanks for the update. Appreciate you dumping that in our laps while you go get coffee. Out." *Asshole.*

* * * *

"Who was that?" asked Taco, knowing shit had a tendency of rolling downhill and their position was below sea level at this point.

"Who the hell knows? Orange. Maybe Agency. Probably Orange. Spooky commo boys flying over the camp. Says Birddog's about five minutes out. Guy on the line messed up. Said first sergeant. That means Birddog is a damn E-8."

"Shit. Birddog's a man of rank. He's been in longer than me. Can they reach him? Images on my display are showing our guys may not have an exit."

"We might need to engage hostiles with the Pred, but if they're outside the wall, they're probably not militia."

"Command has orders from POTUS that this has to be a completely deniable operation. Hostile or not, I'm guessing."

"Ring up the fliers. I'm not hanging our guys out to dry. What a clusterfuck. As usual." Blake slapped the table. "E-8. No wonder Birddog doesn't listen to anyone."

Chapter 4

Nevada, Creech Air Force Base

In the unmarked room off a series of equally nondescript hallways, the military brass approached behind two flight-suited airmen situated in ground-control ergonomic chair cockpits operating multiple visual display monitors. Unaware of superior officers present, the fliers sported mint-colored earphones and flight suits and sat in tan leather high-back chairs as they maneuvered their joysticks to guide flying drones across the global battle space. A phone, more ground-control station panels, and recording systems were the only items separating the two men short of their Yeti coffee thermoses and a candy box of Lemonheads.

The screens streamed the live feed and, among other data, displayed details about speed, altitude, and the terrain below.

"We get a jackpot on the objective?" the colonel inquired, hoping for exciting news of another touchdown, as they termed mobile-device-tracked confirmed kills by drones in his AOR. He tapped the men and repeated himself once they pulled down their headphones.

"Sir, the Delta team in Ain al-Hilweh is requesting a change of target. Their extraction team is potentially compromised."

"Shots fired?"

"Who, Sir?"

"Has CAG come under hostile fire?" he inquired, referring to one of Delta's many acronyms.

"Negative."

"Point me the feed. Who's where?"

"Sir, it's almost a ground fur ball. Other parties converging on our position." The Air Force major piloting the drone pointed out friendlies and the potentially hostile elements near the point of a merge. "This isn't good. We're going to require some top cover here. We *cannot* be caught in that territory," he emphasized. "These men cannot be here. Clear the deck," he announced. "All personnel clear the deck save for Mahoney and Kwon."

Blank looks filled the room. No one moved.

"Now! Out of the GD room!"

The herd of drone operators started to shuffle.

"Sir, what about our—"

"Put everything on auto. We need less than five mikes," the senior man instructed, hoping five minutes would suffice.

* * * *

Both Deltas back in Beirut were devouring every second of the relayed Predator feed in anticipation. The bird appeared to be picking up speed.

"Here comes the cavalry." Taco was cautiously optimistic, his tone showing sign of hope.

"Halo Two, this is Halo Actual, do you copy?" Blake radioed to the team.

"Roger that, Actual, Two here. Looks like Lebanese Army. Think we lucked out. Pretty sure we can chat this out. But someone may want to call the embassy real quick so our get-out-of-jail card is ready. Over."

"Wait. Hold one. Over," Blake nodded to Taco. "Let our fliers know these are kinda friendlies. I'll ring up command."

* * * *

When the flight room cleared, the remaining Creech team stared at the gray screen.

With hands on his hips, the ranking officer inquired over his two fliers' shoulders, "You have coordinates for our team and the bogies?"

"Roger that, Sir."

"Put the coordinates in for our team."

"Sir, that's not right. We put the…"

The colonel put his hand on the young pilot's shoulder.

"Son, we can't be here. POTUS is going to Mideast peace accords next week. There can be no trace if things go south. These men were never here, and this never happened. These are enemies killed in action. That cannot be reported. That was the caveat for the operation."

"But at that close of range, it'll kill everyone. Ours and theirs. POTUS approved the CONOP for the primary objective, not this target, Sir. With all due respect, it's intentional fratricide. That's like...totally illegal. It's murder."

The colonel squeezed the flier's shoulder harder. "The president feels any exposure presents a threat to US interests. We have our contingency orders. You are cleared hot. Shut up and send it. *That* is an order."

"Three, Two, One, Rifle," the trigger-pulling sensor operator confirmed as he fired the missile under hierarchical duress.

"Splash," the colonel quietly mouthed less than a minute later.

Chapter 5

Drake squeezed between the ten-foot concrete wall that separated him from freedom and the ramshackle buildings that protected him from the militia in pursuit.

He stumbled on a pile of rock, construction waste, and random coils of rusted metal wire. His ankle twisted, but that was the least of his worries, and another injury had to take a number at the deli counter serving only vital organs in operational need.

The voices on the other side of the wall told Drake all was not well. The glow of lights emanating from the darkness should have warned him of trouble, but frankly, he'd have to add it to the growing list. Worst case, it was the Lebanese Army, and that issue should be able to be taken care of with a quick call for clarification.

He heard a distinct sound fast approaching.

It was an unforgettable noise he had experienced in Afghanistan at danger-close range. His stomach pitted, and nausea washed over him.

Oh, shit.

Drake tried to turn away but was blinded by a stuttering flash as the initial charge and primary explosion went off in near simultaneous and unperceivable succession. What felt like a tsunami crashed into Drake and felt like his insides were ripped out.

* * * *

"Blake! The feed just went red, they're hot. Are they still—oh shit! Blake! They're—"

The feed cut off from the Beirut safe house FOB.

Taco flipped up his hands in the futility of the moment. "We're blind. Dude. Our guys were right there."

"Ring 'em up!"

"If they launched a Hellfire at that range, they're gone. They're fucking all gone, Blake." Taco covered his face in astonishment.

"They can't do that. It's outside the defined footprint. It would need Joint Chiefs, SECDEF, and POTUS approval. There's no way they could get that so fast. Right?"

"Dude. I got a bad feeling. Dude! What happened?"

"Fuck. Ring 'em up!"

Both men continued to stare at a blank screen.

"Dude... They whacked 'em. We whacked our own guys."

"Ring 'em!" Blake shouted, fists pounding the table.

* * * *

The one-hundred-pound AGM-114P Hellfire missile killed everyone within the fifteen-meter radius and mortally wounded those within another ten meters from shrapnel and secondary explosions.

The concussion knocked Drake from his feet and completely rocked his world. He fell forward and skidded onto the concrete debris, sending a new sharp pain along his rib cage and knees.

Shrapnel jettisoned into and over the concrete wall. An overhead scaffolding blocked Woolf from the hailstorm of fire and steel. Loose particles and tossed metal rained down around his position.

He curled as tight as he could, hoping he would be saved from the rickety structure overhead or other falling objects, and lay breathless in a brief moment of quieted crackles and snaps, knowing the extraction team had been wiped out.

Drake's eyes blurred, and he couldn't blink them to focus. His chest felt like an elephant was sitting on his back restricting every forced breath. The blast's over-pressurization wave had slapped Woolf's ears with phantasmal force he could feel into his throat. It seemed to take minutes for the pressure womb squeezing every part of his body to lessen its sucking force.

"Click, click, click." Drake snapped his tongue. Though his tic was subconscious, he was aware that the sound was muted and realized the quiet was from still-deafened ears. He scratched down on his cheekbone three times as he contemplated his options while still figuring out what had happened. It had been days since he had meds.

Woolf's head and heart told him to go check on the men. But this time he knew what the right thing to do was. He still couldn't move. A distant voice in the deep caverns of his mind called on him to complete the mission with the next exfiltration option. Then, like floodgates, thoughts rushed to presence. He had already screwed the ground team. He had to go with his gut. Something was majorly wrong, despite the fact that he had completely jacked up this op.

As he collected himself and started off in a hobbled and off-balance run, he shouldered the responsibility of the dead. *They got caught waiting for me. I fucked up the plan.*

No, I did it for those little kids.

No. I was selfish. I shouldn't have gone in the home. I wanted to find Dex.

But no one else knew what I was doing in the house. That was a Pred strike on our own team.

An unexpected wave of nausea come back from nowhere, and Drake heaved what little liquid content his stomach would give as it fought to hold nourishment for itself.

The camp in this sector was awake from the blast, and guard towers down the perimeter wall shone bright lights toward the explosion. Doors were opening. Residents were scurrying from their beds to look out windows or open orifices in their walls.

Drake turned back to the wall. He had to check. Gaining an initial boost from a mountain of concrete debris and cast-off construction materials, Woolf scaled up to the point where he could pull himself up and over the lip.

* * * *

The General Atomics-built Predator MQ-1 drone was making a second pass but was now roughly a nautical mile away from the target. Kwon saw the movement in his video feed. He faked a yawn and stretch to see if anyone else was watching over his shoulder. The room was starting to fill again, and rank officers were exiting.

"Hey what's that?" Mahoney bent forward to his own monitor for a better look. "Rotate the—"

Kwon reached his hand over to stop his colleague. "Bro. Redirect outward and elevate to ten thousand feet."

"But it looks like—"

"Bro. They can't know," he whispered.

Mahoney looked to the door as his superior's foot was stepping away from the frame and no longer visible. He wiped his hands on his pants.

"I'm going to have nightmares about this for the rest of my life."

"Me too, bro, but we can't tell anyone. Ever. Rotate east so you create a coverage blink. Keep it more toward the Med. Go back out to sea."

"The feed is already archived. We can't delete it," Kwon recognized. "I'm just saying we didn't see it."

"That'll save our ass, man. Nothing will save our souls."

"Fuck us. Fuuck us."

* * * *

The carnage and glow from the fires showed Drake that pretty much everything in the blast radius had been obliterated. He had to get going. More sounds were drawing close. While survival in the next hour was unguaranteed, he was willing to bet on himself. And that meant he needed to survive the next years, too. That meant listening to both his head and gut before heading west to water for Plan B. Drake snapped a few shots of the wreckage site with his mobile device, then panned with video.

The burning vehicles emitted enough light to capture whatever this was. This video, however, was recorded in a partitioned segment of Drake's device and saved to his personal encrypted cloud database as soon as it added a file to the folder.

Smart move, kid, remarked the vivid auditory pseudo hallucination of Alex Woolf. *Now bug out.*

Chapter 6

Beirut, Lebanon, Forward Operating Base

The main command line rang. Blake snatched it up.

"Major? Colonel Rios here."

"Colonel, what the—"

The head of Delta interrupted, "Blake, there was an attack tonight just outside Ain al-Hilweh. Palestinians launched a rocket at the Lebanese Army. It'll probably be on the news."

"Sir, I mean you no disrespect, but what the fuck are you talking about?"

"I think you heard me, Major; there was a terror attack. None of our forces were affected. And that's because we were training in Jordan. You are expected to be there tomorrow. Close up. Await further orders. We have some aid workers in the area of the explosion. They'll help with personnel recovery and get you anything you need. Do you understand, Major?"

"I don't understand one damn word of it, Sir. There are dead men—"

"Yes. A most unfortunate training accident, but I assure you, our Jordanian partners will investigate it. Now, do you understand?"

"I understand, Sir. Per-fectly."

Taco's eyes were wide, his shoulders hunched up, hands raised. A *what the Hell is going on* look was written across his face as he awaited clarification from his boss. Blake closed his eyes while his head shook back and forth, erasing everything that had come to pass in the last few hours.

"This is not my call, son, it came directly from up top. I'm sorry. We will recover everything and do things properly," promised Rios.

"Roger that, Sir. Out."

"What the fuck happened, Blake?" Taco's expression was empty.

"Nothing. Nothing at all. We're bugging out. What's left of our team will be cleaned up, but really it never happened so their remains are going to be transported to another location. I have no clue. But I know this, if that fucking man from Orange is alive, he's a dead man. I'll make sure of it."

Chapter 7

Sean Havens and his brother-in-law, Lars Bjorklund, steadied themselves in the red-and-gray Zodiac rigid inflatable boat as it lowered from the ship's starboard side. The blackness of the Lebanese coastal waters beside the Heron Explorer seismic research vessel accepted the heavy rubber craft with a subdued splash.

The sea was calm as the near morning tides began to shift. Cloud cover blocked the moon's shine as if playing a part in the rendezvous plan.

The Scandinavian company SaltyPup Exploration owned the eighty-one-meter-long spy ship that was headquartered and registered out of Limassol, Cyprus. Cover for status also played a part, blocking any semblance of a military operation. The bogus corporate setup was courtesy of both Lars and Sean's shady skullduggery and beneficial ownership obfuscation, which they provided as a service to the Joint Special Operations Command through a cutout project of the Department of Defense. Courtesy of one Robert O'Toole.

Havens was a veteran of denied special access programs, while his former detective "binlaw" was more a victim of his sister's marriage and the disasters that had followed Sean in past years.

Lars was a consummate bachelor whose retirement had been disrupted. He had exchanged Arizona golf and spring training baseball for a knife wound to the gut and an exploding drone in a Thai hospital room. Which pleased him about as much as dancing barefoot on glass.

"Seany, you unhitch us and I'll get the engine going. It would be great, of course, if I knew where we were going. Which is?" the inquisitive Swede asked without really caring, but he was interested nonetheless about what disaster would test his fate next.

Havens had to raise his voice to project above Lars's hulking frame fumbling aft. "Yes. Got it about fifteen minutes ago. Can't let you in on it yet."

"Seriously? After everything you've put me through? My home that I'm away from. Missing the Cubs' entire season because of you." He paused. "There can't be a secret left in this country."

Sean couldn't see Lars's face, but he knew his brother-in-law had the same pouty look he'd had going on for the past few months. "Layin' low, Lars. We still need to lay low. On the bright side, not everyone gets a medal for trying to kill a president."

"Not everyone gets blown up by their brother-in-law's cockamamie missions. And if we got a medal, I might not be complaining."

"I already apologized to you in Thailand. And if you had a medal, we wouldn't be having all this fun."

"I never even got a bowl of *chowda* on the Vineyard, either. Strange how New England and Manhattan both have chowder styles but no one else really does. Like corn chowder should have been taken by, I don't know, who makes corn chowder? Santa Fe?"

"Screw your soup, Lars. Let's head out."

"You're a real asshole now that I think of it."

Sean gave another knowing laugh.

Lars started the noise-suppressed four-stroke engine. "Dick."

"Get me as close to the shore as you can without getting us seen I don't want to be floating out there like corn in a toilet."

"You? How about *us*, partner?"

"Change of plans, Lars. I need to do something."

"You're going to kill someone."

"There's about a ninety percent chance of that."

"What's the ten percent part?"

"He kills me first."

* * * *

Drake's mind raced well beyond the pace of his heavy lactic acid-filled legs as he ran through the catacomb of narrow streets toward the lights' edge and the smell of the sea.

His limbs felt like rubber. His lungs screamed for oxygen, and his head pounded almost like the migraines he had overcome before entering the military. The fact that he would have at least a mile swim was simply accepted. But as he scaled the camp wall, he still asked himself again the million-dollar question, *What the fuck happened and why?*

Drake's escape and evasion through Sidon's waist-high overgrown vegetation consisting of mostly weeds, modest agriculture fields, and a half mile of urban terrain was uneventful save for the small pack of dogs that quickly learned the error of their ways.

At the shore, he shuffled through shin-high sea foam, washed up trash, and patches of solid waste before stepping into the tepid Mediterranean waters.

The last hour had indeed been a wade through perpetual shit, but he couldn't deny that the sea lapping at his legs was soothing as it soaked in over the tops and through the seams of his shoes. Drake could only imagine the fecal coliform bacteria spreading disease into his abrasions and cuts. Add diarrhea and more vomiting to his near-future afflictions. But for the moment, it was the first bit of relief he'd had in a long while. His body slowly calmed from post-combat jitters. Tingles ran under the skin of his face, arms, and legs. It could take days for the varied degree of twitchy edges and hypersensitivity to die down, which made it hard to regulate his meds and mindset. Something that was more off than on without a professional's treatment.

Drake Woolf took in a deep breath, careful not to allow hope of a rescue vessel to enter his mind. There was no telling what unexpected horseshit would cross his path next. He retrieved the small earpiece and microphone from his zippered hide. He gave yet another delirious look down the coast and behind his six. From his mobile device, Drake changed the signal channel of the radio and receiver via Bluetooth exchange. He looked out into the darkness of the sea and tossed the small device into the water. "Fuck it."

"That's going to make it pretty hard for Uber Black to find you, don't you think?"

Drake spun one-eighty to find a dark figure drawing closer. Whether it was his pounding headache, diminished hearing from the blast, or his head up his ass, Drake Woolf didn't know how someone had gotten the drop on him on this isolated beach. He had neither weapon nor strength. The man from Orange readied his mind for combat while remotely processing that this was likely an American before him and he had no idea how he could even best a three-year-old at this point. Maybe someone would throw him a bone. "Who are you?"

"You know if you think back to the island," the somewhat familiar voice said in a more matter-of-fact than cryptic tone. "And you'll get no trouble from me. Cavalry's here. Or at least one horseman."

The man walked into the water, taking a step closer to Drake. The dark figure looked down.

Whoever he was, his guard was relaxed. "Sidon's gotten a lot cleaner from a decade ago," he said. "You okay?"

Drake still couldn't make out the stranger's features, but the voice came to him. It was one of the government's shadow masters. "Havens?"

"Yep," Sean Havens confirmed. "Is it really true that if you pee in filthy water microbes and shit can swim up your junk?"

"What are you..."

Sean yawned. "Came to pick you up and help out if you were being pursued. Doesn't look like you are. Didn't bring a weapon anyway." Havens kicked off something washing up in the shoreline against his ankle. "So why you throwing out Uncle Sam's expensive hearing aids?"

"Seriously. Aren't you a bit out of your element?" Drake asked.

"I am. Thing is, someone wants to make sure you get back safe and sound."

"I don't think I'm going back. Was thinking maybe I'd let them think I was smoked in that explosion. I don't have much left back in the States, anyway."

"Well, that sounds like a story we need to chat about elsewhere. I'm not Hollywood's Colonel Trautman trying to bring Rambo back to Bragg. Let's get you fed and cleaned up on my boat. I've got food and water in the Zodiac about half-mile out. We can figure this out. Your uncle was thinking along the same lines of you disappearing. Up for a swim?"

"Wait, my uncle?" Drake reached for Havens's arm.

"Yep. He said you guys had talked about it at one point, and now may be the time. Can I have my arm back? You're squeezing too hard."

Drake remained quiet and released his grip around Havens's formidable muscle. It wasn't an arm pumped from lifting; it was combat strength-trained. Lean, but developed, and task-functional. Command presence under a veneer of who-the-Hell-knows dork-like personae. Drake sure as Hell wasn't hurting the guy.

"Let's go." Sean prodded, "We've got a long swim and we're going to have some sun soon. My buddy'll burn his complexion after six a.m."

"Who's in the Zodiac?" Drake asked.

"The guy who drives the boat. Don't worry. He's good. He's Scandinavian. They discovered Lebanon, so he knows the waters here."

"I'm pretty sure Vikings didn't discover Beirut," Drake asserted with a mix of puzzlement and growing annoyance.

"Huh." Havens feigned astonishment. "Don't tell the captain that."

"If I'm supposed to be dead, then is it really a good idea to have me meet someone?"

"He's read in but doesn't know details of my chat with O.T."

"It can't be that simple."

"Actually, it is. You're already on a military don't ask don't tell roster; we take you off that and input your death across the board. Full honors at Arlington, where you can join the dead and join the living ghosts still doing the dirty deed to the bad guys. You're buried in a program that won't exist. Like you pretty much already are. You can't go back to high school reunions or see anyone you know. Not really as cool as you may think. Let me know if you need help thinking it though. I've been dead for a while. Sort of. More like vanished. But you really need to think about it. I don't recommend it if you have better options."

Havens flashed a quick signal into the night. Drake glimpsed the red light burst long enough to get a visual vector and see Sean Havens respond with a brief flash before fully immersing himself in the Mediterranean.

"Oh, this is great. Just like being in Lake Michigan during the summer," Sean said. "Keep your mouth closed. I think a turd or small twig passed under my nose on the way in. Happened to me at the Indiana Dunes once. Pretty sure that was a shit and not a log then, too."

"Lovely." Drake groaned. "Do you have any idea what I've just come out of to be all chit chatty?"

"Nope. Above my pay grade."

Woolf wanted to just get to the boat, where there was promise of chow and drink. Contrary to what his broken body had been telling him, within mere minutes, Drake found his combat swimmer technique to be rather relaxing as he headed to his pickup craft. He let his ops phone and cameras sink in the sea. They were just shells now that the data had been sent away. He could buy another one anywhere, do a quick cloud backup and be off and running.

Havens kept encouraging him along in between annoying remarks. Drake knew the guy had been around the block and was just easing him out of the field, even if it was in an unconventional way. It was a smart play. Most guys could fake a basic chat after intense field contact and let their mind wander back to the horrors they had just experienced. Havens was sending Drake's brain all over the place. For the first time in a long while, Drake felt safe. He thought the least he could do was be a bit more personable even if the guy was a bit off.

Indeed, Sean Havens was being an obnoxious dick to keep Woolf from shutting down.

"Kinda surprised to see you after Martha's Vineyard and that whole president thing," Drake tossed out to lighten his mood. Not that unsanctioned assassination was light.

"No hard feelings. You were doing your job, I was doing mine. Pretty much a misunderstanding, I'm sure." Sean spoke clearly as he swam, indicating not much stress or exertion for a graybeard.

"Secret Service didn't seem too pleased...." Drake wheezed as his remark trailed.

"They shouldn't," Sean agreed. "They're supposed to protect the president. I sure didn't see you around. At least before it was too late. That could've been bad for me. I'm getting rusty. Been getting a lot of people killed. I'm wrapping up my field work. Time to do something else. Something back at home in the States. Passing the baton to someone younger and smarter."

Drake was starting to fatigue. The exhaustion was apparent in his broken voice and labored breathing. He was having a hard time keeping his thoughts focused. His mind was telling him to quit. To screw it all. It was futile. "Gotta say, for an old guy your tradecraft was pretty damn good. You were CAG or OGA?" Drake referenced two acronyms: Combat Applications Group for Delta and Other Government Agency to signify the CIA. Just another way to do a wink, wink, nudge, nudge to avoid saying what everyone knew anyway, which is stupid, but that's how it works.

"Checks all come from the same place. But I've usually been Clandestine Survey or Support, this and that. CAC ID cards say anything from Air Force to Navy. Can't say I've ever worked for either. Paychecks pay the bills, and they're all checks cashed on other people's lives regardless of the outfit."

"So, run-of-the-mill spook shit."

"Pretty much."

Run-of-the-mill my ass. "You're disappeared but not dead?"

"Yeah. Long story." Havens took a quiet deep breath. The tide current was giving him a little more of a tug than he had hoped.

"Well, I'll say it again. You've got some good tricks up your sleeve working the field." Drake flipped to his back. It wasn't any better, so he went back to combat swimmer stroke. "I didn't even find you for a couple of days. Sure didn't expect you to be wearing those pink shorts with little anchors on them. That was a nice touch."

"Yeah, not my style, but you should've expected it."

"Why's that?" Drake coughed.

"Because that fits the environment. Tacti-cool black hats with flags on the sides and Oakley sunglasses do not. Hey, can we slow up a bit? I think I have a side stitch."

Drake didn't believe Havens was hurting, but the slower pace helped. Lars kept vigilant in the night as Sean and Drake slowly swam toward the inflatable heavy-duty fabric boat. "Holy shit, for a bunch of fancy-pants ninjas, I sure could hear your loud asses. Good thing I'm not fishing, you'd scare 'em all away. They teach you to be loud in spy class?"

"Shut up, how 'bout a little help." Havens spit water. He was wiped and hardly keeping afloat.

"Challenge phrase, please," Lars requested.

"Cut it out, give us a hand." Havens threw an arm up to his brother-in-law.

"Don't get comfortable. Comfortable makes sloppy." Lars grabbed Sean's hand but didn't provide any leverage.

"I get it." Havens pulled himself up and over the wide sides then assisted Drake's exit from the water. "Welcome aboard, Birddog."

Drake leaned over the wall, spitting something that had gotten in his mouth.

"Ugh, probably an Indiana turd," mumbled Havens.

Lars called forward. "You getting sick?"

Drake blinked water from his eyes and squinted to focus on the familiar face. "That's gotta be Lurch behind you."

"How do, Shamu," bellowed Lars, not correcting the name jab he'd heard most of his life and pre-retirement, in his long law enforcement career as a lead detective and forensic expert.

"Been a long time, big man. Gotta say, kinda surprised to see you not locked behind bars, too." Drake staggered a bit while finding a place to collapse, but Sean steadied the younger man and guided him to a spot.

"Can't say I expected to see *you*. Seany said he was going out to kill someone."

Havens turned his head in the darkness. "We'll work on your OPSEC, Lars."

"Well, it's not like you're gunna kill the guy now...."

These guys are crazier than you are. Drake settled into the RIB and gave a few side turns to stretch his back muscles. Everything was starting to tighten up. Havens tossed him a blanket and dropped a medium-sized cooler at the operator's feet.

"This is amateur hour, Havens." Drake pulled at his clinging wet clothes. "People were dying just a couple clicks away and you guys are putting on a circus show to put a smile on my face like I'm five years old and my fucking goldfish just died."

"Sure you're okay? Need a med kit for anything? Any other meds?"

He knows. O.T. told him. He's been assessing me the whole time. "I'm cool. Just need to catch my breath."

"Was I going too fast?" Havens joked.

"Nope, I was just working harder in your sloppy wake. What's in the box? Don't tell me the president's head."

Lars and Sean gave a snicker that was aimed at their last unofficially sanctioned mission on domestic soil.

"There's bottled water with some hydration powder and a bit of green tea caffeine dissolved. Ham sandwich and a banana. It's all you."

"You guys are weird but make a helluva pit crew. Appreciate the chow."

"I'll eat, whatever you don't want. I'm getting a little hungry myself," Lars offered in all seriousness.

Drake fumbled in his pocket and tore open another small plastic bag. He popped two lithium pills despite the fact that with his level of extreme fatigue, he was going to fall harder than a fat kid on a seesaw. "Can't say I'm still comfortable with the conversation, but good pit crew," Woolf praised as he dove into the cooler, fisting the sandwich and nearly ripping the lid off the water. Drake struggled to maintain balance as Lars turned the rubber craft. His hands were shaky and the compound hadn't even dissolved in his bloodstream yet. *Shit. I forgot about offsetting from the microdose.* Drake counted in his head how many tablets he had left and when he thought he might return to CONUS.

"Sounds like things got a bit hairy out there," Sean probed. He was well attuned to post-operational emotions, and clearly something had rattled Birddog.

"You could say that," Drake responded, with a mouthful of sandwich that he forced further in with a banana.

"You solo?" Sean asked.

"You don't know?"

Havens continued to fake being out of the loop. "Just know what we're told, which is pretty much nothing, aside from the...separate call I received, which we already discussed."

"Then I guess I've got nothing else to say. No disrespect, but if you don't know, Havens, you don't need to. You know the game." Woolf downed the rest of the water.

"I do," Sean, the senior intelligence operator, confirmed with more than a lifetime of shitty places and shitshow ops to be able to relate to. Lars tried to enter the conversation. "Sean says you're quite a linguist. Whattya speak?"

"I'm not a fucking parrot," Drake snapped, his mouth full.

"Good talk," Lars mumbled. "Glad your goldfish died."

"Havens, can you kill the engine?" Drake suggested more than he really asked.

"We're almost to the ship. We'll either boat you or chopper you to Cyprus and set you up with a flight home. Just need to get the orders."

"Let's try again. I'm trying not to be a dick. Please kill the engine now. I'm not going back, and I'm not going to be seen by any crew if we're doing this. So, stop the fucking boat," Drake directed to Lars.

Lars killed the engine.

"Thank you. And again, I'm sorry. I've had a pretty fucked-up night. Make that nights, at this point. Sean, I want a no-shit answer from you. Is this a legit pickup? Or is anyone waiting for me on that ship? Or are we really doing what we're doing?"

They're waiting for you. You've got to be taken out. You know too much.

Sean shook his head in the night. "You're good. We have a small trusted crew if you choose to remain in your current status. They're cleared but unwitting to this pickup. Crypto and cyber guys. We were a small leg of your op. I'm contracted exclusive to Sahara Wind," Sean said, referencing the Intelligence Support Activity's latest code name that more or less resembled Benjamin Moore paints by description. He wanted to free this spooked operator of any further doubt. "Most anyone checking on the ship would look to our research on oil, manganese nodules, and other bullshit we made up and then outfitted the rig for."

"I don't give a shit about all that crap. Do you know what happened to the pickup team?"

"Not a clue. Guessing something went sideways."

"That's a fucking understatement. So, I suggest to you to just forget what I said. You, too, big man. Thanks for the chow."

Sean lowered his voice, trying to keep Drake engaged. The guy was in a bad place.

"Hey, we can talk more on the ship. I have a secure area where we can—"

"I'm not getting on your vessel."

"Well we don't have many other options unless you feel like another swim. I'm sure I've dealt with something similar to what you may be experiencing. Let's get you some clothes, let you clean up and rest, and hash through it. You don't need to give me details. Keep it vague."

"Tell you what," Drake started, "you get a message to the powers that be that you couldn't find me. That I never met up. No one will know we connected." He pointed directly to Lars. "No one."

"Lars is good. No need to worry about him," Sean said.

"I don't have any friends, I hardly have any family, but I can't just disappear. I need a certain someone to be able to find me if they need to."

Sean understood—well, thought he understood. At least the emotional part of letting go. The backstory, he had no clue about but was confident he could nug it through with Drake. Later. The dark arts were what Sean did. Not just the physical part but the disappearing act was his forte. This was exactly what Sean was looking for as far as winding down.

"Havens, I know from the Vineyard and your reputation that you're a good man. And knowing you, you also checked up on me. So, do me this solid. If you really know what I'm dealing with, let me go."

Son, go with these men. Get out of this business. Start a family. Stop the search. Let things go.

Drake clicked his tongue only once, and in the blink of an eye, he flipped back in the water and started swimming back to Lebanon.

Lars smacked his lips loudly. "Didn't see that coming, did you?"

"Frankly, I didn't think I'd get him this far. We were supposed to bring him back. Officially. Unofficially, his uncle said given some circumstances he may need to clear his head and stretch his legs and that we shouldn't fight Birddog."

"Stretch his legs in Beirut?"

"O.T. thought Tunisia. Birddog's looking for a ghost. Whether he becomes one or not is anyone's guess, at this point."

"We don't have to go to Tunisia, though, correct?"

"Nope. What O.T. thinks is best for this guy and what's best for us in a shithole like this are two different things." Havens squinted in the dawn's emergence from darkness, looking for Drake. Sean opened a waterproof bag and retrieved a mobile device. He powered it up and waited for the GPS app to kick in. "We just need to go near the shoreline from here."

"How's that?"

"The water. I drugged him. He drank it. He should have gotten some leg cramps and a whole lot of tired by now. I need to get him back on the ship and get an IV in him so the diuretic doesn't mess up his dehydration any more than it is. He's on something or off something, for sure."

"My God, you're an asshole."

"Just doin' our job, Lars. Just the job," Sean confirmed while stretching his neck and arms. "You wanna go or want me to?"

"Where? The water? Swedes don't swim. Give me something to pillage." The Predator drone made its final pass high over the refugee camp, keeping clear of the wreckage, the coastline, and the man from Orange. "I'm too old for this. See if you can find a Starbucks while I'm out." Havens slipped back into the water holding two West Marine inflatable life jackets.

"Hope you can get to shore and back without making a scene. You're not really good with that. Also think about how you just drugged a dehydrated, fatigued, and overall emaciated man. May have overdone it a tad."

"If anything happens, just get out of here. I've put you through enough."

"I know. Don't worry, I'll be here."

"I know, bro. You always are."

* * * *

It was just after dark, and Colonel Rios was driving down Barefoot Road from his home off Fort Bragg's military base in North Carolina. He called his boss, the three-star general of the Joint Special Operations Command, from a secure device.

"Did you speak to our men in Beirut?" the general asked without a greeting, as if it were an ordinary question.

"Yes, Sir. They're working through it. Can't say I've quite recovered either. I'm concerned."

"Then you need to take care of it. Where are you now?"

"I'm heading back to the compound. Not sure I'm tracking what you mean by me taking care of it. This should—"

"Turn around. If nothing happened, why are you headed to the shop at this time of night? Don't you think that's a little out of the ordinary when nothing extraordinary is going on?"

The colonel pulled over to the side of the road. "My bad." His hands were shaking from the adrenaline of fury. His men had been killed, and he hadn't even received the courtesy of options.

"No worries. You're doing what anyone would do."

"I'm reluctant to ask anything more. But I still need to clarify what you mean by take care of it. Take care of it how? You can't possibly mean what I think you mean."

"Good God, no. Are you insane? We're not monsters. I want you to get papers in to promote your men and find some ways they can get publicity with some medals for something they've done in the past. Hearts and minds works for our end, too. If they're married, get their wives involved. See what the wives need. Dishwashers, a fridge, air-conditioning units. Make it all happen. Bring them in close and make their lives so good that they never even consider bringing it up. From my end, the whole op will be scratched from record. No one on the ground can confirm or deny anything. Once the feed recordings are reviewed, they'll be scrubbed and deep-sixed. It never happened. That's how SECDEF and POTUS want it. Period. It was an unfortunate incident that was simply unavoidable given the on-the-ground tempo of events. Understood?"

"No." He sighed, expelling a full breath.

"This is new to both of us. It's never happened in my career, and I've never heard of it historically," he lied. "Let's just hope we never get in a pinch like this again. Keep tabs on any news or reports that may contradict our narrative. Got it?"

Part II

"Truth Overcomes All Bonds"
-Intelligence Support Activity Motto

Chapter 8

Washington, D.C.

A black tactical High Sierra backpack lay under the black fiberglass bus stop bench. The bag was wedged against a steel bench leg and nudged to the Plexiglas wall alcove of the headquarters of the United States Department of Defense's Pentagon Metro and Bay U3 bus stop. The Pentagon was home to approximately 23,000 military and civilian employees. Hundreds passed by the U3 bus stop in the early morning rush to the five sides, five floors, and five ring corridors of the strategic and tactical battle building. "Ground zero" it was called during the Cold War, referencing it as a likely conventional attack by the Russians if a nuclear war ever kicked off. It was no irony, therefore, that one hundred eighty-nine people were killed in an unconventional attack on September 11, 2001, a day equally uneventful as today, which would soon be etched into history.

Within the Cordura nylon and cotton-blend shell of the backpack, smokeless powder, three handfuls of three-penny nails, about fifty medium-sized ball bearings and the pressure cooker itself waited for a command. A command to be received when the target arrived—as scheduled.

Bus 42 from Ballston pulled up to the curb. One man on the bus, Jake Vanderaa, had his eyes above smartphone level and caught sight of the abandoned ruck. His shoulder rested against the window, a Special Forces long tab and US Army Special Forces Command (Airborne) patch, with red background in the shape of an arrowhead with black sword in the center, pressed against the glass. After three tours in Iraq, the scanning, searching, and constant situational awareness was imbedded in his day-to-day behavior. Imbedded deeper by his training others in foreign lands to be able to do the same. Still, his voice never uttered a word to his fellow commuters, who remained oblivious and focused on their devices. Instead, his hands quaked, and the ghostly pictures returned to his mind. The sweats came next. And he closed his eyes. He was home, his wife had said. Safe. Nothing to worry about, she had reassured him. No more bad days. And still he had them.

He didn't know what was about to happen but perversely hoped it would and embraced the peace it would give him, and knew in his heart that what was coming would cause extensive casualties. Karma was a bitch. Yet, he was tired. So tired.

General Reza Shirazian, deputy commander of the Army of the Guardians of the Islamic Revolution (IRGC) Quds Force, was nervous as he, too, scanned and searched the area from a lofty floor at the Ritz-Carlton Pentagon City. A leader of extraterritorial military and clandestine operations, General Shirazian's his hands were clammy in expectation of the first direct operation against the Great Satan after the president designated the Revolutionary Guards Corps as a whole a terrorist group and imposed new sanctions on the organization.

The Americans had previously sanctioned individuals and entities associated with the internal and external Iranian security force tasked with foreign espionage and paramilitary activities. This new designation as a response to Iran's missile tests was unacceptable. Further, it came at a time when his own country's leaders were limiting the power and reach of the military arm. Coupled with the fact that a lucrative business arm used to circumvent sanctions and generate funds for operations had been siphoned away, the sanctions put the IRGC in a precarious situation.

In return, the Revolutionary Guards now further considered the Americans to be in the same threat category as the Islamic State. Especially those American soldiers who had fashioned explosives in Iraq to appear as the workings of adversaries and who created the businesses in Iraq to do their bidding using local talents. Delta Force and the CIA. He squinted, looking for the black plume that had yet to arise across his view of the large Defense complex.

As the bus came to a stop, Pentagon employees rose without a care. They queued like cattle and joined the other herds pounding across the concrete where they would line for screening before a day of armchair war-fighting could begin.

Across from the Pentagon's lot, a former Iraqi aide to the Americans in Mosul held a cell phone in both hands. It was an old-school technical application compared to the infrared light beams he had used with Delta operators in Iraq to trigger IEDs. He contemplated his attack and wept for his children and his wife. He wept for the American soldiers he had served with. The men he called brothers, who left him against the sectarian factions. They forced him to this point. "Help us, and we'll keep you safe," the Americans had promised him. Even as his Iraqi countrymen volunteered to be translators to the soldiers and were then killed by Al-Qaeda as retaliation, he believed in the dream of coming to America. "We burned in Hell working for you. Our families—we put their spirits in our hands trusting," the man said aloud to himself in Mesopotamian Arabic. He drew a deep breath and pressed the key, triggering a line-of-sight electrical firing circuit to the explosives. He was still proud to be a special-operations-trained Mohawk. But the irony of the target was not lost on him. In fact, it was his mission. To kill his mentor. They would kill Jake Vanderaa and all the Delta advisors they could find.

It was time.

Rapidly expanding gasses of gunpowder detonated under tight atmospheric force resulted in a brilliant burst of light as the pressure cooker erupted, sending shrapnel in a violent rupture of blast fragments into passersby and ripping bodies and the former tactical advisor to pieces.

As the sight and sound of the explosion met General Shirazian's senses, he cracked a smile of deep relief for both his mission and reputation. "*Khoda bozorg ast*," he exclaimed, giving praise to God in his mother tongue. When the second and third detonations reverberated, he became giddy with his Iraqi recruits' first operational success...of many planned.

* * * *

"JEEZUS," Robert O'Toole cursed as the explosion's sound boomed into his office, causing a tremor with visible effect to desk-side trinkets and wall hangings. His hand jolted and coffee splashed from the mug. "What the hell was that?" he shouted from across his desk to anyone within earshot of the Special Operations and Combating Terrorism Department while shaking hot black coffee from his hand. Instinct directed him to look out the window for evidence of another airline crash.

"Sounded like an explosion," the deputy assistant secretary of defense shouted back to the ASD with complete seriousness.

"No shit, Mark. I knew I could count on your policy-planning astuteness." Under different circumstances he would have laughed, expecting nothing less from his colleague whom he considered to be the little angel standing on his right shoulder day and night. Mark Watley represented good judgment and morality. Morality was the imp on O.T.'s left shoulder who consistently fought against proposed aggressive and dark operational plans. And that shoulder was the imp of O.T.'s black mission mindset, which usually won the contests.

The desk phone rang, and O.T. knew he would have an answer to the sound.

His left fist clenched, expecting validation of a homeland attack on his palace of war. That validation came to both his pain and pleasure.

Chapter 9

President Ross slammed his bony, liver-spotted fist down on the desk. "We're not going to turn this country into another London or Paris on my watch!" White wisps of hair fell over his glasses. He lifted the strands back over his perspiring forehead in a measured attempt to remain calm and focused.

The room was quiet. Eyes were on the CIA and FBI directors. Both men looked at the floor, nodding their heads in embarrassed agreement.

"I campaigned against this." His eyebrows rose as if they were testing the room's memory of past speeches and slogans. "When I took office, I swore I would direct additional measures to exercise this nation's right to self-defense to protect our *people* and our *interests,*" he declared. "And dammit, I'm going to do so. But this happened on YOUR watch!"

The president made direct eye contact with each person in the room as his words set it. "From my chair, this attack was clearly planned. And you're saying we had no intel?"

President Ross leaned forward, his suit jacket ballooning out over his shallow frame. "Gentlemen. As a former Marine, I know intel, so don't pussyfoot around with buzzwords and finger-pointing. I want a no-shit answer."

"Mr. President," Ron Deluth, the CIA director, started, "we've gone over this before. Our intel continues to produce indicators of threats across the US, but on-the-ground counterterrorist intelligence capabilities can't confirm, and frankly there is so much controversy on the use of the communications we've collected that—"

Sean Mullins, the FBI director, cut off his intelligence community peer. "Ron, we're not going down that hole again. If you had something credible, it should have been pushed to us. What did you have that was credible? We're all entitled to NSA's Special Source Operations and everything the PERPETUAL INTENT system can provide on internet and phone metadata. If you had something, don't say you couldn't share it."

President Ross regained the floor, "Sean, the Bureau has jurisdiction on this one. Counterterrorism capabilities fall to you, state, and local. Did you have anything? Anything from NSA that your people on the streets could have used? Anything?"

"No, Mr. President, we did not. Nothing we could act on."

President Ross tilted his head. "So, you had something, but what, your hands were tied? Are you all going to back me into the corner saying some civil liberty bullshit got in your way of doing your sworn duty jobs?"

"Mr. President, what I'm trying to say is that we have at any given time a number of leads that we evaluate for building a case for further investigation or determining credible threats. In this instance, there is nothing that we were working on or receiving intelligence on that would have pointed to an attack on the Pentagon. That's not to say that we have not been looking into groups or individuals or that something would not have materialized about this attack as we continued to run down leads and develop data points. Hell, we have more requests for court-ordered surveillance than actual approvals. It's not like we're not beating the bushes with the strained resources that we have. We'll have to see what comes out of identifying a bomber, or…"

The president raised his hand. "Okay, Sean, I'm not blaming you. We already know how this works with your turfs. If Ron gets something, he's going to sit on it because he's working foreign. You're going to look for something to prosecute or that fits within the legal apparatus."

The FBI director started to protest but stopped abruptly when the president crossed his arms.

"Hold that thought, I know what you're going to say."

The director didn't back down. "That legal *apparatus* happens to be the Constitution and civil rights. Mr. President."

"Fair enough. I'm not picking on you, and I know what I stated is not exactly how it works. John, I know you'll say the same with Homeland, and General Mathieson, as SECDEF, you have your own hands tied with how you can't deal with threats on American soil. I know you are all working jointly with great success on a regular basis. So wipe your noses and primp your ties. I've given you all the love you're going to get today." President

Ross slurped his coffee. "Gentlemen. We have indeed painted ourselves in corners, but you can't tell me that we can't uphold the Constitution and still do better. Our adversaries, foreign and domestic, transcend borders. Via communication, finance, beliefs, what have you. National security is not just a global affair. Clearly, it happens on our soil, domestically. And on our watch. The question is then, how can we identify and hit them before they hit us? Without our laws and ourselves getting in our own way?"

CIA Director Deluth cast a discreet glance over to the president's chief of staff, Ben Steele. Owen Mathieson joined the silent conversation of conspiratorial gazes but broke connection and rubbed his eyes when FBI Director Mullins became an unwanted guest in the exchange.

"Mr. President," Chief of Staff Steele rose as if to speak on behalf of the group, "I think these men have an idea of the task at hand. No doubt, they are needed back at their respective quarters. Might I suggest we adjourn until we have a clearer picture as to what has actually occurred and who is potentially responsible? We'll need to prepare a response. Although, I think we should take a moment with Director Deluth and General Mathieson for their two cents on the plausible international front, after the FBI takes its leave." He waited for a few seconds, and with no protest from POTUS, continued, "Thank you, Director Mullins. Keep us apprised, and we'll be in touch."

No one rose from their seats, but all eyes fell on Mullins to get his unwanted ass up and out.

The director looked to the president as if asking, *Really, are you sure?*

"Homeland can go, too, for now," Steele suggested, but he really meant *take this other unanointed eunuch with you.*

President Ross fidgeted with the corner of his desk as the FBI director left the room, then raised his head long enough to give a curt, awkward nod to Homeland while the pointy end of his Cabinet's spear remained in the Oval Office to discuss the terror event. This was not lost on those leaving the room, who felt like the favored children were staying up late while they, the younger siblings, were sent to bed.

The chief of staff held a raised finger until the room cleared and the door shut. He motioned to the Secret Service detail. "Boys, would you mind giving us a moment, please."

President Ross looked puzzled, but given the audacity of his chief of staff, he let it ride out.

The group waited again for all nonessential parties to exit.

The president held out his hands, palms up in dismay. "I'm giving you a lot of latitude here, Ben. It'd better be inspiring. This is not how I build my teams."

"I understand, Mr. President. General Mathieson, would you like to kick off this conversation?" Chief of Staff Steele offered.

"Thank you, I would." Mathieson, in his olive-green uniform, leaned from the couch toward the president. "Mr. President, to your point, we've been working on a proposal that seems to be rather timely to your interests and commitments to the people."

"A proposal. We're hours into an attack, and you all have agreed on a proposal. Meaning, this isn't the first you've thought of this, so, I'm odd man out...with the Bureau's director and Homeland, too. That's not good." He heaved a sigh. "I'm listening, and I already know I won't like it."

"We would like to propose a specialized capability, or task force, that is similar to the work of both the CIA and JSOC."

The president slowly shook his head, not wanting to hear what was coming next. He took his seat behind the large mahogany Executive Office desk to impose the full power afforded to him by the people. "No. We're not doing this. We fix what doesn't work. We don't build something new that can screw up, too."

"Sir, if you could just hear us out," Steele pleaded for time.

"I don't like where this is going. I know what's coming." The president guided his drooping hair back again. "No deep state bullshit on my watch. It blows up and does more harm than good in ensuring public trust."

"Mr. President, we agree. You see, under a covered identity, we could enable a team to track persons of interest throughout the country legally. This, uh—hypothetical—team would use its own sophisticated signals interception technology after receiving technical targeting provided by the collaborating domestic interceptors of the CIA and NSA. Whereas we would normally use a team like this to pave the way for Delta or SEAL Team 6, this team would be able to make tactical decisions on the fly to develop new targets when and where we have limited access or limited target knowledge."

The president looked at his chief of staff. "I'm missing the legality point. This will never fly with current oversight and the level of scrutiny this administration is under. If it's illegal it won't fly with me. The FBI can do this with proper legal methods."

Chief of Staff Steele nodded in agreement. "It's legal, because these, well, suspects could be malicious foreign actors. But the Bureau can't really finish it like we are proposing. We need to be more aggressive to completely eliminate threats. To make them go away, if you will, without concerning the public before the threat is neutralized." Steele received varying forms of positive body language from the men confirmation that he was on the mark. All were on the same sheet of music.

"And if this shadow group you are speaking of 'unknowingly' target a US citizen?" The president used air quotes, "I'm sure that's where you're going next. I appreciate your efforts gentlemen, but I need more."

"Sir, you could enable a Presidential Finding. It would give the general limited power for an exploratory covert action that we would describe as a feasibility study of say targeted foreign...preparation of the battle space." Steele looked to the general and CIA director for additional comments, but he was on his own this time. He shrugged his shoulders to test the concept, although they had already agreed on a framework behind closed doors. They were constructing their individual rebuttal or disavowal plans as fast as they could, depending on how POTUS reacted.

Director Deluth capped off his remark with the icing. "We have the tools and the data, but no one to give it to."

"You give it to the FBI. We have processes in place for this to expedite actionable intel. I'm guessing you're talking computer and phone communications, correct?"

"Yes, but the process in place is pull, not push. It's more responsive and less enabling to a point of predictive. Bottom line, it has no teeth. You could tie this to Executive Order 12036 as a special activity, but clearly we would not be doing this abroad. But the same principles would apply. We need to harness a capability to transcend borders in communications, money movements, and...well...ideology, to be frank."

The president crossed his arms. "And what do we do about EO 12333 prohibiting assassination by an employee or agent of the US government? Let's not cherry-pick what suits our needs. I assume you are not arresting anyone or the director could have stayed in this room." The president knew the answer before asking. "This is a bullshit targeting program that is completely out of the question. With the billions we spend foreign and domestic, you're telling me that in all our wisdom and all the resources we have around the world, we could solve our problems now with your little hit squad."

"I don't believe we mentioned assassination." General Mathieson cleared his throat. "Although, this would not be just an intelligence activity. Per se. To hit them before they hit us, we would need to have a Proactive Preemptive Operations Group, and it would be beneficial if kinetic engagement was within their mandate—or at least toolbox."

"Owen, really. Like I said, a kill squad." The president said it like a Trivial Pursuit answer he was trying to convince the room of but with absolutely no enthusiasm in return.

The general raised his hand at the president's accurate inference. "Sir, this would deal with finding, fixing, and finishing the targets, but would also exploit and analyze intelligence with an ability to pass the warning to the FBI, so they could act on items in their jurisdiction, too."

"Owen, I'm warning you. Don't treat me like some young dickhead, I'm a seasoned Marine like you. Lest you forget," he warned. "And in case you did, I was leading the Raider Regiment when you were a pimply-assed sailor. So, level with me. Would you bring the Bureau into the fold of a black op?" The president pushed out another huff of air, not waiting for a response. "Can't happen. And Congress can't know about this. There's no way. You're recreating the Vietnam Phoenix Program. And who would you use? Delta? Not SEAL Team 6. We'd have a book out in a week. A movie in two."

Chief of Staff Steele stood and walked to a window. He briefly toyed at the lace sheers. "Mr. President, we were thinking this would have to be an accepted Special Access Program that wouldn't even unofficially exist. Our thought was, and I am speaking collectively here, we could tuck it under with another Unacknowledged Special Access program that has been waived. That clears us of standard reporting requirements and audits. The congressional chairperson, ranking members, or committees already know of the core program. But a USAP hidden behind another SAP, well, you get the picture."

POTUS laughed as he shook his head at the nonsense filling the room. "Hidden under hidden under hidden. So, what do you propose if it isn't a JSOC program?" The president tested the idea, surprised that he was actually growing a bit more comfortable with the concept as he processed it on his own.

"That's just it. We do use a JSOC program. The Intelligence Support Activity. Gray Fox. Task Force Orange. We just take this little offshoot, and"—he shrugged again—"find it a new home. ISA, it could be said, is growing redundant anyway between Delta and CIA's SAD. Even NSA's been going more military. We could take Orange and use it for our purpose and let the others continue to develop the capabilities that the activity typically held as their niche."

"Building it a home. And a new program." The president spit in detest of another budget add.

"No, Sir, Mr. President. It already exists. Like I said, we are simply redirecting—or directing, what already is established. The NSA SHOTGUN program already tracks anyone who carries a cell phone globally. It's mapping billions of daily records and relationships or movements and intersections with other mobile device users. Its sticks it in the—"

"FASCIA database," Ron Deluth assisted again.

"Thank you, Ron, I know I'm getting overly technical here, but essentially, anyone protected under the Fourth Amendment is technically in the clear. But if someone is plotting against the United States, technically, they're an enemy of the state, and for us to examine their interactions, relationships, and travel time portraits, that's simply due diligence. We wouldn't be targeting US persons, and if we did, those persons would be foreign agents."

"Clearly, despite my position, I'm outnumbered, and you increasingly sound rehearsed, Ben. I just can't tell who's feeding you all this techie shit," the president accused the room. "Deep black programs. I never liked them. Hidden budgets, cost overruns, and lack of oversight. It would be different if it wasn't a whole unit that would be conducting these operations. One guy, maybe, two or three, but this. This is a problem waiting to happen."

The SECDEF shifted a bit on the sofa, took a drink of coffee, and straightened his tie. "Very well. I'll find it a home and let's start with one, maybe two or three to support him. But one man from Orange for this denied activity, no pun intended. That's all we'll need. Thank you, Sir," he reaffirmed, despite a concept plan already in the works for weeks, albeit unwitting to the recent attack.

Director Deluth fought the smile. One operator as the focal point would still work. They would still go forward with more once the program was cleared to go. The SECDEF had already set that in motion.

The president rolled his eyes, not fully knowing how he had opened Pandora's box. Yet he wasn't going to be pushed around. "But," he added.

It was the president's turn. He wasn't a pushover, and he was going to get something out of this hidden agenda as payback for the little coup he had sitting in his office.

"I want the Bureau somehow involved for now. The director and his Counterterrorism Division are expected to have a role in this attack. For any terror act responses, it goes Bureau first. Even if it's some sort of oversight that you work out with them. They absolutely, positively must be involved. And I will not waver on that. Understood?"

Chief of Staff Steele had waited for a pause. "Mr. President, the FBI Counterterrorism Division is woefully understaffed. They don't have enough Arab linguists, they don't have the cultural knowledge for this type of response, and they just don't have the funds to do this effectively."

"I'm so glad you see my point. As of today, Task Force Orange or ISA or whatever it's called now is going to be phased out." The president paused to let it sink in. "They're done. No longer a unit. And I don't mean covered up, I mean vaporized."

Their collective eye bulges looked like an Afghan poppy field.

"Take their budget and their resources and split it up among the community, but half the budget goes to the FBI Counterterrorism unit. We'll have to let Congress know and it will be part of our terror event response. That's settled."

President Ross circled around and re-sat against the edge of the desk. "My first choice is to do a reassignment for Orange's personnel. Just like we did with all the defense intel contractors going back to DIA years back. Task Force Orange is now one man. He has the job to preempt. And if it means it requires more men at some point to support him, you will not come back to me, you will take the funds from the black program that you're tucking this under. But it will never grow beyond a half-dozen people or the funds that you have already supporting the current program. Ever."

President Ross squinted his eyes as it looked like the chief spook was going to say something. Deluth remained quiet. "Clearly, these black programs aren't currently working or you wouldn't come to me with a new program; you'd just share the success story and ask for more money. So, Owen, you bury this program somewhere. I leave it to you how it's structured. But they have to be men who are dedicated to being lifelong soldiers. It's too risky otherwise. And..." The president raised his hand. His Marine voice commanded the office now.

The men cowed before him, knowing there was more to come. They had blindsided him and it was payback.

"I don't care if it's only going to the FBI director, or someone on his staff, but this man from Orange will need to get intel somewhere. Since it's domestic, the Bureau will need to benefit from the intel. We're breaking a silo, not creating new ones."

All the men looked around the room at one another like elder scolded children who learned the hard way that parents weren't so easily fooled. The battle wasn't won yet after all, and they had lost ground. But they had their program with blessing despite a high cost. That would have some seriously pissed-off folks. It meant this dark program would have to go even deeper lest drowning rats scurry to find sanctuary as they often did with killed DOD programs and new skunk work upstarts.

Director Deluth took a hard swallow and spoke up. "It's your call, Mr. President," he appeased easily, since he hadn't lost skin in the reorganization. "But I'll tell you one thing, if we give it to the FBI, Justice will have their nose in it. It's a bad idea. The more people we include, the more people that can get buried in this."

The president huffed. "Your idea, boys. I'll be holding the shovel. And that's a promise. Now if you'll excuse me, we've got a terror attack to deal with. I expect answers as fast as we'll get extremists and whack-job wannabes claiming responsibility."

Steele stuffed his hands deep in his pockets and exhaled. An ass-chewing was coming his way after the room cleared. But he had placed chessmen on the board and had a game of his own to play. His ass might just get brought in from flying vulnerably in the wind.

Chapter 10

Ahmed al-Yousif sat cross-legged knee to knee with the other clean-shaven Iraqi Mohawks in the cramped Alexandria, Virginia, apartment. They were very far from home, but for most of them, home no longer had anything left but bad memories, broken promises, and lost families.

Ahmed leaned over his lukewarm bean soup and took another small square of the cut naan bread from the center of the makeshift floor table. Four other Iraqis, former foreign assets to the American SOF tier one elements, tore at their baked dough and sopped it in the shallow bowl of liquid filled with lentils, zucchini, onions, and other legumes.

"When will the lamb be ready?" Ali joked to the others.

"Mister elite counterterrorism Gold Division member"—Tamer dragged out majestically—"here is your goat," he said, throwing a piece of clay oven baked bread at his former teammate who has just executed the first attack on U.S. soil.

The room erupted in a hearty laugh mocking the paltry meal.

Ahmed hoped to stoke the fire and added, "Perhaps we should ask to rejoin the American-Iraqi training academy for better food and a promise of visas." He smiled, looking left and right to see who would laugh first and loudest.

The room fell silent.

A fart in an elevator, the Americans would say, Ahmed thought.

None of the men, nor their families, had received Special Immigrant Visas in time while still living in Iraq. According to letters each of them had received within days or weeks of one another, they were rejected by the Americans due to "a lack of faithful and valuable service," according to the US Embassy memos, and further, there was no clear evidence that the individuals or their families were under threat.

And when the Americans left, the reprisals began. Blood flowed from those who helped the infidels. Other bodies were burned alive. Heads severed. Families forever destroyed. Children had premature funerals, never to see what life could offer in war-torn strife or beyond. *Allahu Akbar*, their killers chanted, the same phrase the families had used in time of joy and thankfulness.

Adding insult to injuries, the businesses they had set up for and with the Americans were stolen from underneath, their assets and ownership given to others in the community. Most of the "others" being wealthy Shia sympathizers puppeted by local Iranian agents or the IRGC.

"Dogs," Ali accused. He took the bread that had fallen in his lap and scooped more soup and beans into his mouth.

"*Haramat*," Tamer said to express the regrettable shame of the situation.

"Monkey's pussy," Mohammad scolded Tamer, instructing him to shut up. "It is deserved. It is our duty."

"Poison to them all with a thousand dicks in their asses," Ali added, using more local derogative remarks.

"Sons of flip-flops. Fathers of dicks, the Americans," Ahmed cursed as they went around the circle exclaiming insults. "They will know our pain, *inshallah*."

The group nodded with stoic expressions. Their motives were different from their own Iranian tasker, but marriages of convenience furthered common objectives in less than ideal situations.

Ahmed contained a laugh. The Americans had teased them for years about the phrase sons of flip-flops. "Bitches," the US soldiers would correct, not always considering the Iraqis' own cultural reference.

Ali raised the small juice glass filled with tepid water. "And may our brother American warriors feel the rotted fruits of their labor as our deadly talents strike their open necks and leave venomous marks on their country. A thousand curses to their graves."

Ahmed raised his glass. His emotions surfaced in his broken speech. "And may our departed sons, daughters, sisters, brothers, and wives spit down upon them with a thousand curses in Hell when we arrive in Fayetteville." He looked around the room as his words struck a chord, and warmth filled his chest.

"Fayettenam, they called it. Ha! It shall be done," Tamer piled on. "And by my hands will their blood drown their false promises. May God be with us tonight."

Jahmir cleared his throat. His eyes bulged and appeared to be floating on small lakes of tears. "I'd like to propose a change to our next target." All eyes turned to the quiet one of the crew.

"I can't go on, my brothers. We've found the greatest planning difficulty with how I escape once we go to Fort Bragg and I complete my task. My brothers, there is no need. Let me go and martyr myself. Let me make the greatest impact by giving myself. It will help our cover looking like these Muslim zealots we've fought and who have destroyed our families. Our lives. I have nothing left. There is nothing more for me in this world. I am not a praying man, so let God do with me what he will. May he see mercy on my soul and allow me to join my loved ones. I plead with you, let me do this to ensure our next attacks are successful. It is my gift. Please accept it."

A buzz from the loudspeaker caused all of the men to look up at the dated yellowing door chime. The sound signified not a threat in the apartment entryway but yet another mail order electronics delivery from China, clothes from Rothco Tactical, and miscellaneous apparel and techno-gadgets from Amazon.

There was much work to be done. And there was a new proposal to share with Mohsen.

"Coming!" they called down on the intercom with enthusiasm. Kids in candy shops were the Mohawks and their communication equipment.

"Quickly, fools. We're hungry," the tinny but gruff voice demanded through the speaker.

"Open," another voice ordered. "Come grab our bags, you women."

The men upstairs gasped in unison. There were more in America than they had been told, and those in the entryway were not Mohawks.

* * * *

Tehran, Iran

The salt-and-pepper hair and trimmed beard of Major General Qasem Soleimani mirrored the features of other senior military officers of the Army of the Guardians of the Islamic Revolution Quds Force who gathered around the late dinner feast. Other Iranian leadership gathering in the entryway soon seated themselves at the head of the grand table. They had larger beards and waistlines, to boot. Soleimani's IRGC boss, Mohammad Ali Jafari physically looked as though he could be Soleimani's brother. The two were close and had formed a considerable bond over the years in both strategy and resolution.

Soleimani regarded a near-perfect date in his hand before popping it in his mouth.

"Haj Qasem. Congratulations are in order," lauded the IRGC QF first commander.

Brigadier General Mohammad Reza Yazdi, Tehran's IRGC and Basij leader, raised a date in toast. "Hear, hear." He smiled.

Soleimani gave a respectful nod. "Thank you, commanders. But, in truth, it is the work of General Shirazian, who is the living martyr who has the right to pride and success of the initial attack against the Americans."

Iran's top cleric, the Grand Ayatollah, rested both hands on the table before him. He swiveled his head slowly from side to side, gaining the attention from the presiding military leaders. The room silenced.

"You are a stubborn warrior, General, but your fruits of labor have benefited us all. You need not be so modest. You should accept the praises of your peers and superiors in this first of many accomplishments in the new battleground. The Americans will choke on their prejudiced accusations and sanctions."

With Soleimani's eyes drooping to the sides and his tight lips, he almost looked sad. He nodded respectfully to the Ayatollah's accolades and addressed the group. "The pure and exemplary principles of the Islamic Republic are not similar to the principles of our enemy." Referring to Sunni extremists, he continued, "The fiery beliefs of the *takfiris* under authority of our deputy commander in the United States will bring terror to the homes of our adversaries. It will not appear to be a provocation by Iran, but rather a response to the betrayal of Iraqi soldiers whose families were slaughtered as a result of their assistance to the *kafir* Americans. These *takfiris* are an Arab and Islamic Army that we now control, and they will be adventurous for Islam and for us. It is a just punishment for the Americans' meddling in the Arab world's affairs and their unlawful impositions on us and our economy."

"Major General, respectfully, what assurances do you have for General Shirazian's continued success against the Americans? Surely, the special operations arms of the Americans will be able to find these men if they have not been discreet and if appropriate precautions are not followed. Can evidence of their actions return to the Islamic Republic? We cannot endure further accusations or sanctions."

Soleimani was comfortable addressing the concern of a top commander from the Iran-Iraq War. The commander, now finished with his expression of curiosity, dove in to a meaty portion of lamb.

"These men's hearts are not foremost concerned with defending Islam or the Republic of Iran. But they will be victorious through their drive for vengeance. Their jihad will continue until their own deaths, be it at their hands, ours, or the Americans'. They have nothing left but to financially secure their living families and the taste of revenge. To them, there is nothing sweeter. They have been selected, because they have nothing else." The Supreme Leader chimed in. "Major General. Thank you for your delightful insights as to the fire and spirit of the martyrs. But I do not believe you have satisfied my"—he regarded the guests and lifted his arm up and across with flair—"or *our* assurances against these men being captured or failing at their missions."

"Certainly. I beg your forgiveness. General Reza Shirazian is located in the United States, as planned. He is under false papers and identity. It affords him, shall we say, extensive freedom of movement. With these freedoms, he can act as the operational commanding arm and communicate to the ancillary planning and support cells, which have no contact with the martyrs. The support cells have lived in the US for years. They will provide all necessary funds, equipment, and logistical support according to their current access in America. They have no contact with one another. The general also has secured communication through one of his subordinates to the execution cell. Our martyrs. The general has no contact and no definitive link between the cells. If this is too much information, I can respect your desires to be less witting."

"Continue."

"As you wish. The general's subordinate had also worked with the martyrs to establish decoy cells of unwitting *takfiri* martyrs, praise be to God, who are bait and distraction after our initial attacks. They will conduct a second wave of attacks. Reza, General Shirazian, will remain abroad for the next two years as we complete the stages of operations. Does this alleviate your concerns?"

The Supreme Leader nodded. "And the men. Tell me of the men. Have they been properly trained to evade the American counterterrorism efforts?"

"Indeed. These men were called by the Americans 'Mohawks' in Iraq. They are called by a name of American Native Indians entrusted after the colonist invasion to the Far West. As a bit of history, the colonists used the Mohawk natives to kill other Indian tribes in the area so the colonists could expand acquired territories. In our times, the American Delta Force, CIA, and other elite units trained these particular Iraqi men to find and kill their own countrymen in the cities. These men learned from the Americans surveillance, countersurveillance, intelligence, device tracing, explosives and other lethal skills. Simply, the best of the American military trained them to be their brothers in arms. The Americans promised protection and citizenship to these men and their families."

Shit-eating grins ran wild across the table.

"The elite American forces left their Mohawks with empty promises. Daesh and other *takfiri* groups slaughtered their families in reprisal." The general left out the IRGC influence in instigating these events. "It is unfortunate the Americans never told the whole historic story of betrayal to the Mohawks. Yet to our good fortune, we gave these men security for their remaining families and a cause. That and a promise to pay for their surviving families with our martyr funds. Their deaths will pay for their families' survival."

"And how are these Mohawks finding their military counterparts?" asked a commander sucking the meat off a small lamb vertebra.

For the first time, Soleimani broke into a broad smile. He lifted his hands from his lap. "It is what they do. Scout. Track. Hunt. We have database of the Delta soldiers' most detailed personal information gathered from system breaches of their personnel records. We have cross-referenced this information with data searches and linkages. The Mohawks have the names and locations of the American soldiers' families, their homes, and their geo-tagged travel patterns to work, their devices. Everything. This is trusting America, after all, and they do not use false name *kunyas*. The Mohawks even found them on their Facebook. You see, we hunted the Americans just as they hunt us—by peeling back their life story, diagramming families, inner circles, homes, phones, internet sites, and relatives' houses. The students became the masters. The hunters become the hunted."

A round of applause started up but was quashed with the raise of a hand. "And if they are discovered? How do you ensure they are tied to the Islamic State?"

"We do not."

All heads lifted from their food and drink, and eyes returned to the general.

"We will want the American public to know they are the Mohawks. Most importantly, we want them to know the American military has trained their attackers. We will release this information to our contacts throughout Washington.

Ideally, the outrage will, in time, limit the American reach for global training of allied forces and militia groups. By bringing fear home, we hope to reduce their military advisors across the Middle East and Africa. The Mohawks are just the beginning. We have similarly enlisted members of an elite Iraqi counterterrorism unit. Also trained by the best of the Americans. They are already in the United States. Unknown to the Americans, they are being trained right now on their bases. After this next wave, their nuclear weapons complex is next. There is much work to be done. And they will complete the work the Mohawks cannot finish, and they will take care of the Mohawks if they are discovered before it is time."

* * * *

With hazard signals on, the Mohawk named Tamer changed lanes and drove onto the shoulder of Washington Boulevard. The hotwired car from Ronald Reagan Airport's economy parking lot lost tire air with near-perfect timing. Sporting skinny jeans, a striped button-down, and an Under Armour ball cap, Tamer carefully opened the driver's side door and walked to the trunk carrying a medium-sized duffel along the passing Washington, DC, rush-hour traffic. The cut tire valve's hiss stopped as the remaining pressure escaped.

With a burner phone, he dialed Ali, who was similarly dressed in casual American style but driving with Ahmed on Interstate 395 just approaching Pentagon City.

"Our objective, Wagner, is turning on from Army Navy Drive. He is driving the black Jeep with a gray top," Ali reported. Ahmed sat shotgun with a laptop and USB antennae pointed to the windshield. He watched the tracking display that was locked on to OEF OIF veteran Chief Warrant Officer Wagner's mobile phone. Wagner, a former JIEDDO targeting cell COMINT technician with the Defense Intelligence Agency, and previously with 5th Group, couldn't have been any further away from Iraq as he sang to the Steve Miller Band in his Rubicon. His children, just picked up from daycare, giggled in the backseat where they were locked into their boosters. The thought of Mohawks and the Delta squadron he had been seconded to hadn't entered his mind for years. Nor did he think about two men from the Iraqi Special Operations Forces (ISOF) 2nd Special Operations Brigade driving a few cars behind him. The indigenous fighters, or "indigs", like missions, faded away. Working with Delta had been great for his career, bad for his family. His last tour had taken a lot out of him and nearly cost him a marriage.

* * * *

Tamer lifted the popped trunk lid to retrieve the spare tire, which he placed it against the bumper. He scanned the road for any threats and placed the duffel bag in the trunk's doughnut hole as close to the gas tank as possible. God willing, all was in place.

* * * *

Chief Wagner checked both side mirrors as he drove, then looked over his right shoulder as he prepared to change lanes.

"Hi, Daddy," his daughter called from the backseat booster.

"Hi, Pumpkin."

"Is Mommy going to be home when we get there?"

Wagner turned his eyes back to the road. "She sure is."

"And is she going to have a surprise?"

"Like Shake Shack?"

"Yes." She giggled.

"I want Shake Shack too!" Ryan pouted from the back.

"You get Shake Shack too, buddy."

Wagner checked his rearview mirror by instinct. All the cars were jockeying for driving space to include the white Camry that was passing him on the left with a commuter clearly getting in some last-minute work on a laptop—and antennae?

"Geeky war drivers," he said aloud. Beltway bandits were no doubt creating the next commercial solution to entice budget dollars.

"What, Daddy?"

"Nothing, Pumpkin."

"I want a van-ill-a milk-shake," Ryan informed his dad.

"Mommy, got you one. Aren't you a lucky guy?"

"Yay," he beamed.

The white Camry and a herd of other cars zipped in and out of traffic. Ali directed Tamer. "Now."

Tamer shuffled in the trunk and nudged the tire into the road. As the oncoming car veered into the second lane and hit another vehicle, Tamer sprinted onto the exit toward Lady Bird Johnson Park.

Ali and Ahmed pulled to the curb fast enough for their countryman to get in.

Chief Wagner saw the red lights ahead, but it was too late to turn off, and he was committed to the right lane. He watched up ahead as a series of hazard-lit cars pulled over to the side of the road.

"Why are we stopping, Daddy? My van-illa milk-shake is gunna melt."

"Just a little accident, Ryan. Don't worry about the milkshake, Mommy will keep it cold." The chief looked around him and up the road. A petite blond female exited a blue BMW to meet an older, balding white male who had his hands raised and yelled as he walked around his car to look at his passenger side.

"Relax. That's why you have insurance," Wagner counseled to no one.

Ahmed called back to Tamer, who sat in the backseat with his finger at the ready over a different mobile device. "About twenty seconds. I'm getting strong signals. No disruption. Do you see the same?"

"I have good signal."

The blond woman kicked the small doughnut tire out of the road, allowing the black Rubicon to stay in its lane.

The chief gave a casual salute to the woman as he slowly approached an abandoned car with hazards on and a flat rear tire.

"Press," Ahmed instructed to Tamer, who keyed two buttons to detonate the explosives alongside one of their former instructors.

"For my children," Tamer exclaimed without a breath. His finger hovered above the third button as he watched the faces of Americans pass innocently before him.

Chapter 11

Explosive bloodshed ensued, and the Mohawks turned into the Columbia Island Marina. They parked, wiped down their equipment, and left it in the rental car trunk.

As the three Iraqis walked to the docks, passersby running in the opposite direction paid them no attention. The desire for some spectators to help their fellow man overrode any fears. Other gapers' eyes were directed through the clearing to flame and carnage with black smoke rising above the tree line.

The ISOF commandos still on the road continued their driving path in the opposite direction until the third turn-off, at which they would circle back and head off to the next target. The Mohawks had done well.

The Mohawks boarded the Tipsy Canoe, a forty-one-foot Cantius Cruiser, for a short ride to the National Harbor Marina where Mohammed and Jahmir had two more cars loaded and ready for the drive to North Carolina.

Ahmed flipped open and dialed the Thales Teorem smartphone. The secure phone notification light illuminated, confirming the encrypted voice call connection.

"Yes?" Mohsen, the IRGC contact, answered in English.

"It is complete. Proceeding to next," confirmed a Mohawk.

"Thank you. Your families would be proud."

Mohsen turned to Deputy Commander Shirazian. "They have completed another," he said in his native Persian tongue.

It is time. "Your men are ambitious. Very effective. Congratulations on initial success. Contact Daesh. Let them claim it all."

"It will be done."

"Thank you," General Shirazian said in Farsi.

* * * *

FBI Director Sean Mullins played an easy hand on the phone with President Ross, stating the most recent National Capital Region explosion held a strong likelihood of being another terror attack.

POTUS was silent for a moment. "God help us all."

"Indeed, Mr. President. I can assure you, we're on it."

"Sean, I know you're doing what you can, but we're entering a crisis. The media is all over this broadcasting that Washington is under attack. I'm going to have to close the stock markets tomorrow so we don't go in the tank."

"Mr. President, Justice is going to save time by assuming this is a terror attack and engaging the appropriate resources immediately. My counterterror teams are on alert across the country, and my leads will continue to reach out to state and local. We're turned on here and processing the intel."

"What intel do you have?"

"Well...as you know, there are a lot of pieces that may not have meant anything yesterday but may connect to something today...now."

"You don't have shit, do you?"

"That's not quite—"

"Do you?"

"No, Mr. President."

Again, the president remained silent for uncomfortable moments before his reply. "Keep me posted, Sean. We're going to have to go public before too long. And I want facts if I can't have suspects."

Ben Steele disconnected the line for President Ross. "Sir, I'll reach out to Ron Deluth and see what the CIA has. John over at Homeland won't have anything. That's no surprise. We'll just have to wait it out a bit, Mr. President."

"Contact Owen."

"Sir, the SECDEF is—"

President Ross shot the *shut your mouth now* look to his chief of staff. A look that was downright menacing from the old Marine.

"I'll get him right away. Would you like to talk to him or shall I deliver a message?"

"I want two things. You have him get a handful of Deltas up here by tomorrow night. Get them over to Director Mullins. They do not need to be advisor status. Just make sure the media doesn't get wind. See if they can wear FBI jackets or shirts."

"And you want them to do what?"

"I want them to show up. It's protocol and I want to show the Intelligence and Justice arm that I'm doing what we would normally do. Understood?" Ben nodded as he scribbled notes on an official White House paper folio. "Second?"

"Full speed ahead on that skunkworks project of yours. I'm not sure what one man can do, but if red tape is in the way of national security, have this man from Orange start hunting to kill them all. Kill them like we were Israelis finding terrorists in their own country."

"Will do, Mr. President. Oh, speaking of Israel. I meant to tell you earlier, Lebanese forces and our UN advisors...ahem...have taken care of remains of the drone strike outside the refugee camp. We've sent the additional aid funds to Beirut in a separate transaction. The drone fliers and forward operating base Deltas are being closely monitored, and we have assurances of their continued silence. The soldiers who perished will be claimed by the military as a training accident in Jordan. It may be best if you distance yourself from any comment to the families in case it is ever found that, well, you know."

"It was an unfortunate choice, as you know, Ben. One that I will live with as a leader, a soldier, and a man. And between us, I don't think I made the right one. But right or wrong, it can never get out. And if anyone comes forth with evidence from the ground, it has to be taken care of with discretion and certainty of never getting out. We're sure that the soldier en route was also at the blast site?"

"Our reports are that it is highly likely. He was within meters of the target site before impact and never made it to the alternate extraction point."

President Ross turned away. On a sideboard in the office were a few framed photos of himself in uniform surrounded by loyal troops holding up the American flag and their weapons. "God forgive me for what I've done, but it was for the greater security of this country. Not that the last days haven't changed all that, but we had no choice at the time."

"Mr. President, I'll go make the call."

Ross turned to face his advisor. "You're hesitant, Ben. Do you disagree with me? I'd like your honest opinion." He added the reassurance, "Speak freely."

"Sir, you were elected as chief executive. President of the United States. Commander in chief because you can make tough calls. I serve at your pleasure. My role is to handle all matters of a delicate nature that require discretion to protect your interests and manage certain flows of information. It is my job to help advise you on difficult matters, including those you don't want to hear or should never hear. I am your junkyard dog, but you are my master. I know my place, and I could never hold *your* place in making decisions required of this office."

"So, you're saying in a fluffed-up way you don't agree."

"No, Mr. President, I am saying it doesn't matter. I'll keep on this to ensure there are no loose ends. Period. I am not your yes man. I'm your get-it-done man. And that's all I can really say."

Chapter 12

After a five-hour drive south from the National Capital Region, the Mohawks pulled off I-95, exiting to the Fort Bragg area in North Carolina. It was late night. Just before eleven thirty.

With over fifty thousand active duty personnel, Bragg, named after Confederate General Braxton Bragg, is the largest military installation in the world. It is perhaps best known for being the home of Airborne and various special operations forces, and spans four counties. And yet, the Mohawks continued past Bragg to a residential area of choice for many military members, especially those of the renowned Delta Force—Southern Pines.

The night had cooled, and dozens of the unit's team members remained congregated under green umbrellas around small round tables large enough to hold dozens of beer bottles and last-minute waters before it was time to head out for the night. Some of the warriors checked Facebook or Twitter while they sat around bullshitting, others texted goodnight to children headed off to bed, and still others had emails to send to friends, spouses, and the occasional stripper. The bar had great free Wi-Fi and strong cell phone coverage. It was convenient, and convenience trumped real safety with a perception that it was all good.

Roughly a dozen more Deltas sat inside the small white Southern Pines Irish pub that more resembled a two-story home than it did a bar. They followed suit in behavior to those outside, chatting and banging on their devices with conversation and consciousness split between friends and the ease of technology at their fingertips. Despite being the warrior elite, they were still human, and that meant connectivity in this low-key environment. Safe and comfortable.

Delta liked it that way. Quiet, away from Bragg and still within reach of Mackall Army Airfield for those who still helped out on occasion with SERE and Q Course.

The SOF watering hole was set back behind four-foot white brick walls that provided just enough privacy from the street.

When the Mohawks were run by Delta in Mosul, McConnely Pub was often talked about by the squadron members in front of their Iraqi counterparts. Oh, how they had regaled their indigenous team members with stories about stopping in for at least a few to decompress from the day before going home. The Mohawks were told, "When we get you and your families to America, you have to stop by. There are always plenty of Deltas at McConnely's," they shared. "Just remember New Hampshire Ave. New Hampshire, just like the state."

Under tree and darkness cover, one of the Mohawks was dropped off on Northeast Broad Street. There was no shortage of large pickup trucks to hotwire and prep. The plan for five minutes to acquire, wire, and mobilize was reasonable, and Jahmir was up to the task with one minute to spare.

To support or execute technical surveillance and direct action operations in Iraq, the Americans had specifically instructed the Mohawks on: lock bypass techniques, building entry operations, picking and decoding tumbler locks, picking and decoding a variety of automotive locks, transponder bypass, and other access missions. Jahmir became a crack cracker.

Tamer and Ahmed glanced down the street to ensure the elite unit pub patrons were still going strong. Tamer was able to identify and capture the technical details of the mobile devices connected to the pub's Wi-Fi. Four technical signatures were on their list. Equipment identifiers got the Mohawks close; subscriber identifiers gave names and credit card confirmations with physical addresses. Switching from passive "listening" mode to capture the digital signatures, they changed to active "relay" mode and with a few additional commands spoofed the devices' phone screens to be off while cameras and microphones activated, further validating visuals and voices. For the devices they could not access due to heightened security measures, the defensive tradecraft validated users who didn't want to be exploited. They found them.

The Facebook and Instagram images from the soldiers' profiles contributed to a pattern-of-life validation back at home. The Mohawks had created their own baseball cards and Tier One kill list just like the Americans had in Mosul. Tamer worked the Nemo Outdoor cellular survey tool with expertise. It didn't have the functionality of his Harris Blackfin II, but it also didn't cost over seventy-five grand. He had hooked the DTI scanner to his laptop to track multiple networks and devices from the list. Worry about the Title 10 approval to use such a device was of no concern to a man who didn't even have legitimate approval to be in-country, much less surveilling its citizens. Open-source software further outfitted the hunters of men.

Confident in his technical tradecraft, Tamer pinged as many devices as he could with a text message. "HOW MUCH LONGER?" He fired off the patrons' message apps. Tamer knew it would elicit more communications to dragnet more signals from the primary target Deltas and their secondaries. Secondaries being families.

The other Mohawks U-turned on East Connecticut Avenue and headed down Northwest Broad Street, where they signaled to Jahmir that all was a go. Their objectives were confirmed for fixing and finishing the enemy. Just like hunting and geolocating targets in internet cafes back home. HUMINT, physical surveys, networking protocols, and SIGINT. Jackpot!

Jahmir was a go for martyrdom. He waved good-bye to his friends and was met with somber nods. Ahmed raised his hand from the steering wheel in a gesture of the solemn departure. They had trained and worked with each other for years to support the American counterterrorism teams. Both Jahmir's and Ahmed's families had been systematically hunted down and slaughtered on the same day by Iraqi Mehdi militiamen death squads in retaliation for their traitorous service to infidels. More specifically, they were killed by an *inghimasi*, an Iraqi fighter with the intent of immersing himself in an attack, who raided their family compound with firearms before detonating a suicide vest. His wife, mother and children were wiped out in a flash. In addition to Jahmir's mother and children, his wife was expecting in the months to come. Jahmir wiped a growing tear from his eyelid. He was going to do the same now to the Americans, a tactic of the *istishhadiun*, who used grenades, light weapons, and vehicle-borne explosives. He patted the Czech Republic EVO3 A1 series Scorpion full-automatic fire submachine gun. The shoulder stock had been removed so the gun could serve as a single-handed machine pistol with a thirty-round magazine that could empty in less than two seconds and serve up 1,200 feet-per-second muzzle velocity for devastating penetration.

"Go in peace," Tamer praised as their vehicle passed by and turned left onto East Pennsylvania Avenue to Ashe Street, where they parked. And waited.

* * * *

Tamer patted his friend's leg. "He will be with God and his family. He will avenge the betrayal."

"As will we all, my friend."

"It is a true worthy jihad. It is respectable and warranted."

"This will go fast, *inshallah*. Get the address pinned to the map. We have a busy night."

A blue Nissan Altima pulled alongside their car. The ISOF killers gave a nod, pulled off to the side, and awaited their scouts to show the way to the next objectives.

Chapter 13

Jahmir turned right. The bar was up ahead to his left.

A car pulled out of its street parking spot, opening the path so Jahmir could get better access to the building over the delivery drive and curb straight through the beer garden into the crowd and the establishment.

He gave the gas pedal an even push as the heavy Ford neared the pub. Jahmir knew the truck had enough torque that he could stomp the pedal at the last moment for the utmost surprise. And stomp he did, even as some of the familiar faces came into focus and mental images flashed of events in Iraq with the Deltas involving laughter and the unspoken blood-oath bonds of brotherhood.

The large truck's tires screeched as their accelerated revolution thrust the vehicle forward and over the curb, catching some air. Metal met brick and mortar, smashing the materials inward toward the patrons. Men tried to scramble as a ton of impact bore into their position. Those who stumbled from their chairs were mowed down. Others who more successfully scrambled away were trapped within the pub walls.

With the driver-side window down, Jahmir screamed the ruse battle cry to anyone who could hear. "*Allahu Akbar!*" He triggered the hand-held machine gun, spitting rounds into the trapped warriors.

The truck smashed through the thin brick wall of the pub's wing entrance to the beer garden, further crushing its inhabitants and injuring others with flying and falling debris before coming to a steaming halt. The safety bag deployed and sandwiched Jahmir between the powdery white puffed fabric and the front seat.

From a block away, the parked Mohawks detonated the device secured within Jahmir's stolen vehicle. The blast sent fire, concussion and shrapnel out from the wreckage, obliterating everything in its radius.

When the bright flash of light and echoing boom signaled the success to the Mohawks, they exclaimed praise to God and moved out with the digital feeds, prepared to catch all numbers from incoming calls and messages to their targets' devices.

Within moments, the geo-tracer received signals and pinpointed the various locations coming in to the monitor's display feed.

The Altima followed behind like a buzzard trailing a wolf pack.

The Iraqis headed to the closest objectives to finalize the Fayetteville-area attacks. An eye for an eye. A tooth for a tooth.

A family for a family.

Chapter 14

The White House's John F. Kennedy Conference Room, better known as the Situation Room, is housed within the intelligence management center under the West Wing.

The table was cluttered with bottled waters, cans of Coke, Diet Coke, a few juice bottles, and a Cherry 7UP for the president. The staff had been instructed to remain outside for the past four hours. It was just after midnight.

"I know it's hardly settled, but we agree to continue monitoring the situation, and each respective member of the Security Council will continue to be proactive and vigilant. As much as I hate to admit it, it helps that ISIS has claimed responsibility. We now need to narrow down if it's a cell or loosely coordinated lone wolves." The president trolled his gaze around the long mahogany conference table, making sure he made eye contact with each leader present.

The SECDEF, DNI, deputy national security advisor, and vice chairman of the Joint Chiefs of Staff all gave tight-lipped nods. The White House chief of staff raised an eyebrow when he gave his nod of confirmation. Secretary of State Eileen Rous still looked a bit confused as to what she could be doing to assist, which was half the problem of State. The White House counsel, Nicole Wasserman, sat perched like a hawk. She was seething inside from the news of yet another terror attack. The president had brought her into his administration based on her international corporate experience and her JAG duties in the Corps. The POTUS fantasized for a moment about feeding the broken-winged Rous to Wasserman.

"I'll see if the Watch Team has anything by sunup in the Morning Book and when I get my Daily Brief."

Attendees from the National Security Council began to stand from the green leather armchairs. Some men twisted and cracked their backs while others collect their notes and notepads, stuffed them into briefcases, and prepared themselves for the knowing look of wives who had grown impatient with the long hours of the job.

They had their hands tied with no tangible enemy to chase and no new leads on the afternoon's rush-hour attack.

The FBI director felt increasing pressure to come up with something but was dead empty.

There was a rapping on the door, which opened before the invitation came to enter. Watch officers, staffers, and the president's chief strategist all fought at once to get through the door to give POTUS the news.

"Whoa, I'm afraid to ask." The president said with deep concern.

"Mr. President, we've just been informed of another attack," the strategist shouted out.

"Here?"

As others turned, the chief pushed his way through.

A staffer shook his head *no* and belted out "Fort Bragg area. North Carolina."

"At the base?" The Defense secretary probed for more detail while simultaneously seeing if he had missed a secure text informing him of the same.

"No, sir. Outside the base," chimed in a watch officer. "There was an explosion at a bar soldiers evidently frequent, and then... Um." He wiped his face in a gesture of disbelief. He closed his eyes as he spoke, his eyebrows raised as he fought past the mental images. "There was a—"

All attendees' eyes were wide, mouths agape, hanging on every word that this kid was trying to get out.

"What happened? Spit it out," shouted the director of the CIA.

A senior CIA analyst of the "Persia House" Iranian department, Mena Shabpareh, tried to make a comment. She was literally shouldered out of the conversation as the chief strategist took the floor again. "They slaughtered whole houses of people. Families. Children. There was a report of one soldier killed in his house, but he was found tied to a chair. Hacked to pieces. Then burned. Dead kids all around him. We don't know if he was tortured or if it was some interrogation."

"Good God. Pull it up on the news monitor. Find out what the Hell is going on."

With a few clicks of the remote control, panels of television screens lit up all around the room. A conglomeration of eight monitors in the back of the room facing the president's position illuminated with news coverage.

The president shook his head. "We're in a goddamned intelligence center and checking the goddamned news. Are we always the last to know?"

Mena turned her back on the room and went back to her temporary space outside the Situation Room. "To Hell with you all," she mumbled. "No one wants to hear anything but their own voice."

"What was that?" Mark, a White House special operations planner tied to the CENTCOM Special Applications Group, gave Mena a friendly nudge on the arm.

"Hey, Mark. Nothing. Just tried to get my voice in. The usual."

"It's not going to happen in there unless you grow your beard out."

Mena gave an understanding huff. "This is the wrong place for me to be. I'm told to keep my head down even though I may have unique insights. Why they even keep me here is beyond me."

"Let me know if I can help. I'm here to listen if you need to run something past someone."

"Thanks, Mark. I'm good. I'm not going to give you the answers so you can look good."

The Special Forces lieutenant colonel laughed. "It would take a lot for this mug to look good."

She regarded his bald head, bushy moustache, broken nose, and scarred upper brow. He was an old SOF junkyard dog, but there was indisputably a rugged handsomeness about him. But he was married, and too old for her, and, most importantly, he wasn't a Muslim.

"I just wondered if it related to missing Iraqis that we used to track. Iran would have more placement and access than Daesh. Just a hunch, but I can back it up with more than we have supporting ISIS beyond their social media claims."

The lieutenant colonel gave the remark genuine consideration. "You're right. They're not going to listen to a chick with a headscarf refuting a group who's already claimed responsibility. Flesh it out. Let's talk later tomorrow. Deal?" He rose a fist, which she bumped.

"Deal, snake eater," she confirmed with a wink and a grin of appreciation.

Secretary of Defense Mathieson texted on his secure device from the table in the Situation Room. He looked to his left and right for snoops.

NEED TO HAVE OUR NEW PLAYER IN PLACE BY A.M. HAVE MADE NECESSARY PROVISIONS WITH NSA.

The reply came back almost immediately.

ANTICIPATED THIS. JUST SAW NEWS. PROJECT ICE PICK A GO

And just as quickly, SECDEF replied:

THX OT KNEW I COULD COUNT ON YOU

CALL IF YOU NEED. OUT.

* * * *

The glow of O.T.'s television lit up his darkened bedchamber. His wife, wearing earplugs and a sleeping mask, had been asleep since ten. As he moved from the bed, she stirred. "You going to the office or downstairs?"

"Just downstairs. There was another attack. By the Pines down at Bragg."

"Where's that?"

"Down by our home. Where we used to live. In North Carolina," he said patiently.

"Mmm," she contemplated with plugs and eye mask still on. "What happened?"

"An attack. Probably terrorists. There was one earlier this evening outside the Pentagon."

"I think I remember you saying that," she responded flatly. "And where was this one?"

"North Carolina. Go back to sleep."

She raised her mask and focused on the television. "Look, honey, there was an attack tonight. Look. She's reporting from the Pines. Are you going to work? To the office?"

"Yeah, I have to go downstairs and make a few calls." He circled the bed and kissed her forehead. "Can you watch for a bit and tell me what happened?"

"I'll be glad to, sweetie." She kissed the air. "Is Warren home yet?"

"Soon." He smiled as he stroked his wife's cheek. "Soon, dear."

"Is he still teaching English in that place?"

"Africa. Yes. He has a school there."

"His mom must be so proud."

"She's gone, remember? So's your brother." He closed his eyes as his patience waned.

"Where did they go?"

"Nowhere. Yeah, they're proud." Sometimes it was just easier to lie to her. She wouldn't remember the difference.

"I'll have to call her and see if they can come for Thanksgiving."

"Sure, dear." O.T. stood at the bedside faking a smile. His wife watched the television attentively with periodic gasps and "Oh, no"s.

"Goddamned Alzheimer's," he breathed quietly under the television volume. And left the room. He had a message of his own to send and get status on Drake's pending arrival. His nephew would be livid with the way they did the recall, but it was one of the few ways to keep him out of the crosshairs. A few discreet calls, a discreet series of flights, and Woolf would be CONUS within twenty-four hours. Pissed off or not.

Chapter 15

"Come in," Earl Johnson replied to the tinny knock on his office door. The gray government metal opened inward, guided by a tremulous hand causing a drawn-out squeak of the door hinges. Earl first saw the Green Bay Packers cotton baseball hat peeking in through the opening. Under the cap cascaded skunk-striped dirty-blond hair draped behind Tresa Halliday's ears.

"Deputy Director Johnson?" she asked, with a raspy voice fitting her rough but feminine features. She was nearly six feet tall. A bit less conventional looking than what the Bureau typically had in its ranks.

Tresa followed Earl's eyes. He wasn't gawking. He was examining. As she held the door knob, he casually tried to make out the tattoo on her wrist. Halliday dropped her left hand to her side.

"Come in, Ms. Halliday," he said as he rose to stand and extended a hand, which she accepted.

She had a firm grip. Earl's gaze fell to his hand, perhaps not expecting the tight grasp. His probing eyes flicked back up to regard her face. Overset by thick dark eyebrows, her matching dark brown eyes bored deep into his own. She fell somewhere between oddly attractive and a tad menacing— like a professional female wrestler to most men.

"Please sit."

"I'll stand. I thought you were going to be general counsel."

"Hardly. Please, sit. If you care to take off your jacket, I know it's a bit warm in here."

"I'm good," she responded, yearning to take off her white denim jean jacket. It was stifling hot, but she knew her shirt had a hole in the armpit, and deplaning the aircraft had taken nearly forty minutes. She was pretty sure she had enough sweat down the maroon T-shirt that it would make the color look two-tone. "So why did they fly me out here if it's not to come to a resolution?"

"This may be a resolution."

"They took my badge and said I used unreasonable force in a willful act that was in open defiance of the suspect's rights. I'm quoting, of course."

"Special Agent Halliday—"

"Just Tresa. I think I already lost the special agent part."

"You haven't lost your title or badge yet. But still possible. It's your second investigation for deadly force."

"Imminent danger." She shrugged. "Did you not read that he put two rounds in my vest?"

"You shot him in the back." He was cool in his remarks but raised his own bushy gray eyebrows to elicit more.

"I would have shot him in the face if he hadn't knocked me to the ground. He was hiding. My team missed him. I knew he was still there."

"That's not in the report," he said, showing genuine surprise.

She thought cautiously before saying more. "Throwing my team under the bus wasn't going to make things better."

Earl nodded. "It was probably the fact that you unloaded on him that warranted the question about excessive use of force. You know the charter; you can't use deadly force to prevent escape."

"I've been through the training. Been through the debriefing. I'm not going to debate this with you. If I were a man, they'd have a decision sooner and recognize that the suspect still posed a threat to me or others while he still possessed a firearm. It's textbook Deadly Force Policy adherence."

"I think they had come to a reasonable decision, but then you kicked another agent on the obstacle course. Normally, people try to lay low during a period of review."

"He tried to stick his finger in my ass as I went over the logs."

"Well. That, too, probably warranted some force on your part. However, and I want to be sensitive, I think there's more at hand here. Probably most of which, and I agree with you," he softened, "is because you're a woman."

There it is. Tresa cocked her head with her "Duh, what have I been saying this whole time" look. It said it all.

He continued the acknowledgement. "And unfortunately, in most cases, you were probably smarter and better skilled than your supervisor or peers."

"That's an understatement." Tresa chewed at her inner lip. She wanted to play tough, not disrespectful or stupid. She was shitting a brick in reality.

He was alluding to what she had wanted to hear, but she also knew that Earl Johnson, chief of counterintelligence, was a highly regarded agent, and a renowned polygraph instructor. She'd have to keep emotions in check. "Why am I here?" she shifted the ball to her court if only but a minute.

"I was looking over your file. Your annual qualification assessments, in particular. They fluctuate within mediocrity in an interesting pattern. About three years after your EOD. Your Entered on Duty date was almost fourteen years ago?"

Tresa tilted her head. "You flew me out from Milwaukee to DC just to say I was an underachiever while some assholes upstairs are wondering if I was justified for killing a guy who put two rounds into my chest when I followed all the bullshit procedures?"

"No. May I continue? And then we can go back to bullshit procedures when we re-address our bureau's need for rigorous obedience to the Constitution and the protection of civil rights." He continued with a resolute tone, but it didn't come across as terse. It was simply matter-of-fact. Almost as if coming from a professor. "I see that your percentage fluctuations if plotted on a bar line would start the tune 'Jingle Bells' in enough of a pattern that it was pre-thought out. Clever, but…well, let's just leave it at clever." He smiled genuinely.

She returned an equally genuine smile and even blushed that someone actually noticed the little game she was playing. He was indeed a puzzle solver. In truth, it wasn't until she had seen her seventh or eighth marking before the tune and the little game seemed like a fun goal. Sitting across from a person who had figured it out made it much less funny in hindsight. She looked down at her hands and then back up to take in this middle-aged man. Earl was a tall, lean friendly-looking guy. His purple tie probably cost more than his whole off-the-rack gray polyester-blend suit. His gold cufflinks closing the white shirt sleeves had an embossed FBI National Academy logo, but they weren't uniform in direction.

His shirtsleeves had gray rub marks on the cuffs. She deduced they were pencil lead smears. Earl had four sharpened pencils to the left of his blotter. One black pen to the right of his blotter. He wore a black Fitbit watch that didn't go with the outfit either. He was balding, and his partial eagle's nest hair was gray. A few deep scabs on his head might have been from recent skin cancer removal. He wore a wedding ring, but clearly his wife didn't dress him in the morning, or perhaps she didn't care about the details either. He was an odd mix of organized and disorganized. Finally, she answered, while he waited with patience and a perma-grin written across his face. "I was just playing around. When I scored high, it didn't seem to matter. Figured I'd have a little fun."

"Eleven years of keying out a song is playing around?"

"Maybe I'm just not very athletic."

"Partial scholarship for electrical engineering to Stanford paid for by women's water polo. I see you were co-captain and received an offer to join the US Olympic team, which tells me your lack of athleticism probably is a fallacy. Why didn't you go with the Olympic offer?"

"What does this have to do with my situation?"

"A lot. You did two years Army ROTC at the same time to get the state scholarship, but then quit before contracting. Every time you have an opportunity for a promotion or something exceptional that would put you in the spotlight or a bigger commitment, you sabotage it."

"I didn't sabotage Supervisory Special Agent Podasky sticking his thumb in my ass on the obstacle course. I didn't sabotage working in Romania for a year with those criminal thugs we called our allies, and I didn't sabotage getting coffee for people in the Washington Field Office when I stood up for myself after some asshole soldier tried to rape me at Bagram Air Force Base. I'm done here." She scooted her chair back and rose with a nasty scowl. "Screw this place." She took a hard swallow and felt her pits flooding sweat down her sides.

Earl remained calm. "I didn't read much about all that other stuff, but I did read how you broke SSA Hefley's collarbone. I'm curious, why didn't you kick him in the face?"

"I missed," she snapped, still standing in front of the chair.

Earl grinned. "You appear to be a smart fighter. One who knows how to play the game. To a degree. Despite hostile treatment. Despite a mounting body count. I want you to work for me. I'm getting more funding for counterterrorism in our Counterintelligence department. And I need someone who can work it from the sidelines. In the field. In the shadows. You would retain special agent status, largely to support the cover, but you would be designated as a Special Surveillance Group Investigative Specialist assigned to me. I would provide you with extensive entitlements throughout the Bureau so you have literally unfettered access to most everything."

"Why on Earth would I want to even stay here anymore?"

"If the conditions were going to be the same, which you have no reason to believe otherwise, you probably wouldn't want to come back. I wouldn't blame you one iota. But you feel you did your job and could be doing more. You want some order and stability, and you also want some rules. Even though you're breaking them."

"I never broke rules," she hissed, but her expression soon demurred to be less confrontational—with him.

"You were raised by your grandparents. See your actual parents much?"

Whoa, what the fuck, Earl. She took her time answering. "They died when I was young. I'm sure it's in the file."

Earl smiled. "Yes. It is in the file. I'm so sorry for your loss."

"Thank you, I was very young."

"Mhmm. You said that. It says that here, too." He pulled another file from underneath a note-filled pad of paper. It had the US Marshals Service crest across the cover. "Funny thing is this file says they were very much alive in Fond du Lac, Wisconsin, until recently, I'm sorry to say." He tossed the file across the desk to her as her lips tightened and nostrils flared. "And this file shows your search parameters and keystroke logging on FBI systems. It also tells how many times you cross the Wisconsin and Illinois border to go back to your home turf. How you had a much older brother who was incarcerated but was killed in prison. Likely by the Chicago outfit."

"You have no right. That information is sealed. Not even the goddamned FBI has the—"

"Sit."

She did as instructed. "How did you know?" she caved.

"Rino Delaurentis, your father, and the Delaurentis crime family in Chicago was one of the first major cases I worked. I was on the US Attorney team that put him and your mother in witness protection. I knew you when you were Francesca Delaurentis but honestly didn't know you were you until a few weeks ago."

"VIVALDI?"

The agent cringed, "I just like Earl a whole lot better."

Tresa was always guarded and had built a lifetime of walls, but she had never expected anyone to come from behind on the inside of her guarded perimeter. He was surfacing a secret she had held her for a lifetime, afraid disclosure would jeopardize her parents' safety. She let no one get close, so there were no slipups. Earl Johnson had done it in less than twenty minutes.

Tresa was relieved on the one hand and terrified on another. Her eyes started to water, and the saline rolled its way down her flushing cheeks to her lips.

"Don't cry yet. I suspect you killed 'Big Tony' Nero in Cicero, Illinois, last summer. Any comment? Are you a killer like your father and brother?"

Chapter 16

Earl handed Tresa a wad of Chipotle napkins that he had cached in his bottom drawer.

She wiped her pooled eyes and looked at the dark eyeliner smeared on the brown recycled-paper napkin. Tresa figured her face must look smeared and puffy, and God forbid the red splotches appear around her neck. But first and foremost on her mind was wondering if now was when agents were going to crash in and arrest her. They never came.

"Tell me of this UCO surveillance detail you had been doing for Public Corruption before you went to the Midwest. You did a few years in Undercover Ops and did a lot of Title III wiretap recordings. Seems you also assisted in Foreign Intelligence Operations and Espionage tailing foreign operators?" He leaned forward and supported himself with his elbows, arms open to her. "You prefer to go undercover as a man?"

You accuse me of a murder I did and say nothing more? Tresa was utterly flabbergasted. Now she had to defend that little issue.

"Special Agent Halliday?"

Tresa couldn't speak. She felt a drip of perspiration sliding between her shirt and skin.

It's a test. But he knows. Maybe he wants me to confess. Fuck that. He asked about undercover ops. Play the game. "Earl," she dragged out, grasping for words. "I'm almost six feet and weigh over one hundred sixty pounds. I don't have a J-Lo bubble ass"—she raised her hands, palms open, to breast level—"and I don't have big boobs. Chest doesn't get in the way of bowhunting. So that's a plus. Unfortunately, I got my dad's body. Square. Like a boxer. Northern Italian. Not like those greasy southie Sicilian shrimps. And if I'm working the street, I can put my hair up and stay in shadows looking more like a regular guy than I can a woman. I tend to stand out. I also prefer to wear running shoes or boots over flats and heels, and that would stand out as well, with me clunking around trying to follow someone while I trip over the littlest thing."

"Suppose a tall blonde following...or tripping along after a guy does tend to, well, it would stand out."

"I dye it. It's really light in summer and darker brown now." She pulled her hat off and tilted her head down to show the dark roots.

"Okay. Thanks for that," he muttered aloud. "You are exactly what I need."

She was wearing a long skirt and lifted a leg up to cross over the other, showing a bit of skin between her knee and a low-rise Timberland work boot. Tresa watched Earl to see where his eyes went or if he became uncomfortable. "If this interview is a Tinder test, I don't shave my legs either if I have to wear shorts."

Earl sat speechless. In such meetings, Earl Johnson always remained composed. He adjusted his shoulders and back uncomfortably, looking desperate not to break eye contact.

Let's dance, Earl. Tresa leaned over to the desk and knocked. Johnson tilted back as she entered his space. "Messin' with you Earl. I shave 'em. I can duck away and still gussy up as a girl, and then I force multiply my surveillance capability. Especially if I'm in a van and can change out."

"That's what I'm hoping for." He leaned in.

"That I shave?"

Earl backed up.

She gave him a wink, knowing he was feeling a little heat in the kitchen again. Tresa just needed him to back off some. She wasn't into controlling men and didn't want to be owned by this one either. Not unless it was mutually beneficial or unless she was completely backed into the corner.

"So, I'm looking at your history...." He raised a couple of white paper sheets and flipped between them. "I'm guessing that on your geo-preference survey out of National Academy, you picked Wisconsin first, then Michigan or Indiana, and you had Chicago dead last." Earl sucked at his teeth. "And of course, we put you in DC and New Orleans, and an overseas tour, all of which is why you messed up a few times, didn't excel, so you could get passed around until you made it closer to home. Although you freaked out a bit thinking that you had done so well in UCOs and surveillance that they might make you an SSA in Chicago over Public Corruption."

She was back in the hot seat. Tresa held up both hands. "Guess it takes a good CI guy, huh?"

"No, enough people upstairs knew you were not what they thought they hired." Earl thrust his tongue against the bottoms of his front teeth, deep in thought. "After the duty shootings and the incident, you lost." He looked up from the paper. "Incident meaning sexual assault, but no one here is going to call it that. Clearly not your fault. But they used it as an excuse to ostracize and get rid of you. Meanwhile, back at your designated office, you volunteer for upper Wisconsin Indian Reservation matters." He lowered his shoulders and craned his head toward her. He smiled. "No one in their right mind does that. Unless their name is Johnny Whitefeather. Sorry." He lifted his eyebrows, readjusted his tie, and turned his cufflink to face the uniform way. He looked up, "That was inappropriate. Even if I didn't offend, it wasn't an appropriate remark."

"It's not like you stuck your finger in my ass, Mr. Johnson."

It was a Cold War silent battle between the human lie detector and the survivor from Cicero.

"You wanted to disappear. And use national resources for personal gain. What were you doing when you came back to Chicago? I want truths. We're not going to prosecute anything. I need to build trust here."

"I was using our signals technology to try and find individuals that my father thought could still be a threat to our family. When I located them, I tried to capture their phone numbers and technical IDs so we could monitor them if they ever linked to anyone coming up to my folks' house. I just tracked them. They killed my family shortly after."

Earl leaned in and rested his elbows on the desk. His hands folding over the files. "Did they ever spot you before you killed Big Tony?"

Careful. "I never put a hand on anyone and I have never been recognized in any way that leads back to the Bureau or my former identity. I'm no little street paver, but the outfit never had a clue."

"Were you actually assaulted in Romania, Iraq, and on the course? Or were you sabo—" The color draining from her face stopped him dead. He looked down. Clasped his hands and brought them up to his lips. "I'm sorry. I do believe you."

You win. You had to make me want to do this. To back me in a corner. Obliged. You smug asshole. Just like the rest of them but smarter.

Her heartbeat fluttered at a hummingbird's pace.

Earl sat back. "That said, I have to ask for the intent and purpose of this role. Are you in a relationship? Male or—otherwise?"

Where are you going with all this? Tresa readjusted her ball cap pulling at her pony tail and tightened the hair rubber band. "Back to Tinder, huh. Not married. Nobody. Male or otherwise. I'm guessing you mean 'otherwise' as a girl and not a German shepherd, right?" *Stop your talking, girl.* Earl remained silent.

He wouldn't get rattled again. And she knew it.

She felt compelled to talk. Tresa felt a need to defend her status, to defend everything. She had to shut up, but he had compelled her to talk by his silence and blank expression. She was emotionally exhausted. "I don't like basketball players, I've got a lot of guy friends, but they all see me as a pal until they've had a lot of drinks. Good thing I can out-drink them." She winked with a half-smile that didn't convince Earl that she thought it too funny. That game was over. He had let her play her hand. She tightened her lip and pushed a shoulder out in a shrug. "Thought I'd have kids. Guess I just...was seen as one of the guys. Hunting, fishing, snowmobiling, mountain biking, baseball hats"—she pointed to her head—"camping. I'd say I sleep too hot to want anyone in my bed but that doesn't explain my Newfoundland, Kodiak. She keeps me company." Tresa exhaled slowly. She bit her lip as her eyes pooled again. She pointed across to him. "Shit, doc. You're good."

"I'm just Earl, Tresa—Francesca Delaurentis. And it's my job to break you and put you in a position where you feel compelled to work with me. But really, I need us to trust one another, and I want you to do this of your own free will. You will be free to walk if you want."

Her nostrils flared. Tresa felt trapped. "What do you want from me?" she asked. The volume of her voice was much louder than she had anticipated.

Earl relaxed in his chair and looked at the closed door. He said nothing at first, waiting to see if anyone came knocking to see what the outburst was. They never did.

"I think I found my newest ghost." He stood up and reached out with a new tattered stack of brown restaurant napkins.

She shook her head no. Her nerves were shot.

"Mind if I ask what your tattoo is? Is it an Indian with a bow?"

"Sort of." She sniffed. "An ancient huntress. Northern Italian Neolithic warrior. My grandfather on my mother's side said we came from a long line of hunters."

"Good. That's what I need. You were cleared, by the way."

Tresa looked past Earl, wondering at exactly what point he had taken full control of her. Oddly, she was excited about the new gig. Then again, she knew she had no choice—and even with no choice, she still wanted it. Fucking Earl Johnson.

Chapter 17

Helen O'Toole had five pieces of bread left in the Butternut bag. She could make it last a few more minutes before heading home across the half-mile wetland boardwalk and then another quarter mile to their modest estate in Fairfax County's Hybla Valley, Virginia. Her husband, O.T., would check on her by five thirty to ensure she made the walk back safely. It was still light in the National Capital Region until seven thirty, and she had maintained the same routine for years after retirement. O.T. was comfortable with the route and repetition, despite her dementia.

Huntley Meadows Park had a decent enough amount of foot traffic and a few visitor center volunteers who knew to keep an eye out for Helen. Her husband made sure of it. It was a nice place with nice people who watched out for one another. Which was why the smiling, pony-tailed man wearing round spectacles and beaded beard posed little risk, at first glance. Especially with a clear plastic bag of dried fruits and nuts and a tattered hardcover of *Treasure Island* beside him on the bench. He, too, had a bag of bread. Wholesome whole wheat. The worst he was going to do was burn a joint and get a little high.

Helen turned to the big granola man when he first sat and offered her a warm, toothy hello. She turned back to the waterfowl, calling them by name as she pulled small pieces from the sliced loaf and tossed them into the water. As the ducks paddled over to her, she scolded the mallard, Romeo, for being too aggressive. She tossed a piece onto his back, knowing Clarabelle would give him a good peck on the hind end. Sure enough. "Serves you right, you little asshole," she reprimanded.

The seated man couldn't contain his laugh and turned away.

She started singing the hymn "It Is Well with My Soul" and took a few steps away from the younger man.

He reached a hand into his green denim jacket. When he turned back to the old woman, she stood before him holding the Airweight J-frame .38 Special six-shooter right at his head.

Drake smiled. "You going with the revolver now?"

"Your uncle thinks it's better for me."

"And what do *you* think?"

Aunt Helen gave him a wink. "Well, you know me, I'm not supposed to think. Now get your bag of bones up and give me a proper hug."

"Anyone around?"

"Don't test me, child. I was doing this when you were still pooping your little train diapers."

"I never wore train diapers." He laughed as he stood to embrace his aunt. She held him tightly. "Ugh, I could smell you as soon as you sat. I missed you." She squeezed.

"I missed you, too."

"You're more and more like your father each time I see you," she whispered. As they separated, arms locked, Helen asked, "I don't suppose you're staying long?"

"I'm not sure. He called me back. I may need to disappear."

"Oh, good heavens, Warren. This is about enough. Your hard-headed uncle has always been a loon, but this is just too far. You need to settle yourself down and stop all this running around. I know why you do it, and you don't need to. Let things stay in the past. You're not well."

Drake shrugged. "I can't stop until I find him. The work I do gets me closer than any other way."

"Warren. He's a ghost. And if he ever wanted to reach you and clear things up if he wasn't involved, he would have. He's gone." Helen tightened her lips, grabbed the last few pieces of bread, and tossed them into the water whole. "He was gone long before you all even went overseas."

"I can't get him out of my head. I can't stop. It's all I've done in life, either preparing to be able to find him or hunting for him."

"It's what you've done because your uncle made you that way. He could give two knuckles about your brother. It was dishonest of him. He wanted his goddammed army of his own. Pardon my French." She stepped in. "You're a smart boy. Well, a full-grown man, now. Don't waste it on these war pigs. You can be so much more."

"What, a cryptologist?" He rose a brow. His dark eyes searched his aunt's.

"I had that coming. I suppose I did some pushing of my own. You were always so good with numbers and puzzles. I knew it would also be less dangerous."

"You deployed. Still dangerous even during the Cold War. Or was it the Ice Age?"

"Hush, you." She smacked his arm. "War was different then. Mine was different from your uncle's. Certainly different from yours. I was safe. I had a shower, hot meals, and a glass of wine most nights. And to tell the truth, I thought maybe the puzzles could sort out your mind and whatever's going on up there."

A heavy silence fell over the two of them. The ducks quacked for attention.

"Oh, you shush up." Helen swatted at the air.

"How's *your* old bean holding up?"

"Better than your uncle thinks. Worse than I had hoped. The medication is supposed to slow it, but I know I'm slipping more. I keep working word puzzles and those…" She paused. "Oh, you know, those thinking games."

"Memory?"

She touched his arm. "Memory. I've been good since we've been talking."

"As far as you know," he jested.

Helen reached into her bag and retrieved a small cylinder of pills. She stuffed them into his pocket. "I'll say I misplaced them again. But one of these days, you're going to need real help."

Drake ignored her remarks. "Still putting Post-its all over?"

She laughed. "I hate the mess, but I'm actually needing them more and more."

Drake changed the topic. "You should have just left him."

"That's not how my generation does things."

"Puleeze."

"That's not how I do things. He was a good man. He still cares for me. I know he does. He just struggles with me these days. I act it up a bit more so he has an out in knowing how to care for me. How to talk to me anymore."

With thin hands, Aunt Helen grasped her nephew's lapels and gave them a shake. "It's these wars. It changes men. And you keep going back thinking the next one will be different." She let go and smoothed the lapels to no avail. "I've said my piece. Don't let me ruin our time. Have you seen him?"

"I'm meeting him later tonight."

"Mmhm." Helen turned back to the pond. She stepped closer to the boardwalk rail and rested her hands on the weathered wood. "Did you bring me something?"

"I was reaching to get it when you pulled the gun on me."

"You saw me."

"I did. Approach was good but right in my periphery." Drake handed a small piece of paper to his aunt. She examined it intently. She tightened her lip more and reviewed the paper like an elementary teacher to a student. "Kirchhoff's principle of cryptography applied. Complex cipher text. Not Caesar cipher. Well, not pure. Several shifts in the code. Not transposed." She stared intently at the paper puzzle. "Hmm. Maybe arbitrary. No, a permutation." Her gaze hardened on the cipher letters. She looked over to her nephew. Then to the paper. Then to the ducks. And back again at the paper. "As important as the mathematics and deciphering capabilities are, it's always most important to have context."

"What is it?"

"DONTFEEDTHEDUCKS. Shame on you."

"Still took you a while. Almost a minute." Drake opened his loaf of bread and fed himself while tossing whole pieces into the pond.

"Glad you came to see your loving dope dealer." Helen smiled at him with the love of a mother. "I'm enjoying my time."

"Me too." Drake looked around, and with no one in the area, he embraced his aunt again. "The voices keep coming when I'm not on the meds. Even when I am, sometimes I still hear his voice," he confessed. "I know it isn't real."

"If your father's voice is keeping you alive and giving you comfort when you are alone, it's real. He loved you very much. And so did your mom. As for the other voices, that's the sickness."

"I don't have time to be sick."

Ignoring the remark, Helen stood on her toes and gave Warren Drake Woolf a kiss on as close to the cheek as she could get. "Will I see you at your funeral?"

His eyes widened.

"Your uncle tells me things now that he thinks I'll forget the next minute. I know his secrets." Her smile was sad. And she looked tired. "Stop this madness."

"I can't."

"You won't. None of you will. To tell you the truth, part of me can't wait for this affliction to just erase it all until my own funeral."

"Neither of us is having a funeral anytime soon. I'm not getting erased."

"You're as good as a ghost as it is. If you can't quit, do it if it will keep you safe. If you can walk away from all this, rest your mind, set roots, meet a nice girl, and get me some grandkids." She looked up at her nephew.

"I know what you mean."

Both knew she technically meant grandnieces or -nephews, but she had never looked at Drake as anything but her own. At least as close to being her own without being able to make demands of him.

"You've been an amazing mom."

"It's time to let you go. I wish your uncle could do the same. I just can't tell if he's going to get you killed or put you out among the wolves to have you save mankind."

"That may be a stretch."

"Not the way your uncle thinks about this world. And not the way he thinks about you."

Chapter 18

The Mohawks entered the Friendship Heights, Virginia, safe house a few blocks from American University. Their counterterrorism counterparts similarly departed to their temporary housing lair.

The Mohawks were physically and emotionally exhausted. Their demeanor was somber. For some, shamed. While killing their proclaimed adversaries' families was a righteous retaliation, it was harder to cope with the reality of it than they had imagined. They had never imagined what the ISOF men of the Golden Division would do. It was beyond revenge. Beyond human.

At the time the Americans had deployed to Iraq, many of the soldiers' children had just been born. Proud parents, the special operations soldiers had shared their excitement through videos and pictures with their foreign counterparts, the Mohawks and ISOF. After all, they were a team. And the men from differing sides of the world quickly developed bonds of friendship and brotherhood. It was because of that tightly built family that the Mohawks and Golden Division felt so betrayed when promises of citizenship were broken. It was also because of that bond that when the Iraqis and their families were mercilessly hunted down and slaughtered by local Sunni militia groups and Daesh, they vowed to make the Americans pay in blood. But the Mohawks were not religious fanatics, nor were most of ISOF. The Mohawks were not hard-boiled killers. The Golden Division men whom the Iranians had recruited were. For the men in the safe house feeling extreme emotional discomfort, their bloodlust for revenge hadn't filled the void in their hearts. Now, in the silence of their murderous acts, they questioned even the martyrdom of their colleague.

Mohammad was the first to speak in the small safe house bungalow. "We should gather for a hotwash before we sleep." The term hotwash referred to what the Deltas had instilled in their counterparts as a necessary post-operation recap of what had gone right and wrong. As Mohammad interjected the word, he could tell the team cringed as they reflected on their trainers and the supporting intelligence units. Good times and bad, they operated as one. The Mohawks had gone rogue.

"There will be plenty of time to talk more, Mohammad, please, we should rest," Ali suggested, trying to create a rational reason for avoiding any discussion. They had already driven for hours in complete silence. No one wanted to talk. Save, apparently, for Mo.

Ahmed spoke next, "Yes, we should sleep. I agree with Ali. It is best. We will remember more with rest."

"No." Mohammad pulled a kitchen chair out from under the six-person table. "We sit and we discuss."

Tamer kept his head low, avoiding eye contact. "I don't think I can talk, Mohammad. Listen to the others. We must rest. We should be alone with our thoughts."

Mo pounded on the table. "No. If you are alone you can question our actions. It had to be done. It was our duty. It remains our duty to continue until we are with our families again. Our relatives depend on our success for their survival. We are justified in our cause."

Tamer lifted his slumped head, his face wet from tears. "I saw those children when they were infants. I spoke to them on Skype with our American brothers. Those…murderers who…"

"No!" Mohammad pounded again. "The Americans are *not* our brothers! They did nothing for us. They broke their vows. They are responsible for the deaths of our own children. Our wives. Ali, for even your parents and sisters. The division came in because they know we are weak. We are not the same. We have not been trained the same. We hunt, they kill."

"Brother, but the Americans did not kill our families with their own hands. I…we all were…prepared to kill. I murdered that boy who was the same as my own son. I smashed his…" Ali stopped in midspeech. He walked into the adjacent room and collapsed in an armchair, sobbing with remorse.

Mohammad arose in rage. "Do you think I am a monster, Ali?" He spun to address all of the men. "Do you think I took pleasure in their deaths? The Americans left us to die. They came and killed tens of thousands of our people. Do you think they shed a tear? Do you think they did not kill children? We witnessed it. We were recruited to do it."

"Like we have been recruited now?" Ahmed's shoulders were shrugged, his voice hollow. His hands were folded below his waist as he stood limp in a corner of the kitchen.

The Mohawks were silent.

"We were toys to the Americans; we are toys for Iran. We have been equally given promises by our new masters. And who will hunt them if they do not deliver on their agreement to protect our families once we are gone? Who is to say the men who tore and burned those bodies will not do the same to us?"

Chapter 19

Despite still having his mail sent to his aunt and uncle's home, and their address listed for all his personal affairs, Drake Woolf stayed at the family farm when he was in town, which was rare in the past decade. A time or two a year, if that. The farm, hidden off Goby Lane and buttressed against Crow's Nest Natural Area Preserve and the Potomac River, still on the Virginia side, had been co-purchased between his father and uncle years back so the men would have hunting property, their own little safe house, and a place of solitude for meetings and international guests. Drake normally met O.T. there when they needed to chat if it wasn't a Sunday dinner at the house. Pressed for time, O.T. insisted the two meet in the Arlington House Museum of the Arlington Cemetery. The caretaker was a Vietnam veteran O.T. had served with who accommodated the dark ops master upon request.

O.T.'s sand-colored Chevy Suburban was parked out front. The hood was quite warm to the touch. Drake checked his watch before opening the landmark's front door. When it creaked, operational instincts kicked in, and he immediately stopped and waited for a reaction. He wasn't even juiced up, but his senses didn't care until he took a slow breath and de-escalated the fight or flight minions surfing his bloodstream. He entered the familiar spot. There stood O.T., a formidable figure, pacing in the entryway and talking quietly on his mobile device. Upon seeing Drake, he lifted a finger and checked his watch with a scowl.

Woolf shrugged his shoulders and pointed to the ceiling, to which O.T. nodded. The signal meant yes, they were going up to the attic. The attic of Robert E. Lee's former home ironically had housed Union soldiers stationed on the property. Many of their names remained on the attic's wall panels. Drake knew the drill. He mounted the steep stairs and plugged into an outlet that obviously had not been part of this Civil War relic. Drake twisted the dials and flipped the switch of a device that disrupted all signals in a twenty-meter radius.

"Dammit, Drake!" O.T. cursed up to his nephew, who had just disconnected his call. "I was still on the damned phone!"

Oops. Drake smiled. "My bad," he called out, sending down a middle finger to the seasoned war pig.

Drake liked to mess with the old man to get in some passive-aggressive retaliation without significant confrontation. He heard his uncle's loud footfalls as the larger man mounted the creaking stairs. The stairs gave Woolf a brief chill, as they sounded eerily similar to those he had climbed and fled down in Lebanon. He heard the woman's scream in his mind. And then that of his own mother's. His bowels sank and his body flushed with heat. Drake cleared his mind with a breath, cursing life as he knew it.

"Did you bring up any chairs?" O.T. huffed.

Drake snapped back to the present and quipped back, "There are chairs over there in the corner. Small folding table, too. Why don't you grab them while I just test this quick, unless you brought an aide with you."

"I don't think you need to test your techno-spy gear. It shut down *my* phone, didn't it?"

"Suit yourself." Drake grabbed a chair and the card table end leaving his uncle's extended hand hanging in the wind. "Hey, don't be an asshole. It's not like I'm trying to hug you. Show a little respect."

"Respect would be you not pulling strings around my life without me knowing. Or maybe showing like you actually give a shit when I walk in the door after not seeing you for about a year when you know I was almost smoked in the field. As always, I can be your little operator or I can be your flesh and blood."

"Both would shake my hand."

"Both would have gotten a little more respect when recalled home and neither would have been drugged to do so."

"And you can't go AWOL, MIA, or pretending you're killed so you can try to find a goddammed ghost with every free minute of your life when you can be helping hunt real threats to the American people."

"I hunt real threats twenty-four seven, three sixty-five in the shittiest places of this earth. You made me, you deal with it."

O.T. sluffed over to his nephew. He outstretched his arms and invited the younger man in. "I'm sorry," O.T. conceded. "Got a hug for your old man? I suppose more often than not, I know you're going to make it out. Wherever you're sent and no matter the ends of the earth. You've been trained with all I have to teach you, all my contacts can teach you, and everything officially that I can get you into. You've overcome incredible odds in your life, so my faith in your abilities and survivability likely supersedes my inner snowflake expression toward you." O.T.'s body language and words were as genuine as Drake had seen in years.

Drake opened himself up for the embrace. But O.T. brought down his left arm and forced his right toward Woolf's chest. It stopped Drake in his tracks. "You can shake my hand. Don't mistake me for a pussy," O.T. chastised. "I'm no snowflake. And neither are you."

"God, you're an asshole."

"It only seems that way because you'd really rather have a hug from a grown man since you can't get your stuttering, blinking, and clicking ass put to bed by anyone anymore."

I will kill you some day. Take it to the bank.

* * * *

Tamer wiped at his still-tearing eyes. "The Americans are going to kill us. The Iranians will certainly not keep their promises if we fail. I cannot kill another child, but I am willing to find the other Deltas. Mohammad, what names are on the list?"

Mo retained his scowl as he thrust a hand into his pants pocket and retrieved a bloodied paper. He unfolded it and read the names. "I have Trevor Peterson and Ted Gossling as now dead. They were on our first list. From call sign list, we just learned the valid names of Prescott Draeger and Sean Havens. We will have to contact the Iranians for their locations. And the other names we just learned were at the camp, Roe Kraemer, Steve Cera, and Drake Woolf."

"That's the guy." Ali snapped his fingers. "I said it wrong. I recalled 'Scottay' Drake. The Iranian contact said they had no Scott Drake in the database that was viable. This is the Birddog man."

Tamer nodded. "The Birddog. Orange man."

"Nay. The *man* from Orange," Ahmed corrected. "We thought it was a place when our team heard it. But it was another elite military group that advised our Delta trainers. The Birddog. He was a crafty one."

"That is a very accurate way to describe him," said Tamer. "I have no quarrel with him. Same with some of the others. They rarely spoke with us. They never made us promises. The Birddog trained us, but he preferred to walk alone."

"Then he should go first." Mohammad's fire rekindled. "He may not have promised us, but it is he who would consider us dogs to fight America's war. A man like him would make no promises and would not care for our families or people. He came to kill and to make us kill. We find him next." The men were silent. Tamer spoke up. "It could be very dangerous."

* * * *

Drake begrudgingly sat at the table with O.T. and heard his spiel. Woolf learned of the attacks, of Orange's dissolution, and of the president's executive order.

"Drake, can you imagine the power we would have against hostile networks on US soil if we had target packages coming in already ranked by priority, already assessed on the potential risk impact they could have without removal, and the kill team could make the decision for lethal action over capture?"

"You aren't looking for anyone to make a decision. You only want a kill team."

"Not true. You would need to also send intel to us that we would get to the Bureau."

"After the fact." Drake pushed himself away from the table. The weight on his chair made a scuff mark on the historic floorboards, at which he grimaced. "Look. I get the concept of fast-paced preemptive SIGINT targeting cells working with CIA or NSA. Whole thing makes sense with sensor-driven ops monitoring phones, getting and giving geolocation, locating targets, and then call or contact chaining or SSE after taking down the targets. Concept is fine with me. It's going to be harder than you think. It's going to move faster than you think when we get a trail. It'll turn into rapid termination and be even harder to cover up."

O.T. jumped on the perceived opening. "I can work with you on that. This is one of the most major operational stand-ups since JFK green-lighted Special Forces," he beamed.

Drake rolled his eyes and leaned back in the chair, wondering how long this would go on. "You didn't let me finish. I was going to still say no thanks. I'm getting out. Perfect timing if they're dissolving the unit. I can be the first to go. I've got plenty of money saved, and I can get out of everyone's hair."

"What kind of person are you if you think you can just walk away?" O.T. scrunched his face, not hiding his disgust. "We were attacked. Your command was attacked. That means nothing to you? You're nothing like your father."

"Screw you. He's dead, and no one did anyone about it. All I've gotten about the attack is resistance or silence. There's nothing on it even on the high side. It's been wiped."

"He was on diplomatic cover."

"Whatever. Then nothing has been done about *the diplomat* who was attacked. I've seen our guys get smoked before. No one cares. What happened in Lebanon? That was our drone that fired on our men. I'm guessing simply to cover up our involvement. Maybe it's on me, maybe it's not. But this man's game tells me that nothing I do really matters. And the one thing, the one guy who matters to me, no one has any information on, and no one will talk to me about it. Still, with all my access, I can get nothing even on my brother if he's on any global watch list."

"Damn you and your stubborn witch hunt. How can you be so selfish at a time when your country needs you to step up? And don't you think someone is going to want answers on Lebanon? It could turn into a very dangerous situation for you. This would take you out of the equation."

"Answer being for everyone to just pretend I'm dead, so my job can be covering up with other dead guys in order to kill more guys." Drake gathered his thoughts for a moment while distracted by a previously undiscovered sliver on his thumb. "That's a really brilliant way to run national defense. Do you even hear yourself and this deep state bullshit? You've made it really clear. My country couldn't give two shits about me. Never did, never will. And as far as guys from my command, show me the list. I'll bet I can't find even one. Pass it over. I'll humor you."

O.T. wrestled with a potentially failing mission before him. He knew he needed a better sales pitch. His nephew could be a stubborn as stubborn gets. It made it hard getting leverage for discipline and inspiration. In truth, manipulation. Drake reached over and grabbed a printed Excel spreadsheet from the table to prove his point.

O.T. said nothing.

Drake's head cocked to the side. He squinted and drew the paper closer. His face tightened. "Hmmm...I actually know a lot of them. Shit." He looked up at his uncle with a blank face.

"Keep reading," O.T. encouraged.

"No, you don't understand. Hand me the assessments." Drake grabbed for the papers. His head moved as he read and shuffled them and then reshuffled them.

"What? Iraq or Afghanistan with them?"

"Iraq," Drake replied, not looking up from the papers. "That's not it. Hand me your pen."

O.T. fidgeted around on the table between papers and files. He knew he had a pen somewhere.

Again, Drake remained focused on the words before him but directed, "in your jacket pocket," and extended his hand for the pen without looking up. Drake snatched the cheap hotel ballpoint and started writing furiously on the back of a sheet. Drake flipped back to the names and wrote more. He stopped and looked back at O.T. "You were telling me that NSA can supply us a feed with communications and signals picked up that may signify a heightened risk or interest, right?"

"Correct."

"What did they find around these attacks?"

O.T. shrugged. "Not sure if it's the same feed, but there were some captured signals. I think probably evidence of time and geolocation. None of those devices were used for anything other than that. Right after the Fayetteville attacks, there were similar signals that coincide with DC. We don't have much more. We can triangulate out of the ordinary calls, and I don't know what you call the real words, but identifiers. Most of the actual communications are secured. I also remember hearing communications were shut off in the area for about ten minutes before emergency response showed up. What's churning in your head?"

"Of the people on the list, some I've worked with a number of times. But of the ones I recognize, all were in Iraq when we worked the Mohawk program. Remember the internet café targeting and kill squads?"

"Of course I do. I put you on that program. Right after you went to Belvoir so you could work with Orange," O.T. said referring the special mission unit SIGINT work Drake was selected for.

"Exactly. And the families killed. Look at the names." Drake pushed the paper over and scooted his chair closer. He didn't bother to worry about scuff marks. "All of them were Delta families or those men and their families who had been assigned to Delta. These guys were definitely involved with the Mohawks. They rolled in and out based on duty time, but each one was involved. My guess is, someone was on the receiving end of the Mohawk program and is retaliating. Probably Daesh. You don't need me. This isn't a national threat. It's a military targeting threat. You need some analyst at the Pentagon or JSOC to find out who was read in and on the ground carrying out ops at the time. Find them and you have likely targets. Get some Deltas to smoke these guys."

"Then that makes you a target. You're involved and could help, right?"

"Doubtful." Drake slid his chair away to create more space. "We trained the Mohawks in the tech and tradecraft, but I never stayed in the same safe houses as the D-boys and pretty much was in indigenous cover. Locals wouldn't know who I was. I knew some Mohawks, but it's not like they're hunting us. Those guys loved us. Shit, they wanted to come to the US, but they got the same royal treatment as the 'terps. Promised asylum then buried in paperwork and denials. I think we're done here. Just get a couple of Deltas to hunt these guys down. That's all you need."

O.T. stared at the papers and reread the names. Drake had circled all the ones involved in the Mohawk program and added names he could recall. "Drake, I still want you to seriously consider the program. At the very least, just say yes, and help us with running these guys down. I'm also not sure how to address Lebanon. It would be easier if we tucked you under this program and took you off the books."

"Listen to yourself. Why didn't you ever do it to yourself? I'm sure you had the chance to go fully black. It's not so easy throwing your life away and saying goodbye to anyone who knows you."

"I wasn't like you. I married early. Then took care of you." O.T. shook his head. His tight lips spoke of regret. "If I had had this kind of opportunity, I would have jumped on it. So would your dad if he hadn't gotten married."

The epiphany came to Drake. "Holy shit. That's it. That's what all this bullshit is about. That's what my life has all been about. When you were pulled from the field finally, you needed someone else to do what you wanted to be doing. This isn't about me, it's always been about you. That's why you give such a long leash to Aunt—"

"Shut your mouth right there. Don't you say it. Yes. I want you to be out there. And yes, I wish I were doing it, but if I can't still do it, I helped shape you to what this country needs. You're the solution to the next battle space. We've always been able to keep you on the next ridgeline to meet the next threat. Don't tell me you haven't enjoyed it. It's in your blood. I've heard stories and read reports about you. You're not exactly running from the fight. Even with all that mixed-up shit in your head, you're today's hunter."

"I'm through. Not only that, but you'd need more than one guy doing this concept. You'd need to set up front companies, aliases, safe houses or at least the means to fund equipment and logistical support."

"We can have that."

"Sorry."

"What if—"

"Don't say it. Don't say you've known."

"I need your commitment first. But, yes, I may have something on your brother."

* * * *

Mohsen was able to provide a last known address to the Mohawks in minutes. According to breached Office of Personnel Management records, Warren Drake Woolf was listed as living in the DC area.

Tamer keyed the laptop and adjusted the knobs on the twelve-by-fourteen-inch black device. The COMINT application on the screen displayed wireless and cellular interference. All levels on the monitor flattened as he terminated communication service within nearly one hundred meters of their position.

Within range of the Mohawks, Helen O'Toole sat at the kitchen table blowing the heat from a spoonful of homemade bean-and-bacon soup. Robert wouldn't be home for another hour. He could reheat his own damned soup.

The door chimed for the first time in months, drawing a sense of excitement from Helen, who hoped to have another pleasant surprise visit today. She wondered, while she sipped the soup and stood, if Girl Scouts still sold cookies door to door or maybe, just maybe, if Drake might have come back for a brandy and a nice little chat.

* * * *

Drake left the mansion with his uncle. The two had remained silent as they straightened up the room, post-meeting.

Before they parted, O.T. finalized business. "I need you to call me tonight. If you're still unwilling to take on this opportunity, we need to get you back to Lebanon. You're MIA now but a deserter if you're found. Come with me and we wipe you or I jigger the books and paperwork so you do the duty but basically go off-grid."

"If this information you're dangling about Dex is substantial, you owe that to me regardless of whether I take your wet-work job. So, you feel free to call me tonight, too. If not, we don't have much to talk about. You can put me back on a plane and I'll do what I need to do to get out."

* * * *

Helen pulled at the front door's thin highlight sheer and peered out the small window pane. Under the overhanging porch light and faux-flame side sconces, a man wearing a tan baseball hat waved with a smile. She depressed the intercom button but shot her gaze to the purse a few feet away atop the upright piano. Their indoor and exterior camera switched frequency to accommodate for the network communication outage.

"Yes?" She questioned the stranger.

He leaned forward to the outside speaker. "Hi, Ms. Woolf, I'm looking for Drake. Does he still live here?"

It took Helen some time to process what exactly to do. The man spoke again in the silence.

"My name's Mo, I served with him overseas. I wanted to let him know I was in town, and this is the only address I can find. Does he live here?"

"Warren isn't here. He doesn't live here anymore," Helen shouted toward her own monitor.

"Do you have his address? I'm only here a couple more days and would love to say hello." The man kept smiling. He looked friendly enough, but in all her years of taking care of Drake, no one had come to the front door looking for him with the exception of those doing background checks for his clearances and periodic reviews.

"Tell me your number and I'll give it to him."

"Sure, unless you want me to give it to your husband."

"No, he's not home right—" Helen stopped as Mo's head tilted and his smile shifted to a menacing scowl.

Mo nodded back to Ali, who remained a few feet back and out of view. He then signaled with a slight head movement toward the slow trolling Altima on the street behind them. "If we do not do this to their satisfaction, it could be us. Remember that," Mo hissed.

And then it was go time, and Mo was just as ready to put on a show as he was to exact his revenge. He kicked to the right of the door handle. The heavy wood connected by both door lock and deadbolt snapped backward. Helen tripped as she stumbled backward and fell to the floor. Ali jumped from the shadows into the house with Mo. He slammed the door closed, although the hardware was broken and the frame's edges splintered.

The door sensors triggered a text alert to O.T., warning that his mentally failing wife had sought to leave the home.

Helen rolled to her side, hoping she could get up to her purse. A sharp pain in her hip caused her to shriek. She grabbed at her upper thigh and fell back to the wooden floor.

Mo drew his own leg back and shot another powerful blow from his boot to her fragile fractured side.

She shrieked in agony.

"Where is Drake Woolf, woman!"

"I don't know," she cried. Again, he sent a forceful shock to her broken hip. She wailed and tried curling herself into a protective ball, but the broken hip would not cooperate. She remained vulnerable and exposed.

He stomped down on her upper femur, breaking Helen's pelvic bone and dislocating the leg from the hip joint.

Her howls turned silent and she convulsed under the shock.

"WHERE?"

"He's overseas. He works for the military. He never comes home anymore. Please," she bawled.

"Where overseas. Iraq? Afghanistan?"

"I don't know," she sobbed. "My...phone...and address book. They're in my purse. I can show you."

"WHERE?"

"Piano."

"I see it." Ali hopped over the old woman, grabbed the soft leather bag, and tossed it to the ground in front of Helen's face.

Her eyes were blurred, but she could make out the stainless steel Smith & Wesson revolver tucked behind her wallet, some packaged saltine crackers, and a few wads of Kleenex.

* * * *

For as many men as O.T. had led, interrogated, manipulated, turned against their country to spy for the US, or just downright intimidated, he could never find much leverage to control his nephew. Through Drake's military service and special mission unit qualifications and deployments, it was the ghost of Dexter Woolf that drove the Birddog. Nothing else.

O.T. knew he had slipped up by not playing to that sheet of music. He'd have to contact SECDEF about Drake's observations about the list. That would buy time, using a couple Deltas before building the program. And ultimately, maybe Drake wouldn't be the one to fill the billet. He would be of no further use if not. Drake was just a reminder of how Alex Woolf had held so much promise but had shared with O.T. that he was considering moving over to State with his wife and trying the diplomatic side for a while. Alex wasn't supposed to be at the embassy housing villa that afternoon. What a Greek tragedy that was.

As O.T. started the engine, he contemplated his shitshow. "Hang tight, Helen. I'm almost done for the night." He spoke to himself while checking the time. He noticed the alert message and sought to check the home monitors, expecting another exhausting conversation with Helen as a different war ravaged his wife's mind. He pressed the mobile home security app to ensure Helen had made it home and thumbed the Touch ID function to log in to the home feed.

The hallway was the first to display, and O.T.'s chest caved at the scene. Two men stood above his wife. One stomped on her leg.

"NOOO!" he shouted, drawing the device up closer. "GET OUT OF THERE! DRAKE!"

O.T.'s head spun to the window. Drake was nowhere in sight as the darkness cloaked the grounds. O.T. was locked on the device screen as he fumbled for the door handle. "Drake!" he screamed.

The Tesla Model S P100D was not low-profile. Yet, for a man who had few earthly possessions, spending over $100,000 on a car that had twelve short-range ultrasonic sensors, semi-auto driving, and forward-facing radar suited Drake's justification just fine. He could hear the old-man's tantrum as he closed the car door and shut out the noise of this pain-in-the-ass world. Woolf had replied that it wasn't much different from most operators buying a Camaro or Mustang with their re-up bonus. He was just doing it with more resources and style.

Drake was more than slightly amused that Robert O'Toole, a man who men feared as much as revered, had very little say in the years that the man from Orange found his own independence and voice. Still, Drake was rattled, and his mouth clicked with the decision he had to make. He hoped the answer or the words of his father would come to him as he sped away and merged onto Interstate 395 back to the farm of solitude.

Drake's phone rang, stealing his attention from deep thoughts. "UNC," the shortened letters for uncle, illuminated among the vehicle's other glowing digital displays. Woolf cast an annoyed glance at the device but refused to answer. *You need to sit on this for a bit, Bobby O'Toole.* "Fuck you."

As quickly as the glow faded it reappeared. *Are you kidding me?* And again.

Drake flipped the phone over, but the alert of a call still emerged on the display console. "Are you a child?" He shouted at the device, looking down and feeling the car pull to the right. "Damn, you're going to kill me if I don't put this thing on auto-drive."

On the seventh or eighth ring, Drake answered. He let his impatience show in both volume and voice, "Are you seriously not going to let this drop?"

"Drake, they're killing her."

"What? Killing who? Where? What are you talking about?"

"I'm on my way now. Drake, they're killing her right in front of me. Oh, God. I'll kill you."

"Uncle Bob, what the hell is happening? Settle down."

"Drake, ISIS. ISIS or whoever…oh God, no…oh, God…"

"HEY!" Drake yelled to the phone speaker.

"Your aunt. I called 911, I'm driving. I have the camera on my phone. They're killing her. She has a gun. Yes. Kill him! She shot one. No. Yeah, he's… Again. Oh, no. No. He shot her. He's…"

Drake lowered the volume on his phone. His mind was raging, his empty soul screaming. But he tried to work the problem. An unauthorized vehicle sign approached on the left. He slowed just slightly to time the oncoming traffic headed back in toward DC. Turning and then gunning the engine, he catapulted into the left lane with a slight fishtail that he deftly turned out of. Gravel crunched and dust plumed in the darkness behind the Tesla.

"What's happening now?" Drake asked, slowing his heart rate with focus.

"She's not moving. They're bending down. Maybe talking to her. SAVAGES!" There was a brief pause before O.T. started up again. "Two more men just came into the house." The play by play stopped, and Drake heard his uncle's muted crying. "Oh, God. Please, don't. Oh, God." For as helpless as Drake felt, he sensed the utter despair O.T. was wallowing in. Whether actual love or the powerless feeling the old warrior had over the situation, it was as broken as Woolf had ever heard his uncle. It still didn't change things.

"I'm on my way. I'm coming. I'm coming." Traffic began to slow, but the Tesla only accelerated. Onto the shoulder, it sped into the city. Drake flashed his brights in rapid succession, emulating a speeding police car. Drivers pulled to the right and the man from Orange blew past, praying he could make it in time and plotting how he and his uncle would find these fucking crows, and how he was going to kill them one by one.

He would stab their eyes out with the ice pick in his mind's eye. Over, and over, and over, and over. And he saw his parents again for the second time this night.

And the men. And how he attacked them.

He flashed back to his brother and dad screaming one day. Mother was crying. Drake came in the room to help but was told to get out. Dex had looked at Drake for but a moment and raised the fingers of his lowered hand and gave a small wave like he always did. It was months before the family heard from Dex.

Drake's mind flashed to almost a year later when he saw Dex in the medina. It didn't look like Dex, but it must have been. He had looked through Drake, and his hand was lowered and he waved with his fingers and turned back to the man. *The man! The man that was in the back garden! That was the man. The one Dex was with.*

Drake slammed his foot on the brake as an abandoned car on the shoulder emerged in his vision. The Tesla's accident avoidance system kicked in with the front radar. Cars still cleared to the right, and Drake swerved back on track. *My brother was with the man who was outside our house during the attack. But he waved to me when I saw him earlier. He didn't warn me, but he waved to me, hand by his side. He didn't know. He couldn't have known. He may have known some but not all...did he really want to kill me? Never. Mom? No way. Dad? Probably not. He didn't know. He didn't know. I know it. Where are you, Dex? Where are you, my brother?*

And then Drake's mind returned to his aunt. Their talk at the pond. He had caused this. They had come to kill him. She would be dead. He rationalized it. She would be dead. It was his fault—again.

Lost in a whirlwind of thoughts, Drake turned onto his aunt and uncle's street. A cacophony of lights and sirens assaulted the night. He pulled up as far as he could and raced to the house. His uncle was being pushed back by officers. The old man was trying to punch his way in, and they had gotten ahold of his arms. But they were trying to be gentle and understood the reactions of grief and anger. "Uncle Bob! I'm here!" Drake shouted.

O.T. squirmed through the officers' hold and craned his neck to Drake. "Don't come up, Drake. Don't come up." In the porch light, O.T.'s face was awash with tears. His lower jaw was quivering. "It's unthinkable. It's GODDAMNED UNTHINKABLE!," he screamed into the doorway. His legs buckled, and he collapsed. Some officers tried to hold him up, while others tried to gently let him sink to the ground. O.T. swatted at the men pulling on him as he was suspended like a cornfield scarecrow. He folded his legs and let it all out.

Drake sprinted up the walkway and touched Robert's back in a gentle pat of assurance that he was there, but the man from Orange's eyes searched those of the officers. He'd seen those eyes. Amateurs' faces of horror. And he knew it was as bad as he could imagine, and Drake Woolf cast to the far corners of his mind all the horrible thoughts entering his war-weary brain. He pushed away burnings, decapitations, eviscerations, and found his aunt tossing bread into the pond. Scolding the ducks and smiling at Drake and mouthing, *I love you.*

Alex Woolf stepped into the scene in Drake's head. He was chipping ice at the counter. *You have work to do, son. The other questions can wait. Trust your head, find your brother, but for now, kill these motherfuckers, Drake. Kill them all.*

Drake's mouth started clicking. He stepped forward to the officers, entering their personal space. "I'm going into that house." He looked down at his uncle, who lifted his head and extended a hand up.

"I'm coming with you, Drake."

Drake nodded to his uncle and pulled up the Deputy Director of All Things That Get Snuffed.

"Sirs, you can't. It's a crime scene now. I can't—"

Drake stepped into the officer. "It's my crime scene now."

Chapter 20

The officer wasn't backing down regardless of Drake Woolf's bravado. "Sir, don't make this worse. I can have you arrested for obstruction."

"Officer, this is a matter of national security," Drake growled. "This house is under the jurisdiction and control of the Department of Defense. It's a secured compartmentalized facility that you are not cleared to enter. You'll need to contact the Department of Justice immediately."

Drake barreled through the men with his uncle's arm in firm grasp. As they crossed the threshold, the overpowering smell of burned flesh hit Drake like a Mohammed Ali phantom punch. He looked back at O.T. with a long face and gave a tight squeeze. "This is going to be real bad."

From the shadows, Tamer continued to scan all new signals entering the area. His position was covered as he sauntered down the parallel street behind the O'Tooles' home. He sent the screenshot technical network identifiers via secured chat to Ahmed.

Ahmed texted, "Two devices just connected to the home Wi-Fi connection point that popped up. Scanning. Three. One is personal. Two are registered to Department of Defense. This network wasn't up earlier. It had another set of devices connected." Ahmed's face was ashen. "Cameras."

Tamer picked up the pace with an increase of traffic buzzing past the intersection. He dialed Ali and Mohammad for extraction.

Ali's hand shook as he answered, but his other hand remained firmly compressed on Mohammad's abdomen. "I am here," he answered in Arabic, "but we have a problem—"

Drake stood over the burnt and broken remains of his aunt. His arm hung loosely around his uncle, who was rigid with fists balled by his sides.

A uniformed man stepped into the home. "Mr. O'Toole, Sir, one of my officers has filled me in, but we'd like to speak to you, please. I am terribly sorry for your loss." What many would describe as seasoned or well-weathered could be a fair statement about the chief of police, whose hands were spread on his hips and who had what seemed to be a fist-sized rock stuck in his throat at sight before him. The chief had seen plenty in his days on the streets, but this took him right back to the sights and smells of Vietnam and the Huey crash that took most of his squad's lives after surviving a seven-hour firefight in the suck and muck of rice paddies.

"Drake, you go on back to your farm. Do whatever you want to do," O.T. suggested, meaning beat it before someone asked questions.

"It's not my farm. And I'm good staying with you."

"It's yours now. Was never my money to begin with. We used your dad and Helen's inheritance when both families bought it. It's yours now. Your aunt had already signed over papers when the dementia started up. I'll take care of this. Just go home, get some rest. Figure out what you wanna do next. Just do me a favor and don't spend more time on those maps of yours all over the living room there. It's an obsession and it's getting unhealthy. You sleep out back, I cleared out the poison ivy. It came back so we gave it some scorched Earth weed killing. I'll make a call when I'm done here. I'll also let folks know you used alternate logistics to get back CONUS to minimize footprint and any exposure." O.T. patted Drake on the bottom like a star pitcher being relieved in the eighth. "I'll be all right."

Drake nodded okay but was slightly distracted by an alert showing up on his phone. He leaned into his uncle and said something out of the chief's earshot.

O.T. turned to the chief. "Cartwright, isn't it?" O.T. extended a hand.

The chief nodded. "Don't believe we've met." Chief Cartwright accepted the gesture, and both men exchanged a firm handshake with full eye contact.

"You need my nephew? Neither of us were here. He just came to check on me when he heard."

"I think we can get a statement from you, and as long as mister..."

"Woolf." Drake outstretched his own hand to the officer. "Warren Woolf."

The chief, who had been around both military and local Beltway connections, took a double take at both men. The faces he could not place, but the names seemed familiar. "Pleased to meet you, Mr. Woolf, again, my condolences." The clutter of additional officers and emergency response was building outside the entryway. "If you're going to be around the area for the next few days, I think it's just fine for you to step out." The chief unbuttoned a top breast pocket and withdrew a business card, which he extended to Drake. "My contact info and direct line. If you need anything."

Drake took the card, pocketed it, and gave a nod to his uncle. "Give me a call when you can. I'll get started."

"Thank you," replied O.T., knowing he and his nephew would in no time be killing whoever was responsible for making this a very personal new war.

Drake was hesitant getting in the car and leaving. Something wasn't right with how he was feeling. He was exhausted and hungry, but that wasn't it, and he knew the ping on his device meant someone was tapping into his signals. It validated the Mohawk theory. Aside from that, his head was clear, and for the first time he wasn't dehydrated. Drake struggled to find what was off beyond the norm. His uncle was devastated but trying to hold back emotion. He got that. No problem there. The scene was horrific to anyone who would have seen the aftermath. Again, nothing shocking about that. And then it hit him. Drake Woolf felt nothing. He was calm and he was relaxed. To a degree, he was inspired. He had something new to pursue with what he had left of a heart, and the man from Orange was excited to be man-hunting again. And he was going to kill every last one of them. But emotionally, he had nothing left to feel bad about.

Ahmed sorted the O'Tooles' Wi-Fi network connections and history. He scanned the most recently connected devices and mapped them to one another for recent activity. The feed identified that both signatures were recently connected to one another using mobile carriers. Ahmed sent a network ping to one of the devices in particular. It hit. He attempted to remotely access open ports on the target's mobile phone but found a significant amount of privacy settings and security features. Ahmed's eyes widened with his growing smile. "Bingo, Birddog, I believe we have you." The signal displayed movement on the geo-map before him as cell phone towers hopscotched the signal. Ahmed's fully exposed teeth showed his elation. He called Tamer and shared the news. He neglected to mention the camera feed.

* * * *

Fort Meade, Maryland NSA Headquarters

Manmeet Singh's steel kara bracelets clinked against his desk as he ran computer scripts against PERPETUAL INTENT and Y-LOCKCHECK, the wide-reaching systems that provided communications intelligence. His task within NSA's Special Sources Operations unit, or SSO, was to parse the daily surveillance activities of communications data such as

Dialed Numbers and Digital Network Intelligence. His black turban held a traditional small *shastar* decoration. The common *shastar* of Sikhs was a weapon. Manmeet, or Mojo, as his friends called him, wore the decoration of a bejeweled MP5 submachine gun, courtesy of his father. His dad, a former intelligence officer within India's military, wore a custom Colt 45 *shastar*. To say the Singhs were fully invested in counterterrorism was an understatement.

Manmeet sang to himself while scanning telephony metadata as the cherry red Beats flooded his ears with Johnny Cash cranking out the lyrics. "It burns, burns, burns. The ring of fire, the ring of fire," Manmeet sang.

"Todd the new consultant," as he was called by his peers, leaned out of his workspace and tapped Manmeet on the shoulder. He signaled with hands toward his ears and moved his mouth, saying something.

Manmeet spread the cups. His face, what little that could be seen under heavy brows and beard, held a quizzical look. "Yeah, dude?"

"Sorry man, but your singing. It's kinda loud. What's on fire?"

"Your mom's dick's on fire, bro." Mojo let the headphones snap back. He turned away from the annoying "Todd the new consultant" and sorted the data before saving and sending to Deputy Director O'Toole at the Department of Defense. He winked at Janine, a young African American woman who hailed from George Mason University. Neither of them cared much for Todd. The colored badges of the Defense and Intelligence apparatus segmented tribes. Piece-of-shit consultants, especially overnight badge flippers, never had the right color.

Mojo typed a memo that would be sent to Robert O'Toole on behalf of a new task force support request. The requests were to be beyond close-hold. Manmeet was the only team member in SSO who had access or the mandates for the collection tasking. "Supercool," he had said to O.T., and was met with the response, "Superkeepitthefuckquiet if you don't want to disappear." Mojo's simple reply, "That'll work."

Mojo proofed for a second time the note that would be highly technical for O.T., but from working with the old man in the past, Mojo knew the master of black arts would have a henchman really reading the feeds anyhow.

It read:

TFO/ICEPICK: DOD SAP INITIATED TARGETING AT HOMEFIELD FAA911 (TS//SI//NF) THURSDAY, 2017, DDIR

SIR. GOOD TO BE BANGING BAD GUYS WICHU AGAIN. HERE ARE THE FEED ID'S WE PICKED UP AT THE STRIKE SITES. PROVIDED IN YOUR FUTURE TARGET PACKAGES WILL BE THE FOLLOWING: DATA & TIME, DURATION OF CALL, CALLED/

CALLING NUMBER, IMSI, TMSI, IMEI, MSISDN, MDN, CLI,
DSME, OSME, VLR. IN SHORT, ALL THE PHONE ID AND TEXT
MESSAGE INFO YOU NEED TO HUNT AND TARGET MALICIOUS
FOREIGN ACTORS RE BRAGG AND NCR IF NOT ENCRYPTED
OR UNENCRYPTABLE. YOU WILL SEE I HIGHLIGHTED THE
ONES THAT CORRELATE TO ONE ANOTHER. GLOBAL SEARCH
GAVE NOTHING PRIOR. PING ME THE QUESTIONS. ALL FUTURE
TARGET PACKAGE WILL ALSO INCLUDE RELATIONSHIP OR TIED
CONNECTIONS BETWEEN TARGETS TOO TO WIDEN APERTURE.
HAPPY HUNTING. WITH YOUR PERMISSION I WILL START
ENGAGING SEBASTIAN. V/R. MOJO.

Before hitting send, Manmeet grabbed a handful of almonds, popped
them in his mouth, and gave it one last read. If the man asked for him
specifically, he didn't want to screw anything up on the first formal reach-
out. Whatever this project was, it was huge, especially if he got a seat at the
table with Sebastian the Snake. And if the program was what he thought
it was based on the geo-coordinates of the signals, it was the deepest dark
shit he could possibly fathom being part of. He looked over at Todd the
consultant, bobbed his head to the music, and gave him the bird. *I got my
eyes on you, Snowden junior.*

It was late, he wanted a glass of his newly tapped homebrew mead, and
Xbox was calling his name. Enough spying for the day.

* * * *

Drake remembered taking the turns onto the dark side road up to the
farm, but before pulling up to the overgrown drive, his evening continued
to be a blur of subconscious thoughts. He sat replaying what seemed to
be the longest day. It wasn't so much that he was upset by the death of his
aunt, as he felt that she had longed for an escape for quite some time. But
the fact that she had been so brutally desecrated by these savage extremists
sat as heavy on his mind as he could bear conceptually. He felt bad that
his heart had no more room to accept loss. It was permanently closed for
business. No vacancy.

Drake also contemplated his own world. All he had was the job. Such
that it was. And for better or for worse, his uncle. Such that that was,
too. His mother's side had lost contact with Drake, as their academic
circles didn't mesh well with an enlisted grunt. In deference to them, O.T.
hadn't exactly allowed Helen to nurture that bond while raising Drake
in his teen years. Drake really didn't have many friends, a product of

his own introversion. Of course, there was Tom Mendle, with whom he used to go fishing once a year in Canada, but even that had ended with Drake's successive deployments. There was also Rubin Bernstein, one of Dad's old CIA pals who managed the Woolf trust and moved money for Drake wherever and whenever he needed it. The trust entailed insurance monies from the CIA and State Department, personal family finances and life insurance settlements, and the few millions from now-deceased grandparents, especially that of Montgomery Woolf.

The O'Tooles had left that money untouched while raising Drake and took care of him by their own means and Helen's share of her parents' estate. But he had really had no contact with Rubin since most activity was done through an account number and electronic transfers. If Drake was honest with himself, he practically was dead to the world already. Although he had always hoped that if his brother wanted to find him, he could. Drake had so many unanswered questions. He also had a cavernous emptiness in his sense of self and belonging with his whole family unit gone in the blink of an eye.

Fuck it. If they want a killer, they can have a killer. He sent a quick text to his uncle's secure device. I HAVE AN IDEA. DON'T MAKE THAT CALL. I'M ALL IN.

Once he stepped out of the Tesla and got within the farm's staked-out kill zone, the grounds illuminated. The motion sensors captured his size and movement and triggered the floods around the house and out fifty meters to the tree line. Were the grass cut, the house removed, and goal posts placed, it would be one helluva sports arena. But considering the hidden barbed wire between the tall grass and trees and the rustic exterior of the outbuildings, it was closer to a death camp just short of sentry towers.

Drake entered the home, deactivated the alarm Away and reactivated it Stay. The room was unchanged from his last visit many months ago. As Drake stood in the entry, he backed up against the door, rested his head against the varnished wood, and closed his eyes. *Home.* At least the closest one Woolf had to his own. The feelings he had were mixed. One of being in a familiar setting, the other an anxiety of being out of the field, away from war, and knowing the emptiness and loneliness would set in if he didn't keep moving.

Drake activated his personal home security drone with a few taps on the computer keyboard at a planning desk. Well above him, a rooftop hatch flipped up and a tethered UAV America drone lifted up, attached by a thin cable that gave power and a digital feed to the monitor inside.

At two hundred feet in the air, the unmanned aerial surveillance vehicle equipped with video and sensor payloads was out of sight and earshot.

At two miles out, Tamer and Ahmed were nearing sight and sound of the drone's multi-sensor. Tamer continued to track Drake's signals as they drew closer to the target location. As they drove off the main highway, Tamer received a feed alert that Drake's device was connecting to the same mobile phone signal from earlier that night. Tamer shared the news to Ahmed.

Ahmed lifted his fingers from the wheel and allowed some air to pass through his sweating palms. Mohsen had told the men that Mo was receiving proper care and that Ali could provide any needed technical remote support as they pursued the Birddog. The Birddog, Ahmed contemplated with growing concern. The American soldier had always been quiet, respectful, and gifted in speaking their native tongue, but was rather intimidating. His language and dialect skills were like locals. He moved without effort and could blend in with Middle Easterners effortlessly. And his eyes were hollow. Empty. As if he was seeing right through a man or was completely gone from reality. Ahmed prayed that his aim would be true and that the man from Orange did not sleep with one eye open—if he slept at all.

Drake sucked down a cold can of Heady Topper Alchemist beer while reacquainting himself with the living room's quest to find Dex Woolf. Just as his uncle had referenced, Drake had maps and photos pinned to the drywall. The photos were a series of unknown persons of interest from around the globe that Drake thought could feasibly be his brother, if indeed his brother had gone to the dark side as a fundamentalist Muslim. Also pinned were computer-generated renderings of what Dex could look like today in a number of differing scenarios of weight gain or loss and facial hair or lack thereof. It was really just a series of guesses and mental masturbation so Drake could feel a sense of empowerment within the complete lack of any control he actually felt. With nothing much to add, and recognizing the increasing futility, he started taking it down only to stop to turn on the news and take a pull of his hoppy India pale ale.

As he waited to hear the weather forecast for the evening, Drake listened to the continued coverage of the attacks. He turned briefly to the television as a former so-and-so who did what and whatnot was spouting off as a counterterrorism subject matter expert. "Thank you, Melissa, for that introduction. And thank you for the comment on my service. I'd like to think I'm continuing that service today."

Seriously. Drake remained unimpressed and increasingly less so with the televised expert, but the remote control was now on the other side of the room and he had a handful of pushpins that his OCD wouldn't let him scatter on the table.

The talking head continued, "While I cover events such as the recent atrocities in Qaryatan, Syria, where Islamic State militants have hit lists for revenge killings, there is no doubt in my mind, uh, Melissa, from my many years of counterterrorism with the SEAL teams, that we will see more of this from ISIS. Shootings, beheadings, and burning of bodies that happened in the US is right out of the extremist group's playbook. The roadside IEDs on the Beltway, the IED blast at the Pentagon bus stop, and then of course the tragedy in the Fayetteville area with the VBIED. Melissa, for your civilian viewers, that's Vehicle Borne Improvised Explosive Devices. We saw a lot of them during my SEAL tours in the sandbox, as we called it. But this is hallmark ISIS. No question in my mind."

"Thank you, commander, and what of the attack on the Department of Defense deputy director's home this evening?"

"Well, Melissa, he's lucky to have survived. I mean, Godspeed to his family, I understand from early reports his wife…"

You gotta be kidding me.

The television showed a camera view of Drake's aunt and uncle's home with neighbors starting to congregate around cameras.

"Yeah, Melissa, clearly, someone has been leaking our soldiers' names to ISIS and they have begun to target our countrymen based on the threats they pose to tracking down these cells. It's like a Phoenix Program of Vietnam. It could be that we've come to reap what we've sowed, Melissa. And another reason we should not be allowing these—"

"Refugees, right? Is that what you're going to say next, Mr. Expert? And need to build a wall around each state now? Fucking turd," dismissed Drake as he admonished the television. He shot a glance to the drone's monitor.

Woolf left one picture on the wall and the other printed images in a small pile on the table—as well as a second beer that was still half full—and headed to the back of the ranch-style house. Drake turned the alarm off then armed it again to Away.

Ahmed put the car in park about thirty feet past the gravel road entrance to Drake Woolf's location. He waited in silence with Tamer.

Over twenty miles away, the Nissan Altima's engine started. One of the ISOF commandos put a blanket and spare tire over the weapons in the trunk, because no American officer pulling over suspicious looking Middle Easterners would ever ask to see what was under the blanket with a tire resting over it…. He then joined his team member, who was punching in GPS coordinates.

For the Mohawks, the rush and decline of adrenaline proved exhausting. Their bodies felt like they were back doing simultaneous takedowns in Iraq with the Deltas minus the Rip It energy drinks. They similarly were experiencing highs and lows in their resolve to kill their former comrades.

Tamer plugged the car DC inverter plug into the metal encased socket just under the dash and changed the configuration of the book-sized electronic jammer. He boosted the output power to increase the signal jamming range to over one hundred fifty meters. Wi-Fi, GPS, and Bluetooth, among a number of frequencies, were toast once he flipped the power on. He stared off into the darkness of the rural area while his hands blindly screwed in directional antennae. "I like America," he said with a trancelike flat voice.

"Me, too," replied Ahmed. "It is quiet. Very peaceful."

"Have you noticed that there is nothing to fear along the roadside? And when we visit the market stores, we don't need to worry about suicide bombers?" He laughed uncomfortably. "I would have liked to raise my family here."

"Yes. I was thinking this as well when we arrived." Ahmed expanded the Google Maps view of the farm with his fingers. He leaned over to Tamer, showing him the device image. "If we cut through the forest, it is approximately five hundred meters to the small road connected to house. If we cross just south of the structure we can come back up north to the back of the home. We can separate and see if he is visible through windows. Do you still have a strong signal?"

Tamer touched the mobile app to visually audit the connected devices and networks in range. "Same signal. I see additional devices but none are named and most connected to the house have encrypted signatures." He looked at Ahmed. "It's how we were instructed." His eyes showed fear.

"By the Birddog."

"It has to be him."

"Tamer, power off the jammer. Let's see what goes down and then power back up to see how the devices reconnect. Then wait again."

Tamer did as instructed, flipping the power switch off and on. The power indicator showed red while frequency bulbs glowed green. Tamer refreshed his mobile device screen. He refreshed it again and gave the screen a tap with his finger. In the screen glow of the darkened car, Tamer wore a look of increased concern.

"What is it?" Ahmed asked.

"Nothing in the house went off." Tamer turned the jammer off and back on again.

"Anything?"

"Networks at houses here and here," he pointed, "went down." Tamer turned to Ahmed. "Woolf's devices are still connected. And I see more on now."

"Show me the endpoints." Ahmed stretched to see. Tamer pointed to an aerial view of the home and surrounding buildings with a list of networks to the right side. Pinpoints dotted the screen on the satellite map.

"What's this one?" Ahmed asked, the concern still possessing his voice. "This is the forest."

Tamer refreshed the display. "I don't know. It wasn't there before." Ahmed's voice rose. "It's moving."

The two men were fixated on the blue blip that glided across the aerial map to the symbol that marked their own position. "It's on our position."

The men spun around in the car, looking out every window. They twisted and turned. And saw nothing.

"WHERE IS IT?" Ahmed shouted in desperation.

Tamer looked to his colleague. "It's here."

Chapter 21

Mohsen called General Reza Shirazian from his own hotel room. His right hand held the device, while his left palmed Johnny Walker Red Label scotch. His legs were spread with his lover in between them. Mohsen shook the glass to the tune of the high pitch of ice hitting the crystal sides.

"Mohsen. I was not expecting you."

"Yes, General. I would respectfully appreciate your guidance."

"Is something wrong?"

"The Mohawks took a casualty in the last encounter. He has an abdominal wound."

"Will he live?" the general inquired. "Can we make use of his fate, if not?"

"He needs medical attention. His movement ability is beyond limited."

"And where is he now?"

"He is safe. He and his cell member have been directed to a safe house. One of our sleepers. They have morphine and limited medical knowledge. The colleague has trauma training. Two ISOF members will be dispatched to provide security."

"What is it that you ask?"

"We have levied successful attacks against the Americans. We have left no trace. Perhaps it is time they found the Mohawks. They can have a small taste of victory to buy more time, only they will be crushed to find more attacks exist in due time. We can kill the other two members within the week. By then, our second wave will be ready for the other attacks. The news pundits are already starting to call for final withdrawals of troops from the region."

"I trust you are referring to the ISOF counterterrorism unit as the second wave?"

"That is correct, the others of the Golden Division cell."

"The best of Iraq's armed forces," the general emphasized with pride. Iran now had their fingers in the Iraqi counterterrorism forces as well as the powerful Shiite militias once the traditional army and police divisions collapsed. It created a monopoly for Iran and a vacuum for exploitation.

"As you planned, they will ensure operational assurances until our preparations are complete for the Georgia assault."

"Mohsen, you must not speak of this not even on a secure line."

"As you instruct, General, but I will remind you, the Americans cannot listen to our calls even if they were unencrypted. The CIA and NSA have laws preventing what they can listen to in America. The FBI takes too long of a time to request access privileges to listen. Much longer than we have been operational. Even if the Americans had our phones, the FBI would not be able to unlock and recover evidence of our communications. This is literally the safest place in the world for us to be. They must protect our digital privacy even if we say 'WMD' and 'kill the president.'" Mohsen laughed with utter confidence. He slurped the cold scotch, savoring the burn as it cascaded from throat to belly.

"Perhaps. But don't be a fool. Not all Americans play by the rules."

* * * *

The night sky lit up before the Mohawks as ten thousand lumens descended and shone directly into the car windshield. The quadcopter drone hovered in front of the Mohawks at eye level.

Both men shielded their eyes from the surprise beam of blinding light.

The second flash appeared to Ahmed's right. A simultaneous pop and crash. Tamer's head exploded, his body restrained by the seat belt. Glass and ricocheting steel-shot BBs pelted Ahmed's face and hands as he screamed, late to the game.

Ahmed spit debris from his bleeding lips. With the drone lights still illuminating the interior of the car, Tamer's head was a completely unrecognizable cavern of red and dark flaps and bony edges, a mangled stump protruded from between his shoulders. Ahmed screamed as he saw his friend's headless body.

Ahmed's door opened, and Drake Woolf thrust the shotgun butt into the car and against the frantic Mohawk's face, knocking him out cold.

"You said nothing about my aunt, motherfucker!"

Chapter 22

Drake splashed Ahmed with a glass of water. The Mohawk awoke slowly. The red welt was turning blue. The cut at his cheekbone still oozed crimson life from the ruptured corpuscles. He was groggy but quickly understood that he was bound and unable to move his arms or legs.

Sitting across from Ahmed was the man from Orange. The Remington 870 shotgun lay on the kitchen table and was pointed at Ahmed's chest. "We're going to do this one time. One time only." Drake spoke in Arabic.

"I contacted you just like our protocol in Mosul. I tried to warn you."

"You sent me the message just hours ago. What in the fuck are you doing here? And what is T-bone doing here and why was he coming to kill me with you? Don't tell me you're a fucking jihadi now."

"No, no," Ahmed pleaded. "The Quds Force, they are in America. They are here. I'm still working for the CIA. I'm with you! My family is here. The militias killed many of our families. My paperwork went through before the slaughters. I said my wife and children were missing then found dead. So, no one would know. They are in Nashville. Tennessee."

"I know where Nashville is. That doesn't explain shit! And if you're working with the Agency, why didn't they get word out faster?"

"The Iranians recruited the Mohawks. The Shia through the Iranians. They offered us protection. They thought I was among the victims. But I reported this to the CIA. To my handler. Just like I used to do for you. They have members of ISOF, too. The ISOF team handles the extreme assaults and act as second trigger to ensure we carry out our missions. They'll be coming."

"Who attacked the Deltas? Who fucking came to my house?" Drake roared. He thrust the shotgun barrel into Ahmed's chest with enough force to take the Mohawk's breath.

"We did." Ahmed sobbed. "I contacted my handler. He said they were on it, but nothing happened. No one came. I tried him again when the others learned your name. I had tried to throw them off to buy time. You never responded to your primary contact protocol. I tried. Brother, I meant you no harm, I tried," he cried. "You have to know this in your heart."

"Fuck." Drake pushed away from the table. His mouth clicked. "Give me the passcode to the laptop."

"Yes, yes, of course. We all use America. Use the "at" symbol for the *A*'s."

"Lovely." Drake wrote it down on a small pad near the laptop and typed the passcode on the keyboard. He was in. Ahmed was being helpful. Score one for him.

The Mohawks also had accessorized the laptop with a Harris International Mobile Subscriber Identity-catcher, a black box switch signal jammer, and another innocuous black box piece of hardware that Woolf knew to be yet another electronic signals interrupter.

"How did you guys get all this hardware and software?" Drake inquired as he sorted through the laptop programs. He viewed a sophisticated network analysis visual depiction that mapped names, numbers, and locations on a satellite map.

"Some was made available to us. Some from the internet. Some we sent from Iraq to addresses in the United States before coming here. It was ours to use and never collected when you all left the country."

"And no one flagged the shipments from customs?"

"When we shipped the electronics we declared the items under one hundred dollars and stated it was an amplifier."

Drake buzzed his lips in disbelief. He scanned the map to see his own location with a pin. Zoomed out to see his aunt and uncle's home. Expanded to see the Pentagon, Beltway, and North Carolina targets. He zoomed out further to see Maryland, South Carolina, Tampa, San Diego. They were colored red. Other items colored yellow indicated other points originating in Tampa and southwest Indiana. Then there were the blue items in Georgia, Tennessee, Utah, and along the Orange County, California, coast.

"What is all this? Are they all targets?"

Drake swiveled around the laptop so Ahmed could see.

Ahmed was distracted by something else on the table and then the wall. "First, I would ask how you have a picture of The *Modarris*—The Teacher," Ahmed slowly verbalized, as he stared at aged renditions of Dexter Woolf.

* * * *

O.T. disconnected the line when Drake failed to answer for the third time. His mind was reeling from the loss while still being compelled to work the problem. In truth, he had loved his wife. True, he had not been much of a husband for years, but they had had their differences. Always did. To O.T., after a lifetime of war-fighting, Helen was dear to him; however, this was a new warzone, and she was a casualty like the rest of his fallen brothers. Although this was personal now, and he would make it just as personal back to whoever was responsible.

With the police still working on the ground floor, O.T. was excused to the upper level. His office was on two floors, and both were set up for secure data connections and a computer terminal, but his secured device was able to pick up emails at Top Secret levels. He smiled as he read Mojo's communication. ICEPICK was a go. Drake was on board. He already had others in place to build the program and get it off its feet as quickly as possible. Now, they just had to find these jihadi killers and wipe them off US soil.

* * * *

Drake pounced toward Ahmed, his eyes wild. "Who?" He scrambled around the table and hovered over the papers. He moved the shotgun out of the way and spread the papers across the table in front of Ahmed.

"You know this man?"

Ahmed wasn't sure if he should be hopeful or more terrified. His ruse overall was thin, but thin would work in a world of shadows and subterfuge. And he certainly knew of the man on the picture before him. How much he knew depended on how the Birddog would respond to each nugget Ahmed could contrive. One thing that was indeed fact, Ahmed's family was alive and well. He loved them dearly and would continue to lie and scheme as he had for years just to keep them alive and safe. Both the Americans and the Iranians were liars. He would deal with each as the threat or opportunity presented itself.

Drake shuffled more papers. He now had six images of Dex Woolf laid out before his former asset. "Who is he?"

"He is a Westerner. American. You don't know this?"

"What is his name?"

"I only know he is The Teacher."

"Why do they call him the teacher? What does he do?"

Ahmed attempted to shrug, but his tightly bound arms restricted the motion. "Can you cut me loose?"

"No. Answer me." Drake pressed his hands on the table and leaned in. "Tell me everything." Drake's face softened and he sat down again. His body slumped forward. "He was someone close to me in my youth."

"That's not possible."

* * * *

General Owen Mathieson, the secretary of defense, made the first personal call to O.T. The two men shared a history and friendship, which made reaching out both genuine and as emotional as two career killers could muster.

"So, the cops are leaving you alone for a while?"

"Yeah, I'm just hiding out upstairs. Keeping out of their face and them out of mine. I don't know how to make arrangements and deal with some of what I'll need to do for preparations. That was Helen's type of thing. I need someone to handle this so I can focus on hunting these sons of bitches down. It's frustrating when you don't have an XO for your own personal shit."

"Let me know if you need help. My girls handled most of it when Ann lost her fight."

"I appreciate it, Owen."

"Not at all. Now, I know we can't speak of other matters, but I needed to share something with you before you saw it on the news or heard it from somewhere else."

"Another attack?"

"Not here. Lebanon-Syria border. Two Deltas. They were heading to Jordan to return with others killed in a training mission."

O.T. said nothing.

"You still there?"

"I'm here. Not much I can say on this line. Two you say though, huh? I'd heard about the ones in—uh, *Jordan*." O.T. emphasized the country to suggest he knew more of how that went down. "This new info's a surprise. Not how I understood things would go down." O.T. paused again to avoid a sticky situation. "Guess only thing I can ask you is, were you surprised?"

"Completely. On my honor."

"I'll take that. Thanks." O.T. was relieved for just a moment. "That's not good though, if you were surprised."

Owen stifled a chuckle. "I'll admit to you. I was feeling out whether *you* were really surprised."

"Question is whether someone leaked their transit, planned it, or got careless." O.T. heaved a breath of exasperation. "I don't like it when someone's in our black waters. Given that situation there, I'm ruling out carelessness."

"I am too. There's chatter about another operator. The tech."

"Owen."

"Yeah?"

"Not on this line. That's my guy."

"That's not good."

"Why's that?"

"Powers that be played back the Pred's video feed. They're looking for him."

"Who's *they*?"

"Up to the White House."

O.T. relaxed a tad. The White House had no involvement in the attack on the Deltas. They wouldn't even know what to do if they found out Drake was the runner. That was his department, and he made sure everyone else stayed in their lanes.

Chapter 23

"Why do you say I couldn't have known him?"

"The man you are talking about is Muslim. He was raised in North Africa. He teaches jihadists English. Now he works for Iranians. He teaches men how to talk like Americans, act like Americans, do business like Americans."

"How do you know him?"

"I don't know him. I just know of him. I met him once."

"Where?"

"Let me go, Drake Woolf."

"Where did you see him?"

"Untie my hands."

"No."

"Untie my hands, Drake Woolf."

"TELL ME!" Drake pounded on the table.

"I cannot. You must untie me first."

"I won't think twice about killing you."

"I think not."

Drake crossed the table and yanked the shotgun out from under the papers. He leveled it at Ahmed's forehead. "As far as I'm concerned, you came here to kill me. I think you were scared shitless about it and tried to cover your ass and you sat in that car waiting for the cavalry to come and do your deed. So, I have no problem blowing your head off just like your pal Tamer. And because I assume your family in Tennessee is here to commit acts of terror, too, I have no problem wiping them out or sending them back to Iraq. I'll sleep like a baby. Right now, all I really have are my own ghosts, and they'll love me for it. Adding a few more spirits to haunt my thoughts just keeps the party going until I decide to call it quits on my own. And I've gotten to enjoy the taste of steel and oil in my mouth when I lie in bed."

"My family is dead too, Drake Woolf. I was trying to save myself. But now I see you will kill me, regardless." Ahmed tightened his lip and raised his chin. "Too bad you didn't check my pockets."

Ahmed gave a sudden jerk and pushed himself up with the chair.

Drake fired instinctively.

The shotgun popped and flung Ahmed back in the chair with a smoking black hole in his chest. Blood frothed from his mouth as he tried to speak. Ahmed's eyes bulged as he coughed and struggled for breath.

"Where is he? Where is my brother? How many of you are there? WHERE'S MY BROTHER!"

Ahmed's teeth were covered in blood. He smiled as he tried to force words from his mouth. "Fa—"

"Fa what? What's Fa?"

Ahmed nodded.

Drake lifted Ahmed back up, and the Mohawk coughed a mouthful of blood and gasped. "What were you going to say?" Drake shouted. "Say it!"

Ahmed turned to Drake, inhaling from his nose and taking deep swallows to clear his throat. He sputtered, sucked in more air from his nose, and spit a large glob of blood in Drake's face. "Fuck...you...man from Orange," he mustered. "The *Modarris* is...here."

Death did not come swiftly, and no amount of shouting, shaking, or slapping would get Ahmed to reveal anything. Drake turned him over violently in frustration and probed the Mohawk's back pocket. It was a wrinkled photograph of a family. Ahmed's.

"Oh, no." Drake's heart sank. "Ahmed! Oh, shit. Shit!" *What did you do?* Drake frantically tried to revive Ahmed. He checked the Mohawk's pulse. It was gone. No breathing. Drake started CPR. Blood erupted with each compression. The air he blew into Ahmed escaped somewhere in the damaged cavity. The lungs remained deflated.

Ahmed's expression of extreme sadness had faded to the glazed-over stare of death Drake had seen so many times before at his hands.

Drake's mouth clicked. A sense of panic battled internally with news that Dex Woolf might actually be alive and the fact that he had killed an asset who had knowledge of the threat to America. If Drake's brother was CONUS and tied to the attacks, it would solidify the decision to take on this one-man-task-force role. He owed it to Ahmed. But if Sean Havens was also involved, and already contracted to Orange, maybe Drake could convince O.T. to make it a team of two. And even though Drake didn't care much for Lars, the ex-detective, logistics would be key. Couldn't hurt to see if he could provide support and handle the funding and procurement. And such were the worries, concerns, and cross-validations going on in Drake's mind. Ultimately, he came to a simple conclusion—this could work. There was one thing left of Drake to do. He had to die.

* * * *

O.T. answered his secure line on the first ring. "Where the Hell've you been?"

"Targeted," Drake replied. "You doing okay?"

"I'll manage. Bigger question is are you okay? What's going on? You need me to come out to the farm? How many came at you?" O.T. scarcely left and opening to respond.

Drake seized the opening as O.T. took a breath. "When I whispered at the house that I was getting pings on my phone, they were the same dudes that killed Aunt Helen. She got one of them, though."

"How do you know for sure?"

"I've got one crow in the yard and one in the living room. They're dead." *Because I screwed up again,* he said to himself, looking at Ahmed's still body on the floor. "And before you jump in with a bunch more questions, I need to be dead too. Bad news is I need to torch the place and make it look like what you described happened in the Pines. VBIED." Drake expected some resistance when his uncle heard the plan to destroy the home.

"We've got insurance," O.T. said flatly. "I'll use your life insurance to get another hunting cabin."

"Thanks," Drake said, knowing his uncle was trying to lighten the mood in earnest.

"Drake, I think it's the right decision. Not just for the program, but there's some blowback from Lebanon. Two of the FOB Deltas were killed leaving the AO. Don't know if it was coincidence or not, but when an op is approved for some cover-up, some folks don't know when to quit."

"Holy shit," Drake exclaimed with a heavy tone of dread.

"Yeah, holy shit is an understatement. What's up with the raghead jihadis that came after you? You're sure you're okay?"

"I'm okay, but my mind's reeling thinking about those guys. If I had made it to the extraction faster... Shit."

"Drake, they didn't know you had another mission. The money wire and account information was critical to our interdiction of funds. It was one of the big puzzle pieces making a fit to terror funding in the region."

"I get it," he conceded. "And about my attackers, it's bigger than that. I was wrong. It's the Mohawks. Meaning the Mohawks themselves from Iraq. A good handful of them. Maybe more. My guess from what little I've learned is that Iranians are involved. So, if I'm going to do this, I'm going to need some things. And some manpower."

"It's my turn for a holy shit. We should have eyes and ears on the Mohawks still. I haven't seen anything that would have come up like a risk. CIA should've had something if a bunch of Mohawks up and left the country. I've got a guy, Mojo, at NSA who's going to be our ears. He's cuddly with a little Iranian girl over at the Agency's Persia House. She works the White House Situation Room. We'll see what she has."

"That works. So, how about a team?"

"I can't get you much. As I said, we have Mojo, who's a trusted asset. I handpicked him. He can report in to another NSA special projects resource who will act as a cutout and be the custodian of the funds and overall program. Aside from that, if we're going to keep this program buried in black, we'd need another ghost. They're hard to come by. And right now, no one comes to mind unless you have some thoughts."

"Havens," Drake dropped. "Can't say I like him. Especially after the asshole drugged me, no doubt at your request, and shanghaied me back to the States. But, I'll tell you this, I'd trust him to pack my parachute any day. He seems pretty straightforward. Plus, he's on the list. Gives him a vested interest. I'd take that Viking ogre he has with him, too. Lars. The ex-cop. Could come in handy. Although he does stand out a bit."

O.T. couldn't be happier with how the task force was coming together with Drake. His nephew couldn't be forced; he had to come up with things on his own. It just took some nudging. "That guy Lars was a dirty cop," O.T. warned.

"Perfect. He probably doesn't have anyone who trusts or likes him, except his brother-in-law. I'm having a hard time believing Havens would keep a guy around who could be risky. Especially on close-hold Defense work. There has to be more to the story. I think we give it a shot."

"In theory, it could work. Sean Havens has been through a lot. His wife's gone. Daughter is in an exclusive technical program for crypto under a new name. I'm not sure he's the right guy if you want another shooter. Frankly, and don't take this the wrong way, I don't think I've ever heard you ask for help. You sure you're all right to do this? I can't have you going tits up and ruining a program like this and my reputation."

"Yeah. And thanks for my personal considerations. But since you asked, just feeling a bit out in the wind lately. I'm not sure how to process Aunt Helen. It's like it's not even real. I've seen so much that I don't know how to feel what I should feel. Sorry. I know you know. I just don't know how you deal with stuff like this over all the years."

"We bury our dead and move forward, but they're always with us. Your aunt wouldn't agree, but we go after those who have taken our own. Now if we move forward, we're going to have to do it fast. No whining about being sleepy and hungry, and I better not hear one goddamned time about those fucking voices or meds. So help me you will never work with me again. I'll make some calls right away, but I need to make sure you can make this work. It's going to be a clusterfuck scramble for a while. Innovation and flying by your ass until we put this whole program together with some resources for you. I know that's another one of your hang-ups. So embrace the suck. Some things are in the works, but I'll need to get final approvals and turn the lights on. And don't get me wrong about your shortcomings. They hang you up, but I've made you the best hunter-killer of any man I've trained. Can't imagine how effective you'd be if you could get your head straight."

"God, you're a dick."

"Curse me as you will but know this. When they brought you to me nearly twenty years ago, you were a mute drooling vegetable that most doctors wanted to just stick in a padded room. Since you weren't doing anything with yourself and no one else could get you to talk and engage with the world, I took you on like a vacant piece of land nobody wanted. The way I see it, it was fully in my right to build what I wanted on that land. And I built you. If you didn't like it, you should have done something about it. Now, what do you need for the task force?" Drake tucked the words away with his hate. The old man would never change. It wasn't the first time he had heard the abuse speech of "You make me do the things I do to you," and it wouldn't be the last. "I don't need anything more than someone to watch my back and teach me some new and old tricks. I need to learn more. No one teaches me anything anymore. I need to be as sharp as I can be. Havens doesn't know it, but he gave me the slip a ton of times in Martha's Vineyard. I wouldn't have gotten the package back if Murphy's Law hadn't shit on his day."

"Fine. I'll make the call. And don't second-guess the past. You've always made it out of scrapes and figured out an acceptable approach.

I'm not selecting you as the best operator in the world, I'm selecting you because you're going to finish the job and survive. That makes you the best for the job. Make your exit clean even if you have to level that place to chopsticks. You know the FBI will investigate whatever you do, and they'll find shit that stinks."

"Roger that. I saw you still had a little C-4 left here in the linen closet above the comforters."

Drake could hear his uncle chuckle on the other end.

"Not the best place to hide explosives, Unc."

"Who's hiding anything? That was a good Fourth of July. Your aunt put it there so we'd stop."

Guilt for his aunt rolled to the forefront of Drake's mind and hovered above his thoughts like a dense fog over water. He held it there so it would block any new thoughts from emerging. So he could try to find and feel pain of loss again like normal people.

"Drake."

"Yeah, I was just thinking. Sorry. If we do this, it'll be the last I see you in public. I won't be at her funeral and won't be around to help you."

"I can't give you a better gift than that," O.T. rasped, then cleared his throat. "I know I was never easy on you. Maybe never even good to you. I don't raise children, I train warriors. And for that, I am very proud of and honored by how you turned out. You're today and tomorrow's warrior, Drake. The world needs men like you. I admit, I may have exploited you for that reason. But you've excelled."

Drake rolled his eyes at the same speech that usually came in the home basement on Christmas Eve in Uncle Robert's wood-paneled officers' club bar after too much bourbon. "Make the call to Havens. I'll take care of things here. I'm sure someone will call 911 when they hear the place go up. Can't hurt if you reach out to the police chief and say you can't reach me."

"Good point. Obviously, I dialed you on secured."

"Better try a few times on unsecured comms. Well, I don't need to tell you."

"It's a new world, kid. I'm old-school. Havens will be a good mentor to you. I'll stay top cover and figure a way to get you hooked up with my guy, Mojo, at NSA. He'll feed you the target packages through a new protocol, but you task him for any data you need. Do you have a cover and some funds that'll get you operational for a bit? No one can really go off-grid needing the type of resources to get this done. You'll need a new identity and you'll need to stay clear of people and areas you know unless you're disguised. It's not like we have a plastic surgeon in the backroom to give you a new nose and shit."

"Yeah," Drake replied, realizing there was quite a bit he would need to get set up. Even getting off the farm would be an issue. It wasn't like the movies, where everyone had spare passports, credit cards, and gold coins. He'd have to check the bodies and see what they had on their persons.

"Hey, I meant to ask you," O.T. started subtly, "how did you find out Iranians were involved?"

It was an odd way for O.T. to ask the question. He was much more direct. Drake was leery of the slant. Clearly, this was not shocking news despite initial suspicion of Daesh. "Ever hear of The *Modarris*?" Drake just as flippantly tossed the name to see what reaction it would yield.

O.T.'s silence bored a pit in Drake's gut. Birddog closed his eyes. He knew the old dark warrior had held his cards tightly all these years.

"What does he have to do with this?" O.T. spit.

"He's here."

O.T. said nothing. Dead air between the two men was heavy. Finally, he confessed to Drake, "All I can say is that he's not supposed to be here, and you can't ask any more questions about the matter. Drop it, Drake. He's not your target. He's not your problem. Leave it. That's an order."

* * * *

Mohammad groaned on the bed, gripping the mound of bloodied gauze pads and towels in pain. He called out again. "Ali, have you heard yet?"

"Nothing," Ali replied from beyond the bedchamber. "Keep quiet. You need to rest."

"You mean I need to die. My bandages and the towels are sponging life from me. I'm no good dead, Ali. They should know this," Mo bitched.

Ali stood from the couch, but his host pulled him back down. "Sit," Hassan said softly. "He must rest. His wounds are bad, but not terminal. The doctor will be here with the others soon."

"What others? Mohsen said nothing of others."

"Protection. Mohsen would like armed men to keep you safe while your friend recovers. They will take you to another location before light. You can't stay here. My neighbors would suspect something."

"We're not staying. Mohsen said nothing of others."

"Take more tea. It will relax you." Hassan poured hot, fragrant liquid into the porcelain cup and handed it to Ali.

"You are not having any?" Ali asked. His sheepish expression indicated he was hardly the confident warrior he once was in Iraq. He now wore a veneer of shame and fear, which could be costly to the success of an operational cell.

Hassan smiled. "I've had plenty today. I'm sufficiently relaxed," he said as he intently watched Ali sip another cup.

"You are Iraqi."

"I am. From Fallujah. We left when the Americans left. I was an interpreter."

"You work with the Americans?" Ali tensed and straightened. His hand jostled the cup, spilling tea into the saucer.

"No," Hassan shook his head then bowed it as if looking for something on the floor. "The men I worked for left Fallujah. I was promised a visa. It never happened. There was a raid shortly after, by the Americans. They were told by locals that I was Sunni militia. My son was killed in an explosion when they blow open the door to our home. I was taken. Beaten. When I was released it took me two weeks to return to my wife and daughter. I missed the burial of my son." He looked at Ali with heavy, tear-filled eyes. He smiled. "No, I do not work for the Americans. I do not work for them at all." Above Ali's right shoulder was a wall clock. Hassan flicked his eyes periodically to the minute hand as time dragged on and he awaited further instructions.

Ali did not care to ask how Hassan and his remaining family made it to the United States. He knew the story to be the same. He knew there were more. And he was afraid. While not a deeply religious man, Ali knew that if one kills a believer unintentionally or by accident, there should be blood money or compensation due. The Americans had killed Ali's family unintentionally by not protecting them. But Ali knew from the Quran that never should a believer kill a believer. Iraqi believers had actually killed his own family. Not unintentionally, not by accident. It was his fellow countrymen who had fallen astray from Allah. And nothing could guide them right. Ali was getting drowsy. The day had been too long, he thought. And in that moment, he thought of the Iranians who had given them the opportunity to make things right with their help. Why then did they not first find the true killers in Iraq? The Americans. They would have remorse. His friends. The Deltas. They would have remorse. They broke promises, true. But they did not murder families of the Mohawks. Ali's heart was heavy. Who could he warn, who could he tell? He was so sleepy.

* * * *

Drake had no time for bullshit. He removed the SIM card from his device, snapped the small piece of black plastic and circuitry, and smashed the phone under a metal kitchen chair leg. The C-4 explosives he wrapped with duct tape and then inserted two blasting caps. Most American households held neither high explosives nor igniters. It was the one benefit today that Drake recognized being raised by Robert O'Toole. For his aunt's part, a kitchen timer of hers rested on top of the oven. That would do just fine.

He kept Ahmed in place but not before rifling through the Mohawk's pockets. He found money, a couple of credit cards, false ID, mobile device. And then it hit Drake. Mohawks scouted the targets and did light engagement. Ahmed said ISOF finished the job. This was a *job*, Drake realized in an afterthought.

Fuck me. I forgot about ISOF.

Two dark figures stood in the shadows of the illuminated perimeter. Their firearms were loaded, their heartbeats only slightly elevated. The ISOF commandos nodded to one another in affirmation then communicated in a series of hand signals before slinking in tandem to their target, Drake Woolf.

Chapter 24

The problem with black operations is knowing who is friendly and who is a foe. It was a problem Sean Havens had wrestled with for well over a decade in the field, it was a problem like wresting through the damned barbed wire that he was neither expecting nor did he see until it was too late, and it was a problem now as he watched two armed men headed for Drake Woolf's cottage or whatever the hell it was in a jungle of thorns, downed or rotted and fallen trees, probably poison ivy, and then of course the barbed wire. But at least it wasn't that godforsaken Burma.

Vague orders from O.T. such as "keep an eye on Drake until he's on board" inconveniently left out "and be sure to bring automatic weapons in case there are killers with automatic weapons." To be sure, when he and Lars had rolled up to the property entrance and seen shattered glass and blood residue, Havens had a pretty good inkling it was best to let Lars drop him off at the tree line and drive a bit farther to stay out of the way. After all, Lars was a post-crime scene guy. Sean just hoped that fact wouldn't mean Lars would conduct a forensic investigation of Havens's own death in the moments to come.

From the shadows, Sean calculated the situation. He was pretty sure these guys were up to no good. Unfortunately, they didn't move tactically like amateurs. They moved like Delta or other SOF elements, which really sucked. There was no option to contact Drake without being heard. And for all he knew, maybe these guys were here to help Drake. Or so he mused for a split second knowing it not to be true from the onset.

The wind shifted slightly. Sean had been trained to use smell in the field, and while in the field to ensure he didn't smell out of the element. Trying to catch a waft of their scent, he thought he smelled McDonald's french fries. Would an operator grab fries and a Quarter Pounder before an assault? Probably not. Would a couple Iraqis indulge in it? Maybe. It was a stretch. Plus, he could just be hungry. He was almost certain it was french fries.

As Havens slow-footed just a hair closer to the men, his foot landed on a rock, which gave him an idea. Given events in the news, it was likely these guys were Arabs. Or if Arabs were after Drake it could be FBI SWAT or local SWAT here to help, but there were no official vehicles and only two guys, which meant the only friendlies in low numbers and low vis footprint would be Delta. Delta trained with other foreign troops regularly, so a warning would have to apply only to them and no one else to avoid confusion, or in this case, casualties.

Sean picked the rock up, tossed it up and down a couple of times to sense its weight, mustered his preteen Little League pitching arm, and whipped the golf-ball-sized rock. Probably registering between a sixty-five and seventy-five mile an hour fastball, the stone flew just over the assaulters' heads and into a glass window.

"DIE LUNTE BRENNT!" Havens yelled the equivalent of "fire in the hole" hoping if they were Deltas that they had trained with GSG-9 or more likely KSK, Kommando Spezialkräfte, the German elite military counterterrorism unit. If they hadn't, they should have, because they were about to take lead.

The two men spun, startled at the voice behind them, then turned back to the house when the glass shattered.

"Oh, well." Havens quick-drew his Heckler & Koch 45, carried for its compact size over goon shwacking. The four-and-a-quarter-inch barrel length was shorter than he would have liked and the ten-plus-one capacity also a little less firepower than he would have liked. But the rifling boosted accuracy and his focus to kill or be killed upped advantage to a reasonable handicap.

Havens squeezed twice, advancing toward the targets, his aim to the head. Moving less than six inches in his point-and-shoot sight, he double-tapped the head to the left then shifted back to the right, putting two more rounds center mass then two more to the left center mass. As both men deflated and collapsed into a converged heap, Sean Havens put two more caps in each head. Both men's lives were stolen from the Maker in eight seconds.

Upon closer look, their Middle Eastern features gave Sean comfort that his instincts and rationale were on point and had saved him from the death penalty to maybe only life in prison, worst case. His gut and his mind could just as easily have been off, however. And Sean took but a moment to realize he cared a lot less about that possibility than he should.

Havens also realized he had no idea how someone had gotten the jump on him as a metal gun barrel pressed against the back of his head.

"Havens, your timing is getting suspect," the voice from behind challenged.

"One of these days you'll start with thank you," Sean replied.

"Thank you," Drake said. "But for what it's worth, I had this."

"I figured." Sean turned around as Woolf lowered the weapon. "Just thought that I hadn't killed anyone in a while. Figured I already have a life sentence, so why share it with anyone."

Drake was stoic. He wondered if Havens's cavalier attitude was coming from a man who was good and who knew he was good, or if it derived from a man who just couldn't give two shits anymore. Woolf suspected the latter, yet he knew the guy was professional enough to still be giving a hundred and ten percent. And for a relative stranger. "For an old man, you handle yourself pretty well."

"Didn't hear you coming," Sean confessed.

"Payback."

"Or maybe I'm just getting old and rusty. Sounds like we may be working together. You cool with that?"

Drake nodded. "I suggested it over an hour ago. But seeing how you're here, it means I'm actually the last to know. My uncle works that way. He seems to know what I'll do before I do. He just lets me think I'm calling the shots—"

"So it sits better," Sean finished.

"No." Drake countered. "So I'm put in my place later by feeling he was one step ahead the whole time and that I really had no choice. But anyway."

"I understand," Havens said. "Look, if we do this together, you have a choice. You need to be comfortable with me, with Lars, and with Sebastian. Speaking of which"—Sean retrieved his device midsentence—"let me ping Lars and have him help us with the bodies."

"Who's this Sebastian guy?"

"He's just a guy who did in Belfast years ago what we're trying to do now."

Chapter 25

The 256-bit encrypted text from Sean appeared on Lars's Beartooth app, relaying from a Bluetooth off-the-grid paired device in his pocket. It was safe for Lars to move in and bring the car up the access road. The two preferred to communicate, when possible or within ten miles of each other, using the 900 MHz IMS band of the smartphone-connected device. It was an unconventional and unexpected means, which meant it was perfect for staying on the down-low for casual conversation.

Lars pulled the gray Ford Transit van up the drive and slid the windowless cargo door open. A year ago, Lars had been settling into a retirement home in Scottsdale, Arizona. Two things had screwed that up: the money he had siphoned away tax-free from people who ended up being on the wrong side of the blue line and a brother-in-law whose secrets had come home to roost. Funerals, plane tickets, hospital stays, stitches, and an unmentionable amount of Cubs games missed were a disruption to Lars's original plans. But Sean Havens was family, and for that Lars Bjorklund would go through Hell and back. Because that's how Norders did things. Til' Valhalla. Still, he wondered what kind of mess he was in store for now. Loyalty was one thing. A glutton for punishment was another.

Drake, for his part, was feeling a bit like he was back in the Mediterranean with Sean. "Havens, are you even going to ask for my opinion or plans?"

"Sure," Havens replied, as he shuffled along upholding his literal end of a double-teamed body carry. "I'll ask you plenty when I have a chance and when it matters."

"We're doing stuff now."

"I know. But that doesn't need your opinion or plan. We need to just get a few things done first. I'd like to get moving on wherever these guys came from. Especially if it means more would come out here. I'm not too heavily loaded with any hardware here."

Drake couldn't get himself to just drop the body, but he needed Sean to stop. Things were going a bit too fast for his taste. Woolf had a plan that would support his death, and this was going to screw it up. He followed Havens, stewing in his own thoughts as Sean brought the body up to the car that Ahmed and Tamer had arrived in.

Drake's mouth started to click.

Sean looked up. "What're you doing?"

"Nothing."

"You're clicking your mouth."

"So."

"So." Sean dropped the body. The weight pulled the dead assaulter from Drake's grip. "So, pal, if you want to say something, say something."

"What? I'm not—"

"Drake. If you're thinking something and trying to get it out of your head, just say it. I don't need to tell you what you're doing or why you're doing it. We've all got our issues. It's how we work with each other that makes things work. I don't plan to do things like your uncle does, but some things to me are easier done than said. If that doesn't work for you, just let me know. I'm cool with that."

"I'm thinking that somehow I have to come up with a viable way to die without it being a huge pain in the ass and without—"

"You're not dying. That was a stupid plan for where we're at right now," Havens said. "When did this all change?"

"O.T. can tell us what to do, but I tell him how to do it. What he has in his head and what's reality on the ground since he's taken a desk are two different things. And it's stupid to come up with some way that you died, when at some point or another, you're likely going to bump into someone or need to use your true personal history to get out of a jam, or something. You're not dying, Drake. That's storybook shit."

"But you said—"

"Doesn't matter what I said on the little dinghy or swimming. I did what I needed to get you where I needed you, and I said whatever I needed to say so I could get into your head to get a picture about how you think and operate. That was then. This is now."

Drake was dumbfounded and had to concentrate on not letting his tongue click. At this point, his mind was ricocheting thoughts all over his skull and his tics wanted to strike up a hundred-piece symphonic orchestra. Somehow, he was relieved—a concept he couldn't fully comprehend. His mind was ten steps ahead, stressing about how it would all come together. He needed to be a ghost. Needed to be off the books. But still needed access to things, or so he thought. And people to be able to access him, or so he hoped. The more he thought, the less he knew. But Havens knew; Drake just didn't know. O.T. wanted it done, Drake thought it should be done, but now they weren't going to do it, and now something else was going to happen, but no one shared what that was going to be or how it was going to work. Drake needed time to think but didn't have time to think.

He took a deep breath and controlled his exhale to the count of three. "So, how do we do it?"

"We've already got someone working on it. They just don't know it. We're doing the next best thing to killing you." Havens paused, looking at the body and the car. "Do you have anything we can use to make this thing blow up somewhere to buy time on identifying the bodies?"

"Yeah, but finish your thought about me dying but not dying. I'm struggling a little with how this works and why things have changed."

"Sure." Havens approached the car and assessed the broken window. By now Lars had walked up, after giving them some space to talk. "Did you by chance, Lars, see if that Nissan we came up on was open?"

"I didn't. I was keeping clear, waiting for you, as you said, and seeing if my castle was complete on the Clash of Clans app."

Drake shot him a look, replaying whether he had actually heard the guy say he was playing a game while he and Sean were dealing with armed shooters.

Lars shrugged. "I can check now. No traffic coming through here. Next house seems to be a quarter mile or so away." He looked to Drake. "Duck-boy," Lars addressed Woolf, "how nosey are your neighbors? I heard a few of the pops that I assume went into these guys, but the tree line muffled quite a bit with my windows rolled up."

Drake shook his head. "We should be good with neighbors. Sean, you were saying?"

"Yeah. Usually when we put together a covered backstopped unit, we have more time and resources. But this one's going operational faster than we have time to get a lot of things set up. We need to sort out logistics, the intel flow, the targeting, a whole shitload of things before we can make you, Pinocchio, into a little boy, or vice versa. It's taken me months, and most of it I had done years back in preparation. We're doing you like we would if a SOF dude was doing a stint with OGA. But in this case, I'm going to make sure you can keep rank, get promoted, keep pay and benefits and still stay Drake Woolf, and yet allow you to disappear. Unless you have a huge nest egg and can figure a way to pay for everything through Bitcoin, you're going to stay on the grid until you learn your realistic needs and see how that works with any life plan you may have or that you could have in the coming years. It's not just an on- or off-switch."

"That seems to make sense."

"You're getting assigned to a Reserve Unit. Thing is, you're never going to show up. There's a few units that are composed of nearly half ghosts. Guys that are on the rolls but never show up for drills. Nothing black. Just a bunch of lazy losers. It'll take a year of you not showing up before the commander will administratively transfer you into the Individual Ready Reserve. It's easier to do that than for them to deal with a no-show so they don't have to report losses. That way you also keep your retirement. They also may not notice, since budget constraints are killing the funds for training anyway. We'll put you in an active status so your pay keeps coming in and we're assigning you to a training role that gives you base access across the country. That gives us housing, airfields, a secure safe haven, and if we need, a place we can get our hands on more equipment. I think we're going to put these dead guys in the car, drive it into that ravine a ways away from the exit, and then we can blow it up like they ran off the road but were going to crank out another jihadi bada-bing bada-boom. How many guys inside?"

"One." Drake was still trying to process the operational concept that Havens had dumped in his lap. It was not too different from things he'd heard in the past. And it took out the need to have a covered unit. It was truly hiding in plain sight. And it bought Drake time to get things together and see what would work best. In short, it worked with how Drake worked. He suspected that Havens knew that. "How did you know there was a guy in the house?"

"You mean, because there's a dead guy in the passenger seat and the two here probably carpooled together?" Havens didn't wait for an answer. "How does the plan sound?" Sean stepped over the second body they had just carried to the front. "Is this your Tesla?"

Before Drake could answer either, Havens asked, "Don't suppose you have anything we can actually blow this shit up with, or do I need to go MacGyver and see what's available?"

Chapter 26

Drake smiled, for the first time entering a comfort zone. "My turn for a change in plans. I'm all about blowing stuff up, but there's a road not far from here that will take us along the Potomac into the Chesapeake Bay. There's a service road that takes you up to a concrete boat launch that hasn't been used for…I don't know how long. Not for decades. It drops off to thirty or forty feet easy. I used to fish out there. Maybe it's better to just dump them. Buys time. No one's going to the authorities to report them."

Sean turned to Lars. "You're the detective, sound good to you?"

Lars shot his glance to Drake. "The duck's got a good point. Explosion. Feds. News. No good. I'd say buying as much time as we can is best." He nodded to the man from Orange. "Good thinking, kid. And, Sean"—he turned back to his brother-in-law with a heavy brow—"when we finalize the facilities we can use, body disposal should be a consideration. Maybe flameless cremation. We can get a liquefaction chamber that chemically dissolves proteins, blood, and fat, and it can just be poured down a drain after a few hours."

"Holy shit." Drake squinted, absorbing the concept.

Lars shrugged. "If you guys are doing this boogeyman shit, you want to strategically leave some bodies, but if you want to keep authorities at bay, you need to also get rid of the bodies. Black ops or not, if you get caught, I guarantee someone's going to get a murder charge."

"This isn't my world. I leave the Tony Soprano stuff to you guys," Drake said.

Havens chuckled. "Lars, we can talk about this over beers back at the shop, but if you have some thoughts on what we need to do now, I'm all ears."

"Well, I just want to plant a seed before we go too far. Our best bet is alkaline hydrolysis. The units will cost a couple hundred grand, but go cheaper and it takes more time. If there's room in the budget, I'd get a few. If this task force does work across the US, you need to figure air transport of the bodies back to wherever we store these, or take advantage of ad hoc options. I'll be happy to take the lane on disposal advice as it comes up."

Sean nodded. "Cool, let's table the fancy acid barrels for now." Havens paused and scanned the car and bodies. "Let's get this going. Exploit any intel they have on devices or pocket litter. Strip all identification or trails, and head out to next objective. Drake, how does the house look inside? Can we just get the other body?"

"I made a mess," Drake replied, stone-faced. "There's also a laptop on the table. Passcode written off to the side if the log-in timed out. Username shows up Mohawk. Maps of where the Mohawks made contact. Some other stuff I haven't even looked at yet."

Sean turned back to Lars. "You got this?"

Lars was already lumbering up to the house. "You guys get the body out, I'll sanitize. I'll check out the laptop and if I see anything I can put Sebastian on, I'll reach out to him."

"Great." Sean took a slow turn, looking the property up and down for anything that might jump out at him. Figuratively and literally. "We'll load the bodies in one, drive both cars to the river, dump the bad guys and come back. Let's keep the Altima for now. Could help buy us time when we pull up to our next stop. Then we whack a few more of these rogue Mohawks. Cool?"

No resistance.

"Then maybe get some breakfast afterward?" he suggested, hoping for the same support.

Chapter 27

Mohammad cried out for Ali. The plea was futile. His sleeping counterpart lay drugged on the sofa.

The host whispered on the phone to Mohsen. "I've done as you asked. The other man may not survive through morning. They should leave here as quickly as possible. The neighbors will notice so many cars here late in the night and into morning. My daughter's friend comes to the home early to walk to school."

"Not to worry. The others will be there soon. Give Mohammad anything to make him comfortable."

"There is nothing I have for him at the home. He needs morphine. And forgive me, but we have still not received the paperwork. I have done all that you have asked for months."

"You have my gratitude. I will speak to my contact at the consulate about the delay. You should have green cards soon. As promised."

* * * *

What Lars couldn't clean, he removed from the house. It didn't take him long to discover a dual-purpose fire pit and brush burning area to the rear of the home. He scrounged some charcoal starter against an unlocked shed and torched a large, blood-stained carpet remnant, a couch cushion and throw pillow, and all the cleaning rags, towels, and paper products he used to scrub the house. Lars was confident he would confound an evidence response team.

Looking around the home, Lars felt as though he had gained a better sense of Drake Woolf, and the fact that he was a man of secrets and solitude.

Not just on the battlefield, but personally. There were no photos. The home was highly organized but not overly clean. With a lifetime of keeping his own secrets and discovering those of others while being a Chicago police detective, Lars sensed that Drake's proclivities for organization and isolation were based more on turmoil than danger or a lack of family or friends, which could root back to the former.

Retired sleuth Bjorklund hadn't heard back from his brother-in-law after nearly an hour. That meant he had more time to sniff around. And Lars, a man without scruples, would ensure there would be very little left unturned in the farmhouse. The black Hefty bag in the corner would be next to check out. Then he'd get to the laptop.

* * * *

As the two former singleton operators pushed the car filled with American-trained dead Iraqis into black waters, Drake spoke for the first time since they had left his property.

"Tell me about Sebastian."

"He's good. A bit rough around the edges. But good."

"That's a start."

"Here's what I know. He was British intelligence. MI6. He was within a small group called UKN. UKN had spooks and hunter-killers. Sebastian handled pretty much surveillance, countersurveillance, and all things geek. He used to work alongside the SAS Increment. Ever hear of them?"

"Yeah. Wet work and other covert ops."

"Exactly. Sebastian's older than I am but has twice the energy that you do. Married an American who was with NSA stationed in the UK. Now he has American citizenship. From the marriage and because he went through the whole deal. He's not really a military type, although he's been in plenty of scrapes. Survived nearly six months of captivity and torture and walked out with a pocket full of thumbs. They took two of his. The rest he took when he was able to escape. He had a lot of thumbs on him from what I hear. The rest, I have no clue."

"So why is he on the team?"

Sean watched the car bobbing in the water sink to its side as it took on the Potomac's water. In the moonlight, he could see one of the upright shooters fall to the side onto his teammate. There was a time that Sean would have been bothered by the macabre scene. How long ago that was, he could not recall. It was a lifetime ago. "Sebastian worked Belfast. Against the IRA. You probably guessed that. Oh, he's deaf in one ear, too, from the beating, so he kinda cocks his head to one side. Anyway. Stuff he did there in a domestic setting is why he works with us. They got intel and went in and killed everyone wherever they were."

"But he's cleared and works for the Defense space?"

Sean confirmed with a nod; whether Drake saw it or not as they watched the vehicle burp its last bubbles didn't matter. "He also came from industry and has a legitimate cyber company in Maryland. He's badged and can go in and out of NSA and military facilities, so he's our interface for the target packages. Fits his coming and goings. Wears a suit, has access to a ton of equipment for evaluation and training, and most importantly... keeps his mouth shut. People are used to him shaking hands and doing things on the sly."

"Just can't believe we're using a Brit for some of the highest sensitivity ops."

Sean patted Drake on the back. "Your uncle loves him. Let's head back. I'll text Lars. All I can say is 'much to learn, young Skywalker.'"

Drake gave Havens a sideways glance. "Didn't take you for a 'Star Wars' fan."

Sean cracked a smile, his mind distant to battles of the past. "No, not me. An old long-tabber named James was. Used to say shit like that all the time. He was a good man. Had a lot to teach me. Wish he would have taught me more."

"Had a guy like that myself. I'm guessing yours is gone, too."

Both men watched in silence as the rear bumper still listing below the surface finally sank out of view. The conversation stirred memories of those lost along the way, as it often does for men of the sword. The softness of sorrow and self-doubt and loathing came first. Then came the guilt of survival. But these two men had another option, the option that drives warrior soldiers on. It was the glowing fire that burned, kindled and stoked by the thought that evil men who would still kill others remained at large. And such men needed to die to protect innocents. Some would be killed tonight. Surviving sheepdogs would ensure it.

Drake slapped Havens on the back. "Game time, boss."

* * * *

Tresa called Earl Johnson from her temporarily assigned black Chevy Tahoe.

Earl answered promptly, fresh and eager, which was surprising since she was calling well after midnight. "Yes," he answered without the slightest element of annoyance. "How are you, Tresa? Everything okay?"

"Hi, Earl. Sorry to call."

"No problem, I'm just catching up on some reading."

After two in the morning? "Okay, good," she responded, now realizing this whole thing could have waited until working hours. "What are you reading?" she asked to be polite.

"Hemingway. It reminds me of the art of brevity."

Unfamiliar with exactly what he was saying, she made sure he wasn't hinting. "Nice. Well, I'll be short. I just want to make sure I'm doing what I'm supposed to be doing. I was at the scene down at Bragg, I responded to the call here at the Defense deputy director's, and I'm keeping my eyes peeled but also staying out of the way and keeping a low profile. I'm just sitting here parked, wondering what I should be seeing."

"Sounds like you're doing great."

"Seems like I'm wasting taxpayer dollars."

"How do you like your new service weapon?"

"I haven't fired it at anyone, if that's what you're worried about."

"I wasn't."

"Well that's another thing. I've been re-outfitted like I'm on the SWAT and surveillance team." She stared out the windshield at the lights, cars, evidence trucks, and news crews that still came and went in front of the National Capital Region crime scene. "I mean they gave me an extended capacity Glock 17, and in the back of this beast of a truck, I've got the green rail automatic M4 and Tactical 870 shotgun with all the tactical lights and collapsible stock. And then I have half of a surveillance truck in two huge Pelican cases." She flipped her hands up and back down on the steering wheel as if she were having an animated conversation with the odometer. "And I'm driving this monster, which is hardly discreet."

Earl laughed. He said nothing. It didn't exactly validate Tresa's feelings on the matter. "You can blame that on me, Special Agent Halliday. I put the paperwork in, and based on your duty assignment criteria, it likely defaulted to some less-than-optimal equipment. In all honesty, I never even thought about it."

"Yeah, well, I probably should have said something sooner. I didn't really know if I should just roll with it." Tresa opened a search screen on her rugged Toughbook laptop. She accessed the public records view through an FBI virtual private network connection.

"Tresa. You've been on the defensive end for a long time. Let me know if you have questions or have issues with something. Even if it's…late. Bask in the autonomy."

"I guess I still can't figure exactly what I'm looking for and exactly what my job is?" She typed in the address of the deceased. Helen O'Toole. She toggled a tab for associated family for kicks and giggles.

"It won't be apparent at first. Give it time. And patience."

As he spoke, she scanned the name Robert O'Toole and his position within government. It sure seemed to be another terror attack to Tresa, but maybe that was what Earl was talking about by looking at things deeper.

"I want you to be an uninvolved agent at the scene. I want you to be the one who's out of focus. Stay on site as long as you need. Go onto the crime scene if you think you should. Talk to people as you need. But remember, you are a public relations observer assigned to Counterterrorism within the National Security Branch of the Bureau. It's not sexy, it's nonthreatening, but gives you entrée."

"Yeah. A blond girl job." She read the name Warren Woolf. His address was the same as the O'Tooles.

"You and I know that's not what it is."

"I know. Okay," she puffed, swallowing that watermelon-sized pill called pride. "Thanks. Sorry to call, I just—" He also had a residence south of here. She cross-referenced the address to see any other owners.

"Don't apologize. This is your time to shine. Shine you will when the time is right. If you want to go back to the motor pool tomorrow, tell them what you want. If we don't have it, ask them to check if the other field offices have something that may be more suitable. I'll sign off on it. But Tresa…"

"Yeah." Names popped up on the monitor. Again, Robert O'Toole. And Alexander Woolf. *Who's Alexander Woolf?*

"Keep the firepower. You may need it."

"Wait, what?" She hadn't really been listening now that she was distracted by her searches.

"Good night. We'll let you know when it's time."

Tresa didn't hang on his words. Alexander Woolf deceased, she read. She searched family. His wife was deceased, too. Two sons. Dexter Alexander Woolf. No known address. Warren Drake Woolf. Two addresses. The other was a temporary military address. *Military family. Looks like they took him in. But not the brother, wherever he is. But where are you now, Warren Woolf? Let's go for a drive.*

Chapter 28

The ride back from the Potomac boat launch took just over twenty minutes. Neither man spoke further. Drake sat in the silence wondering if Havens felt the same degree of dirtiness ditching bodies in the river. It didn't feel like war. The whole night felt like murder. They were hiding from the law. Drake and Sean had killed the men for a reason. National defense. He took pause with that thought. The killers had tried to kill him for a reason, too. O.T. used to tell Drake something to the effect of, "When you're on the battlefield, remember one thing about your enemy. No one in battle, no matter the side, thinks of himself as the enemy. To each man on each side, their actions are just and their opponent is the enemy. And they will engage that enemy with fervor and righteousness to protect themselves, their comrades, their family, county, or beliefs. You are someone's enemy, Drake. And while you view the opposition as the enemy, remember that when they attack you, they are defending something. Because they see you attacking them. Try to rationalize a conflict with a man who you think is the enemy who sees you in the same way."

The Mohawks attacked us when we became the enemy.

In those silent minutes riding alongside Havens, Drake's conscience took him back nearly a decade. The Mohawks had been like puppies. Those hand-selected Iraqi men followed around their American "friends" wherever they could. When the Mohawks were moved inside the Green Zone areas to live on coalition bases for protection, the Iraqis became brethren to the men of JSOC. To work successfully in war, men had to build trust. The Deltas trusted the Mohawks, and vice versa. Whether the Task Force North's Kurdish Mohawks, those Iraqis in Baghdad or Mosul, or even those in Afghanistan, the model was the same as it had been since Vietnam or even World War II. Locals were befriended to commit acts of Unconventional Warfare. The by, with, and through model. Drake reflected on the fact that in the end, Americans left foreign lands and the local indigenous forces were eaten alive by the adversary, short of the Resistance in Europe, for the most part.

Drake had lived off-base while in Iraq. His unit worked better in the shadows and through safe houses outside the wire. But he knew the Mohawks. If not by name, by face. In truth, he was a bit jealous of the closeness, the camaraderie that was built between the other Tier One counterterror units and those of the indigs. The Mohawks were indeed treated the same. Maybe better. Woolf rationalized that the Mohawks were likely given promises for safe passage to America. That's how the Americans did things. And when those promises fell through, the Mohawks and their families were slaughtered.

Drake stared out the windshield as the headlights cut through the turns and the darkness. It was an easy route, and he was glad Havens drove by recollection from the way in. Havens had been the money man and a logistics guy in operational support. Sean didn't know the Mohawks quite as well, but he had trained them to make businesses look more legitimate. How to navigate corrupt officials. In fact, Sean Havens had helped to build the cover for status and action lie that the Mohawks executed as they outfitted camera cars, infiltrated internet cafes in the Iraqi cities with surveillance and tracking software, and enabled killer drone guidance through emplaced tracking devices the Mohawks had planted.

"Do you blame them for wanting to kill us?" Drake asked out of the blue, his voice surprising him as if he thought aloud.

"The whole world or just Muslims? Or do you mean the Mohawks?"

"Mohawks, for the sake of this conversation." Drake turned to Havens so he could read his colleague's expressions and body language illuminated in the glow from the dash display lights.

After a pause Sean replied, "No. Not at all."

"Would you do the same?"

"I've done worse," Havens confessed. "Are you questioning our mission?"

"Not really." Drake refocused his eyes to the front headlight panorama of asphalt and greenery framing the road. "I'm just thinking about how I'm feeling. How I feel every day. And what I want to do to people who've wronged me."

"You ever see *Old Yeller*?"

"Heard of it." Drake felt himself in the hot kitchen watching his father chip ice. His muscles relaxed, and a calmness passed over him with the comfort of family that he hadn't felt in years. No, since Lebanon, when the same solace washed over him.

"This kid finds a stray dog and brings him in. Kinda like we did with the Mohawks. Mohawks saw hope in something and needed someone to care for them. Or at least we convinced them of it. And that Old Yeller dog, he was like a golden retriever or something, I don't know."

"I got it."

"Anyway, in return for the love that the kid gave that dog, Old Yeller fought off this big-ass cougar—"

"Wolf."

"Huh? It was a wolf? I thought you hadn't seen it?"

"I did. Just wanted to hear you tell whatever you were going to tell me."

Sean glanced over to Drake. A hint of disappointment showed but quickly faded. "Well then you know the fucking dog got rabies and was going to kill the kid, so the kid killed him first."

Drake laughed aloud. "And the moral?"

"You can care for the Mohawks, but they made a decision to help us. They protected us and did what they had to in their home country because it was right for them. They didn't do it because we were going to bring them here. So, when their families were killed, yes, we should have been there. But it's not like they fled the country when we left. They stayed. But now they're rabid. They want to kill us. And we're going to kill them so they don't hurt others. And yes, like the kid in the movie, we're going to get another dog, and when that dog gets sick or we get tired of him, we'll kill them too."

"And you're okay with that?"

"No, I'm not okay with that. I'm a dog guy, not a cat guy. But this is the team we're on. You like football?"

"No."

"All right. Whatever. No judgment. I do, though. Bears fan. And more often than not, they really suck. But they're my team, and every season they lose, I still hang with them because they're *my* team. So, did we betray the Mohawks like we did the Montagnards in Vietnam or wherever else we've dropped in and fucked things up for some indigs? Yeah. And does it suck? Yeah. But it's not like we're car salesmen or own a yogurt shop franchise that we're pushing on foreigners in their own economy. We're killers. And we're America's killers. And we're protecting our team. And if they turn against us, we have to kill them."

"Havens. I don't think you really believe that, do you?"

"No," Sean admitted. "But it helps me sleep at night."

"You sleep well?" Drake hoped that maybe this guy could help with the sleeplessness. The images. The violent playbacks.

Sean remained quiet.

"Yes? No?" Drake pushed.

"I wonder how Lars is doing with your little mess."

Drake thought back to the contents of his bag. He needed to keep those papers safe with him wherever they were going, especially if he wouldn't be back to the ranch for a while.

I may be on America's team, but I'm still keeping options open as a free agent, Drake affirmed to himself.

* * * *

To say Drake was taken aback with the way Lars had cleaned up and staged the house was an understatement. It might have been effective from a forensic standpoint, but it was highly unsettling at face value with the changes that had transpired inside. Drake felt anxiety building but suppressed his feeling to say or do anything. Furniture had been moved to new locations, and pictures and other wall hangings were also changed. It was all wrong. Before, it was just right. Things were even. They worked optimally for Drake. But this was operational, he reminded himself. And operationally, he could let more things slide. Or so he told himself repeatedly.

The big man was seated at the casual dining room table with reading glasses stopped at the bulb of his nose. He was leaning over the laptop screen and simply raised a hand, motioning the men to come over. As Drake's mission mind took over, his compulsions fell off like late autumn leaves.

Lars looked up and broke a wide grin. "Do you guys have enough firepower for the two of you to raid a house in the next couple of hours? And take out five people, maybe?" Lars Bjorklund ran his big sausage-like fingers through thick strawberry blond hair. "I think we've got a real mess on our hands."

Drake and Sean huddled behind the large Norder.

Lars double-checked his scribbled notes before starting in. There were two pages of handwritten assumptions, questions, and linkages.

"Let's start with these guys on the coasts." He pointed to the screen. "California, Georgia. They converge in Utah and have a couple other touch points that come in. About a year or so ago, I read about nuclear power cleanups going on, and there were supposed to be routes to Utah. A mountain or something where they can store nuclear waste. I guess the Mormons are gunna keep it safe or something. So that's one possibility—or things we don't know. But that's my two cents. This"—Lars pointed as he zoomed in—"is us. I wrote down these numbers that I didn't recognize that are central to our exact spot. Called each one from my burner. They all match the phones you guys took off the bodies. So that's good."

"Click this one." Drake pointed to a green dot with a number of data points in a small box on the map display.

"Hang on, youngster, I'm getting to those. These dots match to—"

Drake interrupted, "Good potential about the nuke waste. I've gone through some of these with one of the dead Mohawks. These converged numbers must be a safe house. I'm guessing that's what you think we should hit quick to potentially disrupt some of the other unknowns."

"Exactly," Lars confirmed.

Sean reached over. "Zoom here." Havens was pointing to two separate indicators in the Arlington area.

"I thought you'd like that. Both numbers are geolocated to two pretty nice hotels right now. If you look at the history, they don't tend to move too far from those locations. One of those numbers is the hub of all these other numbers. He's—"

"The handler," Drake and Havens said in near-perfect unison. They nodded to each other. Drake added, "And that guy right here is the ringleader here from where I can tell calls break off and centralize at regular intervals. We need to see who guy number two and guy number one are talking to."

Lars tried to turn around to his two team members. His ample belly and generally wide frame made a slight head turn a better option. "Look, I know you guys have this new secret squirrel killer club going on, but shouldn't we get backup? FBI? Some more G.I. Joes?"

Sean shook his head. "Too many questions. We can't do domestic collection. The two ringleaders probably haven't done anything that—"

"We'd be trying to arrest and prosecute and that could cause other bad guys to go into hiding," Lars finished and capped it off with an understanding nod. "Brings us back to the mission. Task force kill team to move faster. Kill the snakes. I get it."

"Sean," Drake leaned over Lars's shoulder, "We're going to have to do this quick. We can't split up, so do we do a lightning raid and just kill everyone in sight at this safe house here?" He pointed, looking for guidance. "Then jump over here to the hotels, hoping they don't expect us?"

"Crap." Sean walked away to throw around his thoughts.

"What?" Drake echoed with concern.

"We don't have time for breakfast," he pouted. "What kinda stuff you have here to kill people with, Woolf? Guns, explosives, gas." Sean checked the working mechanisms on the ISOF arms now lying on the kitchen counter. "We won't have our arsenal ready for a couple of days. I think we need to hit these guys fast. That means we need to be wheels up an hour ago." Lars cleared his throat. "I don't want to piss on the party, but you guys can only use what the bad guys used. Unless what you've got is unmarked and unregistered. The FBI'll be all over this."

"True," Sean added. "Drake, O.T. said we need to leave a lot of the site intel for the Bureau. Doesn't mean we don't take the good stuff. But there's some type of tacit under-the-table agreement he made with them. So, it also means we leave plausibility that the FBI conducted raids if we can't make them look completely benign. Basically, do some of the work for them but don't leave work for them to do on us. They're covering down on that with a ringer somehow. It just can't be glaringly obvious that a Tier One outfit's working stateside." He added, "when we can help it," as a disclaimer. "Aside from that, our ass is wholly in the wind."

"I haven't gotten to those details." Drake laughed a not-so-funny laugh. "I've learned I'm the last to know and the ideas I think I'm coming up with have already been cemented. So, here's my ask."

"Shoot."

"Havens, I've never worked with you. I don't know your moves, and I don't know your blind spots or tendencies, good or bad, under contact. Until that happens, I go in alone."

Chapter 29

Final preparations and closing up of the farmhouse didn't take long. The plan was to head to the identified safe house but reconvene at a determined point before the takedown. Lars wasn't happy about driving the compact Altima but understood the need for Drake and Sean to coordinate plans. He sped down the long gravel drive and made a swift rolling stop as he turned onto the public road.

Blinding oncoming lights caused him to momentarily shield his eyes, but he stuck the turn and accelerated out of the near collision.

Special Agent Tresa Halliday stomped on her brakes. Nearly six thousand pounds of SUV bucked and fought to move forward as mechanisms and rubber tried in vain to hold the monster vehicle back. Her Dunkin' Donuts cup sent a tsunami of hot coffee splashing onto the panel. Cell phone and laptop jettisoned from the passenger seat into the glove box door. "Jeezus Christ!" she yelled. Her right arm hung paralyzed in midair, unable to decide what to stop of all the loose articles flying around.

The red Altima sped off with a fishtail turn. She made out a massive human form squeezed into the driver's side. The motorist's face looked overweight, eyes wide in a moment of terror then transformed into intent with focus. Maybe someone in their fifties. Obviously a local wasn't expecting anyone coming down the road at this time of night—or was it considered morning?

The only thing within Tresa's power was to flip him the bird and shout a flurry of curses as his taillights faded from her mirror's view.

"You suck, too," she said to the white plastic coffee cup lid that she had pulled off only minutes ago to let the hot liquid cool. It hadn't moved. While she bent into the passenger footwell to retrieve fallen items, a second vehicle sped from the drive and jolted her hand, causing the aftershock to her coffee cup. The second car drove more slowly than the first, and when she looked at the occupants both had their heads turned away from her.

"Little late for a poker run, boys."

The cars exiting the driveway roused her suspicion, but without backup or intel on who else was on the premises, she forced herself to let it go. Tresa took a few minutes more to clean up and reorganize. She checked the navigation display and the map showed that she had arrived. The hidden entrance was not well marked, and the mailbox didn't have an address or box number on the side. Very private. Likely designed that way.

She put the vehicle back into drive, gave some gas then stopped abruptly with a new concern. That was him! Maybe. Was one of the men Warren Woolf? Maybe someone had come to get him after learning of his aunt's death. None of the cars' occupants looked notably Middle Eastern, from what little she could tell. That had to be it. He was just leaving. Probably to go to his uncle's. What lousy timing, she thought.

Can't hurt to just take a peek at the place.

Turning onto the drive, the Chevy Tahoe's lights caught glimmers of crystal light on the narrow shoulder. She flipped on the headlamp brights and exited the SUV to approach the curious debris.

Tresa stooped to examine what appeared to be broken tempered glass. She tried to reposition herself to get out of her own shadow and nudged a few larger granular chunks. Training at the FBI National Academy and more than enough crime scenes told her she was looking at blood spatter on the fragments. It had not yet fully discolored darker, which made the evening's curiosities more apparent.

* * * *

While Tresa was initially cleaning up her own car mess as Drake and Sean passed, Havens instructed Drake to turn away. He, too, did in kind. As they passed, Sean looked to his driver's side mirror. "Big black SUV. Like a Fed Suburban. Couldn't get a good look at the driver. Has brake lights on."

"Is it moving yet?"

Sean shifted from eyes on the road to eyes on the mirror. "Still there."

"Iraqis?"

"I don't think so." Sean could still see the lights a mile down the road. As he turned the vehicle to the right, he lost the view but renewed processing of the potential risk. "You didn't speak to authorities after hearing news of your aunt, did you?"

"No. Can't imagine my uncle would either. I'm guessing Feds are coming by the house. Probably someone from Counterterror. I think we're good. But now they've seen the transports."

"That's exactly what I was thinking. What a start to a low-vis operation. Fuck me now."

"Fuck us, partner."

"Yeah, welcome to domestic ops. Can't call in an airstrike on this battle space," Sean reminded him.

Let's hope not.

* * * *

The host entered Mohammad's room. He carried a glass of water in one hand and an armful of clean towels in another. "How are you feeling?" The frail Iraqi asked with little actual interest. It was clear the wounded man would die soon if he didn't receive proper medical care. A sedative would ensure this, but orders were orders and the former Iraqi translator knew to keep his head down, eyes low, and mouth shut. The Iranians had given him money for a home, a new life, and all he had to do was run a small local office of an electronics import business. It was a pleasant enough job. Easy. Receive packages, create a new invoice based on size and weight, change the content description to one of ten selections on the point of sale and inventory software, reship, and confirm. Done. The work was neither exciting nor intellectually stimulating, but he was working for security and a better life, not professional satisfaction. He snapped out of his reflection with the sound of car doors slamming. *Finally,* he thought with relief. *I can be rid of these men.*

* * * *

Tresa parked her car up the drive and just in front of the Tesla. She noticed the electric extension cord coiled tightly on the side of the carport and wondered how often an owner needed to charge their vehicle and how much a car like that would cost a family full of soldiers.

Agent Halliday strolled the grounds. What she was looking for, she hadn't a clue. A low-toned snap caught her attention, compelling her to investigate farther to the rear of the house. She ambled to what looked to be a large firepit. Cinderblocks formed a wide circle with chopped tree stumps for sitting all around. She loved campfires. A cool night such as this would have been perfect to sit around, have a beer, and listen to the stillness of the night.

There were ten large logs situated outside and around the embers. Each appeared to be precisely spaced from the next by about three feet. Then they were spaced about two feet from the block perimeter. Two of the wide seating logs were toppled over and pushed aside. She shone her light on the dirt gap and eyed a roughly four-foot area where the ground revealed a dragging pattern or skid up to the blocks. There was about a four- to five-foot mass of smoldering debris. She walked up to the ash, coals, and glowing embers and stirred the larger pieces with her boot. Carpet, some clothes, maybe towels, a cushion. Tresa approached the large upholstered chair pad and touched the unburned remnant. It was dry and firm to her push. She suspected it hadn't been just lying out here in the elements waiting to be burned. It wasn't dirty or damp. She smelled her fingers. There was no mildew.

Tresa took a few pictures of the large firepit and the remaining items. She moved as many large pieces out of the fire as she could, hoping they would smolder out and she could have forensic technicians check it out, if needed.

The rest of the front area appeared to be as normal as normal was in a place that was foreign to her. She appreciated the serene property and found herself envious to the point of fantasizing that a place like this would be great to live on. She could see herself walking around over crunching leaves with a warm cup of coffee. Her dog by her side, and not being dog-sat back home. Kodi would love this place. It reminded her of Wisconsin.

Her flashlight was hardly necessary within the first twenty feet of the backyard with the large spots shining across the property. *Definitely going to see the Indians coming to the fort with these security lights.* Tresa wasn't much of a tracker, but she had followed more than one wounded buck into the brush and had examined the area around her tree stand for prints, bed-down marks, and the like. So, it wasn't out of her knowledge base by any stretch to recognize bent grass coming from two people. Maybe three. Possibly four. She was equally attuned to the fact that there was blood and trail across the grass. No one shot deer back here, but someone had definitely been shot. She turned to the prints that came from or went to the tree line. It didn't appear that someone from the road had come through bleeding. She walked farther to the tree line and was surprised to find the barbed wire designed not to keep animals in but people out.

Tresa spun herself around, orienting to the layout and the road. She bet herself that if she followed the trail into the woods it would emerge at the street. Likely right about where she had found the broken glass. If they weren't wounded coming in, others were wounded once they were in.

Given what she knew of the evening and the latest attacks, her initial hypothesis unfolded. *They came for you, too. But you were ready. Either by yourself or with those other men. Unless.* Tresa slowly twirled around again, playing out the hypothetical scene. Now it was a crime scene. *Unless that was your cleanup crew. Did you lure the terrorists here? Were you waiting? Does that mean you know who the attackers are or did they contact you?* Tresa's teeth emerged from the tight lips of problem-solving. Now she was having fun.

* * * *

Drake's ability to track the location of the devices was unfettered with the advanced technical outfitting of his former students. The Mohawks had either acquired or customized enough technology that Drake was familiar with and most likely, in one shape or another, had instructed them how to use.

"I can't believe we're hunting down the Mohawks and that they came after the units. That's not an easy task," Sean mused, more to himself than directed to Drake. "I mean didn't most guys you worked with keep decent OPSEC?"

"I didn't spend as much time with the Mohawks as others did. I stayed outside the wire."

"Okay, well, perfect example. You're not the most outgoing guy I've ever met. I can't see you hosting dinner parties in the hooch." Sean glanced over to his partner. "That's not a bad thing, but I'm guessing you didn't put too much effort into becoming their pen pal or hooking up with them on Facebook, right?"

"Correct."

Sean tapped on the steering wheel as he drove. He was thinking. Backtracking. Replaying the mission from years ago. "No one knew my real name. I came into the camp and outside the wire to meet with some of the Mohawks who were running the businesses." Sean clarified for Drake. "Businesses meaning front companies we built to give ourselves and the Mohawks legitimate reason for being places, shipping and receiving items, to have access to places we wanted to monitor, right?"

"I get it. We completely knew what you guys were doing and how they were set up for placement and access."

"Exactly. So, that Mohawk piece of shit you killed in your house, I recognized. The other two, not at all. We put your guy up with a little cell phone and computer shop a few storefronts down from one of the internet cafes."

"I know exactly where you're talking about. I've been in his shop. Technically, he was one of my guys. About as close as anyone I spent time with, but he still only knew my call sign."

The coldness of Drake's demeanor seemed to switch off and on. "All right, well he knew your call sign. Any other name you would have told him?"

"I mean, maybe someone would have said my name. First or last. But I didn't give out addresses and I've not found much information on myself online when I've checked. Can't speak for the Deltas, but I think they may have shared more than I did. Probably full names. Some guys got pretty close."

"Yeah, but it's not like we have a Tier One Personnel Directory lying around with our work and home addresses and shit like that." Sean looked to Woolf for affirmation. Drake's light shrug translated to *no shit*, which was close enough. "And if these guys were pissed off that we left them behind, and their families got smoked, it's not like they just hopped on an airplane, found an Airbnb, went to Radio Shack to pick up some geek ware, and started hunting operators down. Right?"

"Most of the reconnaissance Mohawks I worked with could get in and out of places like the local social fabric and never raise anyone's eyebrow. They could load surveillance software, do recce, use shit like this." Drake raised the laptop and devices from his lap. "But not that many were killers. They could make IEDs. Went on some nighttime takedowns, and plenty of snatch-and-grabs, but they ended up being translators or putting things in context for us if anyone was left alive."

"That's what I thought. Deltas or ST6 did the raids, and if they used Iraqis as shooters, it was mostly ISOF, like the dudes at your house."

"Your point?"

"My point is, how many of those lazy Iraqis…even the best you trained and worked with…could get a bunch of their bubbas together who just had their families killed, sit down and make up a dead pool list, get to America, get safe houses, get funding, and not royally fuck something up?" Sean paused only for a moment. "Aaand, enlist a few knuckle-dragging ISOF thugs to come along on the road trip like Harold and Kumar Go Hunt Delta?"

Drake was starting to like Havens. The guy was smart. Clearly, he could shoot. And clearly, he was a good lurker. But instead of weaving a big conspiracy web, Drake was more concerned about how two guys were going to go in blind to a safe house filled with at least a handful of trained crows. Drake had conducted more than his share of ad hoc surreptitious entry and termination assaults, which some may call murder, but this felt rushed, uncertain, and rife with variables. He clicked his tongue and counted the tracked devices again on the map indicating the destination as it neared. This wasn't going to be easy, and it was outside his comfort zone.

Drake sized up his new partner with more of a scrutinizing assessment than before. Warm fuzzies were one thing, putting your life in someone's hands another. At first glance, Havens, with salt-and-pepper hair, had to be mid-forties, maybe fifty. He was more spook than shooter, which concerned Drake regarding Sean's breach training. The way Drake saw it, Havens would probably have learned in a shoot house how to open and close the gate. It was pretty standard approach for a combat clear to take each room. Drake could be first man acting as shield. He would pan room and Havens could come in from behind for the quick dirty clear. Muzzle points would do all the commo. Drake and Sean would switch out who picked up long cover. Clear seventy-five to eighty percent of the room before entry and stay out of halls. Then again, that was also what the green beanies all taught the ISOF. So maybe it was stupid and a trap in which the students would know the teachings of the masters. What the Hell were they thinking?

Ask him, Drake, don't wrap your head about something you can talk out. The surreal sensation of Alex Woolf's voice gave Drake a needed nudge. Drake realized that he felt some of that same calmness each time Havens had materialized in the past month. If this was his new teacher, then let the man teach. *The Teacher. Modarris.* And just as soon as a sense of calm had come to him, it was lost.

* * * *

The farmhouse was locked from what Tresa could see, or rather sense, though a few unshaded windows in the darkness of the home and the glare of the security lights illuminating the perimeter. Her gut told her that what she would see, if she could see, would have been a scrubbed scene. And thus, the burning remnants in the yard of the crime or its aftermath. *Hmmm*, she thought, would that mean the large vehicle had the bodies? And who the Hell exactly was Warren Woolf? She wondered if bringing a coffee and some doughnuts to Robert O'Toole in the morning might yield answers if he was willing to talk despite his grieving. And where was Woolf heading? To dump the bodies? "What the Hell." She dialed the FBI field support line. "May as well see if some camera jockeys can see if my suspects went anywhere." Tasking the support team only took a few minutes. She gave the name of Earl Johnson as the approving requester to get things moving. *Let's play this autonomy thing to the max.* And then she asked that the support team send her a copy of Woolf's military records. Tresa was informed that the team would search official military personnel files and send what they could find. Having this kind of power to get things done was a new world to Tresa. It was nice being able to do the work as she saw fit and to make requests that she deemed important. It validated her.

As she walked to the big black beast of an SUV that absolutely screamed FBI or Secret Service to her—and anyone else around—she said, "Fuck it. We're rolling heavy, girl." And hoped she would keep getting some more goddamned respect.

Respect. Tresa returned a look to the Tesla. That's got to be Woolf's car. And if it was, she had just the thing in the back to see where he came and went. A nice little GPS tracker.

* * * *

Drake navigated, giving Sean final driving instructions as they approached the target area. Lars listened in via the Beartooth connection and had slipped his vehicle to the rear, tailing his two colleagues. "Hey," Lars radioed the team, "I haven't heard you guys talking much about how you were actually going to pull this thing off. Think it might be a good time to ask each other to dance?"

Sean chuckled. "I've got some thoughts. It's not like we have a lot of options here, but I'm thinking about steering away from conventional if that's how the bad guys were trained. Drake, any thoughts? Especially since you're probably the most experienced for this sort of suicide mission."

Drake hid his rising smile. "I agree. I think they aren't expecting us, but they'll be able to react to us better if we attack like they've trained. While we were driving I pulled up some visuals of the house and found some sold homes that have what I would think to be similar layouts. The homes in the area are Bungalow raised style. That keeps us on one level, from what I can tell. They have a slight advantage of elevation point if we come in the front or the rear, but that's negligible if we have surprise upon entry. So it's a pretty level playing field from that standpoint. I'm guessing you guys don't have flash-bangs or a door ram anyway, and we're not wearing greens," he surmised, referring to typical assault tools and night-vision goggles.

"Nope. We don't. We'd have to kick or shoot the entry depending on the door. We're going in cowboy."

"That's what I figured." Drake puffed out some growing stress. "According to the specs on most of these homes, they have fuse boxes in the basement and centrally wired fire alarms. Code requires that the basements all have emergency escape windows, too."

"I like what I'm hearing so far," Sean said.

"And you guys need me to just stay in the car and call 911, right?" Lars joked from behind on the radio link.

"Kinda." Drake smiled.

* * * *

Tresa received a text from the FBI support center. The message confirmed that traffic analysis was still working on locating the two described vehicles. There was an end note, however, to call a direct extension number for further clarification about the military records.

Curious, she did so.

"That was fast," the voice answered. "Special Agent Halliday, I assume?"

"It is. And who am I speaking with?"

"Reno Manis, ma'am."

"Well, thank you, Reno Manis. I'd say you were just as fast. And you can call me Tresa. It's late and I don't need the fanfare. What'cha got for me?"

"Not much I'm afraid. Just a number for your guy."

"A number?"

"Yeah, he has a Department of the Army Special Roster designation. They don't list names at that level. Just a control number. I can't see anything administratively about his career history or current assignments. He's buried."

"So, he's Special Forces?" Tresa asked. "Well, that's a common misconception, ma'am. Tresa."

"Just Tresa. What misconception?"

"Well technically, Special Forces is a designated Army command. Not a catchall, and usually not special roster. He's special operations for sure. Now which one, I haven't a clue. But if he's Army, that limits it. Probably Delta or Orange or some CI group. Sorry I can't help more. I see we're working on traffic for you, too. Let me just send them a note for status. Hold one, please."

Tresa's skin tingled with intrigue. She found herself with gooseflesh. This was getting not good but great.

Reno returned to the line. "Looks like they have a few hits. They're sending them now to your device. It'll have another direct line to them if you have more questions. Sound good?"

"You've helped a ton, Reno. Thanks so much!"

"Alright ma'am, you have a good night. Pretty late to be looking at SOF personnel," He laughed. But not too hard. Indeed, he recognized that a designation to DASR wasn't just a way to mask names and histories of special mission unit personnel—it was a notice to piss off and sniff no more.

It was all coming together, whatever it was. Tresa wanted to call Earl but figured she'd wait to see what the traffic surveillance would provide. That and she had to pee.

Chapter 30

Lars Bjorklund remained in the Altima idling down the street until he was alerted to make his move on the target location. Drake and Sean parked their vehicle two blocks over and followed a brush-lined property easement to the target house. Short of having to cross one open-view street, their weapons hidden under shirts like deviant teens smuggling a bong or booze to a pal's house, the two men worked the shadow and shrubs to their concealment.

At the residence's perimeter, Drake checked the signals again for any change in device endpoints or increased activity. Fortunately and unfortunately, the war party inside appeared to remain the same size. The man from Orange gave Sean a nod and motioned that they continue their movement to the designated back blind side of the house. Their optimal point of entry was where one of two basement emergency exit wells were located, to satisfy local egress codes.

It gave Drake a sense of security that he was breaking into a residential safe house in the middle of American suburbia. He suspected—and hoped like Hell—that he was walking into a traditional safe haven situation where an individual or family was giving temporary asylum as opposed to a house full of goons armed to the teeth and trained for high-speed takedowns. This the Birddog prayed to himself as his fingers probed the sides of the window well cover in search of booby traps that could alarm the safe house habitants or explode and cut men's bodies in two.

Clear.

Drake nodded to Havens as he lifted the plastic cover and set it on the grass. Lights in the basement were off, and a quick illumination from a mobile device flashlight showed Drake that there was an unfinished room, nothing obscuring his entry, and the window was a slider with a locking clasp in the middle. He slid into the tight well and found the window was only secured in the metal framing by two metal pins. Drake wished he had an electrical probe that could sense if a window sensor was present. That said, he was reasonably secure with the thought that they had moved around sufficiently without tripping a motion detector, and had some validation seeing no security system signal warnings posted to deter would-be cat burglars over elite, trained assaulters, which didn't happen much in the 'burbs.

Although, Drake thought in hindsight, a hardwired alarm system would be another issue they might have to contend with in the future. Put that down for items to explore if this domestic gig was really going to take shape.

Drake inserted his Griptilian Benchmade AXIS knife between the two window panes and lifted up with extreme care and caution. As he opened the seal between outdoor and within, he felt cool air escape, which was also a subtle sign that there was likely no one sitting in the basement waiting. Or so he told himself. He double-checked Havens, who had his head on a swivel providing cover. Rust on the window lock prevented an easy slide, so Drake had to hammer with his hand against the handle.

The frame collapsed.

"Oh, shit." Drake whispered with presence of mind to keep it quiet. The securing pins of the frame released, and the window toppled inward. Woolf missed grabbing a handhold as the glass tipped and fell. His long legs were tight to the crescent cavern he was stooped within. Just as the bottom lip of the window became exposed, Drake jammed this thumb through the gap then secured his fingers around the thin metal over glass. He flung his arm out and up in a wave to hijack the momentum and float the window away from knocking against the wall.

Phew!

Drake looked up at Havens, who was still scanning but had a thumbs-up lowered to Woolf's eye level.

Holding the window, Drake used his light to rescan the visible area of the basement. Normally he would have liked to have a weapon outfitted with a torch to do his scanning so he could see and shoot. But this was abnormal. And stupid. And unplanned. And it felt more like a crack-fiend robbery than a counterterror assault.

The basement still looked benign, so he slinked in on his back through the opening until his feet touched the floor. Once inside, he waved Havens in, rested the window against the wall, and took both weapons.

Sean made a less than graceful entry but remained quiet.

It was go time.

The assault was to start with a ruse. Havens located the whole-house, wired fire alarm overhead and went to push the test feature. As he reached for the button, two shots rang out from overhead and throughout the house, their source unidentifiable from below.

The gun report was somewhat muffled through the floor overhead, but it certainly caught both men's attention.

"What the Hell was that?" Drake whispered to Sean.

"No clue."

Two more shots cracked overhead.

Both men heard shouting, then screams. Two more shots. One more shot. Another. Another.

"Get moving," Sean quipped. "I'm hitting the button." The smoke detector's high-pitched beeping screamed throughout the home. With the noise confusion, Drake climbed to the top of the wooden basement stairs and waited by the closed door.

The two ISOF commandos were startled. Most American killers would have known it was a fire alarm. Iraqis not so much. This Drake and Sean had not planned on but capitalized on.

The commandos started shouting at one another in confusion. They could see the tiny red alarm light flashing as their senses drew them to the origin point of the sound. The main floor smoke detector was higher than their reach. One commando, a lean, clean-shaven, and handsome Iraqi wearing a cotton Henley shirt with khaki 5.11s took a shot at the alarm. It stopped, but being an integrated system the others continued the incessant beeping.

The men shouted at each other, trying to figure out if the sound was an alert to police.

With less than a minute timed, Sean pushed the reset button on the alarm, and with two chirps, it ceased its alert.

The two Iraqis looked at one another, eyes wide, and started to laugh. Still, they wore concern that their shooting might have sent a signal.

Havens hit the circuit breaker, and the lights went out in the house.

Drake could hear the same two men shouting. He heard no one else. He turned the basement handle and slowly opened the door. The house was dark. Drake could see movement coming into view. The two Iraqis were starting to panic, unsure how to turn on lights, concerned that the military was going to raid them, and arguments over how the Army couldn't kick in doors of a home of Americans and how no one would have called police.

Havens sent a text to Lars, who started the cruise a hundred yards to the house.

Drake knelt low, weapon raised. He turned his wrist slightly up and looked at the faint glow of his watch's second hand and closed his eyes to save his vision.

Havens flipped the power back on, leapt over to the fire alarm, and pressed the button again.

Lars pulled into the drive and pressed the car alarm on the key fob.

Drake opened his eyes and within the slight halo of light snapped off two rounds at one target, two more at another. He pounced up and out toward the men as they fell and continued to send more lead love their way, ensuring each was kissed on the head with a quick double-tap.

Havens was up the stairs and behind Drake. "Got you long!"

Drake swept to his left and fast-stepped to the next room.

"Dead man on couch in here," Sean called out, looking into the living room and seeing Ali with a wrecked forehead.

"Same in bedroom," Drake shouted from the side bedroom to the left. He was in the next room almost before Havens could register his movement.

Drake called out. "They must have taken out the family who lives here. Fuck. All accounted for. You just had to kill a kid," he said to the dead.

"Kill it and wipe it down," Sean radioed Lars, and the honking stopped. "Get the van and pull it to the parallel street. We'll be there in five."

"Roger that," Lars responded.

"Drake, we gotta roll." Sean entered the room half expecting Drake to be standing over the family. Instead, he was stuffing items in his pocket. Was stuffing cell phones and an iPad into what looked to be a woman's purse. Drake brushed past Havens and returned to the second bedroom, searching for electronics. He pushed over the large man with the abdominal wound. "Mohammad, you always were a piece of shit." With a free hand, Drake punched the dead Mohawk in the jaw. As the man's head slammed lifeless and limp to the side, Havens could see the blackened blood and brain blow out on the pillow. Sean looked back at the family. An Iraqi man lay facedown on the floor, an Iraqi woman and teen girl on the bed. The woman was pitched forward, her leg tucked underneath; the girl lay slumped over on her left side. The blood spatter was low on the wall. Not much spray. The wall color was the same as the bedroom in Havens's Chicago home. Close enough anyway. The blood spatter also seemed to be the same silhouette as his own daughter's. But Maggie had lived. Sean walked around the bed and reached for a pulse on the young girl. There was nothing. She was warm. Soft. She had one eye partially open, and

Sean gently brushed it closed. Emotions started to bubble deep from his core, so he moved out to find Drake.

"I have all the phones I can find." Drake stood beside the kitchen table with a fistful of purses. "And another laptop. Looks like it was the resident's. It was still open, screen on. Passcode-enabled, but it hasn't timed out. I can't change it. But we need to roll, Brother." As Havens cruised down the hallway, images of the wife's head wet with blood flashed before him. The terminal wound was agape. It struck Sean for the umpteenth time in his career doling death how inhuman people could look with massive battle wounds. The young girl, however, took her position with all the other children tucked in the back of his mind. They were the ones who he felt could open their eyes at any moment and come back to life. He hurried toward the basement stairs, not looking back and hoping not to see them in his dreams, but he had to check things out in the living room. He could already feel their souls weighing heavy on his heart.

Drake was staring at him. "They're going to think we killed the kid."

"Leave the weapons. Let's give them a wipe," Sean said.

"I'll put one in the hands of the dude on the bed. You put one on the guy on the couch, and let's get the hell out of here. Let ballistics and tech whizzes figure it out. It won't add up, but they can handle that."

"Good call," said Sean.

"Back out basement."

"Right behind you."

Sean was first out, with Drake to follow. Havens agreed to move out ahead while Drake closed up the window. If authorities or any other surprises came along, it was best to create space. Daybreak was coming.

With the window closed up and the grate being the final touch, Drake was sure they were out of danger. Light and movement caught his right eye. He looked up over his shoulder to see a closed shade flop back in place from the window on the second floor of the house next door. The light went off, and as Drake waited, the shade moved again. He saw a dark shadow in the window, and the shade whipped closed.

"Great." Drake huffed as he gathered the large handbag and bolted after Havens to the extraction...minivan, or whatever the term for that ugly-ass car was.

Chapter 31

Tresa Halliday was at a literal fork in the road. She had traveled for nearly an hour along the route the FBI's support unit provided. Both vehicles she had spotted earlier in the evening had followed the same route. Red-light cameras were unable to produce anything with the exception of license plates. It had turned out that the white van had plates not registered to that vehicle. Probably stolen. The second was also a plate not registered to the same Nissan Altima. In that case, the Nissan had been listed as stolen from an Enterprise Car Rental lot in North Carolina weeks ago.

That was the definition of "you'll know it when you see it." Tresa tried to wrap her head around what she knew. Or thought she knew. There had been a series of attacks. Muslim terrorists in the homeland. The targets had been military men. Fort Bragg was the home to not only military units but, more importantly, special operations units, and of course the National Capital Region had all sorts of defense personnel. Warren Woolf was one such man. He could have been a target or possibly his uncle. Someone might have tried to attack him at his own house, but he was ready for them. Now, he was in the middle of a Virginia suburb, or had continued on somewhere out of camera range.

Tresa gave a big yawn. "Not bad for a day's work, girl."

She wiped the grime off her teeth and rotated her watch hand to view. It was five a.m. What military man didn't get up before six? She sent a message to the support team requesting any new updates on the vehicles, threw the truck in drive, and headed off to the Dunkin' Donuts closest to Robert O'Toole's home.

* * * *

Drake gave a double take when he arrived at the street. The sprinter van was where it was supposed to be, but it wasn't the same van. The side door slid open, and Sean Havens motioned Woolf inside.

"Let's go," he encouraged quietly.

"Where did you? How?" Drake stammered as he strapped in.

Lars was inconspicuous with his acceleration, but they were without question getting the Hell out of Dodge fast.

Sean gave a thumb in the direction of the rear, where white vinyl auto-skins lay crumpled in a heap.

Drake was impressed. "You covered the car. It's black."

"Nope," Lars called back. "Midnight blue. Looks dark blue in the day and black at night. Two-fer. We can skin the vehicles to be anything."

Woolf turned to Havens, who was sitting next to him on the passenger side. "You did this at Martha's Vineyard. I thought you had two cars."

"Not my first rodeo." Sean smirked. "Hey." He reached over and nudged Drake's arm. "Nice work in there. I'd say that lil' plan of yours did just fine. Bad outcome, but we did our part."

Drake said nothing.

"You all right, Woolf?"

"I was seen."

"Seen?" Lars turned his head back to the crew.

"You just drive," Sean scolded. "Seen by whom?"

"Don't know. Someone next door. Up in a bedroom. I was still in the shadows, so they didn't see much. But they know someone came out of the house. Someone very much alive."

Sean let his head fall back against the seat. "Well, that's not good, but it's not horrible. Until we stop running behind an eight ball, we're bound to have setbacks. We made it out alive with a half-assed plan, no offense, and took out two more crows. Number's going down."

"Besides that, I'm good." Drake unbuckled, reached over to the passenger seat near Lars, and snatched the laptop. He patted Lars on the shoulder. "Thanks for the ride. Again."

"No problemo, amigo."

When the computer rebooted, Drake pulled up the matrix of mobile devices. "We got all the phones. Now the question is when we're going to get a call."

"If the goons we took out were tasked to clean up loose ends, I think we can expect one soon."

"Agreed," Drake said. "We need to get to what I'm assuming is the cell leader."

"Let me know where I'm going. Chicago boy here. Not too familiar with things out here yet."

"Yeah, pulling up a screen." Drake fingered the keys and zoomed in. A realization hit him like a Muhammad Ali phantom punch. "If this guy is heavily armed, what are we using to take him out?"

Sean smirked. "You."

* * * *

Tresa walked into the unlocked O'Toole residence without a knock. There was still an evidence van and two Suburbans parked out front. Her entrée was a dozen doughnuts and the box of joe.

Special Agent Halliday was dressed in standard khaki pants and sported an FBI-issued Outdoor Research black nylon jacket over a navy knit polo shirt. Blending in could mean standing out to others and fitting right in with colleagues. She peeked a head in to ensure the techs were cool with someone entering their scene. Had they insisted she stay outside of the home or perimeter, she would not have protested. They had their job, she had hers. That, Tresa understood and respected.

The tech motioned Tresa in. "Please sign in. List is right over there to the right, on the stairs."

"Thanks. Is Mr. O'Toole up?" She smiled. "I have breakfast for you guys."

"He's gone. Left just after five a.m. Headed into work."

"Don't suppose you know—"

"Pentagon," he interrupted. "But that's all I know."

"Great." She faked the best smile she could. "I'll just put these in the kitchen."

"Thanks," the tech replied. "Hey, Dan, doughnut chick's here with breakfast if you want to break for a sec."

Assholes.

Chapter 32

Getting into the office at five a.m. isn't uncommon at the Pentagon. A number of men and women show up early as part of routine. They were trained that way, and for most, it became programmed into their biological alarm clock.

Robert O'Toole planned to start the morning with black coffee in a black JSOC ceramic mug and then figure stuff out on what he considered home turf. As a career military man, he spent most of his time away from home. To stay at the house now felt foreign. He was a stranger in his own skin at home and longed to be back in the SCIF if he couldn't be in the field.

"Bob." Mark Watley rose from his desk, surprised. His coffee was already half drunk. Watley wore nylon running pants, running shoes, and a Kelly green T-shirt with a SOCCENT crest on the left breast representing the special operations command central, a sub-unified command where he had supported the war efforts in Iraq. "I, uh, I heard about Helen. I'm so sorry. Can I help you with anything?"

Bob motioned to the ASD to have a seat by patting an outward hand in the air like a basketball dribble. "Thanks, Mark. It's being taken care of. I've gotta make some calls. May not stay here long. Just needed to be here."

"Let me know what you need. And, uh, if there are services, Joan and I will be there."

"Yeah, it's going to be a couple hours south of here. Down at Hollywood Cemetery. Her family's there. She'll be cremated, what's left of her, and interred in their mausoleum. It's what she wanted."

"Oh, good. Well, we'll be there. No question."

"Sure, Mark. Thanks. Hey, I do have something you can help with."

"Anything."

"I've got a personnel redirect and an IN-SAP that needs to be submitted," Bob said, referring to IN-SAP as an Intelligence Special Access Program that required a final stage of establishment along a set timeline for funding and billets. "Did you already do the proponent submission, slides, and all that manpower request stuff?" Mark asked, knowing O.T. cut corners where possible, but times had changed. There were processes for processes. Even for things that didn't officially exist. Because that was the process. And such was progress.

"Yeah, it's just another phase under a program I've already got running. No biggie. The personnel change is for Drake. He needs a rest. Thinking of his options for the future. He's sticking around CONUS for the time being. I pulled some strings," Bob shrugged, feigning qualms about the nepotism play. "Let me get my notes from my desk."

"Sure. But won't his new unit send out the confirmation first?"

"I need to move him in, Mark." Robert's tone was flat.

"I understand, buddy. So, if I understand, you just need me to slot him in, and then basically open the funding funnel for your program, too."

"Yeah, if there's some admin that can update the records and I can give you temp access to the program so you can submit the SAP change."

"Anything I should know about?" Mark was delicate as he probed. He wasn't a secret weenie who wanted to be read in on everything for egotistical purposes. Rather, he remained one of the few people to protect Robert O'Toole from himself and his proclivities for the dark side of war that often tossed out rules, morality, and accountability. But such was the game of war for those who wished to win. And evil it could be, but a necessary evil, nonetheless.

Robert just saw it as shit needing to be done. Sometimes you rolled up your sleeves and got a little dirty.

O.T. contemplated what Mark should know, which was nothing. "Program code name is ICEPICK. Aside from that, run-of-the-mill project for some collection work. I'll be surprised if it ever sees light."

"Ha," Mark laughed. "Is that a euphemism?"

Time to shut up, Mark. "You know how it goes with approvals these days."

"I do, but what approvals would you need if your program is tucked behind an unacknowledged waived SAP? It's already exempt from Congress or committees. Sure you need to put it there?"

O.T. moved from the doorframe, stepping closer to Mark. Robert's smile evaporated, and with it, so did Mark Watley's. "If we're playing some kind of game here, *buddy*, I can't even say 'no comment' because the program doesn't exist. If you don't have time, I can do it."

"I've got time. I just know, and you know, there's that memo we got. We're not supposed to be increasing USAPs. I'm assuming SECDEF is at least aware?"

"I know a lot of Eagle Scouts, Mark. It's a pleasure having you police my camp and telling me where I should piss and where I shouldn't. But remember, I was a Scout too. Not as high level, but experienced enough to know that *you* should know where not to piss too." O.T.'s smile returned with *fuck you* written in invisible ink but plain enough for Mark to read. "Can I refill your coffee, Mark?"

"I'm good. Thanks."

"Okay then. Thanks for your help." Robert gave his colleague a wink and turned on his heels, wishing to high heaven that such a dependable guy didn't need to sniff O.T.'s shorts so much.

Within thirty minutes, Drake Woolf was pulled from a gray program that hid his identity to a black program where he was assigned to a reserve unit in full view of anyone who accessed his file. Hidden in plain sight. And ICEPICK was fully operational. As soon as O.T. received the administrative email confirmation that a program had been updated, he started moving the rest of the funds, added monies to purchase cards, and shifted some unit resources to new owners. He filed the urgent request to JSOC to move specified equipment to a delivery location, then specified the recipients to move the content into a digitally secured storage container. That information was sent to Sebastian, who, in turn, sent it to Sean Havens.

Sean read the message just as Lars walked in through the hotel lobby.

"May I help you?" a twentysomething Ethiopian woman asked retired detective Bjorklund.

Lars yawned and twisted his frame. Two cracks sounded, and the hotel desk clerk winced. "Yeah, young lady, you can." One reddish blonde bushy eyebrow rose. "Where can I get about thirty years back of my life and about a hundred hours of sleep that I've lost?"

She giggled. "I can provide you a room for some rest, but I don't think you look much more than a young boy." She played with him, her heavy accent making the appeasement sound that much more truthful on her part.

Lars gave a louder than needed bellow. "You're a smart one." He pointed to her as he leaned over the desk and pulled a thick brown leather wallet from his back pocket. The cowhide was well-worn and deeply scuffed. He opened it up and surprised the clerk with the flash of a badge, which he quickly closed back up and returned to his rear pants pocket.

"I need your help." Lars looked to his left and right dramatically, playing things up a bit. "I'm looking for a Middle Eastern man." "Sir, many of our guests are from the Middle East. We have many who stay at this hotel. I could not tell you just one."

He knocked on the desk and stood back up to full height. He tipped up his tweed Irish Donegal cap. His eyes were wide and his mouth soured to a pucker. "Oh, I have no doubt." Lars cracked his back again, hands on hips. As he delayed and the clerk waited for his next words, he hoped she was probing her mind for someone in particular that she might think looked suspicious. Unfortunately, she was distracted by the protruding belly and deep navel that were saying hello from under his maroon sweatshirt as he twisted.

"I'm looking for someone who may have been staying here for a couple weeks. Maybe more. Someone probably pretty average-looking. He might keep to himself. He probably doesn't come or go at any set time like a businessman on a repeat schedule. He may not even come down into the lobby much. He may just stay up in his room. Anyone come to mind?"

"We do have a guest who has been here for nearly two months. He has a suite. He is a very nice man; I don't think he is a criminal. He is a businessman and is staying here until his personal items and family can arrive. He is looking for a house. There is another man..." Her face scrunched as she contemplated the details. "No, I don't think he is a bad man." She laughed.

"Why is he so funny?"

She covered her mouth as she continued to laugh. The clerk tried to regain composure. "He loses everything." She bit her lip, trying to keep control. "He can never find his room key and leaves his bag in the dining area. He leaves his phone at the bar." She shook her head and finger amused at the instances that apparently struck her funny bone. "One time he came back to the table after breakfast looking for his phone. He went to the table, right over there"—she pointed across the corridor to the open dining area—"and took our other guest's phone and wanted to look at it. Ah, it was the other guest I spoke of." She laughed again. "He was not so very happy that the phone was taken. I have never seen him get so mad. He must have been expecting a very important call." She flushed struggling to regain composure.

Lars tilted his head. This was interesting. In Lars's extensive law enforcement experience, it was patience and probing that got answers, not intimidating posture or badgering questions. He gave a laugh to share in the moment. "I think if he was expecting a call from his wife who is so far away, he could get very mad." Lars lifted his brow again, waiting.

"Ohhh, yesss. I can speak a little Arabic, and even though I could not understand all of his words...I knew he was mad." She made a hand gesture that looked like she was brushing something from her shirt.

Lars got a kick out of how enthused she was about the incident, but he wanted to know more about a point she made. "It wasn't Arabic?"

"No. I teased him, too. He says he's from Dubai. Yes, Dubai. But he was very mad in what I think is Persian. He says he speaks too many languages to remember what he says. I like him." She shook her head. "He is not a criminal."

"It sure doesn't sound like it. I'm guessing he's not a criminal either and that he's downstairs every day for breakfast at the same time, too. You are a great judge of character, I'm sure."

The clerk couldn't have shut up if she wanted to. She had an audience, and she wanted to ensure this detective knew how innocent her guest was. "Yes. Yes, he is. Every day. Seven thirty in the morning. You can set your watch to him. And he sits in the same place, every day. Fruit, an egg, sliced tomato, and two cups of black coffee. At eight thirty, he goes back up to make some calls. He always reminds me. No cleaning service." She started to giggle again and covered her mouth.

"He doesn't like cleaning?"

"Not that, Sir." She covered her mouth again. "He says that is his bathroom time. He is very funny man."

"Well I hope he doesn't get stuck in an elevator here. That would be embarrassing if he was on camera with a bathroom accident."

She laughed again. "No, sir, I don't think this would happen, and there are thankfully no cameras."

"Oh, c'mon, you have to at least have cameras in the hallways to see who eats people's leftover room service."

It was an odd question that she struggled a bit with, but one thing she knew. "No, sir, no cameras in the hallway."

"Well, I am happy and sad." Lars extended his hand. "It sounds like I have the wrong hotel, but it was a pleasure to be entertained by you. You have a very wonderful day. I'm sorry to have bothered you."

"Pleased to help, sir."

He turned away knowing they had a solid suspect. Lars walked out to the parking lot and did a little wiggle dance. It wasn't flattering. But he now also knew they had an hour to toss a room, and a likely pattern that could be timed for termination. It felt good to be a cop again.

* * * *

When Tresa answered the phone, she was excited to find Earl on the other end.

"Late night?" he asked.

"Still going, Earl. Pretty exciting, too."

"Oh?"

"After we spoke last night, I decided to go for a drive. I headed out to a second home belonging to the O'Tooles. Turns out it's where his nephew lives."

"I hope you weren't knocking on doors in the middle of the night."

"Didn't have to. He and his crew, well, I think it was his crew, Warren Woolf, that is, he flew outta his drive like a bat out of Hell." Earl said nothing, so she continued without a beat lost in her excitement. "I wasn't going to follow them and decided to pull into a private drive. And here's where it gets better. I notice broken glass at the driveway entrance. Check it out. Blood on it. I head up to the house, and guess what I find?"

"If I guess, it'll spoil the story if I'm wrong. Continue, please." His voice was calm. It was hard for Tresa to read. It was pretty damned exciting to her, even if Earl's personality was two pumps away from being a fully embalmed corpse.

"I found shit burning in a firepit. Blood-soaked towels, rags, and a seat cushion. Some serious shit went down."

"Why didn't you call it in? Perhaps the men you saw killed Drake?"

"Drake Woolf? It's not Warren?"

"You were going to tell me why you didn't call it in."

"Can't say that didn't cross my mind. Except the footprints in the back leading to the house and the broken glass also led to more blood."

"You should have called our people to the scene. Maybe have forensics take a look. Technically, it's a related potential crime scene."

Tresa brushed it off for the moment. "There's more. Turns out, Warren Woolf, Drake, the nephew, but it sounds like you already know that, is on some military secret roster. Special ops stuff. Maybe you know that, too?"

"Continue, please."

"All right, whatever. I was curious about where he was going, and he and another car were headed out of the area and back toward DC."

"That *is* interesting."

"Which part?" she asked, her tone hampered with the weight that she deserved a bit more validation of her goddamned efforts all night long in the darkness, driving all over the place, being seen as the doughnut chick, and having to pee in two filthy locations where they could have at least cleaned it once a month. Oh, and spilling coffee all over herself and the big-ass ride.

"The part that he drove to the NCR after potentially having some sort of sordid altercation, if I am understanding you correctly."

"I lost him. The video and camera feeds lost him. I tasked surveillance support."

"I am aware that you tasked them. Good use of resources."

Tresa thought about the approval flow and that even if she had the approval status, her boss would have been made aware. Checks and balances, plus, she had been caught using Bureau resources for personal use. He had given her a long leash, but she knew he would be fine strangling her with it if she screwed up. "I guess in the end, what I think I have is the terrorists were either looking for Mr. Woolf or could have been looking for both him and his uncle. I think they headed over to the second home and Woolf took 'em out. I think he and his guys are either looking to ditch the bodies or warn someone else or find whoever is responsible for maybe more attacks. I'm not really sure, but I know it's a lot more than I had eight hours ago."

Earl said nothing.

"Well, how'd I do?"

"I'd say it's a good start."

"Good start? Tell me who else would have figured out what I did and run it down like I did in that short a time?"

"Agent Halliday, it's not a competition. Your efforts are commendable, but they don't stop there. There's been another attack. I need you to check it out."

"Oh my God. I had no idea."

"It's not public yet. It's different."

"What happened?"

"Some foreigners were killed early this morning. They were undocumented. Middle Easterners."

"Is it related? The attacks have been against military personnel. Or are you saying someone—"

"I'm saying," he interrupted without raising his voice, "that I want you to check it out. From what I saw from the traffic camera reports you were receiving, the crime scene is in line with the route you were pursuing."

"Oh my God. That's awesome!" Tresa was elated and made no efforts to hide it. She'd high-five the rearview mirror if it wouldn't leave her hanging.

"A young girl was killed, Special Agent Halliday. A woman and man, likely her parents. Four others. We can't confirm who killed whom, but if you believe Mr. Woolf was involved, I need you to pursue it." Earl's tone was one of genuine disappointment. Sorrow. Tresa was a bit surprised at that. His typical demeanor spoke to her as one who could remove himself from death, even that of a child. It softened her judgment of the boss.

"I'm sending you the address. Usual protocols. Be discreet, don't mess with the crime scene, but get the answers you want."

"Yes, sir. Thank you, sir."

"And Tresa, call in the Woolf location. Let's get it checked out."

"Will do." While Tresa remained excited about her work, she was refocused. Another kid had been caught in the middle. She only hoped it wasn't at the hands of Warren Woolf. If she was going to be honest with herself, it was because the guy seemed pretty damned cool on paper and she adored his wooded property.

Earl's next call was to General Owen Mathieson, the secretary of defense.

"Didn't expect to hear from you. How goes it in the cesspool sewers?"

"You couldn't even pull this off for a month!" Earl screamed.

"Whoa. Earl. Relax." The SECDEF was fully amused with the calmest man in Washington's complete unhinging.

"You fucked up. Fucked it all up."

"Earl, I have no idea what you're talking about, but clearly if it's a secure line, you have my attention."

"The program. I agreed to put someone on your program so it would be on the Bureau books but so no one else would be able to look into it. I put the biggest fuckup I could find. And in one day she got a scent. Shut it down."

"You need to take this up with O.T."

"His wife was just murdered. I'm really going to call and bitch him out? Shut it down."

"Tell me what happened. I'm listening."

For the next five minutes Earl Johnson briefed the Pentagon's head dog on how the FBI's most unlikely ghost was on their trail. "I was willing to cover for you guys. But you got a kid killed. That's going to draw attention. This program was a bad idea from the start, and if it's going to overtly disregard the Constitution and conventional rules of war and good judgment, I want no part of it. Even behind closed doors, the Bureau will have no part in it."

"I'll shut it down. I think it achieved what we needed it to in the short term anyway. O.T.'s wife's ceremony is tomorrow. I'll give him a day. Meanwhile, I'll get with Ben Steele. He can let the president know. Can't say it didn't come at a cost. You all are getting funds, and we just put in motion the closing out of a unit to save some high-brows' skin."

"Spare me," Earl hissed. His blood pressure slowed to a Class IV category of powerful rapids and boiling eddies coursing through his body. "You assured us it would primarily be an intelligence collection team, and if necessary they would terminate if there were no other options. It was a hit squad all along. I knew it as soon as O.T. was involved."

"It's done, Earl," Owen placated while fully bemused. "Done. Now call off your dog."

"I can't."

The tables turned, and the SECDEF's bureaucratic role flipped to a much younger infantryman that still lived inside the general. "Why the fuck not? I said it's done. I killed my end, you kill yours."

"Your program left trails. It wasn't supposed to have trails. That moves them from operators to criminals. If it leads to me, I did my job. The Bureau does its job."

"You're being a cunt, Earl," the Marine barked.

"I know," the spy hunter conceded. "Redskins opener on me."

"Football is into the fourth week."

"Next year then."

"You don't even like sports, Johnson."

"But I value my allies. And they respect my duty. As I do yours."

"You're a real sonofabitch. You at least going to the service?"

"I'll send something. Robert O'Toole won't miss me. Send my genuine condolences and envy. I'd trade spots with him in a second," Earl Johnson said, his pulse back to a normal chill heart rate of sixty-five beats per minute.

Chapter 33

Mohsen was irritated but not concerned. The operation had yielded great success despite the associated risks and losses. Frankly, it was a miracle that things had gone so well. He tried the phone numbers of Phase I Mohawks and USOF one more time. On the third number, he had success. The team from Indiana was nearly in town. "Your target is to be executed tomorrow," he confirmed, and then it was time for breakfast.

When Lars re-entered the vehicle, Drake and Sean were hovering over a laptop and talking a million miles a minute. "Good news," Lars presented to the team.

"Hang on, big man," Drake said. "Phones are ringing off the hook. They must know now."

"There's another one." Sean pointed to the screen.

Drake banged on the keys, bringing up two three-by-four-inch white, framed boxes. "Same guys he was in touch with yesterday. Came from Crane, Indiana. Isn't that where the Navy does sniper school training?"

"Yeah. They do quite a bit of odd stuff out there. Question is, how many Iraqis are there and why."

"Training. We bring them over all the time. Could be more USOF. Maybe we can find someone who would know. I mean, what else could it be?"

Havens shook his head. "Who knows what's next?"

"Hellooo." Lars sat in the driver's seat, facing out the window. "Either of you knuckle-draggers care to hear what the only real detective here was able to uncover?"

Drake and Sean chuckled at being called knuckle-draggers. Each had experienced quite the opposite coming from the Intelligence space, where they were most often deemed the "plant eaters" or "booger eaters" but rarely mistaken for the knuckle-dragging shooter types. Knuckle-dragger was fitting now, but the irony was not lost on the intel weenies who just happened to kill a lot of people these days.

"Go ahead, Lars." Sean reached over and patted his brother-in-law on the shoulder in an overly done apologetic gesture of kinsmanship. "Sorry about that."

"I got him." Lars turned around. "He'll be downstairs shortly having breakfast. I know what he'll order, where he'll be sitting, and the clerk didn't realize it but she started doodling his room number while chatting me up. Weird chick, but she was happy to talk. He'll be out of his room for an hour. Who's the bigger geek for tossing the guy's room? I can't go back in there without raising suspicion."

Drake's eyebrows rose with the big win. There was indeed something about this big oaf. He liked to play dumb. And of course, Sean liked to play the guy off like he was dumb. But Drake sensed the shining on. Lars Bjorklund was not a man to be underestimated.

Drake volunteered to go check out the room. "You keep an eye on him when he eats breakfast." He turned to Lars. "He eats in the hotel?"

"Right through that window." Lars pointed toward the atrium, which was built off the side of the structure and overlooked a large pond with multiple small fountains.

"Cool. I can go up, see what he might have upstairs, and wait for him to come back to the room. If I find enough stuff, I take him out. If not, I sit down and chat with him for a bit."

Drake's proposal was clear to everyone in the van. He had no qualms with dirty work. It was a little unsettling to Sean and Lars. Each could see something deeper in Drake Woolf that was much more than a killer, but something had been lost along the way. And it was a long way away. Guys like that usually lived by the sword and died by the sword before they found their way back. Or they took themselves out on their own—a tragedy Drake could be on the path toward.

Sean agreed. "I'll go keep an eye on the guy. Give me the deets. Drake, you wanna download the Beartooth app? I can radio or text you when you're inside. We should be connected." Sean cast an eye that was meant to tell Drake he was on a team now, and he would act as such.

"I'm good with it." Drake nodded to Lars that he would accept the device. "I just download and pair it with Bluetooth or something?"

"That's it. Should work anywhere in the building. All secure, won't be blocked." Lars handed the small gray device over to Woolf.

Drake fiddled with the electronics. "Do we know if he's alone in the room?"

Lars pursed his lips.

"Lars?" Sean questioned.

The big Swede grimaced. "I forgot to ask."

"That's awesome." Drake said sarcastically and reached out a hand to Sean. "Sidearm, please. Any edged weapons in this short bus?"

"Screwdriver." Lars shrugged. "Guess you're out of luck. It's an up-and-coming program, if you couldn't tell."

"I'll take it," Drake replied without a flinch.

Sean was the first one in the hotel. He walked with purpose to the restaurant, giving the desk clerk a slight smile and nod before finding an optimal table for eyes on target. There were only a few patrons dining: a businesswoman who appeared to be settling in, a large businessman settling up the bill, a young man wearing a flat-brimmed ball cap hat tilted off to the side, which pissed Sean off to no avail, and a family of five where the dad waved a fork full of sausage at a toddler and a mom cut up pancakes while a teen daughter ignored everyone and tapped on her mobile device. They must not have known what sort of hotel this was when they booked. Havens stared at the pancakes.

"Coffee?" The server startled him.

Bad Havens. Screw up when you're solo. The war-weary spook chided himself for being slow on the uptake. He needed to fine-tune his game, but frankly, he was losing his edge. Sean Havens had worked discreet programs for years as a civilian under the cover of a traveling businessman. He'd moved money, established safe houses, planned social cultural uprisings, and taken out his share of threats to national security by proxies and by hand. He was good. And he'd been trusted. But he'd also been lied to and betrayed. The latter had turned his family upside down and left more than one friend lying faceup or facedown filled with lead. It was a life he'd chosen but couldn't escape. Whether it was duty, fantasy, or some other categorical bullshit reason, he didn't know and didn't care. All he knew was that while he was in the dark world he could only think of getting out. When he was out, he wasn't himself until he was back in. It was a cyclical mind-fuck that addicted him like a crack whore and similarly destroyed all those around him.

"Sir? Coffee?"

"Yeah," he responded to the tall, blond, rather effeminate male hovering above him. The lean man had an armful of woven friendship bracelets and a number of large rings on his hands. They reminded Sean of his now-deceased aunt and the custom jewelry she wore. Large stones. Some carved wood. Myriad metals. He found it odd that this kid had similar taste, but the familiarity of it all brought Havens to warm childhood memories, and he passed neither judgment nor critical eye.

"Anything else?"

"Pancakes. I'd like some pancakes, please. And if you can please make sure the world doesn't blow up before I eat them, it would be amazing."

The server crinkled his face, not really understanding what yet another weird customer was saying—whether trying to be funny, being mad at the world, or whatever else people were thinking when all they had to do was say what they wanted and not complain when they got it. Was it too much to ask?

"I'll tell the chef you want four buttermilk pancakes," he said with a glare. He bent a hand to Havens. "And I'll tell him to hold the rapture. Or Armageddon, or whatever your heart desires." The young man smiled.

"Thanks, Sherman," Sean said reading the name tag.

"Just Sherm. And you're?"

"Hungry." Sean extended his hand. "But you can call me Don."

"You don't look like a Don."

"You don't look like a Sherm."

"Faaair enough." Sherm rolled his eyes. What that meant, Havens didn't know, but the kid was nice enough and Sean might need eyes and ears where he didn't have them. The waiter would do.

And like clockwork, the target arrived in the dining area with a rushed gait. Body language told Sean the man's concern seemed to go away upon seeing his table free.

Mohsen surveyed the room. He spent a little more time taking in the man with salt-and-pepper dark hair. He looked at the guy's shirt. His pants. His watch. His mobile device and its case. Shoes. Hands. How the stranger held his posture. Where his eyes went as he drank his coffee. Mohsen craned his neck to see if he could see the color of the man's coffee. And then regarded the number of sugar packets torn and crumpled on the saucer, a spoon atop staining the white paper, the creamer close at hand, and the fact that the man sat in the open with his back not to a wall. The man was clean. And handsome.

Sean sipped his coffee and controlled the wince from the sweetness. *The shit I do for tradecraft.*

Drake Woolf entered the common area of the hotel and checked his watch with overt annoyance. He messed with his mobile device and lifted it to his ear. "You coming down or what?"

Drake paused speaking and listening to no one. "You still need an hour? What've you been doing?" He chuckled aloud. "Never mind. I don't wanna know. What room number?" Woolf paused again. "Put some coffee on. We can do a conference call from the hotel room then head over. I'll be right up."

Drake pressed the up button at the elevator bank and waited while the car came down and the clerk went back about her business.

Lars remained in the vehicle. While he waited, he toyed with the laptop Drake had found at the house. The computer was left unlocked so the ex-detective could rummage around files and whatever else he could access.

The keys were standard. The filenames in My Documents basic. There were fewer documents in the files than there were in the desktop display. Whatever the reason didn't matter. Lars started opening files and hunting. Within minutes, it was clear that the laptop was used to store business files. Invoices, transactional export and import spreadsheets, business ownership documents, etc. For kicks and giggles, Lars Google-searched on his mobile device the name of the company. It was legit. Lars searched a little deeper and found other affiliate companies. They, too, appeared legitimate. The breadcrumbs showed him the way, so dive he did into the interwebs. And it was nothing. Maybe something. Curious for sure. The dead dude's business spun all the way up to a US State Department-endorsed multinational corporation. According to what Lars was able to discern, it started in Baghdad, enveloped a number of small businesses ranging from electronics to auto parts to date palm processing to soft drinks. Now the ownership structure was located in Dubai. Lars did a Google Maps search of the address. It wasn't what he expected. There was no corporate headquarters. The address was just a suite in what appeared on the satellite map image to be a series of buildings just outside an industrial port. Lars opened another search string and pasted the address to see what Google would pull up.

"You dirty shits," Lars exclaimed. "You dir-ty little shits."

Lars went back to State Department declarations and initial funding. He scrolled the document to the bottom. It was endorsed by Ambassador Benjamin Steele, administrator of the Coalition Provisional Authority of Iraq, with an acknowledgement by blah, blah, blah prime minister, ministers—Iraqi, Iraqi, Iraqis…and finally, Lieutenant General Owen Mathieson, director of the Office for Reconstruction and Humanitarian Assistance. "Oh, shit. Here we go again," Lars mumbled with the dread of yet again going after an apparition that came back guns blazing.

Drake got off the elevator two floors lower than the target's room. Before could exploit a room for sensitive intel, he needed access. He found exactly what he was looking for and excused himself while a rushed businessman wheeled a suitcase into his way and jockeyed around Woolf in the corridor. His new target was a cleaning attendant. She whistled as she tidied, her cart outside the room's open door. Drake eyed the cart, not seeing what he was hoping to find lying on the top of the shampoo, conditioner, and other complimentary mini toiletries.

He rapped on the open door. "Excuse me. Can I have a few more towels, please?"

A smallish sixty- or seventy-something Asian woman turned. "Okay, I get for you. How many you need?" She moved quickly, faster than he expected. He was forced to make eye contact with her when he really wanted to scan her pocket area, waistband, or something that would hold the keycards on a retractable cord. At least that was how it usually worked.

He saw nothing.

"How many you need? One? Two?"

"Six."

"Six? Why so much? You no so big, you have big family?" She laughed while bending to count and pull towels. He thought he saw a bulge in her cleaning smock pocket.

Drake leaned in to get a better look, his hand moving slightly toward her.

She spun abruptly. "You say six, right?" She looked at his outstretched hand. "I get for you. What room? I bring up."

"Uh," Drake turned to where the traveler had exited. "1126."

"1126?" She pushed her glasses up her nose. "You no stay in 1126. That room check out."

Drake clicked his tongue. "I'm just checking in."

"It no clean yet. I clean and bring you towel. Come back twenty minutes. You go get breakfast. Come back I have room clean and new towels." She tried to shoo Drake away, but that would seriously jack with his plans, timetable, and the fact that he had limited time to kill a far-from-home terrorist in this way-too-warm hotel.

"Yeah, I need to shower before my meeting. Can I just get in?"

"You need six towel for shower? Just you? Or you have party?" She laughed, which was not very funny at the moment.

He stepped toward her and spotted the card on a red elastic coil in her pocket.

Bingo.

"Lemme check. I see what room open now. Lots room open now already clean. No too busy now."

Drake seized the moment as she reached to her left for a clipboard and room roster. He stepped in and grabbed a handful of shampoo with his left hand while he slipped into her smock pocket with his right.

"Hey! What you do? Why you push?"

"Sorry, just need some shampoo." He slipped the coil into his pocket.

"Room have shampoo." She clawed the small bottles from his hand with a deep frown.

"So sorry. I'll go get my bags from the car and come back."

His clip was quick as he headed for the exit stairwell at the opposite end of the hall.

"Elevator faster!" she called. "Too many stair."

That was pretty pathetic, Alex Woolf taunted his son with a laugh. *You're going to have to do better than that.* The same vivid memory flashed in Drake's mind, as always. His dad turned from the counter with a reassuring smile. Scotch glass in hand. Ice pick in the other. The kitchen was hot, and Drake Woolf felt the heat of North Africa upon him despite the coolness of the hotel corridor.

Drake leapt up the stairs two at a time, three on the landings.

He checked his watch. Not what he had hoped but still plenty of time.

Woolf found the room but took a moment to assess the surroundings. No one was in the hallway. He examined the door in its frame. Privacy notice on the handle. No filament. He looked in the gaps between wood and metal. There it was. A small, folded piece of paper. It told Drake a number of things. One, he was at the right door. Two, the target wanted to know if someone had entered the room. Three, while it wasn't the most sophisticated approach, he wasn't dealing with a complete amateur.

* * * *

It was a scene Tresa Halliday had come upon a number of times. Gaping neighbors talking to one another on sidewalks. News vans and cordoned-off reporters talking shit like they knew what was going on but were being as vague as they could until they actually were told something. Then there were the law enforcement cars and officers, like a piece of lettuce stuck between two teeth. They were a part of something good, but by being in the wrong place at the wrong time, they were a real nuisance. And then the Bureau's entourage played their part, which was like a turd on the plate of the person who just got lettuce stuck in their teeth. You could see them, couldn't avoid them, and they too were somewhere no one wanted them to be. And you sure as Hell didn't want to get too close.

Tresa exited her vehicle, parking it where she wanted because she, too, was a turd on the table. And that was fine with her. At first, she just stood outside the home, feet firm on the sidewalk. The neighborhood was quiet save for the sideshow. What was inside the victims' home, she hadn't a clue. Aside from dead people. And a girl. That, of course, weighed heavy on her as it would most people. Children should be kept safe while crazed adults killed each other. It was a written global rule, but it was one that was often broken when bullets and bombs were involved.

Special Agent Halliday had been feeling the adrenaline rush of success wane as her fatigue fought with her mental and physical state of near exhaustion. Emotionally, she was afraid to enter the crime scene and show weakness. A walk around the house could be justified, like she was really investigating, when in reality, she was scared shitless of what she would see inside. She had seen bad aftermath shit in Iraq. By accident, really. Real bad shit. She never could make sense of it, nor did she want those memories to resurface.

As she passed the front of the home, movement caught her eye. It came from above. Drop shades moved hiding the glimpse of a face. Tresa played the little game of being spied upon, the shades shifting in a succession of hide and show. It dawned on her that to get new information, she would need a new approach. *What the Hell. I'm secret agent girl these days.*

It took a couple of minutes before someone answered the door. A thirty-, maybe fortysomething blond woman answered. Her husband, or at least a man of about the same age, peered from a kitchen down the entry hall, coffee cup in hand. He looked away, pretending to be busy, and then engaged again in a conscious effort to be nonchalant. It wasn't working and rarely did for people.

"Hi, sorry to bother you, Mrs....?"

"Excuse me. Who are you?" the woman asked.

"My apologies." Tresa pulled out and displayed her newly reunited identification and badge. "Special Agent Halliday. And you are?"

"Barrens. We're the Barrens. Are you able to share with us what happened? They're our neighbors. Nice people. So nice."

"Yes." *I know they're your neighbors, which is why I'm here and not five miles away knocking on doors,* Tresa thought while wearing a nonthreatening *I'm here to do you no harm or inconvenience of your time even if it will help solve a murder* smile. "May I come in?"

"Yes, of course. Please." Mrs. Barren offered but only stepped back a few feet. "What can we help you with?"

"Standard procedure, really. I've not been inside your neighbor's home. I understand that there may have been a homicide. I'm very sorry."

"Oh, my God. We...well, we suspected something was very bad, and there were ambulances that came but never left." She turned to her husband, who stood and walked toward the women.

"Do you know what happened?" he asked with the morbid curiosity of people gaping at a bad road accident hoping to see a dead victim and then wishing they had never seen it.

"I don't. Not yet. I'm sorry. But I wanted to introduce myself if you had any questions. Or had any information."

"I'm sorry. We were asleep, and when we got up emergency vehicles started coming in. At first we thought maybe something had happened, but nothing too serious," Mrs. Barren offered. "We literally awoke to this whole thing that just never stopped." She gestured out from the entryway. "Then we knew."

From the door highlights and front window, Tresa could see the not-so-everyday staging on the street. "Mrs. Barren, is it just you and Mr. Barren who live here?" Tresa turned to a photo on the wall that captured children not yet of an age to fly the coop. She kept her gaze on the framed picture, sending the "don't lie to me, lady" signal loud and clear.

"Well, our children. We sent them back up to their rooms. I know it's a school day, but we"—she looked to her husband, who was standing by her side—"well, we thought maybe they should stay home for now."

"I understand." Halliday's fake smile was working overtime. "Whose room faces your neighbor's house?" Tresa addressed the Barrens then looked back to the photo on the wall.

"That would be Rosie's room. I'm sure she wouldn't know anything. The kids just woke up."

Tresa started to climb the stairs. "You said she's in her room, mind if I go say hi for a moment?"

The Barrens gave each other blank looks not knowing what to say, what to do. They were good parents with nothing to hide but saw no reason to bring the truths of an often violent world into the hearts and souls of their children. Kids would have plenty of time to learn the ways of society. Today wasn't the best day for that. It simply had not been discussed, and good people discuss such things beforehand. At the very least they text an article to their kids and type, "You should read this."

"Thanks," Tresa replied to the blank stares and shrugs and looks.

Special Agent Halliday moved as fast as she could while the parents collected themselves. They hurried up the stairs behind her to serve as advisors, translators, and stopgaps.

Tresa knocked on the door.

A young teen answered. With the shades closed and lights off, the room was dark. The only light came from a small reading lamp lying on its side on the bed. It was resting on a book.

"Hi. I'm Special Agent Halliday. Are you Rosie?" Tresa stretched out her hand. The expression she wore for the girl was warm and genuine.

Rosie shook her hand. "Is Miriam all right?"

"Can I come in?"

"Sure." Rosie flipped the switch on the wall, and the room was hardly awash in what must have been one, maybe two, forty-watt lightbulbs in an alabaster-covered ceiling sconce.

"Reading anything good?"

"Yeah. I kinda like to read a lot."

"Me, too." Tresa stepped into the room and pulled the book from under the light. "Silva, huh? I haven't read those, Mossad guy main character?"

"I just started it."

"I like Lee Child. Ever read any of those?"

"Reacher." She nodded. "He's pretty cool. I didn't like the movie so much."

Rosie's mom was mouthing something to her father. The husband couldn't read lips, and Tresa couldn't give two shits.

"Yeah, Tom Cruise was so-so. Didn't bother me too much about the size thing."

"Yea, I watched it with my dad on the plane to Florida last year."

"Where was I?" Mrs. Barrens asked the room. Mr. Barrens tried to keep up with the conversation between books and shows. He thought the Reacher movie was pretty kick-ass.

Tresa sat on the bed and patted the cover, beckoning the young teen to sit. "So, I need to ask you some stuff, kiddo."

"I figured."

"What'd you see?" the agent asked matter-of-factly.

"Two men. They came out of the basement."

"You never said you saw—"

"Sir," Halliday interrupted, "the big picture here, please. Sorry, you were saying?" *Holy shit*, Tresa thought. *I've got a witness.*

"I saw two men coming out of the basement. I think one saw me."

"Someone saw you?" her mom verified, two octaves higher in the *I'm going to panic now* pitched voice.

"Mrs. Barren, please." Tresa held up her hand.

"What time was this and how do you know they saw you?"

"It was late. Maybe four?"

"Four? What were you doing up at four? Reading?" Mr. Barrens popped the dad hat back on.

Halliday fired the look of death to the parents, which effectively choke-held them both for the moment.

"What did you see?"

"Pretty much just what I said. They came out of the basement. The first guy took off. The second guy was slower, like he was putting stuff back together. Then I think he saw me and just sat there."

"But you couldn't see him?"

Rosie shook her head. "Too dark. I heard little pops before they came out. Miriam's dead, isn't she? They killed her. I know it." Rosie looked away.

Tresa reached out and pulled Rosie in at the shoulder. "Rosie, I'm not sure yet. But I'll find out more, and I promise that I'm going after these guys. You understand?"

Rosie wiped her eyes and nose. It made a squishing sound. "I understand. We were friends. She and I used to pretend we were going on, like, *America's Got Talent* or something and sing and dance in her basement. We were the High Heeled Heroines but then it was like heroin, so we needed to change that because of all the heroin in our school. I mean we never did it. Just the name sounded like it." Rosie looked up at Tresa, "Are the men going to come back?"

"Never," Tresa promised. "They're never coming back here. Got it?"

* * * *

Sherm passed by Havens's table after setting two breakfast plates by the target. One was covered with a metal heat retainer.

"Sir, your order will be up shortly," he promised Sean.

"Hey, Sherm, not that I'm complaining, but that guy over there, don't look."

He looked.

Crap.

"Bro. Eyes on me. The guy came in after I did. How did he get not one but two plates of food first? My other question, out of curiosity, is why he has two plates? He isn't a very big guy."

"Mr. Habib calls down first to preorder. Then once he's finished, he brings the second plate up to his...colleague." Sherm pointed up to the ceiling and lifted an eyebrow.

"Colleague?"

Sherm bent down and whispered into Havens's ear. "You know. Associate," he purred.

Yeesh. "Thanks. Sorry to bother you. Just getting hungry."

Sherm patted Sean Havens on the shoulder. "Sure you are." He smiled. "That's why every fella comes here." He winked.

Jeezus.

Mohsen cast a heavy eye of scrutiny at Havens. Sean was back on the radar.

Havens raised his eyebrows. Softening his jaw, he smiled and gave Mohsen a wink.

Mohsen bashfully turned away with a bashful smile.

Havens started texting his ass off, then raised the phone to his ear.

Drake opened the room door and bent to retrieve the paper that had fallen from the doorjamb.

He heard the faint sound of a shower deeper in the suite. Drake drew the pistol from the small of his back and followed the room's layout flow, weapon ready. There was a small toilet room to his immediate right. A quick glance in proved clear. Down a roughly ten-foot hallway, he gave a fast check to his right as the room opened up. The immediate room was a vast eating area. The table was long with eight leather chairs pushed in. It was clean. No papers. No electronics.

To the right of the table was a broad marble wet bar with a bottle of Johnny Walker Red scotch atop, an ice holder, tongs jutting out, and a glass-faced refrigerator underneath the black sparkling stone. Nothing of intel value there either.

A sitting area butted against the dining and drinking area, separated only in the open-concept floor plan by two large area rugs, each with a sofa, overstuffed chairs, a low cocktail table, mirrored fireplace in between, heavy drapes, and small end tables.

A laptop.

The running water silenced. The last of the shower flow trickled audibly on shallow standing water. Woolf could hear from his right that in the large bedroom someone was sliding what must have been a heavy glass door, and the muffled snap of a towel being shaken out. Drake advanced to the laptop. He remained out of sight from the bedroom. The laptop shell was closed. He snatched the computer just as his own device squawked Havens's voice up through the thin earphone wire.

"Second target in room."

Drake needed to remain silent. Using the radio function through a cell phone didn't give an opportunity to confirm with a key click response. *Add this to the list of program improvements.*

Drake tucked the weapon between his left arm and the laptop. It was a good thing, too, as he hadn't noticed a trailing power cord that must have been hidden between the long purple drapes.

Retrieving the phone, Drake viewed the text message that displayed within the opened radio feature. Drake precariously thumbed a "K" and Send and put the device back in his pocket.

Woolf glanced up to see a naked young man with a shaved head standing before him. Maybe sixteen, seventeen. Not much older. The kid was olive tan in full Monty skin color. From the lighting, maybe Hispanic, could be Middle Eastern. Either way, the ripped youth lunged at him, holding nothing back.

Drake's left leg slid back, and he twisted his torso, reducing his target profile. His free right hand was now extended forward and met the flying kid just at the rib cage. Woolf ducked an arm then finished his left leg pivot back to follow the kid's momentum and used a free arm to slam the boy down on the floor, just missing the fireplace seating stone.

Drake's movement was restrained as the computer cord became tight, held firmly into the wall socket and pulling at an angle against the end table. The momentum of Drake's full turn stopped short and caused the pistol to fall to the ground. The youth sprang up with gritted teeth, from them emitting a growl as hands rose to clawlike stance. Drake drew his weight back to his left leg then raised and flung out his right foot, kicking the kid squarely in the chest.

The boy's hands snapped in and grabbed Drake's leg. Momentum sent the kid backward, the fall and clamp causing Woolf to spread into splits. The kid climbed his way up Drake's leg and was met with a discus swing of Woolf's right arm holding the laptop. The impact shocked the kid, and Drake could see the boy's eyes widen in surprise. As the youth swayed, trying to shake the stars and blackness, Drake yanked out the cord, let the computer drop, and spun the power cord around the boy's neck.

In the blink of an eye, the boy had flipped himself over Drake's shoulder and positioned for a sleeper hold. The kid was strong, and Woolf was wedged to a point where he had few options. Drake reached back to try and grab the kid by the balls, but the boy felt the shift and moved to the right.

It put Drake into a locked position. His windpipe was getting squeezed. Woolf tried to move to the right and fought against the long screwdriver in his pocket stopping his turn. Drake got a thumb between his waist and the screwdriver, pulled the tool out from the side, and hammered it down on the kid's bare foot.

Woolf immediately sprang back, launching himself into the air, his passenger wrapped tight around, and crashed down onto the glass coffee table.

* * * *

Mohsen pawed his ringing phone from the tabletop, covering a visible number. "Yes," he answered in a hushed voice. "I am waiting to hear. We have additional resources coming. Please, let me get to a more private location. Call me back in five minutes, please," Mohsen stated in English.

Sean Havens had been watching the target through his device camera, which appeared as though he was reading mobile news as he sipped his coffee. Mohsen had been careful not to make direct eye contact but played a close flirtatious game.

When the target started shuffling around, Havens knew something was up and he'd better get into better position.

Sherm exited the kitchen, holding a tray with the plate of fresh pancakes. Sean's mouth salivated as he discreetly withdrew twenty dollars from his pocket and tucked it under the coffee cup. He signaled to the server pointing up. "I'll be right back down. Just have to get something from my room real quick."

"It'll be here. I'll go get a cover if you want to bring them up."

Sean glanced at the target, who was still fumbling at the table, taking a last drink of coffee and putting a napkin-rolled silverware set on top of the covered plate. Havens knew he had less than a minute but also didn't want to look too coincidental getting up at the same time. He looked at the pancake stack coming toward him. *Always.* "I'll just be right back," he lied. "Thanks, though." Other men congregated near the elevator. By their dress and mannerisms, Sherm's comments made more sense. Either this was a down-low hotel or there was, well, he didn't really know. The elevator came to the ground level, letting out a stream of guests, and the others crowded together to pile in.

The target was hurrying, and Sean weighed whether the mark would wait or squeeze in. Havens looked to the descending car lights above the nearby elevator shafts. He rolled the dice and opted to wait.

Eyes were on Sean from those holding the door in the elevator car. He turned before anyone could create a greater spectacle by asking if he was coming. As the mark moved to the elevator, Havens slowed to let the car pass by. Sean approached the front desk. "Can I get a cab in about fifteen minutes, please?"

"Certainly," the clerk replied. "May I have your room? I will call when it arrives."

"I'll be right back down," Sean informed the clerk loudly enough for the Middle Eastern man to hear.

The elevator car came down with doors opening at the lobby. Fortunately, a few guests turned right into the high-value target, allowing Sean to slip in. Havens pushed the mark's floor number as if it were his own, held the door, and smiled. "Here, let me help you. Looks like your hands are full. What floor?"

Mohsen probed the button panel. Upon seeing his button already lit, he looked up at the American.

"Thank you. I have got it," Mohsen replied in English with a hint of a British accent and pushed for the floor above his own.

He's either on to me, cautious, or creeped out, Sean thought. Others were headed to the elevator. Havens hit the door close button.

The two spooks rode up in silence. Floor by floor, both stared at the floor-level lights and the polished silver door. From time to time each man could see the other glancing over in the reflection.

The doors to Mohsen's actual floor opened.

* * * *

As the kid's arms relaxed, Drake twisted himself and rolled to his right, preparing for the next melee round. The boy lay motionless with his eyes opened wide with terror. Large glass shards had cut deeply and collapsed at such an angle that they trapped the youth within the broken table as blood spurted in low arcs from his limbs.

"Aw, shit, kid."

Drake popped up to his feet and ran to the bathroom, where he grabbed all the towels he could. He yanked the bedsheet off and fell back to his knees before the boy.

In a flurry of motions, Drake ripped and spun fabric. He pulled on the kid's body, freeing the boy from the jagged snares, and quickly bound those wounds, as well. He freed the boy's neck of the power cord and used it as a tourniquet high on the thigh to stop the femoral flow through the ruptured artery below. Tears rolled from the boy's cheeks as he lay sprawled, naked, and field wrapped.

The young man mumbled incoherent sounds. Drake noticed dark blood emerging from the kid's mouth. Not good. Woolf leaned in and put a gentle hand on the boy's chest. "I didn't hear, can you say again?"

The kid spoke again. This time more clearly. The words came from the Middle East.

Drake responded in the same Pashto tongue, "No, I'm not going to let you die."

Woolf caressed the boy's head as life slipped away. "I'm sorry," he said to the Afghani boy. "I'm so sorry." He kissed his forehead after closing the kid's dead eyes.

The pain of war and death had returned to Drake Woolf. It lodged somewhere between his throat and his sternum.

What is wrong with this world? Drake asked himself as he wiped the tears from his eyes.

* * * *

Given this was a fast reaction makeshift op, Havens figured he should play this one out a little longer in case their three-man death squad had made a mistake. Drake might have rectified it but been incommunicado. It was a new way of doing business for both of these intel singletons to be working with a partner, and both needed to adjust to the learning curve.

Sean stepped out from the elevator, willing to let the target go for just a moment longer. Already committed, Havens looked back to see the man holding the covered plate in one hand, an outstretched pistol in the other.

"If you wanted to get in my pants, you could've just said please."

"Move." Mohsen motioned Sean forward, which he obliged for only a raised step. The elevator door started to close, causing Mohsen to flinch. Sean grabbed and twisted the weapon to the weak side of the man's hand, pulling it free.

Havens trapped Mohsen's wrist with his right hand, jerking the man from the elevator and into the hall. The plate fell with a clank. A consummate foodie, Sean couldn't help but look at the contents as they descended. It smelled so good. Mohsen in turn looked to capitalize on the moment, making a move that was immediately countered.

"Nice try."

The fact that the man didn't have an immediate death wish told Sean he wasn't a martyr, which was a relief. They might be able to get some answers. Whether Sean and Drake decided to kill him or tie him up and stick a note on the body for authorities, in theory, was still up for grabs, however unlikely. Sean knew the guy was a dead man in one way or another. The task force simply hadn't yet developed a protocol for prisoners, and the mandate was, from the charter, to judge in the field and rule with death sentences.

"We're going to have a chat in your room. This little pea shooter of yours won't kill you, but it'll paralyze you until my second shot," Havens threatened, with the muzzle pressed firmly to the suspect's spine.

Sean used the push-to-talk feature, mobile device in his left hand. "If you can read me, I'm at the target's door. I have him here. How copy?"

"Roger that. Coming to you now."

When the door opened, the look of Drake covered from hand to shoulder in blood gave Havens and Mohsen a start. Woolf's face was sunken, his eyes puffy and bloodshot. A laptop was in his hands.

"The man from Orange," Mohsen wheezed. His eyes bulged, his mouth dropping open in fear.

"Mohsen," Drake's voice rose as he gasped the name at the sight of a most familiar face. "Motherfucker."

Mohsen shoved Drake to the side and ran full tilt down the short hallway of the room, but he didn't turn. The unexpected rapid movement took Havens by surprise. Sean's finger remained off the trigger as he and Woolf watched the target run straight for the large window.

"His phone!" Drake shouted before the crash.

Woolf raced to the broken window opening soon enough to see the aftermath occur in real time as the target landed on the edge of a moving box truck, severed at the midsection and ruptured in a splash of red before an approaching car transformed the man's torso into a long brushstroke of blood.

Drake's tongue started to click. He turned to Havens for a response. They needed that phone.

Sean Havens was casually leaning against the doorframe. "Holy shit. I did not see that coming. Most hotels have better safety glass," he said, retrieving Mohsen's mobile device from his back pocket. "Did you mean *this* phone?"

Havens glanced down at Drake's leg. "Dude, is that your blood?"

Part III

"If you have nothing to hide, you have nothing to fear."
-NSA Branch Motto

Chapter 34

Tresa Halliday displayed her credentials upon entry to the home. The special agent tried to deny her, at first, it being a closed crime scene, but she informed him that they had missed something. She brushed past the other agents along her way down to the basement.

"You need to sign in," he shouted as she disappeared into the stairwell.

Tresa pulled a number of white twine strings, turning on exposed lightbulbs that illuminated the concrete expanse under the subfloor and its support beams. The unfinished basement was barren save for boxes along the side of the wall and a large square of carpet that hosted two beanbag chairs. One green. One black. There were a couple of wireless microphones lying at the front of a black plastic karaoke set plugged into an orange extension cord that ran its way to an open junction tubed up to the master fuse box.

Halliday oriented herself to the neighbor's home and zoned in on the most logical of the utility windows before her. While footprints were not visible, there was enough evidence of light grass-stain smear and dirt that trailed faintly to the fuse box, then to a point in the basement, then toward the stairs. Two sets seemed apparent to her, but she had to fight whether they were actual or based on her knowledge that there were two men. Facts, fantasies, and forensics could spin a case in multiple ways.

Tresa explored the random area on the concrete floor that had some dirt residue. She looked up to see the smoke detector. "I'll bet we can get some prints if you two didn't use gloves." She flicked her gaze to the fuse box. *You assholes turned out the lights, maybe disconnected the smoke alarm, killed everyone in the house, and then bugged out. Let's hear upstairs what the guys have to say and whether they needed to turn on lights down here.*

A moment of dread passed by her. *Unless our own guys had to turn on the lights down here, walked to the window, and left tracks of their own. Shit.*

Tresa stared at the karaoke machine. She could envision the girls singing and dancing, laughing and making lifelong friendships. Her chest tightened, and she caught a double breath that took her by surprise and stuck in her throat. The two empty beanbags shared the now silent and empty narrative of a dead little girl upstairs who was no longer able to make as much noise as possible down here with a friend. Parents who had been so happy that their daughter was lucky to have made such a good friend next door now lay dead beside their child.

Tresa Halliday swallowed hard and wiped pooling tears from her eyes. Her hand shaky, she fumbled to find a wadded Kleenex in her pocket. Her forearm rubbed against the Glock sidearm. She raised her hand, feeling the grip. Tresa quick-drew and sighted to a dark point in the cement wall, then holstered the firearm.

She was going to get Drake Woolf and everyone that son of a bitch worked with.

"I need prints!" she yelled.

"I need some damned fingerprints," she said to herself, "because I'm working a case."

* * * *

Sean Havens had completely forgotten about Mohsen's returning phone call. The vibration and low ring startled him, and he struggled to remember how the target had answered in the restaurant and whether it was actually English or if Havens had immediately translated whatever language it was to English. Sean had a large language repertoire to choose from in the catalog of his mind.

The phone rang a third time.

"Yes," Sean answered flatly, rolling the dice again.

"Mohsen," General Shirazian said, before starting a frustrated tirade in Farsi. "I have received word the Americans have a task force to stop you. Let the final operation continue as planned. I have arranged to deal with matters tomorrow, so there are no further failures. You will return and we will continue without your further assistance. You have done well. We cannot afford to have them find you."

Drake was leaning in to hear the call. He was impressed to see Havens understanding the Persian language, or at least pretending well.

"Mohsen? Do you understand? It's not like you to not interrupt."

Drake motioned to Havens, pointing to his own chest and reaching for the phone.

"By my chin hairs," Drake said, his voice sounding nearly identical to the target's. It was clear to Havens by the initial recognition and response of the target that the two and now three men had history. "General, I've heard enough of your tantrums to know I cannot change your mind. I only ask whether The *Modarris* will remain involved."

Havens was lost, but he didn't question.

"He will remain until Atlanta. This does not concern you."

"I think it does."

"After you kill her, you have completed your task. You must return and handle matters for Dubai. Everything is complete. What is this nonsense?"

"I am not coming back. *Allahu Akbar.*" Drake hung up.

Sean shrugged. "Nice touch. These guys your friends?"

Drake shook his head. "I don't have friends. We need to bug out. This shit is just getting started."

"Let's find another room and get you cleaned up."

"Yeah," Drake responded, looking at the young man's blood that had stained his skin.

"I didn't get the impression that Mohsen guy liked you very much."

Drake shook his head, looking down. "Nope. But stuff I just dealt with in the room here now makes a lot more sense."

Sean didn't push.

"And we're not going to be able to pull shit off on the fly like this anymore. We need real equipment, real plans, real intel and real support. Quds Force is here in America. And things just got very real."

Sean put his arm around Drake. "I got a note from Sebastian while I was downstairs. It's all in the works, amigo."

"I've heard that before." He gave Sean a wink.

"Dare you to wink like that in the lobby." Havens grinned as he reached to the wall and pulled the fire alarm. "This alarm stuff is habit-forming."

* * * *

General Reza Shirazian redialed Mohsen's phone numerous times to no avail. He was at a loss, not knowing what the hell was going through Mohsen's head, where he was, and what he was going to do. The general had received intel about a task force charged with running down the active terrorist responsible for recent acts, but it was highly unlikely they would have gotten to Mohsen. Counterterrorism was chartered to the

FBI, Homeland Security, maybe the Secret Service, and state and local authorities. Even if a few counterterror soldiers were tasked from the military, they would have to work within America's rules. To Reza, that would mean the task force would always be steps behind. If Reza was caught, he would have diplomatic ties to intervene. Mohsen, on the other hand, would be fine if his head was in the right place. He could manipulate anyone with his charisma and determination.

Perhaps Mohsen was drinking. The little monster certainly had his dark vices. Perhaps the demons had caught up with him. Perhaps the Americans were closer than Reza thought. He'd have to take extra precautions. The fact that Mohsen may have been compromised mattered little. He was compartmentalized and Reza had taken over the final attacks; the second phase had been kept away from Mohsen. No, the greater concern for Reza was simply telling his superiors that he didn't know what happened and that he hadn't learned if the Americans were on their trail.

The general stared out of his hotel suite window. The sun was bright, the sky cloudless. He decided to take a walk in Georgetown, change hotels, and have a nice lunch overlooking the water. It would help him craft a plan to trap the task force. Then he would contact his superiors with a report. Should news break of Mohsen, he could quickly formulate an excuse. The plans for tomorrow and the following day would be much more newsworthy. Yes, he was done with Mohsen. Reza pulled the SIM card from his phone, turned the phone off, and tossed it down to the bushes far below his hotel suite.

* * * *

Tresa was pleased to learn that her colleagues hadn't entered the basement prior to her arrival. That increased the probability of at least some of her initial hypothesis. Heavy fatigue was setting in on her mind and body, but a new surge of adrenaline fed her resolve to keep pushing on.

The other agents in the home were actually quite pleasant. They listened attentively to her ideas and called in to request another tech to cover the Altima parked out front and the basement for prints. In turn, she learned of the way her colleagues perceived the events to have unfolded. While ballistics and autopsy would confirm their hunch, weapons were logically accountable on the scene. Impacts matched the caliber, position, trajectory and blood patterns of the crime scene.

The agent in charge of the scene sat at the kitchen table with Tresa. He opened a notepad for the tête-a-tête with Special Agent Halliday from Counterterrorism. It was refreshing for them both to be taken seriously.

The agent in charge was new in town from New Orleans and was happy to meet with one of the Counterterrorism leads, meaning Tresa. Or so she had told him.

He scribbled on the pad and circled a few words. "What I don't understand, Agent Halliday, is that while inserting your two suspects into the equation is plausible, if I look at the evidence before me, it confounds the logical. Even if I draw in some conspiracy, it makes more sense that there was an internal dispute or vendetta or, I don't know, maybe some silencing if I'm following you." He winced and drew another circle and a couple lines on the paper. His actions made no sense to Tresa, but she could see it helped the agent think through things from another lens.

"Okay, it does make sense given the position of the two men we found outside the doorway. You're right." He processed. "Someone coming up from a basement would have surprise. And trajectory would support that. So, maybe there was another Middle Easterner sleeping in the basement on the rug and he heard commotion, took out the other two, and then escaped?"

"Why go out the window? You said the doors were all locked when the police came on scene."

The agent rubbed his forehead, trying to wrap his mind around all the possibilities and permutations. "You still think someone came in the basement knowing there was a conflict and tried to help? Or you think someone came in and didn't know what was going down and took out whoever was left standing?"

"It's possible, right?" she tested further.

"And how do you explain weapons? They or he or someone came in unarmed hoping to obtain a weapon?"

I think Drake Woolf took the weapons off the men who tried to kill him, killed someone in this house and then confounded the crime scene, she kept to herself. Tresa stood. "I think it's another question to add to the puzzle. What we know for sure is this is not as simple as it appears. And someone probably walked out of here alive."

"That's a pretty hard stretch without a witness."

"I know." She smiled. "So, our witness will have to be forensics. Can you please keep me posted? Here's my card."

Stretching out a hand, she noticed for the first time since the start of their conversation that he wore a wedding ring. Tresa put her hand on the agent's shoulder in a friendly gesture. "And let me know if you or your wife would like to go out on the town sometime. I'd be happy to show you around."

"Really?" He smiled. "She'd like that. She—"

"Sir." Another agent came into the kitchen. "You still need us here? We got a call about a Middle Eastern man who just did a swan dive from his hotel window. Arlington police called it in because they thought it may have something to do with terrorists. Maybe because he was an Arab. Guess there was a dead kid in the room, too. There was a questionable scene there. Maybe related. We're going to check it out and need to take a guy from Evidence Response."

Tresa's brows rose. "I'll follow you guys out there."

The agent heading out looked confused. "You are?"

Tresa stretched out her hand.

The lead officer remained seated, held her card, and read. "She's Special Agent Tresa Halliday, she's a counterterrorism specialist just assigned to NSB. She came in to advise Violent Crime," he vetted, referring to the National Security Branch that combined a number of disciplines. "Help her out, Dave." He turned to Halliday, stood, and extended his hand. "Thanks again, Special Agent Halliday. I'll keep you posted. Anne will be happy to hear of your offer. Maybe you come on over for dinner in the coming days if you're not too busy."

"Thanks, Mike. I'd like that," she replied with surprising interest and sincerity about actually getting to know more people at the Bureau after all these years. "I'll let you know if anything at the hotel could be of interest to you, too."

As she followed the agents out, tiptoeing and sliding across the crime scene, careful not to get in the way, she finally felt like she was part of the Federal Bureau of Investigation. It felt good. This was what she had signed up for. This was what was missing for her. Professionally.

* * * *

Drake and Sean separated in the converging streams of hotel guests filling the stairwell. Emergency vehicles arriving in response to the jumper added to the confusion, laying a perfect cover for the two operators to flow into the parking lot and hop into the waiting van.

"You guys set the place afire or what?" Lars threw the vehicle in drive and drove off chill-style to avoid unwarranted suspicion.

"Good thing we didn't have a plan. Because it sure as Hell didn't go according to one," Drake responded. He was warming up to the big man.

And to the idea of being on a team. He was getting tired but still keeping his shit straight for now.

"Drake's right," Sean added. "I know it feels like we need to save the world in a day, but we need to lower the op tempo and actually get our heads together. We can all use some sleep." He thumbed to Drake. "I think this guy's been going for—"

Drake Woolf had slipped away from consciousness into the house of terrors that most people would call sleep. He tried to avoid it at all cost, but the demons demanded their time for retribution and pulled him in when their powers channeled enough strength and he could no longer fight their spell. The shadows longed to show Drake their faces, their wounds, their sunken blank eyes. It was the children he feared most. There were not many who had fallen by his hand. None when he had the choice. Most in his dreams just cried and reached out, pleading for his help. He could never reach them, and he watched them all die again until he awoke, felt for his pistol, and wondered if he had the guts to make it all go away for eternity.

After driving for nearly thirty minutes, Lars turned off the Dulles Access Road to Fairfax County Parkway and then off to Sunrise Valley Drive.

Drake awoke with a start, self-conscious as to whether he had cried out or shit the bed with any other embarrassing sounds.

Havens closed his eyes quickly to save Woolf some face until he gained more confidence and trust in the team.

"Where we going?" Drake asked Lars as he slowly reoriented himself to the surroundings.

"Home office," Bjorklund replied. He checked the rearview mirror to see Havens playing possum and went along with the ruse. Woolf had been mumbling and pleading with his night terrors for the past ten miles. Lars and Havens had chatted quietly about them as they drove. Havens had never been afflicted with the terrors—or depression, for that matter—but it didn't mean he hadn't had his share of the past revisiting him in his sleep nor did it mean he didn't still have his own set of battle scar issues.

Sean opened his eyes and gave a yawn and backstretch. In truth, he, too, had almost fallen asleep as soon as his eyes closed. How Lars was holding up was a miracle. The guy was usually out minutes upon hitting a La-Z-Boy chair with a baseball game playing on the television to his peaceful slumber.

Drake blinked his eyes, trying to focus on the approaching green and grey sign. "USGS?" He continued to read by squinting. "US Department of the Interior...US Geological Survey?"

"Yeah," Lars responded. "We got a good spot. GSA had a rental opening here with a dock and bay, separate from the main building. We've also got these." Lars pointed out the front window, and Drake contorted his body to see over the front seat. Sitting in the back parking lot were two storage containers. "We can give our suppliers the code, have them deliver without seeing anyone, and change the codes after we get whatever we receive and bring it inside."

"You did this in less than a week?"

Sean jumped in. "You know your uncle, he keeps his eyes out for these sorts of things all the time. Snagged this a while back and held it for the right opportunity. We've been sending things over here for a couple days. Mostly O.T. and Sebastian. Sebastian's bitching a bit since it takes him over an hour from Fort Meade, but from this place as our home base, we can get to Dulles if we need to fly commercial, hit the NCTC or Agency real quick, and it's less than an hour from Fort Belvoir. Probably an hour and a half from your place, Drake."

"I'm not going to be staying there anymore."

"Well, let's all talk this out when we get inside." Lars pulled into a space, put the van in park, and turned to face the guys. "I've got some shit to show you guys. I think I have a pretty good idea about some things that bring this whole mess together."

* * * *

Tresa followed the lead Bureau SUV into the hotel parking lot but held back a bit and parked in the far side of the lot. There was a shrubbed knoll that crested and dipped before the main road that ran alongside the building. From what she understood, the man had fallen from one of the topmost floors onto the road below.

Her thought was to continue trusting her instincts, but when she reached the top of the small hill and pushed through the bushes to get a view of the hotel face, there was little left to the imagination. There was a big-ass broken window at a helluva height. While she never considered herself much of a physicist, it didn't take a rocket scientist to know the jumper had to have some momentum to get to the heavily trafficked street about twenty yards out from where building met ground. She'd seen the aftermath of suicides from high jumping points before. Either this guy had wings, he was thrown by someone with major anger issues, or he had launched himself like Evel Knievel over the Snake River.

Her biased perspective was that two angry men could have given him the old heave-ho with requisite strength and hate. Fucking Drake Woolf and his crew. Goddamn, this guy was a savage. Time to check out the launch pad from the inside.

The two best ways in Halliday's mind to clear a path through people were to fart or flash a badge. Her badge raised, she cut through remaining emergency responders who were evidently clearing a fire alarm, waded through the journalists hoping for a statement, and pushed through a gaggle of men hanging out in the lobby drinking margaritas and dancing. *The fire alarm.*

The jumper's floor was taped off, and other guests had been relocated. She was stopped by an officer and then an agent, but to both she responded, "I just need to see one thing." That was, until she learned about the boy once she saw the window and the distance from below. Regarding the window, she was puzzled. There wasn't much room against the wall and in the opening of the entry hall to the eating area where two men could have coordinated hurling a man out the window. Tresa asked to have the sheet over the boy pulled down so she could take a peek.

"Someone took a lot of pains to try and save this kid," the agent offered from behind.

"Unfortunately, not enough. Was 911 called?"

"We're checking, but he bled out fast. This glass is razor-sharp. It's thick too, so it didn't have much give."

"Tourniquet, huh?"

"Tourniquet, hemorrhage control, someone did the best they could do."

Tresa leaned in, looking at how neat and even the wraps had bound the wounds. "Think it was possible someone wounded the boy, he died, and the jumper ended it?"

"If the jumper was trained in Tactical Combat Casualty Care, maybe."

"Hmmm." Tresa twisted her mouth. She wanted the events to fit the narrative in her mind. They didn't exactly fit together so nicely, she admitted to herself. What if they were protectors? Cool idea, not as fun to investigate Batman and Robin as it was hunting a rogue black ops unit killing everyone indiscriminately. *Shit.*

"You said you were counterterrorism?"

"Yeah." She perked up. "Why?"

"This isn't an act of terrorism. You can leave now unless you're bringing us some lunch."

From the top of the mountain to the shit in the sewers. "I'll get lunch, can you guys pitch in ten or twenty each? A couple good places down the

road. I can be back in fifteen minutes with some mind-blowing chow."
She smiled and flipped her hair.

"Can I get in on that action?" asked an officer standing against the window still looking down below.

She counted fifty-five dollars in the kitty after all the men anted up. "I'll be back, boys."

"And don't forget drinks," someone added.

She smiled with a wink—a gesture that must have been contagious in the no-tell hotel. "Drinks, right. Got it. I'll try to hurry."

"That's what he said." The officer winked to the others, smiling and making eye contact with the boys club, trying to get a laugh. Tresa laughed the hardest as she left the room.

Douchebags. She stuffed the cash into her pocket and gave it a pat, proud of her little ruse. The cash would get her a good steak and an excellent six-pack for dinner. Time to check in with Earl. Then get some shut-eye. She double blinked to clear the image of Drake Woolf sitting across from her at dinner. *Where did that come from? God am I desperate. But if he's not killing all these people, what's he doing and who's leaving bodies all around town?*

* * * *

Drake was impressed with the possibilities of their operations center. It was large enough to house what they needed and leave room for growth, storage, or the possibilities of a small workout area or post-work bar. With so few men involved, it was perfect for a comfortable Forward Operating Base. He nosed around the dimly lit, unfurnished building and checked out what the guys had already brought inside. There were dozens of large, medium, and small Pelican cases lined against the inside wall closest to the delivery ramp. Offices had been framed. There were two large fence cages, a large metal table with no chairs, and a half-dozen whiteboards folded into each other leaning against a metal support column. Drake couldn't tell if this was what it looked like after everyone left or if it was progress being made.

When Sebastian opened the biometric lock with a thumbprint and code. A fitting symbolic sunbeam forced itself in and paved the Brit's first few steps in the bright light until the door slammed shut and the smallish man was shrouded in shadows. "Aye, lads. Busy huntin' trolls all night, are we?"

"Not sure about *we*, Sebastian, but *we* sure as Hell have been." Sean walked up, shook the man's hand, and gave him a pat on the shoulder. Sebastian did the same.

"Ya look ten years older than you did yesterday, Havens. Missed your breakfast?" Sebastian chided.

"I sure did. Feel a bit older since yesterday, too."

"Baaah, just the weariness of the kill. Just like a Thanksgiving turkey. Ya just need a lil' nap."

It surprised Drake first off that the man was likely no more than five-seven or five-eight. He was lean, and from what Woolf could see as he moved to introduce himself, the man was hairy as Hell. Except the top of his head, which was shiny bald. His brows were like small black bear pelts mounted above his eyes. The other odd aspect was Sebastian might have been a Brit, but he had a heavy Scottish accent. So, was he a Scot or English? Probably a question Scots had been asked for hundreds of years.

Sebastian gave Lars a big slap on the back as the detective leaned over a laptop he had just opened on the long metal table. "Aye, big fella. Fit as ever." Sebastian pounded up the big man's back to the shoulders as he passed him by, Bjorklund making no efforts to stop booting the machine.

"Aand this must be Oh-Tee's boy. Put 'er there, lad. Welcome. Welcome, Warren. Great to have ya with us."

"Good to meet you, Sebastian. Drake's fine."

"Ah, Drake. The Birddog. Great name. Trade ya." He laughed. His handshake was firm, his eyes direct. The confidence Sebastian exuded wasn't overbearing. He was outgoing to be sure, but it was a man who wasn't full of shit, just a man who had seen and done shit. And that worked just fine with the man from Orange.

"Okay, boys," Sebastian started. "Pleasantries aside, everyone okay? Life and limb? Still have your cocks?"

Sean and Drake nodded. Lars continued his self-driven task.

"Perfect, glad you made it back all right. Rough night to be sure, from what you reported there, Sean."

"It was. Drake has some great thoughts on how to turn an otherwise shitshow into something workable. He did great."

Sean's comments weren't patronizing, and Woolf didn't take them as such. Still, Drake wasn't much for attention and kept his head down. "Fortunately, the contact was coming from us. So, we made some luck and it worked out. Hopefully, we didn't leave much trace. It was still a bit of a shitshow."

The chat was informal, but Sebastian, Drake, and Sean were used to the format of a hotwash debrief. It wasn't a time to blow smoke up everyone's ass; it was a time to walk through what happened. What went right, what went wrong? How could individuals and the collective improve? All were reading from the same sheet of music. That's how the tip of the spear worked, and it didn't get much more pointed than where they were now.

"Well, you all made the best of a fluid response, and you sure as Hell didn't have much to work with but your minds." He tapped his head. "Drake, apologies. You were brought in with less to work with than we've asked. It was a danger to you and to the mission. I don't take that lightly and welcome the burden."

Drake looked up long enough to give a nod of recognition and appreciation for the words.

Sebastian outstretched his arms, "We've commandeered some toys, but remember, to be light and nimble, we don't want to have much because we can't afford to leave much." He brought his arms back in making a gesture of small with his fingers and thumbs. "Lean is the name of the game when killing men without sanction. You're doing your country honor, but by all laws that make this beautiful country great, and which I am honored to now be a part of, we're criminals. Murderers even. But by God, it takes monsters to kill monsters…. Or maybe a fucking duck." He laughed and backhanded Drake across the chest. It ruined the speech, but it kept things real. It kept them mortals and not so much shiny armored crusaders spearing dragons in their lairs.

"Okay, guys." Lars turned to the men and raised his eyes to the team but remained fixed over the laptop. "I need you to come around and take a look at this if you're finished." With his size, it would still mean all would be leaning two feet in on either side to see the screen. The men tried to crowd around the mass that was Lars.

"Sebastian, we're going to need a screen and projector," Havens suggested. "Unless we want to sit on each other's shoulders."

"Noted," Sebastian confirmed. He typed something in his device, which Drake assumed to be a running list of needs. "Done. Oh, before I forget. Phones. They're ordered and coming in within a couple days. Codan Sentry. Gives you VHF analog and digital networks, plus secure voice and data. Looks just like a commercial phone. Who loves you, lads? Your Uncle Sebastian does." He smiled, eyebrow-hair bundles raised as high as they could go. "Sorry. Continue, please."

Lars gave Sean an elbow, nudging him over like a bear swatting at a cub. "Great news on the phones. We're not good as we are now. Anyway.

While you guys were playing guns in the hotel, I took a look at the laptop Drake snagged from the home this morning."

"God, it feels like that was a day ago," Sean interrupted.

"I checked files, read a few things, yada yada." Lars opened one of the desktop files and pointed at the screen as the pdf opened. "But this. This right here. I think this means something."

Sean leaned over Lars's arm.

"Yeah, it's one of the companies we set up other business under in Iraq." Sean reached in. "Scroll down here." He read the document further. "Yeah, this was the parent structure covered by State Department and Reconstruction teams. Since our money was already going into local business development, we used this as a holding company. It's legitimate, Lars."

"Right. And remember that. Foot stomp by the teacher here, kids, you'll see this again on a test." Lars clicked on another file and held up a finger. "Now look at these names, carefully. Recognize any of them?"

This time Drake squeezed in. He had been standing behind Sebastian, who didn't pose much of a height obstruction. "I know these names." Drake pointed to the display. "He is one of the guys I took out in the car. This guy, my house. These two were in the house this morning. This guy, I know but haven't seen. Then, these guys marked as deceased, I know those names, too."

"Same," said Sean. "I wouldn't know their faces with names in a lineup, but I do know some of the names from payments we made."

Drake looked directly at Havens. "Mohawks, Sean."

Lars was ping-ponging his head, following the back-and-forth between the two spooks.

Sebastian just soaked it in like the sweet smell of a good pub curry. He was beaming as he watched the men interact and the pieces fall into place.

Drake continued to flesh out the emerging rapid thoughts as synapses fired, linking memories long forgotten. "They were turned. Each Mohawk was supposedly motivated by revenge. It's too big of a coincidence that the ones coming after everyone were the prime business owners in the AO. And the only people who would really know that they were business owners back in the States were the Deltas and one-offs like us. And then, of course, the powers that be."

Lars scrolled to the bottom of the page. "So, you guys don't think the folks listed down at the bottom of the resolution...these muckety-muck generals and diplomats...You don't think they're targets?"

"Not so far." Sean looked to Sebastian, whose facial expression and head turning back and forth, negating Havens' observation, gave away his desire to make a grand splash with some new intel.

"Boys. Look. Fairness here, you've been rattling the cage night and day. We just took on our new mate and haven't even welcomed him on with a proper night out. Meanwhile, we're...well, I"—he blushed—"I've been getting the pieces you've been looking for. Spot on. Brilliant. Now, here's something that stays with us. Agreed?" He searched the men's expressions, which were stone. Lars turned to affirm his understanding with a nod. Sebastian expected nothing less.

"Not so many months ago, we took in some intelligence. Fort Meade intelligence. Got me? There was a list. A couple ambassadors, our boys in brass"—Sebastian pointed to the screen still showing signatures—"the lot of them and a couple others in the mighty towers of our leaders. And I'll tell you what, they fucking shit their pants they did. And I'll tell you another, they knew if they weren't traveling the globe, someone would be coming for them."

Drake nodded in understanding. "Can I ask a question?"

"Of course, boy. All one, here. Speak your mind."

"Was this task force set up to go after domestic terrorism or to protect the asses of a few bureaucrats?"

"Ha, ha." Sebastian slapped Drake on the back. "Speak the mind you did. Well. Fair enough. You, Warren. Smart as a whip."

Drake let it go. "So we are?"

"Initially, that's what got the ball rolling. These guys were calling down to the fort almost every day to see if there was more intel about them getting snuffed. Lost a lot of sleep, some of them, for sure. Especially that putz Steele. Fucking twat, he is. He works directly for the president—if you don't watch the news."

"He's made a career off the backs and blood of others, for sure," Sean added.

"Correct. But it wasn't until these Mohawks of yours started coming after the squadrons that the power players really had a shot at saving their own skin. Once they found an opening, they seized it. From there, here I am, here you all are. Mind you, it's a righteous mission no matter how it started. It's got legs, got funding, got equipment. I've got some more numbers and some names of more Muj we need to keep an eye on or feed to the Birddog." He laughed.

Drake deflected the attention by fidgeting with his pant leg. The dampness of the blood was drying. *Child killer,* the voice said to him.

Sebastian's voice seemed distant. Woolf fought to find his way back to the conversation. *You enjoyed it.*

"Drake, you with us, boy?" Sebastian asked before continuing. "I have some new intel about ISOF bad fellas that went AWOL from a training. Good shooters, I'm informed. Coming here to the NCR, most likely. Happy to say, hate to say. You know? Always easier when the prey comes to the hunter."

Lars raised his hand. "Can I add one more thing?"

"Floor's yours, detective." Sebastian took a side step and dramatically waved his arm to give Lars an opportunity to share.

"I did a search of the Iraqi company as it exists today. They were making tens of millions. That's net profit, but the amount of money flowing through the companies is likely to the tune of hundreds of millions." Lars looked up to see if everyone was tracking. He had their full attention.

"Someone stealing or profiting?"

"If they are, they now have business headquarters running out of Dubai. This company literally has dozens upon dozens of affiliates now. All around the Middle East. Huge textiles, beverage companies—I think your guys would've been millionaires if they really were running the companies. But from the time frame you guys are talking about, almost as soon as everyone bugged out of Iraq, these businesses changed ownership."

"Mohsen," Drake hissed.

All eyes fell on him.

"The guy we tracked who was the focal point of the communications. Once I saw him, I knew. Once I talked to his boss, Shirazian, I knew more. Mohsen was a shady-ass Intelligence officer who brokered a lot of local contracts. He made a lot of deals between factions. Worked for the Iranians. Shia factions. His sugar daddy is General Reza Shirazian. IRGC Quds Force. My guess is these companies are multipurpose. Front companies, money makers, and probably being used to evade sanctions. Even if it's making millions, it's probably enabling billions. It would be just like them to have the Mohawks' families killed, blame Americans, get them here to kill anyone who knew of the companies—not that most of us would give a shit about them—and then who knows what the Iranians want next. But if the door's open, they will exploit the opportunity."

Sebastian put his hand on Drake's shoulder. "Shirazian's here."

"I'm not sure. He had a local number. It's one we mapped to a few different locations in the NCR, but the signals are pinging from a number of points in the city. He might have some countermeasures applied to the device. Last we checked, though, the signal went dead. Maybe he ditched the phone, maybe he's going radio silent for a bit, or maybe he knows something's up."

"Warren. Shirazian's here for sure. We know he is. We have his numbers and have been mapping out numbers he's been calling, emails he's been sending secured. We need to match them to what you-all have. He's the prime target at this point."

Sean cracked his back. "This isn't good. We need to get over to the fort and lay it all out on the table. We know something's happening tomorrow, something the next day. Maybe you-all picked up on something but don't know it yet."

"Agreed," Sebastian confirmed. "But as much as I'd like to keep pushing you boys, you need to eat, you need to sleep. Warren, Sean tells me we're keeping you on books, is that correct?"

"Yes, Sir."

"Not a problem. Easier that way. Back in the UK, we learned it did more trouble than good aside from extreme situations like when one of our boys put a pecker in an officer's wife." Sebastian remained stoic, which made it difficult to know if he was joking or not. He told Sean, "O.T. already made arrangements for First Sergeant Woolf. He's fine with it." The conversation validated to Drake that this had been an ongoing topic, but knowing his uncle, he'd like everyone to be a ghost killing people in their sleep and hiding in a cave until night fell again.

"Were you able to take care of the other thing?" Sean asked Sebastian.

"Indeed. Success."

Drake was afraid to ask. "And there's more?"

Both guys smiled. Lars, who had been busy looking at the laptop, turned and smiled too.

Sean pushed Lars. "Go ahead. It was your idea."

With pride, Lars lifted his hands and shook them in the air.

Jazz hands? "I give up," said Drake.

"Sean is the only one whose records have been expunged, but he still exists. All of us do. What doesn't exist any longer are our fingerprints. If someone wanted to track us, they'd need DNA."

"And we could intercept some of that as well," Sebastian bragged. "As long as we know who's putting the lab work in. But we've set up filters for all your names. If someone's doing anything with them electronically, we get a hit. FBI's checking on you, Woolf, but we've got a handle on that from the inside."

Drake was relieved with the fingerprint news, knowing that he and Sean hadn't been exactly discreet in the past—whatever the Hell time it was, last twelve hours-ish. Clearly, the team would be cautious when they could, but when they couldn't it was good to know that Sebastian was on it. "What happens if we're arrested and they run our prints? What comes up?"

"Don't get arrested." There was no questioning of Sebastian's sincerity this time. "It would take some real undoing on our end if you're picked up. But if they found your prints," Sebastian continued, "they wouldn't find a match with either of you. Prints associated with your records have been replaced with deceased."

"Cool, huh?" Lars sat on the large table, arms folded, his feet flat on the floor.

Drake nodded. Indeed it was.

"Oh, Drake." Sebastian was walking to the door. "I've nearly forgotten. Apologies. Your uncle is having a small interment service tomorrow. Hollywood Cemetery. Said you'd know where it was. Small group, he told me. The old man hoped you could be there by eleven now that plans have changed. Lunch after. Meet at the...whatever you-all call the structure that keeps cremated remains."

"Columbarium. I know it. I'll be there."

"Okay, lads. Get some rest. Get some chow, if pussy's your thing, get some fer me." He winked. "You two." He shot a glance to Sean and Lars. "I put three sets of keys on that case over there. Come up to the fort tomorrow. Same protocol. Call when you get near; I'll come get you in my car. I'll have your badges. While Warren"—he turned to Woolf—"I know, you want Drake. Warren's a good name, lad. Polished. I can call you Sally, too, if you prefer."

"Drake's fine."

"Brilliant. While Drake's with family tomorrow, we can sit with the analysts. I'll bring in an Agency girl." Sebastian smacked Lars's shoulder, smacking being Sebastian's preferred method of communication. "Oh, you should see her, big man. Little Persian thing. Mena from Persia House. Smart as a whip. She covers Shirazian. Tell her you're interested because, I don't know, we'll have to come up with something. Then you guys can meet back up here. I'll have them send some chairs to the containers. Drake, pick a set of keys, get some rest, be with family and we'll find some more Muj for you to kill later tomorrow. Right?"

"See you tomorrow." Drake questioned if he was too tapped out to drive back.

"And hey," Sebastian added, "if you can kill 'em all by the weekend, we'll go get right fucked up, ya? And if we can't, we'll drink while we keep killing 'em. Go rest or fuck, boys."

Chapter 35

Drake stayed awake for the first fifteen-minute drive, feeling out the gadgets and handling of the no-frills Jeep Cherokee. According to Lars, Sean had researched vehicles that had the lowest insurance. At first, Drake figured Havens was a cheapskate when it came to spending Uncle Sam's dollars. But as usual, there was more rationale to follow. Lars explained that the decision point was based on low theft, meaning people couldn't give two shits about the car, and it was relatively safe from collision. Sean had researched the stats and data of four-wheel-drive options derived from actuaries to pick out a perfect tradecraft car down to the color. White, gray, and silver cars were pulled over the most. Turquoise was the least likely to be stolen and pulled over, but Lars had opined that the color would be memorable. A dark blue vehicle was less likely to be stolen than a black one but could function as black, and so, Woolf and Havens would be driving the navy blue Jeeps. At least as their nonoperational cars.

Lars used the same insurance principle on his car but added considerations for his needs along with the police pull-over factor. He would drive a 2005 Buick Park Avenue. A big-ass grandma car that packed a supercharged 3800 V6. The car could crank off the line and still feel like it was floating on clouds. Lars's middle age, his pub-stool patron fashion style, and his size made the old boat a perfect choice.

These guys think of everything, Drake mused. And yet they came off as guys who you could see mowing the lawn or heading to the gym only to lose some holiday weight. There was much he could learn. And plenty he could teach them, as well.

The rest of the ride, Drake's mind was a washing machine slogging and spinning thoughts around about family, his aunt's death, the fact that his uncle would rather have a dedicated operator than a nephew—or the son he never had, and the Mohawks. And the attacks. This all led back to his brother. And that he pushed from his mind save for the fact that Drake so desperately wanted to find Dexter—his only real family left.

A psychologist would have said Drake was keeping Dexter hidden knowing that if he was in the United States and involved, he could be a target. He needed to find him soon. But Drake's family didn't listen to psychologists. Shrinks never said anything that the Woolfs, and later the O'Tooles, wanted to hear about Warren Drake Woolf.

As Drake neared his property drive, he saw that the glass debris had been cleaned. Just as Lars had said it would be. Sebastian had an unwitting cleanup crew come out and handle some items that were described as accident debris and renter vandalism. Included in the hundred and eighty dollars—cash—Sebastian had paid the migrant landscapers to mow the lawn, aerate the ground, and trim back the bushes. They weren't paid too much or too little. Just a regular random call for an honest day's work.

Drake pulled into the entrance content that he was working with pros. About fifty yards up, he glimpsed through the foliage a big black SUV.

Feds. They're here for you. You need to run. Kill them if they come after you.

Drake didn't want to surprise anyone and get himself shot, but he also wanted to get a feel for what was going on. He backed up the Cherokee, the tires' somersaulting treads in near silence until they crunched the gravel and Drake drove onto the shoulder grass.

It was afternoon and the property was awash in sunlight. Woolf cut through the wooded path. No one was in the back. The yard looked damn good. He gave it a prideful examination, nearly forgetting the potential threat out front. Drake loved this place. Whether it was serenity or solitude, he felt safe here. At least until recently.

At the back door of the rustic home, Drake punched the numbers on a rather high-end modern keypad and unlocked the entrance. The house smelled clean, and he kept the door open, inviting fresh outdoor air to follow. He slinked from wall to wall into the kitchen, where he peered out the window not knowing if he had pursuers or investigators inquiring about his aunt. Sheesh.

There's ammo for the Remington in the bedroom. You can take them out with the .30-06. Kill 'em.

The funeral was tomorrow. He felt bad that he hadn't given his dear aunt the mourning she deserved.

Drake had a direct line of sight to the front of the premises. He saw a driver inside the SUV, which was parked sideways on the wide gravel drive. He scanned the area to see if anyone else was out of the vehicle walking around.

Goddamn it, Drake, kill those bastards.

Woolf slinked to other vantage points, careful not to expose his movements. He saw nothing more. From a rear bedroom window, his view of the SUV's occupant was more distant and less clear, but while before he thought the driver was looking for something in the side area of the car, it appeared that the person had their head against the window.

After one click of his tongue, he stopped himself. Drake moved to another window. He couldn't see blood, broken glass, or anything that would immediately alert him to danger. If there were ISOF snipers trained on his property, they hadn't taken the Fed out, from what he could tell. Drake moved back to the kitchen.

The guy's sleeping. Get the jump on him.

As much as Drake wanted to hit the rack himself, he figured the best course of action was to put on a pot of coffee. And shave. The voices were getting more frequent. He'd have to think about timing with the meds. He needed the antipsychotics to ease the symptoms of delusions and voice hallucinations, but they altered his dopamine and serotonin levels. Take those out, and, operationally, he was dulling his senses. Hence a need to heighten senses at times with other chemicals. He was frying his brain scrambling an already oversensitive mind with the concoctions of mad scientists and mad war planners.

He wanted to chat with the Fed.

The tap on the truck window woke Tresa with a start. She saw a man holding two mugs up at her door. Her left hand reached for the door handle while her right whipped across her mouth to catch or erase any evidence of drool she had not yet sensed in her abrupt awakening and brief disorientation.

It wasn't until Drake was within a few feet of the SUV that he saw the driver was a woman. Blondish brown hair was covered at the top with a navy blue FBI raid hat. It was a nice fall day, but she wore the daily wear, standard-issue charcoal gray Outdoor Research all-weather jacket. He saw she wore typical special agent khakis. The chick looked big. Not offensive lineman big, but a smaller defensive lineman wasn't out of the question.

When she exited the vehicle and stood, they were nearly eye to eye. He broke eye contact for a split second to double-check her boots, then brought his gaze back to her face. She was attractive. Not smoking-hot attractive. She was more like the girl who was your best friend for life and then you realized one day she was really pretty and you'd somehow missed it all these years.

Her expression was blank, and she seemed to pull her head back a bit. Drake suspected maybe that was a reaction she got from most people who took in the Amazon.

"Hi. I came out to see if you were okay, then figured maybe a long day at the office so far. Coffee?"

"Thanks." She stretched out her hand and licked her lips then wiped them with her hand slightly covering her mouth. "Warren Woolf?"

"I am." Drake extended his hand in greeting. She had to switch hers and take the coffee in her left. She had a firm grip. Pretty big hands, but they were warm. And soft. Definitely feminine. He still checked for an Adam's apple to be sure.

She was looking at him intently. *She knows what you've done.* Drake saw her eyes circle his face. Her probing gave off a puzzled look.

"You're thrown off. My beard? Did you see me with a beard before?"

She seemed to regain her focus.

"And your name is?"

"Sorry. I'm Special Agent Halliday. Tresa Halliday."

"What branch?"

"What? Um. Counterterrorism."

She was visibly off. But counterterrorism was a good thing. Drake assumed she was there about his aunt. His muscles and mind relaxed.

"Okay," he replied, then followed her gaze to the fire pit. Her stare returned to his eyes and hardened. *It was her at the house. She knows.* "So, what can I help you with, Special Agent Halliday?"

Tresa's jawline came forward. "I'm very sorry to hear of your..." She paused and appeared to be either thinking of the relationship or waiting for Drake to say something first. His antennae went up. He waited.

"Aunt," she continued. "If you don't mind, I'd like to ask you a few questions about the incident. Would that be okay?"

"I'd be happy to help." He stood firm as her body appeared to shift toward the house. She stiffened when he remained in place.

"Is there a place you would prefer to talk? It could take a few minutes."

Drake wanted to control the interview but had to present a presence that the Fed before him would believe she was dominating. Let the game begin. Her eyes returned to the firepit, the carport, the pushed-back tree line.

It was Drake and not the voices who did the rationalization. Though both surmised the same. *She's been here. She was the one in the SUV that*

Sean saw. She snooped, came back, and the scene has changed. She's pissed. She has a scent.

"We can sit over there." He gestured to the wood stumps neatly arranged in a circle around a stone ring. "I can start a fire, or we can sit on the porch."

She shook her head. "Porch is fine. No need to start a fire. I love this setting out here in the woods. Looks like you haven't used it in quite a while," she said, casting a glance over to the pit and sitting circle. "Do you use it much?"

Drake turned toward the house. "I've been traveling. I prefer to have the fire going when it's cooler."

"Traveling long? Anywhere fun?"

He smiled as they walked and kept his head forward, tilted toward the ground. "Not so fun. Not too long."

"Place is well kept."

He raised his head as she once again scanned the property until locking back on him.

"Yeah, I don't do much of it. Someone else handles those things."

"Mmm." She nodded in a gesture perceived by Drake as saying *bullshit.* It was a favorite response of his aunt, his mom, and every other woman he had spent time with. Completely universal language. "So, what is it that you do, Mr. Woolf?"

"Army."

"What branch?"

"Signal," he replied, not missing a beat.

He saw her shoulders collapse. Her jaw dropped. "Signal?" Her eyebrows narrowed and cheeks rose. It was a *who farted* look.

Yes. "Yeah, I'm a techie. Little cyber. Lot of SIGINT." He motioned for her to sit on the handmade wooden Adirondack chair. "Careful with your coffee, they're lower than they look." He sat slowly, almost demonstrating a proper technique.

She followed his lead and nodded in appreciation then took another sip. "I could sit out here all day."

Drake just nodded. She was pretty. She was also a Fed who wanted answers. As much as he'd like her to stick around—if she were a veterinarian, or a teacher, or a surgeon, or anything other than law enforcement—she had to go. She was a danger to him and to the task force. "So, what can I tell you about my aunt's murder? Have you found the suspects?"

Tresa tightened her lips. "I'm sorry, I'm sure you can appreciate that it's an ongoing investigation. We're doing our best and we'll do what we can to keep you and your uncle informed."

"Makes sense." Drake stood. He tossed the rest of his coffee onto the gravel. "Well, I'm sorry then. There's little that I am aware of that I can share with you about who may have killed her."

His move by nature would typically obligate another person to stand as well. Tresa gulped the rest of her coffee, then slowly rose to full stature. She took a step toward Woolf. "You aren't aware of anything or aren't aware of what you can share?"

"Special Agent Halliday, you're counterterrorism. I'm counterterrorism. I've spent a lot of time overseas. If anyone I knew was involved, my whereabouts and contacts would be compartmentalized. Most of those people are still OCONUS. This is domestic, and I know very few people living in the States who would do something like this. I've hardly been in the States over the past decade. I'm sorry I couldn't be of more help," he said, with a straight face.

Tresa handed him her coffee cup and forced a smile. She tilted her head and leaned in. He moved his to the side to avoid the ball cap brim coming toward him but he sure as Hell wasn't backing up. *Is she trying to kiss me?*

Drake felt her body drawing near. He could smell the scent of citrus and something flowery he couldn't discern in her hair.

Halliday stopped dangerously close. "You cut yourself shaving?"

With his free left hand he reached to the point she was looking. She turned away still holding her smile and started off toward the black beast of an SUV.

"I'll be seeing you around, Mr. Woolf. Thank you for your time."

Drake wiped at his neck and checked his hand. Nothing. *Bitch.* He smiled, thinking of her smile, a little crooked eyetooth, and those deep brown eyes. He liked her neck. She wore no rings. But she was hunting him and that meant danger, not a Tinder date.

His tongue clicked as his hand waved good-bye. This was an operational twist he hadn't counted on and didn't know how to handle. An ember was glowing in his pit of loneliness, and he had to put it out.

Special Agent Halliday kept her eyes on the road. Her hands tight on the wheel.

As relieved as Drake was that she was off his property, he was disappointed she hadn't waved back.

Chapter 36

Virginia's historic Hollywood Cemetery was located just off the James River with rolling landscape and wooded acreage and architecture that made it not only a coveted final resting place but a tourist attraction, as well.

In the early morning of Helen O'Toole's closed memorial, a few joggers challenged the cemetery's hilly grounds as an increasing flow of dark SUVs wound their way between elongated marble monuments, the modest rows of Confederate graves, and the long morning shadows up to the high, arched mausoleum.

The mausoleum was erected to look out over the majestic property and the valley below. Those who were privately entombed comprised a number of *who's who* and *was was*es. Helen's parents were entombed here, and her surviving husband always insisted he would take the full Arlington honors for his final resting place.

Even as O.T. exited his vehicle officially as a widower, he never really expected that he would be the survivor. Robert didn't recognize the modest Jeep pulling in behind his own SUV but put pieces together when Drake exited the truck clean-shaven and wearing military dress. The image gave O.T. a wave of pride. Helen was a patriot. She would have liked to have seen Drake all decked out. It was a surreal image of the battle-hardened soldier as he walked among the tombstones, a pointed *V* of American flags periodically placed from the structure out toward the dense pockets of trees parting like a curtain to the waters below.

Following behind Drake came Owen, the secretary of defense, Sean Mullins, the FBI director, and a small entourage that included Presidential Chief of Staff Ben Steele, O.T.'s office suite mate Mark Watley and his wife, and a smattering of other defense and political personnel. A few actually were there for Helen and had come from the National Security Agency.

O.T. was touched that so many people had made the two-hour drive during the middle of the workweek. There were still fewer than twenty people present, not including security drivers who hung back by their vehicles.

Drake and O.T. shook hands. "Glad you came, Drake. I would have understood if you were too busy working to come."

Meaning you'd rather your little warrior was out killing someone. "We've accomplished quite a bit. I'll be heading back after the service."

O.T. gave him a wink and thumbs-up. "Go on up. We need to get the show on the road here soon. Have everyone come to the back area and fold in."

Drake took in the view. Autumn had kissed the trees with her cool lips and started the color change of leaves. The flags waved as a breeze blew up and across the hilltops. Drake thought to himself that his uncle had probably splurged a whole thirty dollars for the long line of flags in lieu of any flower arrangements. Typical.

After Owen gave his condolences to his old war buddy, he climbed the slight incline to the open alcove. Drake caught the wince coming from pain in the older man's knees. Hell, it was probably his ankles, back, and who knows how much shrapnel still lodged in the old bulldog Marine.

Ben Steele was following up the path close behind, trying to whisper something. Drake heard the SECDEF, Mathieson, make a reply then nod up to Woolf.

"How's the Birddog doing?" the general asked, extending a hand and pulling Woolf in for a rigid man-hug. Owen had known Drake for years and had given the Birddog more than his share of unsolicited professional and tactical advice over the time while dining, drinking, and smoking cigars on the patio.

"I'm good, Sir. Thanks for coming."

The SECDEF released Woolf from the embrace and turned to Steele, presenting Drake. "Ben, do you know Bob's son. Sorry, his nephew, Drake Woolf?" He turned back to Woolf and gave him a shot in the arm. "The Birddog, ha, ha. Fine soldier, here. He's a techie, but Ranger qualified. A killer with a weapon and a radar. Just as long as the extension cord can reach." He laughed.

"I don't think we've met," Steele said. "I thought I heard him say Birddog. You don't hear that every day. That your nickname? Call sign?"

Drake gripped the man's cold fish hand. "Pleased to meet you. Just something that stuck."

Steele was visibly distressed. "Can't be a common call sign."

Owen Mathieson was talking to someone else but still had an ear to the conversation behind him. He spun back to Steele. "Not common in JSOC, that's for sure. One and only."

Steele's smile looked forced, but Drake let it go as others were starting to push in. *They're right, you're a putz.* Woolf stepped back and bumped his shoulder against a large marble block with an inscribed name of the deceased. Their ashes hid behind the stone. On the ground, Drake felt his foot slightly off-balance. Checking, he found an anthill-sized mound of fine white powder. Looking along the wall, Drake noticed another pile about twenty inches ahead. As he looked at the distance between piles, it was the same width as the stone face. Maybe a fresh stone had been inlaid and they hadn't cleaned it up yet.

Taking a fresh scan of the open room, Drake gained appreciation of the space's curvature. The outer frame was square, while the inside was rounded like a marble fishbowl. It certainly made the architecture more interesting and a bit more intimate.

Drake shook a few more hands of the govies who made their way to the back of the columbaria where he stood. He saw his uncle coaxing Mark Watley and his wife to come in for the short service. Mark gave a wave and a smile but stood fast with his wife. She was nudging her husband up, but he apparently had something to say about it. Drake understood. Mark and O.T. had known each other for years but had disagreed on most everything. Still they had respect and an in-office or in-field loose friendship. Mark was here to show support without intruding.

O.T. flagged Drake over. Not wanting to knock the small urn pedestal in the middle of the room or cut through the globs of chatterers in the columbaria, he followed the opposite wall. Again, his footfall found another powder mound. And, as he guessed while drawing his eye forward, another little pile about twenty inches away.

"Drake," O.T. called. "C'mon up, let's go. Give it a move."

Drake ran his hand against the wall and in the seams of the stones. He felt the grit of fine white powder against the surface. Drake stepped on a mound and dragged it back, feeling a similar light grating texture with his shoe.

"Drake," O.T. shouted over. People now turned to Woolf as he stood at the wall inspecting the crevices of the stone slabs.

Drake scanned the crowd. He looked at the space. The two side walls made a perfect concave claymore kill zone.

"Oh, shit," Drake said, his uncle about twelve feet away looking at him with a deeply puzzled expression. Eyes popped wide, he gestured to O.T. with his hands like a tomahawk to go back.

"Uncle Bob, everyone, please, get out of the building. Now!"

A number of people took a step out, but Bob O'Toole and most others still stood around with hands in the air, blank stares, and questions about the directive.

"People, sorry, but get the Hell out now." Drake opened his arms wide and started pushing folks to the entrance. The sheep started to move. As they backed up, Drake looked to the walls then back out to the hillsides. The guests fit nicely within the angles of the flags. SECDEF Mathieson with his tall stature stood out the most in the center, and it was his head that vaporized first as pink mist rose and dark chunks exploded outward. Director Mullins stood on the side of the structure, perfectly in line with a flag row. He suddenly flew backward. Drake watched as the head G-man's back exploded and painted the white stone wall behind him. Woolf crashed through the panicking crowd and tackled his uncle, rolling him out just as an old relic NSA cryptologist's face split in two, releasing a similarly wide blood plume. Ben Steele tripped over his own feet and couldn't get up as the others stepped on and over him to get back into the open columbaria.

As Woolf checked his uncle for wounds, the flash and explosion burst from the marble building. Drake rolled back over his uncle not from decision but by the concussive force of the primary blast wave. The hill angle allowed most of the pressure wave and debris, people meat, bone, and stone, to pass overhead. Watley and his wife were tucked safely between vehicles. The security drivers didn't know what to do—respond to the threat or locate their principal as body parts and rock rained down on them.

Drake was rattled, but most of the shock had been contained by design. Those within were reduced to pulp and char. Steele was screaming frantically. He appeared uninjured but terrified.

"What are you doing," he yelled out. "What do you think you're doing?" He screamed to no one in particular.

Drake scanned down the flag-lined kill cone for any movement. *Shoot. The flags were tracking wind, too.* He thought he saw something behind foliage. Maybe someone running. He thought he could see a shape in the shadows alongside a large stone tomb.

All Drake had was a concealed-carry handgun. So be it.

One of the SUVs was roughly twenty feet away and had a clear opening to maneuver around the other vehicles and human mayhem. Clearly the driver understood personal protection by gapping the car with ample space to make a fast exit. Drake ran down the hillside, cutting over to the gravel road. The SUV's driver wasn't in sight, but no matter, the vehicle was running and unlocked. As Drake spun the wheels, kicking up dust and gravel, he trained his eye back toward the first area and thought he could see similar dust rising from another vehicle. He floored the pedal, hoping the roads would connect and follow a path down toward the river.

A vehicle was definitely speeding toward the access road running parallel to the river, and Drake sped toward it. He looked to his right at the large tomb, scanning any potential threat or a target to engage. He saw movement then turned back to the road for bearings. A large black SUV was spinning up the road right toward him, then stopped. He had nowhere to turn and stomped on the brakes to avoid collision. He struggled to control the SUV as it bucked and swerved to a jerking stop.

Special Agent Tresa Halliday jumped out of her vehicle, gun drawn, aiming at Drake.

"Get out of the car," she yelled. "Show me your fucking hands!"

Drake pounded on the steering wheel. "You stupid bitch…"

He leapt from the car with no intention on raising hands or standing down. "What the fuck are you—"

"Stop right there," she ordered, her finger now on the trigger. "I'll shoot you, you son of a bitch."

"Tresa!" he yelled. "I'm not the…I'm going after…" He pointed out to the road and then kicked gravel at her out of sheer frustration. "He's fucking getting away!"

Drake heard a scuffing sound from his rear and spun back to the crypt. "Contact!"

The bullet tore through Drake's uniform shoulder. It ripped his flesh. It was a glancing blow but threw him off balance. He looked for Tresa, who was hunkered down by her front wheel, which did no damned good since she was in the open. Drake reached around, grabbed her wrist, and yanked her behind a large tombstone for cover.

"Believe me now?" he growled at the wide-eyed agent. "They killed your boss."

She shook her head, not understanding.

"The director," he snarled, while peeking around the stone. "He was at the funeral. These aren't ordinary Mideast Muj from caves and radicalized mosques. They were trained by Americans and are wiping out Americans. Big difference from me."

Drake heard another crack and ducked for cover. He withdrew his pistol, ready to fire, but saw another figure quickly walking away toward the shadows of another tree line. He flipped his eyes back to the tomb and spotted a body lying on the ground. Exit wound out the front of the head. The man was a Middle Easterner—Drake assumed one of the ISOF snipers. Woolf recognized the weapon as a Remington CSR, concealable sniper "rucksack rifle." It was a bolt-action suppressed 7.62 carbine. Easy pack and go, and lethal as Hell.

He killed the shooter.

Woolf tried to make out the face of the mysterious intervening man who stood over fifty feet away in the shaded opening. Waiting. And then Drake saw through the dark shadows as, hands by his side, the man lifted a hand and waved.

"Drake, who else was killed?"

He turned to Agent Halliday. Her Glock no longer pointed at Drake. Woolf turned back to the figure. *Gone.* Drake's tongue was clicking. He leapt up and started for the SUV. Halliday grabbed his ankle like a bear trap, snaring him in his tracks. She popped up surprisingly fast.

"You're not going—"

Woolf's right cross popped her between the cheek and jawline. But she didn't go down.

Special Agent Halliday discharged her firearm into a grass berm to his right then trained the weapon on Drake. "You call that a punch? I've had worse." She rubbed her reddening face. "You can leave when I learn what's going on and when I say you can leave. Try that again, and you'll join the dead."

Drake said nothing. He felt horrible about hitting her and hardly remembered doing it, much less getting to the point of losing control. Woolf turned to the wooded ridge again. *It couldn't be him.*

Drake saw a flash of light then heard the near immediate sound of a round hitting Special Agent Halliday's SUV. The point of impact was at the top end of the front quarter panel. It surprised the shit out of Halliday, who first just stared at the hole three feet from her and then looked to Drake for answers.

His first reaction was that Halliday had clearly never been in combat before. Woolf was calm. He had his suspicions about the shot. And remained still.

Another round hit the vehicle.

It was a foot closer to Tresa.

"Stay calm, Special Agent Halliday."

She hit the dirt, scanning the trees and deep shadows between hillcrests.

"Why aren't you down? You have a death wish?" She fumed, still clearly scared shitless.

"I don't think he's after me."

Another round moved down and closer to her position. "Woolf?"

"I think you should drop your weapon."

"If the shooter's with you, I can remind you you're shooting at a federal agent."

"I don't think he cares."

"What does that mean? I'm not dropping my weapon."

Another round moved closer.

"Shit!" She dropped her weapon. "Fine."

Drake casually walked over to the Glock, picked it up, and placed the pistol in her SUV. He reached down and offered her a hand.

"I can get up on my own. Thank you."

"I think the guy shooting at you is someone from my past. He killed the sniper who was shooting at us. I'm guessing he didn't like a gun pointed at me."

"You're both going to jail." She ignored his hand and got up by herself. She looked at Drake, deadlocked at the eyes. "Did you kill that little girl? Or that boy in the hotel?"

"No," He half lied. Eyes steadfast.

"Were you—"

He interrupted, "I didn't kill any kids. Any other questions you have for me will just have to remain questions. You seem like a good agent and good person. I know you have a job. I was wrong to have assaulted you. I'm deeply sorry. Do what you need to try to bring me to justice for that, but know this. I have a job, too. And I don't fail. There are very bad people doing very bad things right now and planning more. I suggest you focus your energy and attention on those men. Not me."

Drake's adrenaline was skyrocketing.

Through the wooded shadows of the cemetery and under cover of memorial stones and raised burial buildings, Sean Havens grabbed from his backpack a hat and runner's water bottle. Emergency response vehicles were coming. He stuffed his handgun down the side of a headstone into the earth and started off in a light jog toward his Cherokee.

His chase efforts futile, Drake drove back up to his uncle and the few survivors. He knew a family reunion wasn't going to happen. Best to check on the one family he knew he had.

Security protocol had whisked Ben Steele away from the scene in the black Secret Service sedan awaiting him with the other detailed protection.

Mark Watley's wife was hysterical in the passenger seat of their car. Mark was trying, unsuccessfully, to calm her down from the outside. The security drivers of other government officials were flapping their hands in the air while holding phones in the other. Some sat in their cars like dogs waiting for their masters. There was nothing to triage for field medical support. You were both lucky and unharmed, or you were dead. Drake was glad he wasn't dead. The bullet graze didn't do much physical harm, so he considered that lucky.

Robert O'Toole sat on the grass, his back to a large headstone. There was nothing he could do for anyone. As the futile emergency vehicles arrived, Drake sat next to his uncle.

"I don't need to know why you stopped. I could hear the shooting. Could see some of it. That was a Fed, right?"

"Yeah, you know her?"

"I know her boss. They've been trying to shut us down almost before we even got started. Owen was supposed to talk with Steele about canning it." O.T. turned to Drake. "Against my protest, of course."

"That Steele guy's kind of twitchy."

"Doesn't sound like him. He's either a snake or a hawk."

"He asked me about my call sign. Mathieson mentioned it and the guy's jaw about fell off."

"My God." O.T. hit his head against the headstone. "Owen always did have a big mouth."

"I'm not following."

"Lebanon. They didn't know you survived. They knew Birddog was the operator. They're looking for some tapes. But the tapes disappeared." O.T. patted Drake on the leg. "They won't find them."

Drake knew better than to ask. His tongue clicked. O.T. looked at Drake's mouth. Drake stopped on the second click. He couldn't stop the eye blinks that slipped through. They had returned.

O.T. shook his head and looked away. He continued, "Steele's a problem though. So's Mark Watley."

"How so?"

O.T. rose his hands outward to the aftermath before them. "I didn't send out invitations here. I spoke to people one-on-one. Face-to-face or secure line. Who are the survivors?"

"I was wondering the same."

"I'll have Sebastian send you guys their phone numbers and other details. You'll want to track their recent calls. If it involves this mess, obviously get a fix on the transmitter and do any close target recon that you can."

"So, we're collecting against our own?"

"The charter is to address national security issues that need to be handled quickly and discreetly. It can be a raghead, it can be a traitor, it can be you or me if we're supporting acts of terror. If they're guilty, you guys take them out. The battlefield is here, as you can see."

"I don't have an issue, just clarifying. I can kill people; I just can't lead a normal life. But the other reason I ask is one of the team members drew a connection from the terror attacks to companies State and DOD set up in Iraq. Seems like Iranians are using them now to circumvent sanctions. And bring in cash. Who knows what else?"

"Quds Force."

"Exactly. Steele, Mathieson, even Watley's name was on it."

"Watley?"

"Reconstruction team."

"He knew about the companies. Anyone who knew about the companies that were working with the Deltas or Mohawks who were propped up as business owners was killed."

"That's why these guys were on the first list."

O.T. turned again to his nephew. "How'd you find that out?"

"That's my job, right?"

"I'm guessing we'll find Steele and Watley are talking to each other. I'll see if I can get records of the hard-line dial-outs and -ins for Mark's desk. I'm betting they cut a deal for their lives. Traitors."

"There's still intel about an attack tomorrow. We don't know anything else."

"Who's left?"

"Unless there are other lists, we've narrowed it down to secretary of state."

"Eileen Rous. They'd have to shoot her down. She's heading out overseas tomorrow. Sniper or bombers won't get anywhere near Air Force One. She's going with POTUS."

"Where does she live?"

"Georgetown. Prospect Street. Renovated row house. Two from the end toward the library. Google it to be sure."

"Security detail?"

"DSS. It's light. One rotating agent at the house. When she leaves the house, maybe two cars. Three agents. Maybe four tops. Secret Service could come get her tomorrow since she'll be flying Air Force One."

"But a sniper could take her out on her way to the car."

"Yep. And tell you another thing—Steele would have the schedule."

"I need to move on this."

"Hold one." O.T. looked Drake dead in the eye. "Nephew or not, you best not fuck this up. Don't think I haven't noticed all those tics coming back. You're weak if you let them come back." O.T. pointed to his head. "You have to be strong in the mind. I've seen as much shit as you have. Maybe more. You don't see me crying in the corner and winking uncontrollably and clacking off my tongue like some retard mental patient." O.T. further gestured his arms gimping up and lolling his tongue to the side, mocking Drake.

"The meds aren't working."

"Meds? You better not be seeing any shrinks. Your clearance will be pulled in a heartbeat if they learn you're a fucking nutcase."

"Then why'd you put me on the program?" Drake challenged.

"Because you're a killer, Drake. A stone-cold remorseless killer. Part natural, part, I'd like to think I helped build to get you out of that sorry driveling shell of yours when you killed my brother."

"What bullshit are you talking about now?" Drake waved off the EMTs. Remaining security drivers were speaking to the gaggle of authorities arriving like a literal funeral procession.

O.T. continued his rant. "If Alex didn't have to wipe your nose and tuck you under a bed and entertain thoughts of joining the State Department, he wouldn't have been slaughtered. He was as close to my blood as anyone I've known. Hell, if you were more like your own brother, both you and Alex could've taken those ragheads out. But you're not. So I hold you responsible. And if you can't get the job done anymore, I've got no use for you. The only way you're of value to me is if you can kill. Got it?"

"Damn you." Drake spat as he stood.

"Ha! That's the spirit I want to see. Turn that hate into power, you bastard. Get out of here. I'll handle authorities. I never wanted to have this service for your aunt anyway. At least she went out with a final bang."

Drake glared at his uncle. Hate twisted his thoughts from what he had to go and do now, and what he had undergone under this cold bastard's roof for years.

From a new vantage parked across and up the hill from Drake Woolf, Tresa Halliday lowered the supercardioid shotgun directional microphone back inside the SUV cabin.

She sat stunned and swallowed hard before calling Earl Johnson.

When she connected to him, it was on his secure desk phone from her encrypted Boeing Black Android device. Another perk of her new role.

"Can you talk for a bit?"

"Special Agent Halliday, I'm afraid it's not a good time."

"I'm here. Where the director was killed."

"You're at the Hollywood Cemetery?"

"Yeah. Bloodbath. Long story. I need to leave the scene, though. Woolf is involved with his uncle in some kill squad. They're hunting down the terrorists. They're the guys leaving bodies all over town. And I'm not sure Woolf is well."

"How did you find this out?"

"Which part?"

"All of it. I'm sure they didn't send you a memo," Earl snapped.

"Technology. I was able to overhear a conversation with all the toys you outfitted me with. Apparently, the kill squad was set up because of some targeting lists. It involves Iraqis, Iranians, front companies, seems like a big cover-up."

"So you know."

"Know? You knew?"

"It wasn't confirmed. But I had some intel on it. Sorry if I'm a bit punchy. There's a lot going on here, as you can imagine. Woolf and his crew have been doing foreign work that resembles the CIA's activities. Shooters and spies. They globe-trot with covered identities and hunt people down using intercept tech, surveillance, HUMINT, proxies, and even do their own killing. They're on Special Rosters and now they're working the homeland, building target packages on domestic threats and taking out suspected high-value targets."

"So, if you knew, that's why I'm here, right? That's why I'm following this guy all over Virginia?"

"Correct. And you've done exceptionally well. But they're shutting it down. And we'll investigate and bring everyone in who broke the law."

"It's not shutting down. And apparently, the terrorists are going after the secretary of state tomorrow before she leaves for the airport."

Earl said nothing.

"Earl, what side do we work? I mean, should we help protect her and help Woolf's team?"

"Keep an eye on Woolf and his team. Have you identified the others?"

"Not clearly. I might be able to pick out one, but it was dark and I only caught a glimpse. I think there are three of them. At least operating in the field. No clue how far up it goes. But Robert O'Toole is involved. Sounds like it's his program. God, that man's a monster. And Woolf—"

"Have you spoken to O'Toole or Woolf?"

"Woolf. He's as hard as I've seen. He's definitely combat capable. Something about him, though. Violent for sure, but I see him as a protector. Not just a killer. From what I overheard, there's some serious backstory to this guy mentally. I'm not sure he's okay."

"He's breaking the law. If they are killing people extrajudicially, or if you witness any federal offenses committed in your presence or if you have grounds to believe they have committed one, arrest him."

"And if I can't get cooperation?"

"What have you done in the past?"

"Is that the real reason I'm on this?" She grunted.

"Are we clear?"

"Yes, sir."

"Anything else?"

"My truck's shot up. Functional, but I'm going to pick up another one. Needed to change it up anyway. He can see me coming."

"On the contrary, Agent Halliday. I don't think anyone saw you coming. Good day. And be safe."

With that he disconnected, leaving her to contemplate the next move and to challenge her actual objectivity.

Chapter 37

As Drake was waved through heightened security at the cemetery exit, Sean Havens called. Woolf answered on the third ring.

"Yeah?"

"Did you make it out okay?" Sean asked, as he, too, drove along. Havens was searching for a good place along the road to catch up quickly with Woolf.

"You already heard?"

"Heard?" Sean was confused. "Heard what?"

"We were attacked at my aunt's memorial service. They killed the SECDEF, bunch of retired NSA staffers, FBI director—they knew we were here."

"Drake. I was there."

"That was you in the tree line?"

"Who else? A gravedigger with good aim?"

The news deflated Woolf. Clearly not who he thought or wished it to be. And the more he thought about it, the more enraged he became. At who or what, he hadn't yet processed, but the words were scalding. "Can you just back the fuck away from me?"

"I just saved your ass. I don't expect a thank-you, but what the Hell are you getting all bent up about? And at the very least, you can clue me in on the FBI chick you're trying to get a phone number from."

"Sean, I've been doing this my whole damn life. If it's my time, it's my time. I don't need you to be my big brother or whatever the fuck you think you're doing. You said you were going to be at the fort. And then you pop up again like my goddamned babysitter. Back the fuck off, man."

Sean played Woolf coolly. "Drake, Lars and I met with the analysts. We met an Iranian one and our NSA point of contact, Mojo. Great guy. I'm going to see if we can get him a hotel kit so he can bring an NSA laptop into our space and have him be our on-site Targeting and Analysis Center with Lars. They can build target orders of battle and Baseball Cards so we can prioritize our ops. We also got some great stuff that added context to the raw SIGINT the analysts gleaned from devices. It wasn't enough of a threat to raise before you went to the service. I sure didn't expect anything to happen. We're not much closer to learning anything about the next attack, but we do know where General Shirazian will be tomorrow night. Make sense?"

Woolf's blood cooled to a low rolling boil. *He doesn't trust you,* the voice warned. "Anything come up about The *Modarris*?"

"A few more things pointing to Atlanta area. No clue what it means yet. We probably need to think about heading out that way in the next few days. Seems like that's the site of the next wave of attacks. It's all based on new end points. None of the same mobile devices except Shirazian's. Matter of fact, the analysts are picking up Russian connections."

"Russian?"

"Don't know much other than that." Sean fell silent.

Drake pondered what he was receiving from Havens. It played to the secretary of state being an endgame for now. Woolf trusted Havens, and could see no reason not to, but he withheld the intel he had gained talking to his uncle. Drake needed more time and equipment to figure out how he wanted to work the counter-sniper issue. And frankly, Drake found it easier to think it out himself than have a group discussion. "Look, man. It's been a long week. How 'bout this? I need to go back to my place for some things. Maybe catch a quick bit of shut-eye. If we don't learn anything more about an attack tomorrow, I may stop by the shop and check out some of the gear. I can do that on my own if there's a code or something that'll get me in. Then maybe we reconvene there or wherever in the morning and plan how we'll work Shirazian." He dropped it there to let Havens marinate on the words.

"Well, I don't mind if—" Sean stopped abruptly, then took a different approach. "Sure, let me know if you need anything. If you have questions for Lars, hit him up directly. We're a flat org, but when it comes to Sebastian, at least for now, if you need something, I'd like it to go through me."

Drake was pleased with getting space. Havens's chain of command request was also reasonable. He really didn't think Sean or Sebastian, for that matter, would give two shits about a communication protocol. The reality was, Sean was the team lead and he needed to assert some sense of boundaries if he was giving concessions. Quid pro quo. "Works for me, boss. I'll keep you posted. Hit me up if you need me to scramble. I'll probably just find a hotel room up that way in case someone shakes down and you need me to roll out quick."

"You can crash over where Lars and I are temped for now. We already paid up and have an extra-long-stay suite right next door."

Fuck, Havens. Are you hearing me? "Thanks. Maybe." Drake fought for an excuse but just closed it off to avoid a rebuttal. "I'll let you know if I need anything. If you can just text me the code, that should be good." And with that, he hung up feeling bad about jacking up team trust and cohesiveness. "Kumbaya" camp circles weren't Drake's bag. He might have liked knowing Sean Havens didn't care much for them either.

Drake continued past his turnoff. He was going to head to the shop first. The plan was coming together in his mind. First, he'd make a call to his next-door neighbor, then he'd get a prepaid card and set up a bogus Uber account. He wanted to leave the Jeep up north. For his op, he needed the Tesla. And its autopilot.

Among other thoughts, Drake Woolf thought of the hand that waved to him from the shadows. How he was sure it was Dex who had come to his rescue. He then flashed to the look on Tresa Halliday's face when he decked her, and how she looked hurt beyond the pain of the punch.

His tongue clicked, which infuriated Drake. He slammed his hand on the wheel. "I want to be fucking normal!"

* * * *

Presidential Chief of Staff Ben Steele dialed the number hidden in his encrypted memo app for the fifth time in the past thirty minutes.

"There is a fine line between persistence and panic, my friend," the low, accented voice said upon finally answering.

"I was nearly killed. Someone tried to kill me. We had a deal, Reza," Steele reminded the general.

"You and your colleague would not have been harmed."

"Bullshit." Steele steamed from behind the privacy glass of the Secret Service sedan. "You never said anything about a bomb, you Stone Age cockroach!"

"Ambassador Steele, you are in no position to lecture me. You are not harmed, you will not be harmed. But should you continue to try and contact me, I will be forced to reconsider."

"I got you the list. You were supposed to take me off the other list. I could walk into the president's office right now and have your country annihilated."

"You can do no such thing. Firstly, you are riding in a black Dodge Journey. Do you prefer that to the Secret Service Suburban or are you not important enough?"

Steele spun around in the car, twisting to look out the rear window. He scanned but saw nothing that screamed Iranian Quds Force tail. "How do you—"

"Secondly, such a threat is ridiculous. Even for you, Benjamin. Never call this number again. Or you may indeed become a casualty, regardless of whether you can find our money," Shirazian threatened. "Oh, it appears that you are not turning back to the White House. Have you soiled your trousers? Perhaps going home to see the family? We'd be happy to say hello. Goodbye, Ambassador Steele. Do not call and you will remain safe."

Fuming and panicked, Steele thought to dial the SECDEF before realizing in the next instance that the old Marine's head had ruptured before him. *Watley.*

Assistant Secretary of Defense Mark Watley drove in silence as his wife sobbed. The name Ben Steele appeared on his Bluetooth auto display. Mark answered from the phone handset and not on the car speaker.

"Hello, Benjamin," he answered as quietly as two might speak in the narthex during a church service. "Are you alright?"

"I spoke to him." Steele's statement was clipped. Agitated. "I gave that fucking Arab a warning, but I'm not sure he knew just how damned serious I am."

Mark's wife was mouthing something. Her gestures indicated she wanted to know who was on the phone, which he brushed off with a *don't bother me* hand signal. "Look. We can talk about this some other time. We shouldn't be speaking now."

"I need to know about the task force. And, oh, my God," he continued at a madman's speed, "BIRDDOG? BIRDDOG is Robert O'Toole's nephew? Alive, I might add. Holy shit. The president is going to have a heart attack. I have no idea how I'm going to tell him."

"Listen," Watley said, hushed but forceful. "I can't talk. You say nothing about O.T.'s kid. Something's going on with Warren. I had to do some paperwork, but I have no idea about the task force unless you're talking about O.T.'s newest skunkworks."

"That's what I'm talking about. That's how we were running down the terrorists that had us on their list. That's what the list was for that I had you get me."

"The list?" Mark's hands tightened on the steering wheel. He stomped on the brakes, avoiding a collision as he sped mindlessly through traffic as he neared the Outer Beltway. "The list of the Deltas?" He spoke to his side window, knowing his wife was listening in. "What did you do with it?"

"I gave it to them. I had to."

"To get the money back?" Watley changed lanes abruptly, his wife reaching over and squeezing his leg in fear.

"What money? That's what Reza just said." Ben watched intently as the Secret Service driver's eye showed in the rearview mirror.

"Look," Watley deflected, "you said the list was for a closed awards ceremony. I never even put it together that those are the men being picked off one by one." Mark stopped short of the brewing outburst.

"They would have killed us. Would have killed our families. Mark, they're still following us. They're following me now. How else would they have known we were even at that goddamned funeral?"

Mark swallowed hard. "I have to hang up."

Chapter 38

While Drake found a lot of future value to the weaponry and electronics at the shop, he left it all behind save for one item. The rest fell to the cardinal rule: if you haven't trained with it, haven't tested it, and haven't cleaned it or performed maintenance on it, don't use it for the first time in battle.

Drake knew he would be hunting a sniper from the ground and didn't want anyone else to get in the way or to get caught in the fray. Where a sniper was concerned, less was more in the field. *More* in the field simply provided a bigger target or caused a sniper to dig in deeper. And as good as Havens seemed to be, Woolf suspected the older operator was more of a high-speed spook than a high-speed operator with time in combat. The man was certainly able to handle himself, but Drake thought that to be a good team, they needed to train together first. Until then, he was perfectly fine going it alone and shutting the door from behind without another thought. After all, Havens was making quite a few decisions on his own, so if it was a flat org structure and Drake was running point on ops, this was simply his assertion of management in his lane. Or so he convinced himself to justify his work-style preference.

"Going somewhere?" the deep voice inquired from Drake's blind side.

Woolf spun, startled. Lars Bjorklund stood along the brick wall holding a cardboard cup holder with two drinks and a carryout sack on top.

"Lars. Hey, you scared the shit out of me."

"Thought you ninjas saw everything coming."

"Wish that was the case." Drake walked down the entryway stairs toward Lars. "What's up?"

Lars lifted the tray. "I thought I'd do a little more checking on the laptop files. See if I could get any more insight on tomorrow's potential threat.

The analysts are coming up with some good stuff. Few more blips on the radar. We still don't know what it means."

Drake just nodded.

Lars cast an eye to the medium-sized case in Drake's hand. "Heard you were in another scrape. You okay? You've been through a lot."

"Story of my life." Woolf shrugged. He nodded toward Lars's tray of drinks. "Havens with you?"

"Nah. He's a little more like you than you think. He needs his alone time. Oh, you must mean because of the drink." He gave a sheepish grin. "Milkshake and a Diet Coke. Have some dinner in the bag. Should hold me over for a few hours."

"You don't sleep much either?"

"I nap a lot. Back to old cop days."

"You miss it?"

"I like this. I was a bad cop. Well, I was a great cop," he corrected. "My early years on the streets, I was on the take. Everyone was at the time in Chicago. At least in my precinct. Later, I was promoted to detective. I found my wings. Spent a lot of time with the FBI training. Loved it."

"Why aren't you a Fed then?"

"Polygraph. Didn't think I'd pass it." Bjorklund looked down at the ground with a face of true loss and remorse. "So, I just did the best I could at policing from that point on, but my reputation followed. People thought I was on the take. Then I got a little mixed up in something that put the family at risk. Thought it was time to hang things up. Clean the slate."

"Sean get you back into the game?" Drake asked with genuine interest.

"He did. Probably didn't need to. He's a good man. Good read of character. Probably why he's in the business. He lost a lot. We both did. But he's a loner. He knows I need people. I need to be around a lot of people. Family especially. I think that's why he keeps me around."

Drake nodded in understanding. He didn't ask more about details.

"Hey. I meant to ask you. When I was cleaning up your place, I about threw away a bag of papers."

Drake's eyes widened under raised brows. His head tilted slightly.

"Seems like you're looking for someone. From the drawings and a few pictures I saw, there's a likeness."

This time it was Drake focused on the ground avoiding further discussion. "It's nothing."

"Got it." Lars moved around Drake toward the cement stairs. "But from the locations and dates I saw, his cheeks should be more sunken. Same with eyes. Has to do with diet and vitamin deficiencies. I learned it in Quantico doing sketches. Teeth would look a little more pronounced, too, under the lips. Same principle. Not a big deal, but it would seem to age your sketch and could feasibly look like an entirely different type of person to a witness." Lars looked back. Drake was staring at him intently. "That's just if you wanted to know. We're on the same team. Let me know if I can ever help. Even if it isn't business."

Drake remained expressionless in thought as he took in the big detective and the new details.

"See you tomorrow. Have fun with the drone in the case. Kinda surprised we got a Chinese one. I would have thought they'd think of the security risks. Anyhoo." Lars balanced the food and typed in the code without saying another word.

Drake considered sharing his plan. But in hindsight, maybe it was because he liked these guys that he knew he needed to go it on his own.

An hour later at the farmhouse, Drake retrieved one of his own backyard favorites, a tactical crossbow with scope that delivered a broadhead bolt up to four hundred twenty-five feet per second. For a handgun, he selected one of his uncle's favorites, on which Woolf had plenty of finger time. It was a Sig Sauer P227 .45 auto Tacops. Holding a fourteen-round magazine, Drake filled one more backup and threaded on an SRD45 titanium and stainless-steel suppressor. Finally, he unpacked his own UAV America Eagle XF drone. With forty-five minutes of flight time, autonomous mission planning with auto landing, and a FLIR thermal streaming camera, he had all the team he wanted. Lars was right. Drake only trusted the American-made drone. The Chinese DJI drone from the shop would serve another purpose.

Woolf headed back into his bedroom and took a framed photo off the wall; he tucked it under his arm. From the nightstand, he collected an assortment of pills and micro tabs. The C-4 bundle was next. Finally, the black plastic bag full of artifacts from the endless search for his brother.

Sporting jeans, a gray T-shirt, a black Bodyguard 2A ballistic protection street jacket, a Defi low-profile Scout watch, and Converse Urban Utility Chuck Taylors, he loaded up the Tesla and headed off to Georgetown with a peanut butter PowerBar between his teeth.

Drake, you haven't slept. Your body is weak. Your meds are off. Be careful, son. Alex Woolf's voice was calm. *Please ask for help*, his father pleaded more adamantly.

Drake washed his mind, so he could focus. He'd just have to power through this like he always did. But God was he exhausted.

As the Tesla navigated the road on auto with adaptive cruise working the gas, Drake pulled up a detailed map of the secretary of state's residential area. He noted the high ground of Georgetown University Library's rooftop. It had direct line of sight to the second row house on Prospect Street, that of Madam Secretary Eileen Rous.

The rooftop of the Walsh Building had the same. The other row houses on the street provided much less of an effective overwatch position save for one. Some front entrance stairways could provide cover, but he wasn't expecting a ground assault.

Drake touched the steering wheel to keep the vehicle on auto.

With a general perimeter of possible sniper threats save for anyone inside a row house, Drake started to program the Eagle XF drone for its own autonomous flight sequence. The air pattern would cover primarily three blocks with streaming infrared surveillance coverage, and every third pass would extend to nine square blocks for a sweep before closing in again.

Drake decided to launch on approach as he crossed the Potomac with the intention of parking *by* but not *on* campus. The easement by which campus police and DC's finest would not converge would be his safe zone. College kids coming and going on those grounds would also support a plausible late-night walk from studying, a night on the town, or an early escape after a booty call.

As a final prep, he pulled up a YouTube video of the secretary of state. He couldn't remember exactly what she looked like. Nor could he really recall her age or general health conditions. That would give him insight as to how fast she would be moving down the row house stairs and into the secured car.

You're going to die. You can't stop this.

Drake pushed aside the voices and contemplated the potential attack scenarios: Would she need assistance, would someone hold her arm, would it take her a long time to get out the front entrance. An interview was the first to come up on the screen. Drake immediately recognized the background of the Potomac. She was being interviewed on the back patio of the row house. Interesting. The secretary of state was being interviewed by an anchor whose name escaped Drake. Woolf cursed the cameraman when the video panned in a different direction, blocking the view Drake was trying to assess.

Vargas, that's it.

Vargas was asking the usual interview questions as they strolled through the home like a high-class episode of *Cribs*. The secretary, trying to appear normal to television viewers, talked about her twenty-minute routine on a treadmill at five a.m., taking her shower immediately after, then having her ritual morning coffee outside every day, just as the sun rose, unless it was cold or rainy, and then she'd have it in the glass enclosure. They walked out to the back balcony terrace, and Madam Secretary joked about Vargas not taking her personal seat. Rous went on about some shit about her two dachshunds. She was an attractive woman. Clearly smart, but Drake could tell that she was a typical elite power player who had little in touch with the reality of the world.

Alright, check the box. The bitch could walk fine. Her dogs started yipping in the background. *Jeezus lady, have your people take the stupid dogs out. What the fuck are you people thinking?* Drake shook his head and rubbed his face. His hands were jittery and his heart was racing. He was exhausted but tweaked up.

Take the pills. Clear your thoughts.

No, you need to take the microdose. To keep your edge.

You're going to fail.

Call Havens. You're dead. This is going to be a huge shitshow.

Before Drake realized it, he was on the bridge crossing the Potomac. There was no one around. It was a good time to launch the drone.

Game time.

Drake took a microdose and slowed the car as the large sunroof opened to the night sky. Woolf turned all systems on and was prepared to send it off.

What if you can't get it back? They can trace it back to your credit card. This wasn't supposed to be an operational drone. You'll ruin the program. You'll get discovered. Agent Halliday will find you. She's going to lock you up. You shouldn't have hit her. She'll kill you.

Seeing no one still behind, Woolf pulled over to the side of the bridge with hazards on. He dashed to the trunk and split the C-4 that he had planned on using to blow up the Mohawks' car. He made a quick wiring change so the igniter could be activated through his device. It was more than enough explosives to destroy the UAV if he needed. Hell, it was enough to take out a good ten feet of whatever was in the blast zone. But most importantly, the payload wasn't going to be a weight issue for the drone.

That's it, you've really screwed up now. Cars are coming up to the bridge. If the police catch you with weapons, you're toast. You should have never stopped on the bridge. Stupid. You're going to get caught.

Drake hopped back in the car.

He could barely control the shaking. His eyes were getting twitchy now, too. *You need your meds. You've been off the meds too long.*

A car passed Drake on the bridge, giving him a startle. It was so loud. The night lights shining from Georgetown were becoming more vivid. It seemed like too much. He needed to tone down the stimulation.

Take the meds. You've been off your meds. Drake, dammit, take your meds, his dad shouted.

Drake turned off the hazards and accelerated. Lights coming at him caused him to jerk the car to the right. Seeing the side wall fast approaching, he overcorrected with another tug of the wheel.

Alerts signaled in the car. Oncoming vehicles. One to the rear, one to the side. Drake jerked again, this time scraping the right side of the Tesla. Lights flashed in the car.

Drake fought to regain his bearings.

Launch the drone.

Take your meds.

Drake's eyes were wild. He slowed at the end of the bridge. Still no one around.

Launch it.

Still stopped and with no cars approaching, he stuffed his hands deep into his pants pocket and retrieved two lithium tablets. Drake popped them in his mouth. His eyes caught something on his hand under the light of the streetlamp and glow of the interior display. A microdose tab.

You forgot to take the tab. You're going to crash out. You'll never pull off the mission. She's a dead woman. Take the tab, quick. It's game time, motherfucker.

Drake licked the small dot of paper and headed toward the secretary's street for a quick recce before parking and checking the drone feeds.

Shit, Drake. That was a second microdose. Call Havens. Call Halliday. You can't do this alone. They can help.

* * * *

Special Agent Halliday's phone alerted to the GPS activity. She flipped through mobile device apps until she reached the GPS tracking monitor. Seeing Warren Woolf's vehicle blip in the shape of a green car image heading through Arlington toward Washington caused her to rouse from her sleepless position on the bed.

"It's almost three in the morning. Where the Hell are you going, Woolf?"

She had been staying in temporary housing at Quantico. It was about forty-five minutes to his current position, recognizing that was continuing to travel farther from her location. It was rather late at night to be chasing after someone, but then again, she'd be lying awake binge-watching old episodes of *Grey's Anatomy* thinking about what Warren Woolf and his crew were up to, regardless. The bedside can of Pringles and bag of white cheddar and caramel corn could use a rest from her feeding hands anyway. She gulped the rest of a warm Snapple raspberry iced tea and was out the door.

* * * *

Drake's unmanned system was airborne and had made a full pass over the area of the greatest risk. Nothing. There was a slight read, but it was a person walking out of the area. The visual heat display on Drake's monitor appeared to leave a long tail behind as it flew. The red and blue lights in the car were getting wavy. The double dose of LSD, even at lower levels, had sent Drake on a trip in his weak physical and mental condition. The man from Orange was viewing a wash of colors all around and was completely wigged out with fractals messing with his visual field and warped patterns of kaleidoscopic imagery flooding his mind.

Drake fought to clear his mind, to no avail.

Time to go hunting, Woolf. Get the crossbow. Go kill some Arabs.

The Birddog was slow to turn off the vehicle and collected his things haphazardly and at a snail's pace. He loaded the crossbow in the relative darkness. The bolt bent in his mind and he recoiled, dropping it to the ground. His depth was completely off. The dim reflection of lights changing in colored hues on the ground reverberated in his mind as energy forms. The experience was throwing off his balance as he fought to control the psychological effects. His normal reasoning was completely off-kilter and the LSD's takeover of the imaginary influencers and cognitive processing was increasing strong spiritual visions surrounding him with terrifying images of the dead.

We have to go back. You can't function like this.

Drake stared blankly at the vehicle. *Dad?* Drake Woolf spoke aloud to the memory of his father. "Where are they? They're going to hurt her, but I can't find them. I need your help." Drake looked up to the rooftops. The tree limbs and leaves swayed in the moon's light under the toxicity of his mental state.

"I can't see them," he cried.

Drake tried to focus on the drone app and thought he saw two heat signatures within the radius. He tried to orient himself to their location. "Sappers. They're coming to overtake the FOB. Where's my radio? Shit!" He searched his pockets, not realizing he was not in a foreign land. From down the street, Drake could make out movement. He sprinted to the side of a building for cover, crossbow at the ready. It was a long shot. Woolf raised the weapon, peering into the scope. *I'll pull the trigger extra hard. That'll help it flow in the wind.* The sapper was now within seventy yards. The form was moving closer.

Drake steadied himself, tucking his left elbow into his side for support. He waited. *Where are the others? You're the scout seeing if I'll fire the first shot. But they won't hear this. I can flank them.*

Thirty yards. *I've got this. Check, check, checkmate.* Drake squeezed the trigger.

The pedestrian remained on his course, continuing to walk along the sidewalk at a leisurely pace.

How could I miss? Drake questioned, not realizing he had not retrieved the dropped bolt from the street. He reached to his shoulder harness for a knife and only felt the smooth fabric of his ballistic jacket. Woolf was confused. The shanty Iraqi village transformed back to row houses. Drake pulled back behind the building's edge as the man passed by, completely unaware that he had been in the literal crosshairs of a deranged assassin.

Drake watched dumbfounded as the figure walked out of the target zone.

A decoy. They're getting into position. He's just a distraction. Drake dropped the crossbow and fumbled to find a mobile device with a now-delusional drive. His pockets were all different. Nothing was where it should be. "What's happening?" he screamed.

Drake rubbed his head in frustration and started to sob. "Dad? I'm sorry. I'm going to mess up again. I can't think. I can't figure out what I'm supposed to do." He spoke to the streets. Drake shook his hands down, trying for a reset. He started with his front pockets and worked his hands up. In the right pocket he found the phone and had enough presence of mind to check the drone app. No more bogies in the area.

"Where are they?" He stomped, his foot looking like it had sunk into the pavement. "Where are you hiding?" Woolf slid down the wall, his head in his hands. "Dad? Why won't you talk to me anymore? I'm sorry," he cried.

"Sean." *He'll know what to do.* Woolf dialed Havens's unsecured number. After five rings, Drake got a response.

"Uh, hello?" Havens answered.

"Sean." Drake exhaled in utter relief. "Thank God. It's me, Drake Woolf." Birddog smiled.

"Um, I think you need to call me on another line." Havens disconnected the line.

"Noo. No. No. I need you." Drake redialed.

"Is there something wrong?" Havens answered.

"So wrong. Sean. I'm fucked up. I got my meds mixed up, doubled, maybe tripled, a performance microdose. I'm tripping. I can't turn it off."

"Dude. Where are you?" Sean started dressing himself and gave a light kick on Lars's bedroom door. "Can you sleep it off somewhere safe?"

"No. I'm in Georgetown. Secretary of state's house."

"What?" Sean stopped in his tracks. Lars was getting himself situated. He could tell something was up, never asked, and just stood waiting for more information.

Havens made eye contact with Lars and put the phone on speaker. "Drake, why are you at the secretary of state's house?"

Lars made a face of astonishment, to which Havens just shrugged.

"They're going to kill her. She's next. They're going to kill her before she goes with POTUS, but I'm too fucked up to find them."

"Drake, slow it down. Where exactly are you? You're not in her house, are you?"

"I should go in her house. Sean, I'll go into her house. That way I can stop her from going out."

"No. No. Drake. Don't go into the house. Drake?"

There was no reply as Drake Woolf headed across the street.

Havens shot his brother-in-law a look.

"You said to give him a long leash," Lars said while putting on his tweed cap.

"I'm going to strangle him with it. If we don't get choked ourselves."

"What was he saying about being too fucked up? Is he drunk? Didn't sound slurry."

"Meds. Pills, I'm guessing. O.T. told me a little about it but clearly not enough. I saw some signs but thought we had time to build his trust first. Also figured we're all wiped, so no one's been a hundred percent," he said, as the two walked out of the long-stay apartment.

"Why did they assign him to a project like this if his shit isn't together?"

"Because his shit's together ninety-nine percent of the time. But we may have learned that that small one percent is being accommodated for somehow by Woolf." Sean pointed to a vehicle in the lot. "Let's take the new van in case we need some hardware. I put some toys in it knowing we need to roll heavier. Anyway, I've seen his actual records. Smart as shit. Autonomous operator. He's everything the military and intelligence community is trying to build in their warriors. He's seen a lot of combat." Sean looked over the hood as they neared the vehicle. "A *lot* of combat. A lot of up-close and personal stuff, but I'm guessing he's been hiding some problems. We'll just have to see."

"Well, let's go get our wayward son," Lars said as he mounted the white Ford Transit van. The vehicle had a roof rack, ladder, and new adhesive brandings of VML Security and Fire Alarm Inspection and Maintenance. "Do we need to let Sebastian know? Maybe he can run some interference if we need?"

"Ugh. Yeah. Maybe he can shut down all the comms in Georgetown while we get our curfew-breaking kid, who, if he wanted, can pretty much kill us all."

"I'll let *you* call him. Chain of command."

* * * *

The Mohawk sent the text message to a dedicated number.

DRAKE WOOLF THE BIRDDOG CONFIRMED ON PROSPECT STREET, WASHINGTON, DC. GEORGETOWN. SEAN HAVENS ON HIS WAY.

As the message was sent, Tresa Halliday turned her SUV down Prospect Street, tracking Woolf—or a now-parked Tesla—as she drove. Her breath stopped short as Warren Woolf ran across the street in her headlights like a coyote in pursuit of prey. Drake was holding a handgun and seemed surprised as the vehicle caught him in headlights. He blinked his eyes and shielded them, then seemed to snap back to action and headed toward the secretary of state's home. He appeared to be talking to himself, or maybe someone else if he had voice comms attached.

In the middle of the street, Special Agent Halliday threw the vehicle in park and exited, drawing her service firearm. "Drop the weapon, Woolf!"

He turned slowly and tilted his head, trying to discern the familiar voice, but he couldn't make out the person in the lights of the SUV. Woolf looked confused.

"Warren. Please put your weapon on the ground. I don't want to shoot you, but make no mistake, I will pull the trigger to take you down."

He bent forward at the waist toward Halliday. "I have to save her." He pointed to the door with his gun.

"Put the gun down and we can talk about helping her."

Woolf maintained the weapon level, out to his right. He scanned the rooftops and pointed them out to SA Halliday. "I can't find them, but they're here. I know they're going to be here. They're going to kill her just like the others. We have intel."

"Drake. She left," Tresa lied, playing to his apparent fragile state of mind. "The intel was good. So"—she, thinking of something plausible—"so they left earlier to get her to a safe place."

His weapon fell to the side. "What?"

She's tricking you. You wrecked the program. They're bringing you in. You'll be locked up for good. You have to kill her. She won't stop.

"Tresa?"

"Yes, Warren." She took slow steps closer. Her feet gradually moved over the curb and sank into the grass.

"I don't want to hurt you, Special Agent Halliday, but you have to go. I'm not well, but I'm on a mission."

"Woolf, please put the gun down. I know you're not well. I know you need your meds."

"Who told you!" he screamed. Bedroom lights visible from the street flipped on. The noise from the loud negotiation awakened some residents before their morning alarms summoned them to the start of a new day. Drake turned his body and started to raise his weapon.

"Woolf! Drop your weapon. Now! I want to help you."

Drake. Remember what I've said. Mind memory is still muscle memory. Trust your training. Trust your instincts. Let your own voice, not your head or your eyes, get you out of the problem. Don't fight the sensation. Use what you can sense. Use what you know to be true. Trust your gut. His dad returning to his mind let loose a cascade of emotional comfort. The blurred atmospherics were sharpening. The movements he caught beyond Halliday started as shadow waves along the row homes, but they materialized to his tactical brain as positioning. Advancement. Textbook tactics.

"Tresa, I need you to get into your truck."

"Not going to happen, Woolf. This ends now. Let me help you."

Woolf's head was on a swivel. There were two. Three. A fourth.

"Tresa. They're here." He tossed his head to the right and to the left. His mind was still clouded, but he fought to rationalize what was happening and to connect to his kinetic mind. He had to cut through the mental fog. *Focus on what's real, Drake. Shut off the images like we shut off the voices.*

Woolf sensed that Halliday was steadfast. While he couldn't fully see her features, her voice was resolute.

"You're just going to have to trust me," he said, slowing down the euphoria and channeling it to optimized situational awareness. Woolf directed his weapon away from Halliday and started firing.

Tresa flinched then fired at Woolf. He was already on the move, running parallel to her.

He continued firing down the street, his suppressed pistol still making audible pops, sounds of metal mechanisms and dropping brass pings following in his wake.

Halliday's Glock round hit brick and mortar of the secretary of state's home.

She trained her weapon on Woolf, leading him slightly when the street erupted in fire. She spun to the left and saw the flashes of light flickering and heard the cracks in succession of automatic gunfire.

Turning back to where Woolf was last, she saw a dark blur slam into her then lift her off her feet toward her SUV. Woolf had her by the waist as he fired.

"Get in the truck and stay down," the man from Orange said calmly, a completely different person from moments before. The confusion was gone, and Drake Woolf was riding the heightened senses of the drug now that he was in his element. "What kind of firepower do you have in here?"

Halliday was pushed toward the open driver's side door, and Woolf continued to shield her.

He reached for a magazine to reload. Halliday twisted over him and shot suppressive fire over his shoulder.

"MP5 and a shotgun in the back," she shouted. "If you can cover me, I can get to them."

"Go for it." Woolf restarted laying down fire. As Tresa opened the passenger door and jumped in across the seats, a volley of rounds peppered the SUV, shattering the back window. Drake increased his rate of fire, suppressing the incoming assault from the right. As he fired, he gave a quick glance, hoping he wouldn't see a cabin full of Halliday's gore. Instead of reaching over the seats, she had lowered the seat down and was charging the MP5. She handed it out to him. "HK but this safety is on right thumb, it's off," she yelled.

In one fluid motion, Woolf grabbed the weapon, recognized the armorer's change for ease of use, and started spraying toward the threat.

Halliday was trying to get back into the fray when sparks from the road sawed their way up to Drake. "Contact right," she yelled.

He turned and the incoming fire leveled tracers and made the sound of a hammer tinking as it ripped into the truck and varying layers of metal.

"Agh!" Woolf yelled. He stopped firing for a moment then started up again.

Shots were coming from only two sources now. He must have taken out the others—or they were trying to flank. As he scanned, a vehicle turned onto the street, its lights off.

"There's more coming. Get out of here. I'll hold them off," he shouted to Halliday.

Tresa pumped the assault shotgun as fast as she could pull the trigger, casting more firepower at the incoming rounds.

The oncoming vehicle speed up, heading directly toward them. The hidden assaulters started up again when fire poured from the left and right windows of the vehicle near the Iraqi shooters. Bullets were hitting the row house bricks, tracing in the direction of the kill team.

"Cavalry. Let's go." Drake charged the remaining assaulters in a forward assault, capitalizing on their distraction of incoming rounds from another direction. Woolf directed his fire first to a figure on the right who had gotten much closer than expected. The man gyrated as Drake stitched him up. He panned to the left, spraying the man with metal across the waist.

Sean Havens was firing from the passenger side and was soon on target hitting another man center mass; another gyrating zombie danced in the dimming moonlight.

"Get in," Lars shouted from the driver's side.

"Hang on." Drake reached into his jacket with a wince and retrieved his mobile device.

Havens had opened the sliding door. "Dude, what are you doing? We gotta go!"

"Hang on." Drake pulled up the drone app. It was flashing less than five minutes of flight time remaining. Woolf fingered through the target zone. In the early morning, there was more movement around the area. He checked the respective rooftops.

"Drake, there's no time!"

Tresa was fast approaching the small utility van on foot.

"The sniper. I still can't find the sniper," he said, fingering his device display. "You mean that shit wasn't bad enough?"

"I'll explain later. I gotta find him before—"

"Everyone out of the car!" Halliday had her shotgun pointed at the men.

"Dude, your girlfriend is a real pain in the ass," Havens said.

"Out!" she ordered.

Drake remained fixed on the device.

"You, too, Woolf. I need answers from all of you."

Sirens were drawing near.

Woolf turned to SA Halliday with complete seriousness and simply replied, "Wait."

Havens nodded to Lars to get out of the car. As Lars unbuckled, Havens got out his side, hands raised.

Halliday took a step back, her shotgun pointed at Havens as he moved around the vehicle. "Time, Woolf?"

"Drone's about out of gas. He's got to be here. I don't know why he isn't in the zone. There's no way he can pull it off anywhere else."

Lars stepped out of the van. Halliday raised her head slightly as Detective Bjorklund exited the vehicle displaying his full height. He stretched out his hand. "Hi, I'm Pedro, pleased to meet you."

Tresa took a second to respond, but by then Havens had his arm around her neck. Lars grabbed the shotgun with his outstretched hand. He waved to Special Agent Halliday. "G'night, sister. Just relax. He's not going to kill you," he said, as Sean Havens tightened the sleeper hold amid the large woman's attempts to stomp and twist him off. Sean held on while she resisted with all her might, lifting him off his feet and flipping them over to the ground.

Havens fell hard but never loosened his hold.

"You'll be safe," Sean reassured her as her body started to go limp. The sirens neared.

"Woolf!"

"The interview," he said with revelation. "They've been hunting everyone and then getting close using social media." Drake looked up to the houses. He could just make out the tower of the Georgetown University Car Barn, also known as the School of Arts and Sciences. Drake remembered seeing the nearby tower looking down on where the secretary had her morning coffee. That would be the easiest shot, and the timing was literal clockwork of when she would be outside.

"It's got only a minute left of battery. I have to redirect."

"Drake, we have to go, there's nothing we can do from here."

"Yeah, there is. Put her in her truck. Dump all the weapons we used with her. I'm redirecting and—"

Drake got into the van. Lars and Sean loaded Special Agent Halliday into her SUV's passenger side and dumped all the weapons in the footwell. Lars ordered his younger brother-in-law, "Put Woolf's handgun into her hands. He's making it look like she took these guys out. Then we don't have to worry too much about brass cleanup either."

Sean nodded.

Drake flew the circling drone off course and over the south end of the row houses up to the university building's tower. As it neared, Woolf picked up a heat signature. As the drone approached, he increased its speed at one of the tower windows.

The heat signature high in the tower was moving. Scrambling. And Drake detonated the C-4 payload.

A bright flash and explosive boom further interrupted and startled the otherwise quiet neighborhood.

Lars and Havens had gotten into the car when the burst of light assaulted the morning darkness. The sound set off car alarms.

Sean turned to Woolf with a smile. "Please tell me you're still not all high and blowing up GU before you order a pizza."

"No, but I am shot."

"Kids these days," Lars replied.

Chapter 39

It was late in the afternoon when Special Agent Halliday finished answering immediate questions of the Capitol Police, Diplomatic Security Services, and the Secret Service. Notwithstanding the FBI, before she instructed them to contact Earl Johnson, the director of PR for her division, for additional questions.

She was back at Warren Woolf's home an hour later on the off chance he would be there. As she pulled up his drive, Halliday was met by the wave of a seventy-something man. He was holding hands with a woman of about the same age who wore a smile and waved her own hand at the approaching vehicle, a gray Dodge sedan.

Halliday parked the Challenger behind a red pickup truck. It was the first she'd seen it on the property. No sign of Woolf's car. The GPS tracker was dead. He'd found it.

As she got out of her car, the couple was nearly on top of her. "You here to see Drake?" the man asked.

"Uh, yes, do you know him?"

"Oh, boy, do we ever," the man said with a smile. He had graying hair, a Patagonia green zip-up over a cream turtle neck, and wide corduroy blue pants. A smashing outfit a few decades ago. The older man topped it off with blue and tan duck boots, or so she assumed they were still called.

"Is he here?"

"Nope. Won't be back either."

"How do you know?"

"He left. Are you the special agent?" He looked down at a white envelope. "Halliday?"

"I am."

"Thought so. You fit the description to a T. He said you'd be by. We just came by to check on the place. Figured we'd tape this to the door. We're your neighbors."

"My neighbors?"

"Yep." The man handed the envelope to Halliday. As she opened the papers, he rambled on. "Gave us the papers yesterday. Oh, we've known him since he was a teen. His aunt and uncle used to take him out here until he got right."

"Got right?" she asked while reading the paperwork.

"Oh, yeah, that poor dear. Wasn't right in the head for a bit." The woman was wearing a nearly identical outfit to her husband save for a quilted red jacket instead of the thermal zip-up of her spouse.

Her husband added, "Didn't speak a word to us at first. Came from Africa. Parents were killed there. Helen and Bob took him in. He was slow going at first but sure came around. Nicest boy. A little twitchy now and again, but great kid."

"Stop it," his wife scolded. "That's his business."

"I'm not saying anything out of sorts. Boy's a war hero now. I don't know how many medals he earned," the husband added. "Bob sure did brag on him. I think he was a little heavy-handed with the boy, but he sure did turn into a nice young man. We always told Bob and Helen, if they ever sold, we'd love to expand our property. We live just behind." He pointed through the trees to what could have been Canada or China for all Halliday knew.

Tresa drowned out the words with her thoughts. In the paperwork was a property gift deed. It was a notarized document that transferred ownership of the property from Warren Drake Woolf, donor, to Tresa Halliday, recipient. There was a check enclosed for $100,000 with a sticky note on top with the writing, "for taxes; if you have questions, call my lawyer." A number was written below. Behind it was a list of names. They were Middle Eastern names. It also instructed her to the location of a boat launch down the road.

He was indeed mad. She knew he was wounded, too. She'd check the hospitals but knew she'd find nothing. Tresa suspected the uncle wouldn't be of any help. Either way, Earl had told her to stay away from O'Toole and focus on finding Woolf and his crew by other means.

He was gone.

Halliday was a hero to the counterterrorism unit, especially after the sniper rifle and remains were recovered in the Car Barn tower. The effort had been attributed to her once Drake had wiped the device, leaving the remote flight app functional, and tossed it on her lap. A text had come through on his unlocked phone after she regained consciousness and assimilated the weapons around her. The message read, "SORRY AGAIN."

"We were just sayin' it was like old home days for Drake," the neighbor said, bringing her back to the chat. "You're the second person that's been by since we got here. Probably just passed the other guy as you came in."

Tresa snapped back to full attention and tried to recall who else she had passed on the road. Nothing and no one she could think of. There was a bearded guy driving a car that she at first thought could be Woolf until she realized Woolf was now clean-shaven, but she didn't get a real good look anyway. "I don't think I saw anyone else, did you get a name?"

The older man turned to his wife. "Old friend of Drake's. What did he say his name was, again? Dirk?"

"No, you're thinking of Junie's boy. This was"—she squeezed her chin in thought—"Dex."

"Dex, that's right." He snapped his fingers. "We asked if it was short for Dexter, but he had a way about him. Friendly guy. Didn't talk much. Had a little bit of a foreign accent. But he just thanked us and left."

"That's right, just thanked us and left," the wife echoed. "Friendly."

Ever confused by Warren or Drake Woolf, this new information meant nothing to Halliday.

Woolf had probably saved her life. But he was breaking the law, which put her in the situation in the first place. It was her job to protect American citizens on US soil. Not his. At least that's what she convinced herself was her primary interest in Warren Woolf. But now he had given her his house? She was dumbfounded and didn't know if Earl should be told about the papers. Tresa wasn't into taking bribes, but this could be bait. Now, regarding his team member who put her in the sleeper hold, payback would be a bitch.

Chapter 40

Two weeks later.

The texted instructions for Mark Watley were to meet Chief of Staff Ben Steele in the parking lot of Virginia's Occoquan Bay National Wildlife Refuge. Watley was to leave his car running in the first two rows and walk to the passenger side of the Tesla parked at the back of the lot. Steele had noted, "We have to discuss the list. Come alone." Watley had always found Steele to be a bit of an overreacting tool, but he obliged. Neither could take chances.

As Watley pulled into the lot from Dawson Beach Road, he instantly saw the Tesla in the nearly deserted parking area. Steele's black Range Rover was parked where Mark was supposed to leave his vehicle. Watley noticed that it, too, was left running. The hairs on Watley's neck would have stood on end had this been Iraq, but Steele was a twat, and this Hollywood meet and greet was probably the best the intelligence amateur could come up with.

As he walked to the Tesla, he could see Ben sitting in the driver's seat. Steele was smiling ear to ear. Watley followed the instructions and entered the passenger side.

"How did you pull this off?"

"Pull what off?" Watley answered, annoyed.

"The car. You said, in your text, your contact had presented me a gift as a token of apologies. It's from the general, right?"

"Ben, what the Hell are you talking about?"

Equally confused, Steele pulled out his mobile device and showed Watley the text.

"Ben, that's my number, but I didn't send it."

Watley checked his own device. "I've got nothing in my history that shows anything other than you playing Spy vs. Spy telling me to leave my car and come over to a Tesla here at the preserve. Look." He pointed to the text on his device. "It says you want to talk about the list."

"The list? We gave all the names we could."

"Ben, I already told you. I had no idea about why you wanted it. I don't even know why it matters anymore. The Iranians can't do anything with those companies. The money's gone. That's why they're pissed."

"Gone? There were hundreds of millions of dollars in those accounts," Steele offered.

"Three hundred fifty-seven million dollars. To be exact."

"Wait. I thought the names we gave took our names off the list. They're still after us?"

"Not us, the money," Watley clarified.

"Well, who the fuck has the money? I don't. Do you?"

"O.T."

"Bob O'Toole has the money?" Steele was dumbfounded. "He'd never get away with that."

"He took it, but not for his own interests. He's got a techie crew that can get into bank accounts. They had the monies siphoned out and wired all over the place. His nephew the Birddog used to get side missions wherever he was operating to find illicit funds. O.T.'s funding his black programs with the Iranian money. Through his cutouts, Bob gave the Iranians our names. That way it all just disappeared. He would be the black ops czar with a self-funded program."

"That son of a bitch. He completely played me."

"He played us all."

"He had me give the unsecured cell phone numbers of his nephew and that Sean Havens guy to one of Shirazian's agents. He said that finalized the concern of POTUS for Lebanon."

* * * *

Sean Havens looked over at Drake. They could hear the audio playing on Woolf's mobile device from their location on a small dirt road about a quarter mile from the Tesla.

"My uncle never cared much for me." Drake shrugged with a cockeyed smile.

Havens chuckled. "Yeah, but I thought he liked me."

"Not so much."

"I guess not."

"Your call, Drake."

"I'm ready to be erased for good. And this falls under our mandate. I'll handle O.T. myself."

"I guess we'll see you in Atlanta?"

"That's where the intel seems to be pointing us. I just need to make a delivery in Tennessee. One of the Mohawks has a family there. Those kids need to be taken care of. I've got some extra cash."

"No problemo. So which car do you want to drive? The Range Rover or Watley's car?"

"You pick. You saved my ass again."

"Suit yourself, Woolf. Better send this bird off."

* * * *

"So, what now?" Steele asked.

"Well, when I came here, I thought maybe I was walking into a trap." Mark pulled a .357 snub-nosed revolver from his jacket pocket. "But I need to finish cleaning this all up."

* * * *

Drake flew the Chinese DJI drone up to the Tesla and let it hover below the trunk. As Steele cursed Mark Watley, then pleaded for his life, Woolf landed the UAV and hopped its final flight just under the car.

"I'm going to miss that car," Drake said as he armed the explosive. "But I think I'm going to like being dead." He detonated it with the push of a button.

The ground shook and debris fell even as far as their position.

"Used a little extra to eliminate dental records?" Sean asked.

Lars leaned up. "I had him go with three pounds. We're clear." He slapped Drake on the shoulder.

"Ow."

"It was your thigh."

"Passed through the thigh. But I still got hit a couple times on the ballistic."

"Hope she appreciated it." Sean made a kissing sound. "You can have more painkillers after you eat. Then we'll try your new lithium dosage, too. Road to recovery, brother. But as a team."

"As a team," Drake replied. Then he paused in thought. "Huh."

"What? Wondering what your girlfriend's doing?"

"No. I was just thinking how we need to find Shirazian, but then I was thinking. All the last Iraqis we took out were ISOF. We took out the last Mohawks before the funeral."

"Right?"

"So who made and triggered the explosion at the cemetery?"

Epilogue

Robert O'Toole stood in his kitchen and added another ice cube to his goblet of American Freedom Distillery's Horse Soldier Bourbon. He walked back down the long hall toward his study. The third and final transfer of funds to Project ICEPICK were already solidified and confirmed by Sebastian. That and two other black programs would never see the light of oversight, nor would they ever be at risk for funding again.

He didn't particularly expect either Havens or his nephew to find themselves bullet-ridden on a cold metal slab at the morgue. God knew those two rogue warriors had more lives than a roomful of cats. The house was quiet, which he liked. He had no more worries for Helen. In reality, he missed the old Helen, but the fragile-minded wife of late carried a burden he was unwilling to support.

As he turned into the home office, seeing a bearded man sitting in his leather office chair didn't surprise O.T. as much as it pissed him off. "Who the fuck are—"

The man raised a pistol and shot O.T. in the shoulder.

Bob O'Toole yelped, but not much more. He gritted his teeth and held the bleeding wound. "I said—"

The bearded man shot O.T. in the other shoulder. Bob yelped again and grunted like a wounded bull. He dropped to his knees on the floor. "Go ahead, you Arab faggot, finish me off."

The man rose to his feet and walked around the large mahogany desk. He put the pistol to O'Toole's head. "Where's my brother?"

Bob O'Toole hadn't made the initial connection. He lifted his head, eyes wide in surprise. "Dexter."

The bearded man fired another shot into the top of O.T.'s kneecap. The old warrior screamed and flopped to his side, holding his leg in agony.

"Where's my brother?"

"I don't know," he whimpered. "He's gone. He's a ghost now."

"Who knows where he is?"

Bob remained silent, rolling back and forth on the floor in a pool of blood. The bearded man fired again, hitting O.T. in the side of the other knee.

Bob O'Toole screamed. He was panting but unwittingly cast his eyes up to his laptop. Dexter Woolf followed the look.

"Old man, this is your last chance."

"Go to Hell, Dex, you CIA piece of shit. Go to fucking Hell. I only wish you were home when we killed your parents."

The bearded man fired three shots into Robert O'Toole's head.

The old man flopped to the wooden floor with a thud.

Dex Woolf read the computer screen and scrolled through open windows. He took pictures of each pane with his own mobile device and noted one name. Sebastian Haggerty.

End

Look for the next Task Force Orange thriller,

The Presence of Evil, *by J.T. Patten.*

Available everywhere ebooks are sold.

About the Author

J.T. Patten worked for the government and military community in support of national defense and policy. He has a degree in Foreign Languages, a Masters in Strategic Intelligence, graduate studies in Counter Terrorism from the University of St. Andrews, and numerous expertise certifications in intelligence analysis, cyber forensics, mobile device tracing, and financial crime investigations. For more, visit jtpattenbooks.com or find him on Twitter @JTPattenbooks.

Made in the USA
Coppell, TX
21 January 2022

72028580R00173